the SCAVENGERS

A Novel

Lucas Blexb

8-20-15

the SCAVENGERS

A Novel

LUCAS BLEYLE

Illustrated by BLAINE GARRETT

TIPSY PHOENIX BOOKS

AMES, IA

Tipsy Phoenix Books, Ames 50014

© 2015 by Lucas Bleyle
All rights reserved. Published 2015

Printed in the United States of America

21 20 19 18 17 16 15   1 2 3 4 5

ISBN-13: 9781514154182
ISBN-10: 1514154188

Illustrations © 2015 by Blaine Garrett
Book design by Trevor Brown

Author photo © 2015 Cheri Thieleke

www.tipsyphoenix.com

For Grammy and Grumps

Acknowledgements

I am very indebted to my formatter and cover artist Trevor Brown, and my illustrator Blaine Garrett, whose artwork brought my ideas and characters to life. I'd also like to thank the following people in no particular order: Ron Nelson for his thorough scientific review; Grumps and Grammy for endless support and countless hours spent editing out all my careless mistakes; my mom, Amy Bleyle, for turning it into a bedtime story, and my dad, Dan DeGeest, for hooking me up with almost everyone in this acknowledgment and for his time proofreading; and Todd Hageman, a published author and mentor, for his careful reading and professional feedback.

I am ever so grateful for the endless inspiration from people, such as Aubrey Branch, and from the many books, movies and stories that have given me glimpses into the wonderful creativity of others.

Finally, thank you to my teachers who have not only put up with me, but also taught me everything I know: Tonja Goodwin for pushing me farther than I ever thought I could go; Shannon Fitchko for not only bringing history to life, but also for being the kindest, most generous, and caring person I know; Ron Weber for his wisdom that has done more for me than he could ever have imagined; and Collin Reichert for making science something of breathtaking beauty and wonder and for teaching me that I had the ability to make a difference.

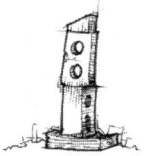

Don't Litter Entire Planets

I don't know why people keep hoping that they will escape the Wasteland. Things haven't changed in the last five hundred years, so why would they ever? But when I look down deep inside me, I find myself hoping, right along with them, that maybe, somehow I might escape to the Clean World where everyday isn't a fight for my survival. My name is Zane and all I've ever known is the Wasteland.

A hideous snarl pierces the silence, a shriek so loud it seems to echo for eternity. Not again, I think, but I raise my bow anyway. The wind howls almost as much as the creature hiding in the darkness, blowing a piece of paper that whips me in the face. The wind brings the stench of rotting garbage and trash. It's a smell I have grown used to. I slip an arrow out of my quiver, feeling the smooth wood as I raise it to the bow. My bow isn't much, only a few pieces of metal crudely welded together with a string in between, but it's still deadly. I hear the snarl again, closer now. It's too dark to see, but I know what it is and, more importantly, where it is. I hear it crunching towards me on razor sharp claws. Then I spot the glint of a yellow eye only feet away. It's a volve, the ugly wolf-like creature that roams the land, killing at will. Its mouth drips saliva and its foot-long fangs hang out of its mouth like sharpened icicles waiting to sink into my neck. I hope it is smart enough not to attack. I'm not in a killing mood. I never am.

We stare at each other, seconds pass, eyes locked in a silent standoff, then all of a sudden the beast howls and sprints towards me. I have a moment before it reaches me, but I don't need it. I've already released the arrow and it thunks out of sight into the volve's exposed throat. The volve stops in mid sprint and howls, blood spitting from its mouth. It stumbles a few more feet, slipping on trash. The volve lets out one last strangled whimper and collapses at my feet—the volve's long purple tongue is hanging from its mouth in the all too familiar image of death.

My brain insists that I should be celebrating my victory, but my heart gets the better of me as I see the poor animal lying in a dead heap. I walk to it. The only sound now is the crunching of my metal-clad boots, which protect my feet from the array of razor sharp bits of metal, glass, and wooden scraps that cover the Wasteland.

The night is dark, but the partial moon lights the night enough to see that the volve isn't even an adult. It was probably cast out of the pack when fresh meat was too scarce. I bend down and lay one hand on the beast's neck. For such a hideous animal, it sure has some soft fur.

There is no blood, except the gentle trickle from its open mouth, around its massive razor sharp teeth to the resting place, mingling with the trash, staining it a scarlet color. My arrow had gone straight down its throat and into its heart. The injury bleeds the volve from the inside, and

if the arrow hadn't killed the animal, choking on its own blood surely would have. I grab the volve around its claws and heave it over my shoulder onto my back, its skin still warm to the touch. Its head rests on my shoulder, and its tail hangs over the shoulder opposite to it. I carry the volve much like the shepherds of medieval times carried a lamb. I am suddenly overcome with sadness. This creature didn't deserve to die. I don't care if it had been trying to kill me. Volves eat meat—that is their way of life—and even if it's an ugly creature, how evil could it really have been? It was only trying to feed itself, following the instinct hardwired into its brain. I had caused this animal such pain, and for what? Another meal? To escape death for another day?

I look up to the sky at the stars, to the moon and somewhere much farther away. Not visible to the naked eye is the planet where the enemy is, the people who ultimately caused this animal's death, and my miserable life. I look back towards the ground, closing my eyes for a moment.

I start the walk through the fields of trash back to my home, the Nomad's wagons. It's less than a mile back, and from here I can see the fires and the steam from the wagons. My boots crunch over cans and bottles. I kick aside boxes, climb over a dented refrigerator and dodge piles of junk. There is no sign of plant life, no sign of soil—there is no bare ground. I know that soil exists somewhere deep below my feet, below the layer of trash where it is of no use. At one point this place might have been a forest. I don't even know what a forest looks like, but I have heard stories about seas of green and brown and an abundance of cute little animals. That is now a thing of the past.

As the wind blows, small whirlwinds of paper form, and

I'm forced to shield my eyes as papers whip against me. It's unusually windy tonight, but I don't take much notice because I am almost back to my home. The volve swings on my back as I take each step over the uneven ground. It's not exceptionally heavy; fifty, maybe sixty pounds. If it were an adult, I would have had to leave it and return later with help.

"Yo, Zane." I look up to see Auburn standing atop the first wagon. I can barely hear him from here. He is but a speck. I immediately quicken my steps to reach him.

The wagon is huge, a giant metal house on tracks, with steam billowing out of its many chimneys, spiraling high into the sky where it disappears into the darkness.

"Got yourself another volve, I see. Killing a whole pack this morning wasn't enough?" It's Auburn yelling again. His voice is low and echoes down to where I am standing.

I yell back, "It attacked me first. I was only defending myself, you know I don't like killing."

"Whatever you say. Now get up here!" I walk up to the wagon and start scaling the metal ladder on the side. When I pull myself up onto the first rung of the thin metal ladder, I can feel the slow movement of the wagon. Its speed is no more than one mile per hour, but it moves us steadily over the trash. Inside I hear the steam engine humming and feel the slight vibration of the ladder as I climb. I reach the top of the moving house—Auburn lends me a hand to help me up the last couple of rungs. I take his hand and look up into his face.

His dark skin blends in with the night around us. His features are prominently African, a large slightly flattened nose, dark black hair that seems to have no respect for the laws of gravity, and bright white teeth surrounded by thick brown lips. Like me, he wears a pair of jeans torn at the knees, and a pair of metal-plated boots. His muscular arms are revealed by his sleeveless shirt that looks as though it's stitched together from about a million different scraps of cloth. He takes the volve from me and then says, "I'll give this to the butcher. It's a runt of a thing, but should be enough for a couple of dinners." I'm relieved to have the dead animal out of my hands as I wipe my sweaty palms on my worn jeans.

"I'll come with you, but you can carry it," I tell him. He just grins at me and adjusts his grip on the volve. I look around. I can see everything from up here. I see all the other wagons moving along with us, twenty in all, each one different from the other. None is symmetrical and they look as though they have been fixed and added onto hundreds of times, because they have.

Some have small gardens on top while others have wind turbines and rain barrels. Imagine every piece of metal you have ever seen, and then imagine it put together into a house-shaped structure and slammed onto a set of tracks. If you can do that, you have a pretty good idea of what one of these wagons looks like; like the bottom half of a tank and the top half of an RV, but much larger and more randomly constructed.

We make our way through the garden atop our wagon to a hinged metal panel in the roof. The gardens are one of the only places on this planet where you will see any kind of plant life, and they only grow with large amounts of work, and soil that comes from the city, Skumford, where there are mines to collect it from under the layers of trash.

We pass through a row of herbs and another of carrots before we reach the rusty hatch.

"Not like you to be waiting atop the roof to greet me, so what's up?"

Auburn grabs the handle and swings the hatch open, revealing another ladder descending deeper into the wagon's interior. It doesn't seem the most efficient entry to climb all the way up the side only to descend back down again, but it's necessary for security reasons—keeping out volves and the occasional unfriendly Nomad group. When it comes down to it, it is more efficient to be alive, so we keep the main door closed after dark.

"I had finished dinner and I was getting tired of Zeleng's complaining so I thought I would get a bit of fresh air and wait for you to arrive." Auburn's voice echos up from his lower position on the ladder.

The hatch clangs shut above me, the sound reverberating through the narrow chute. I lock the hatch behind me with a couple of padlocks as well as the old-fashion bar across the opening. I am fairly sure we are the last ones back, so odds are we aren't locking anybody out. It had happened to me before, and let's just say Ham got an unexpected guest knocking at his window that night. Auburn is already several feet below. Although he is descending with one hand (his other holding the volve), he doesn't seem to be having very much trouble. When we climb to the bottom, we will be in the main room where we eat dinner and spend most of our free time. Many of the other rooms in the wagon can be entered from this main room. As I climb down the last couple of rungs, the metal of my boots against the ladder alerts anyone in the main room of our arrival. There aren't as many people in the room as I would have thought—but then again, it's late at night, and most people are in bed preparing for the early morning.

The room is a rectangle about twenty-five by forty feet, but it looks like a rectangle drawn by a five-year-old. The walls slant slightly and don't always follow a perfectly straight line. There is an assortment of torn chairs and scratched tables scavenged from the dumps as we travel. A couple of older people sit around these tables, talking and playing chess. They have a board they had found, but the actual pieces are scraps of metal, and a fair amount of plastic army men, more stuff scavenged in the unending landscape of trash, which is our source for everything.

Some of the other walkers, who have returned from a long day walking along side the wagons, sit around tables or on couches in the corner. A few eat from bowls, but for the most part everyone seems to have attended dinner earlier. Walkers is the name given to people who walk along the wagons, surveying the trash dropped earlier that week by the Clean World ships called Trash Crafts. Sitting among them is Zeleng, probably the only person other than Auburn I call a friend. He wears his usual volve skin cloak; his spiky black hair falling across his face as if it is intent on covering his eyes. He spots us and walks over.

"Another volve. You know how tired of volve meat I am," Zeleng complains. He has an amazing way of looking sad while grinning from ear to ear.

"Just think, it's almost time to harvest the roof gardens again," replies Auburn, wistfully.

"And as a bonus, we won't have to listen to your complaining anymore," I say, returning Zeleng's infectious smile.

"I know, but why couldn't we just stop at Skumford once in a while and trade for some fish or something?" Zeleng says. "I'm sick of volve. You feel me?" Auburn and I are used to his complaining. He does it jokingly, but sometimes I almost complain about his complaining.

As we head for the kitchen, Zeleng doesn't question what we are doing. I push open the metal door at the far end of the main room. Let's just say the kitchen isn't my favorite place. Carcasses lie everywhere, and the skinned and cleaned volves hang from the ceiling already smoked and salted and ready to store away. The place reeks of blood and organs, but I guess we are to blame for that, since a pack of volves does take a while to cut up and dry. I think back to our scuffle with the volves. It had been early in the day, so Auburn, Zeleng and I had barely been outside an hour before they attacked. There had been six of them, a large male, two females and three volves that were entering their teen years, almost old enough to split and start a pack of their own. They had come out of nowhere, creeping up behind us, quieter than a wisp of wind. Then they attacked with a shriek much like the volve I killed minutes earlier had made, and only my quick reflexes saved us. I pulled my bow and shot the large male in its muscled shoulder. It had continued towards us, slower than before. With the others following the large male's lead and slowing, it had given Auburn and Zeleng just enough time to pull their weapons and put up a fight. With the air of surprise gone the pack had nothing on us, and we finished them off quickly. I had only killed a single volve in the morning attack, Auburn and Zeleng had dealt with the others with gusto, but I still felt the twinge of sadness that is brought about everytime I end a life for my own sake. Auburn and Zeleng had gone off to the wagon to get help transporting the volves back to it, and I had told them I wanted some alone time. I had spent the rest of the day wandering the trash alone. It was a nice change to be by myself in the Wasteland. It gave me time to think without interruption. Of course, until that other volve had attacked, and I had been forced to slaughter another animal. I look to the creature in Auburn's arms and pause for a moment trying to locate our cook and butcher.

At first I don't see the him. He's so covered in blood that he's easily mistaken for a dead volve. The butcher's name is Ham. The name's ironic because none of us has ever eaten ham. As far as we know, there aren't even any pigs left in the world. All of them either died out or were taken by the people who left for the Clean World all those years ago. Ham is a small, bald man with an assortment of knives hanging on his belt. Usually I wouldn't trust somebody that small with knives so big, but Ham has strong meaty arms and is a master at cutting things up—it doesn't matter whether those things are dead or alive. His skin is permanently stained red, which makes his black eyes stand out from his face, sort of like the spots on a ladybug (another creature I have only seen in books). If he weren't about four foot nine, I would be afraid of him.

"When are you going to stop? Volve after volve after volve after volve. You gotta give me some time to sleep." Ham's a good sport about it, but I can see he is irritated. I would be too if I had to spend all day cutting up dead animals, up to my waist in gore.

"Hey. It's better to have a surplus of food than not enough," says Zeleng, trying to sound intelligent. He strokes his chin for extra effect.

"Genius Zeleng strikes again," Auburn jokes. I chuckle at that. That is probably one of my favorite things about Zeleng and Auburn. We can make fun of each other all we want without anyone ever taking it personally, and we are always able to laugh about it.

"Bring it here," says Ham, needlessly gesturing at the volve. Auburn walks up to him and drops the animal onto his counter. Ham pulls out a knife and gets to work, viciously slicing and hacking it to pieces. Blood leaks out of the volve's mouth and from multiple incisions that Ham bestows on the dead creature.

At that point Auburn, Zeleng and I leave, not wanting to see Ham rip apart the innards of the animal. Just the squelching, tearing sounds are enough to make me choke, but part of the choke almost seems like it's from the sadness of watching a creature that minutes earlier had been alive reduced to a pile of meat. I scold myself on being so compassionate. In the Wasteland it is survival of the fittest, and tonight I just happened to be the fitter one. Before I am completely through the threshold, I feel something slimy hit the back of my neck. I don't even look back to see what organ hit me. The last thing I hear before leaving the room is Ham's uncontrollable giggles, as if throwing animal parts at me is the funniest thing ever. I slam the door, eager to block out Ham's laughter, and to prevent any more body parts from flying my way. Zeleng and Auburn are laughing again, and Zeleng's laugh is so contagious that even as I wipe the slime off my neck, I am laughing, but a part of me still aches. I had become a target for a slaughtered creature's body parts. Amusing? Maybe. Degrading? Certainly.

The three of us head back through the main room. It is the height of two floors. Ladders go up at irregular intervals into doors randomly placed higher up. The whole place is made of metal sheets welded together, as well as a good amount of wood and the occasional brick. The walls are lined with cabinets made of every kind of wood you can imagine, filled with just about anything you can imagine—cans of food, wires, paper, boxes of junk, and anything else found in the usual junkyard. Lights hang from the ceiling; some are oil lamps, but others are electric, powered by energy that comes from turbines on the roof of the wagon. There's a very cozy, cluttered feel to the whole place. In one corner there is a couple of old ratty couches placed around a metal-framed fireplace. Seated, leg crossed, in a black armchair—that at one point may have been white—is our leader, Leon. He doesn't sit like an almighty ruler perched on top of a mighty throne, all straight backed and official. Instead, he conducts his work sitting in a torn up armchair, slumped over slightly and leaning against the back, giving the impression that he is laidback and relaxed. He has long black hair covering one eye. He wears a volve skin cloak just like Zeleng's, but unlike Zeleng, he has a belt wrapped around his waist. A sword and dagger rest on the arm of the chair, making it very clear that although he is very laid back he is not off his guard. His face has a long scar across the right side from an incident with a volve. On the eye not covered by this hair, there is a green lens, almost like a monocle. This lens is a device that allows magnification of his field of vision, as well as limited x-ray and night vision. The lens is from the Clean World, a rare piece of technology that was found intact by one of the walkers and is so far ahead of any other piece of technology we have that even Leon hasn't discovered all its capabilities.

As we approach, Leon glances up at us. He seems to have been in a heated conversation with a group of older men about weapons. I recognize them not by name, but as people I have seen before. They must be part of one of the other wagons under Leon's control and have come to inform him about an issue. This occurrence isn't unusual, because Leon lives in our wagon. When there is a problem, people come here to talk to him.

We pass by them and sit on one of the couches. It's old and ratty, but that doesn't matter. It's my favorite couch. I scavenged it myself. It's made of black leather, and if I really wanted to, I could get my first ever taste of cow by licking it. It probably cost a fortune in the Clean World. But typical of the people of the Clean World, they threw it away, probably after it got the tiniest rip or stain. Auburn and Zeleng sit next to me in silence for a bit. I am glad to finally sit after an entire day of walking.

After a minute or so Zeleng says, "Find anything else besides that volve?"

"Not really, I wasn't really looking for anything." I don't usually find anything very useful. A daily scavenge for me usually consists of scraps of cloth, or pencils, or string, or anything you might find in the average trash can. But when I'm lucky, I might find a can of food or two, or a not completely rusted knife. By far the most valuable thing I have ever found is my collection of movies and books.

Zeleng nods. "Just think how our ancestors had it before our world became such a giant crap hole."

"They were fat and lazy because food was so easy to get. They also were idiots. Ruined this planet in a few hundred years after it had supported life for millions of years. And to top it off, they killed off almost every animal that they couldn't eat, and destroyed their habitats to build their own places to live," Auburn says, distastefully.

Bashing our ancestors is something we do a lot, but it always gets me thinking. I try to imagine how it must have been. Is it possible that only a few hundred years ago this world was a prosperous, expanding land of plenty? There is no written account of exactly how it happened, but from stories passed down through generations, we have a vague outline of how it has played out. It started when technical and medical advances had increased the average life span to over one hundred years. With fewer people dying and the birth rate being so much larger than the death rate, population skyrocketed—and so did pollution. Farms were moved to floating islands that covered large sections of the oceans just to produce enough food for an ever-increasing population. As oil and natural gasses became harder and harder to find, let alone to supply, people started panicking. Food and water became scarcer as farmers struggled to keep up. Being the soft-hearted creatures humans are, the easy solution of birth control and allowing the old to die off wasn't an option, so the governments of the world decided the only solution was to reduce the population of earth by other means.

Billions of the rich and middle classes boarded ships

headed for a newly discovered planet and ring of moons with almost three times the landmass of the Earth. The world drained, until only about one billion people remained on Earth. This should have been a great success—the population had been drastically reduced and that should have meant that the earth would recover. One small problem: Earth was already too far gone to return to what it once was. The people left behind knew this. Everyone thought the ships were going to come back, because surely the governments weren't about to leave one billion people to starve to death on a planet stripped of its resources and polluted to the point of no return. Twelve years later the ships did come back. During those twelve years people fought for food. Millions died from starvation, or were murdered for their food – or, in the worst case, for the meat on their bodies. The killing continued without an end in sight, and when the first ships were spotted everyone was hopeful that finally they had come back to save them—but that was far from the truth. The ships' sole purpose, they soon found out, was to bring trash—an endless stream of it at that. No one understood why they would go through the trouble of bringing trash all the way back to Earth, but there were speculations. "The Clean World was shipping their trash to Earth as a storage facility," some said, "using Earth to store resources until they could be recycled." The ships, as far we know, never came back to reclaim any of the trash, so people started to suspect more evil things. The Clean World was bringing trash back to Earth just to torture the remaining inhabitants of Earth even more. With all hope lost, the killing intensified. Everybody was now sure that they had been abandoned. Why couldn't the Trash Crafts take survivors back once their cargo of trash was emptied? The only answer people could come up with to address this question was, that the people of the Clean World simply didn't want us. Trash came faster and faster. They thought surely they would run out of stuff to dump on Earth—but no such luck. The people of New Earth, or as we call it, the Clean World, had learned how to harvest asteroids full of water and minerals, thus it became unnecessary to recycle. Eventually skyscrapers in our cities became buried, and all natural ground was covered in layer after layer of waste. Earth became nearly uninhabitable. In a matter of decades the population went from almost ten billion to less than two hundred million scattered survivors.

The people of the Clean World thought they would help Earth by creating new genetically modified animals to replace the ecosystems they had destroyed. From this came new breeds of fish that could survive in super-polluted waters. They created treefs—herds of scavenging bull-like animals, which spread across the world eating whatever they could scavenge. They also created hybrid animals such as volves to balance out their new ecosystem. But the volves became ruthless killers, intent on eating anything that moved. That is how it was for the next three hundred years. During that time humans became scavengers, living off volve meat and the bull creature's meat known as treef. Cockroaches and humans are the sole survivors of this ruined Earth. The Earth that had harbored millions of species throughout its existence was left as a dead sphere in space, giving home to a small group of humans that still hung on to their survival.

These survivors split into three groups: the Bargemen, who travel the seas (in old ships from the time before everyone left Earth, and sometimes in new ships built in the cities) fishing the large schools of genetically altered fish; the Nomads, who travel the land scavenging and hunting volves; and the CityFolk, who farm as best they can, and make things that can't be scavenged, therefore basing their lives on trading with the Nomads and Bargemen.

Once order and a system of living was reinstated, things started to improve and the slightest bit of normalcy was restored to a life that was anything but normal. Even I, who had been born into this condition, couldn't find it normal. There is a better life out there and we all know it. I am part of Leon's Nomad group which is very large; about five hundred or so people who live in the twenty wagons under his control.

"Stellafilius, you there?" The use of my last name tears me from thoughts of how we have come to be, just in time to notice a hand reaching out to rap on my head with its knuckles.

"Yah?" I answer, shaking my head a little to clear it of thoughts.

"I brought you some volve soup." Somehow, during all my thinking, Auburn and Zeleng had had enough time to finish their conversation, get up, and get me food without my noticing. Auburn sets down in front of me a coffee tin cut in such a way that it forms a bowl shape—the smell makes my stomach roar like a volve on the hunt. Ironically, however, we are the ones who hunted the volve and are now are eating it.

I give him a little sarcastic grin, staring right at Zeleng

as I say, "Oh yay. I'm totally not tired of this stuff."

"You're starting to sound like me," says Zeleng, apparently not realizing that that was my intention. I sip the soup with a slightly bent rusty spoon. The soup is in a tin coffee can because not very many ceramics or glass items survive the trip to the Wasteland, or the fall from the Trash Craft as it flies over, or the treef rampages. The soup is nice and warm—a good feeling spreads through me. I hadn't realized how hungry I was. I stir the chunks around my bowl and think about the animals we had to kill to get it. I remind myself that it is me or them, and try not to feel bad. Finally, I spoon the last few mouthfuls out of the tin and look up. Auburn and Zeleng had been talking about something, but I had been too engrossed in my food to notice. "Dang, I need to get some....," but before I can finish the sentence, I yawn, "sleep."

"Yeah, I know. I can barely keep my eyes open." says Auburn, making a show of rubbing his eyes.

"Am I really that boring to listen to?" laughs Zeleng, also getting up now.

To get to our room we walk through a passage that is cramped and vibrates from the engine. The steam engine is loud, but keeps us warm no matter what the temperature is outside. Metal pipes run across the walls, bringing water to the engine and steam hisses from several leaks. Our door is made from an old refrigerator door, and is only about three feet high, so we must crouch as we walk inside. I share the room with Zeleng and Auburn since they are the only other people my age in all of the wagons—they are really my only friends. We have four bunks on the left wall covered with torn mattresses, ripped pillows and a random assortment of rags and blankets. The other wall space is covered with shelves overflowing with scavenged objects. Old torn-up books, clothing, and metal parts litter the floor, but there are mostly books.

Whenever I see a book lying in the trash, I can't bring myself to pass it by. I always end up picking it up and bringing it home. I find so many that I don't think I'll have enough time to read them all—but it gives me a good feeling to know I have them in case I need them. That is a kind of side advantage of living in trash. You start to appreciate what people throw away, and you become a major league hoarder.

There's a small circular window that looks out over the desolate landscape—sitting right under it is a large box TV and VCR. The thing is at least a few hundred years old, but miraculously, when there's enough power, it actually works. Over the years I have put together a small collection of movies. But movies are kind of rare, because in the age when the world was being abandoned, instant online movies had made owning an actual copy obsolete.

We each walk over to our beds. I lay my bow next to my bed and hang up the quiver that I made from old backpack straps and a cylinder pipe, and crawl in, not even bothering to pull up the covers. The heat of the steam engine has me covered. "Night guys," I say into the darkness. I get no reply. My friends are already snoring. I pull a chain and the light turns off. When I finally get comfortable, I am out in the blink of an eye.

Dueling Questions

I awake to the clattering of metal, like someone had tried to make a drum set using only metal and no drums. I keep my eyes closed even though the sound makes me want to get up and strangle whoever's making it. Why are beds always so comfortable in the morning? One of my arms hangs off the bed. I lift it to my face and rub my eyes, yawning as I do so. When I finally open them, I see Zeleng pulling his weapons from the chest next to the TV, not even bothering to be quiet. He has his gun slung over his shoulder. We never find guns, since nobody in his right mind, even in the minds of the horrible people of the Clean World, would throw away a gun. We are forced to buy them in Skumford, the city that makes guns in its forges. They are very crude, large barreled, one shot rifles. Good for hunting—but in a fight, I always prefer my bow, which, unlike a gun, takes almost no time to get off another shot. Zeleng also has a shield resting on his back. It's made of thick wood with a thin metal sheeting on it. The edges are studded with nails so he can bash the heck out of anything that attacks him. The most deadly weapon he carries is his mace. It's a long metal shaft, wrapped with duct tape and cloth until it is comfortable to hold. On the end is a solid piece of metal with multiple spikes protruding from it. Zeleng's fighting technique includes a lot of bashing, mixed in with some ninja rolls and spins. He swings his mace around, nearly hitting the TV, and notices that I am awake.

"You awake?" he asks, completely needlessly. I nod, and with a struggle I roll out of bed. I slept in my jeans and shirt, so I simply grab my bow and quiver and walk over to him, grabbing a hoodie off a hook as I go. I brush the hair out of my eyes and look down into the weapons chest. In it I see my dagger and sword, two weapons that I purchased at the dingy forges of Skumford with stuff that I had scavenged. I recall I bought my sword with a dozen cans of food and forty pounds of scrap metal. I don't carry my sword very much because it's rare that I would ever have to fight hand in hand with a volve. I much prefer to pick them off at a distance with a gun, or, even better, my bow. Instead, I pull the dagger from the chest and strap it to my belt. I notice Auburn's sword and bow are missing. He must have already collected them and has probably gone to eat breakfast. Zeleng closes the chest and replaces the lock. Locking up weapons in a locked room in a guarded wagon may seem a bit overly cautious, but the weapons are the most valuable things we own, so we prize them.

We stroll into the main room—a quick glance reveals that Auburn isn't here either. The only other place he would likely be is the training room, unless he has already started scavenging without us, which isn't likely, knowing that Auburn isn't the kind of person to get up early and work.

Breakfast is a step off the path of normalcy. We get to eat canned food. You would be surprised how much canned food is thrown away in the Clean World just because it's past the suggested expiration date, which, with canned food, is usually a bunch of bull or better still, treef. Today, when I swing by the kitchen, Ham hands me canned peaches and garbanzo beans. Not the best combination, but I'm not about to complain. This is a luxury compared to the normal breakfast of ground volve bone and oats. For once Zeleng doesn't complain about the food, and we eat fast in silence, making no effort to be polite. Several other people are eating on the couch. I recognize Luke and his younger brother, Paul. They are some of the other walkers and are about the only other people close to my age.

Luke and Paul, Zeleng, Auburn and I are all walkers. We became friends because we spent long days together sifting through trash.

I've lived in Leon's Nomad group since before I can remember, and I remember the day that we found Auburn and Zeleng, half dead and starving after they had been separated from their Nomad group. I was about eight at the time, but I still remember it as though it was yesterday. I remember spotting them and yelling for help. The Nomads had taken them in without questioning because they were only kids—and even the hardened get soft when it comes to saving kids.

I was happy to finally have some kids my own age in our wagon. On the other hand, I had known Luke and Paul for my entire life, but they were older than me. Luke was twenty-four and his brother eighteen, so they never became such close friends as Auburn or Zeleng, but we are definitely pretty good pals. Luke is tall—he has longish blonde hair and a barely visible blonde beard. His face reflects years of hardship that almost every older person wears. However, he is probably the most hopeful and optimistic about getting to the Clean World, often coming up with wild plans to accomplish it. His brother is the exact opposite of him—much shorter, heavier and not as confident. He also doesn't believe that we can ever escape to the Clean World, but he will follow his brother anywhere. Usually I would have acknowledged them, but I am eager to find Auburn, so I continue to stuff my face.

I see only a few other familiar faces as I look around, most people having already eaten, but there's still a buzz of conversation all around us, discussing anything from wagon trails to the weather. Everyone looks pretty happy. All it seems to take these days is some good food and bam—just like that, a wagon full of happy scavengers. I've just scooped the last of my peaches and am about to turn to my beans when I hear a familiar voice behind me.

"Hey, scoot it." I'm roughly pushed to the side as Auburn squeezes in next to me. "So, while you fatties were sleeping, I've already been to the training room." I don't bother to acknowledge his insult.

"And your point is?" I ask, using my dagger to pry open my can of beans.

"I was going to say that I overheard Leon talking to the old weapon master. What is his name even. Kerry? Well, Leon said something about finding another one. I didn't think much of it, but as I heard more, it sounded as if they had found something unbelievably dangerous."

"What kind of something?' I say, not really buying it.

"How should I know? All I got out of it is that they are trying to hide something dangerous from us."

"So. You're saying Leon is hiding something from us?" asks Zeleng, showing off his obvious brilliance.

"Yeah, that's literally what I just said," says Auburn, somewhat exasperated.

"I don't buy it," I say. "Leon is the best leader we have ever had. He wouldn't keep something from us unless the knowledge would disrupt the order around here, or just plain obliterate it," I reply, but even as I say it, I begin to think. I wonder, has Leon found something that could endanger life as we know it? Definitely hard to believe, but not impossible.

"If he were talking to the weapon master, what he found must be some kind of weapon, right?" Zeleng suggests.

"You don't say," says Auburn, rolling his eyes. But Zeleng brought up a valid point. The thing they found must be some kind of weapon that could threaten our existence. I'm not sure if something like that even exists, other than a nuclear bomb. And I am pretty sure they didn't find one of those lying around.

"I trust Leon, but we'll kill two volves with one stone. We'll take a look around the training room while getting in some training."

"Why would we even kill a volve with a stone, let alone two. If it was me I would smash them to death with my mace," ponders Zeleng. Auburn and I exchange eyerolls, but don't bother to say anything.

We climb one of the older wooden ladders up to a higher floor to reach the training room. For Nomads, training consists of weight lifting, body exercises, sparring, wrestling and anything else that might help our survival. After climbing the ladder, I push the hatch open. It creaks on its old rusty hinges. I pull myself into the room and glance around to find it deserted. Usually there are a few people in here shooting targets and sword fighting. "No one is up here!" I shout down through the hatch where Zeleng and Auburn are looking up at me.

"Better for us—nobody to get in the way of our training. And nobody to laugh when I beat you guys," challenges Zeleng. "That also closes the case on exploring what Leon's been up to, that being kind of hard if he isn't here."

The room is roughly the same size as the main room. The ceiling dips and slants randomly from other rooms that have been built on top. To the left side, on the floor, painted circles indicate small fighting rings. The other half of the room is filled with targets to practice shooting, some pull-up bars, and assorted heavy things people can weight lift—among these are tires and even a mini fridge. Once the others climb into the room, we determine who will spar first. For now, thoughts of the strange, life-altering weapon we were going to look for are temporarily forgotten. We sure have our priorities straight. We argue for a little, and then decide Auburn and Zeleng will spar first. They exchange their weapons for the less lethal wooden rods. This sparring prepares us for confrontations with people that we might have to fight. It might even save our lives someday.

Auburn and Zeleng step into the first ring. "Ready to get your butt kicked?" asks Zeleng, shrugging off his cloak, and gripping his weapon with both hands.

"You wish," says Auburn, cracking his knuckles.

If I didn't know these two so well, I would bet Auburn would win. He has size and strength on his side. But I know Zeleng is a demon when it comes to fighting. He's super fast, and has some wicked moves. All in all, I would say, they are evenly matched.

They face each other and start to circle, volve style. Auburn has a three-foot-long wooden stick in each hand. He swirls them around, getting a feel for each. Zeleng holds one stick. It is about four feet long, but he carries a shield to make up for it. "Ready?" I ask, looking at each of them in turn. They nod and I start the count down.

"Three...............Two...............One...............Fight!"

Zeleng strikes like a viper, his stick swings up, barely missing Auburn's face. The movement of his weapon, cutting through the air, sounds like the whistling of wind on a windy night. Auburn steps to the side and takes a swing at Zeleng, who darts out of the way, rolling behind Auburn. Zeleng strikes Auburn's back before he can turn around. There's a muffled thud as the stick hits his back, and Auburn's face contorts from pain and anger. For a second, Auburn doesn't move. Zeleng seems to be considering if it would be too much to hit him again, when Auburn swirls around, rage turning his mouth into a snarl. Their sticks meet. Their faces strain as each one pushes as hard as he can.

I can tell by how Zeleng is trying to find an escape from the deadlock, that Auburn is much stronger and will soon overpower him. As expected, Auburn pushes him to the ground. Zeleng gasps for breath, but he brings his feet up and kicks Auburn's knees. Auburn cries out and falls next to Zeleng. They both scramble to their feet and face each other again. They are both breathing heavily now—sweat is starting to bead up. I can see it on their foreheads. They engage again in a flurry of movement and swinging sticks. Zeleng swirls around Auburn, striking with incredible speed. Auburn fends off the attack with swings that knock Zeleng away. The sounds of their sticks colliding are like gunshots—loud and in short bursts.

At this point I turn away and head towards the other side of the room to the row of targets. I walk to a point roughly twenty feet away. If I weren't confined in a room, I would have shot from much further back. I am somewhat of a prodigy with a bow. Ever since I was first given my bow at age eleven, it has been my weapon of choice, and I have learned to wield it with deadly accuracy. I string an arrow onto the bow as I raise it. I take a deep breath and bring the arrow up to a firing position. I pull the string back to my ear with ease. I spend roughly a second calculating my shot. Over the years the bow has become like an extra limb to me. All I have to do is think about where I want the arrow to fly, and when I release it, it strikes my intended target. I tighten my hold on the string and release the arrow. It flies through the air in a blur of black and gray for less than a second, before it thuds into the target about three inches below the bull's eye. I shoot again and again, until I have used all my arrows.

I hear the thuds of sticks hitting sticks and the thuds of my arrows sinking into the target. Mixed in with the thuds are the grunts of pain and gasps of strain. I don't bother to see how the fight is going, I know the participants too well. If it's like normal, they will exchange blows until they drop—no one winning or losing. I retrieve my arrows,

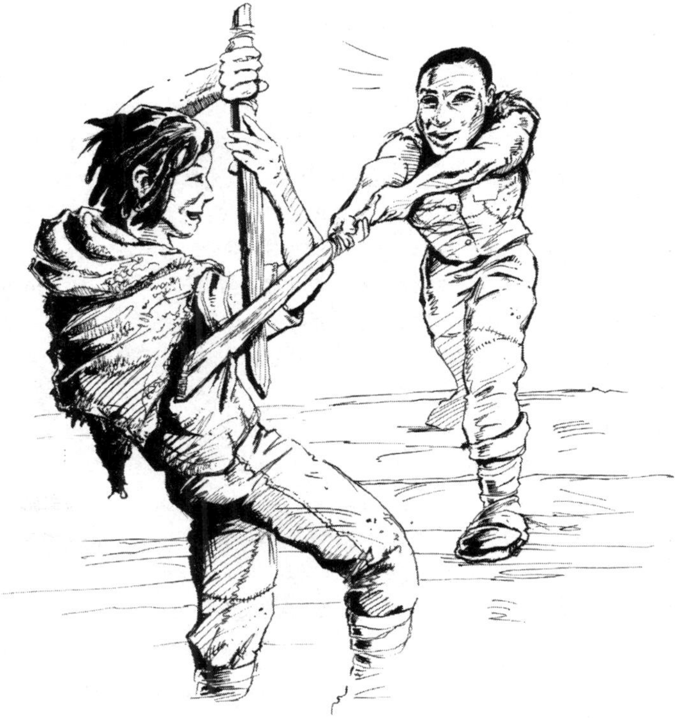

yanking them from the wood of the target, and then walk back and resume shooting. There is something very relaxing about the steady thud of arrows, and I think that's why I enjoy shooting so much.

Shooting also gives me time to think without interruption, and naturally my mind drifts to the mysterious thing Leon is hiding from us. I can't imagine that anything is dangerous enough for him to keep it from us. The whole thing sounds rather ridiculous, and I make a silent note to keep an eye out for anything, but to not actively stick my nose into it. Besides, I trust Leon with my life, no matter what he does. Without him, I would most likely be dead, or stuck in some slave wagon. Ham and Leon had given me a chance I would never have had as an orphan—a shot at an actual life. They always made, and still do, make sure I have enough to eat, and that I am happy. They weren't parents by a long shot, but they got me through my early life to a point where I became self-sufficient, something I couldn't have done on my own. That is a debt that I will never be able to repay—but I'll start by not nosing into Leon's business. With that settled in my head, I shoot my last arrow.

After gathering all my arrows back into my quiver, I head back over to where the others had been dueling—but now they are lying exhausted in heaps on the ground. "I think it's possible that we were a little too rough," says Zeleng, wiping blood from his nose and sweat from his forehead. "You don't say. I feel beat up," says Auburn, using one of his favorite lines.

"Hah, yeah, because I won," Zeleng says, trying to smile—but it looks more like a wince.

"You want a rematch right now?" challenges Auburn, a black bruise already spreading across his eye. He attempts to stand up, but falls back down.

"No way," says Zeleng, a bit too quickly. And we all start laughing, because they're in no shape to fight anymore.

"I guess we should call it quits. I guess I don't get to fight." I'm not exactly mad about it, but I always find it fun to fight my friends, and test each one's skill and strength, while the whole time getting stronger, faster and more in shape.

After Auburn and Zeleng recover enough to stumble to the door, we grab our weapons and head out of the training room.

All in a Day's Work

We pick up a few more things—some thick leather gloves, a spacious backpack, and a canteen of water that we fill with lukewarm water from the rain barrels on our way out. Since the sun is high in the sky, the main door of the wagon is open, and the ramp has been lowered so it is easier to get out. The three of us step out into the Wasteland, prepared for a long day scavenging as walkers.

"Nice day out," comments Auburn, shielding his eyes as he looks up into the sky. It is true. The sun rises higher into the sky, blazing heat onto the trash, creating even smellier heaps of partially roasted rot. It would have been uncomfortable, if not for a cool breeze that dries the sweat the second it forms. However nice the weather is, it is perfect fire weather—dry and windy.

Trash fires are absolutely devastating, burning out of control through the endless supply of fuel. Besides reducing everything to ash, trash fires also send up poisonous fumes from all the plastic and chemicals they burn. The only way to be completely safe from them is to cross a river or just get as far away as possible.

We walk in a diagonal line from the wagon, just enough so that we keep up with the wagon's slow movement forward, while still getting further away. Our metal-clad boots crunch on broken glass and grate against metal, and wind stirs up papers like the leaves of long ago. I search the ground, keeping my eyes out for anything of use. I spot some cans, but a closer inspection reveals that they are empty. We are mostly surrounded by piles of rotting food, crumpled papers, plastic crap and the occasional wire or cracked computer.

We continue to wander farther from the wagons, but we make sure we are always able to see the column of steam that rises to the sky from the many chimneys and steam pipes of the wagons, so we can always find our way back. Getting lost in the Wasteland is probably the worst thing that could happen to a person. It happened to me and Luke a long time ago, and the memory is so sickening that I have shoved it deep into the back of my mind to avoid thinking about it. Just thinking about thinking about it makes me shudder.

For the next few hours we scan the trash, spread out enough so that we can't really talk without yelling. My legs don't get tired because they are used to this exertion—twelve hours a day, everyday—but what does hurt are my head and eyes. After a while of looking at the same dull color, trying to find useful objects, my eyes start to play tricks on me, and everything starts to look like something I might want to investigate.

We take a break around noon, judging by the sun's position in the sky. We take cover from the blazing sun the best we can behind a mound of trash consisting of four couches, two dented refrigerators, and a mound of assorted mini ovens and microwaves.

"I haven't found much," I say. From my backpack I produce two cans of green beans, in cans so smashed they look like plates rather than cans, and a couple of rusty knives still slightly sharp.

"Same. This trash is trash today. Am I right?" Zeleng looks at us as if he expects applause or something. When he realizes he isn't going to get any, his smile fades, and he starts to take out his findings.

I take a sip from my canteen. The water is basically air temperature and does nothing to cool me off—and that earlier breeze is all but gone. Zeleng pulls out a bundle of t-shirts—not in as bad a condition as you usually find, and a rubber ducky that squeaks as he squeezes it above his head. Zeleng is always collecting weird toys: teddy bears with their eyes missing, armless action figures, and so on. As far as I know, he's never found a good use for them. They are still sitting in the box he stores them in, like a giant death hole of neglected toys. It was a little strange, but I had long ago assumed Zeleng just collected them for kicks. Bringing a rubber ducky back to the wagons is a definite way to get some laughs, and that is basically all that Zeleng lives for—that and complaining about food.

Auburn found a three pack of beanies and soy protein imitation weenies, which to my great relief is just another word for hot dog and nothing else. I get excited when he lifts them from his bag, thinking that I might have a chance to taste actual pork—but just my luck, they are for vegetarians. Most people hate vegetarians, but after a life of eating volve, I can totally see their logic. We sit in the shade for a while, savoring the rest before we get back to scavenging. We still have half a day of walking around in the heat. I am about to tell the others that we should actually get to scavenging and stop sitting on our butts, when a wild trumpeting shakes us from our somewhat relaxed state.

I immediately recognize the sound and let out a muffled curse—treefs that scavenge the land, eating any food scrap they can find. They don't eat meat, but they have no problem pulverizing any living thing that gets in their way.

"We gotta hide," I whisper, kind of needlessly, since nothing can be heard over the sound of the treefs' trumpets—a sound produced by the crest on the creatures' heads. I frantically search for somewhere we can hide. I hear the pounding of hooves definitely coming our way, like a thunderstorm suddenly deciding that it hates us in particular, and wants to make us deaf. A cloud of dust and paper appears on the horizon, a trail from the charging treefs.

"Over here!" yells Auburn. He's running towards a beat up old minivan with broken windows. It may have been white at one point, but now it is so rusted it's hard to tell. I can tell it's a few centuries old, not only because this type of vehicle is a thing of the past, but also by the piles of trash heaped on and around it that have clearly been built up through time and many trash storms. It doesn't take me long to decide to follow him—either that, or get trampled into a Zane-flavored pancake. I turn, and Zeleng and I sprint after him. The trash slips under our boots, which are just heavy enough to make it awkward to run. However

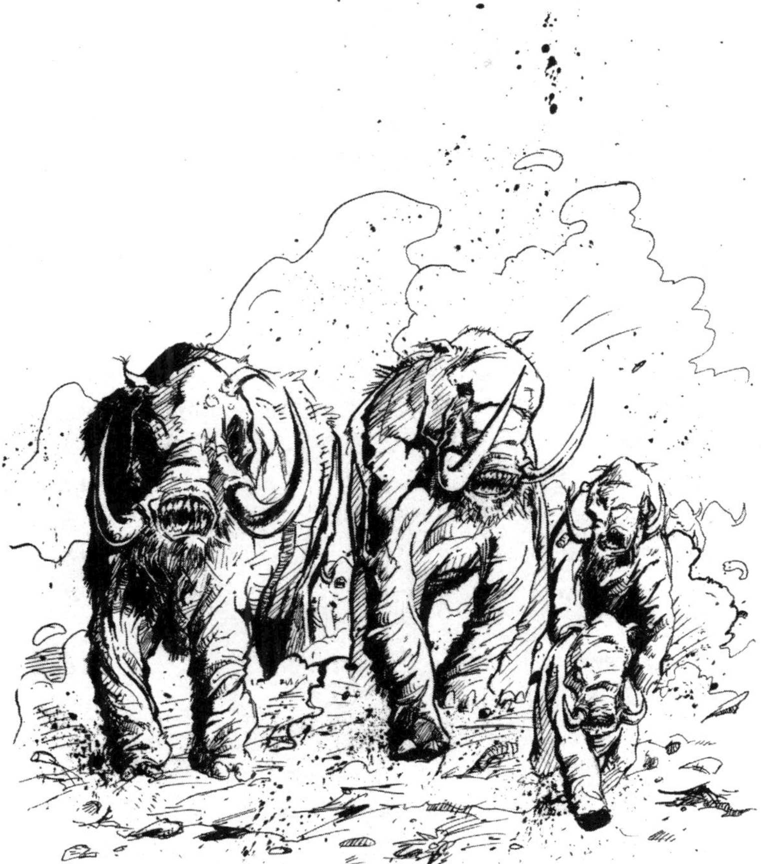

that isn't really stopping me now, and I run as though my life depends on it, because it probably does. I barely register when Zeleng slips on the uneven ground and falls, cutting open his knee, but somewhere in my subconscious, my brain is telling me, 'oh no'. I see him trying to get to his feet. I look left and see a wall of treefs thundering our way, like the lines of a massive army, armed with tusks as long as spears, headed right towards where Zeleng is struggling to get up.

It's kind of one of those moments that happen in movies just to make them seem more epic and unbelievable. What are the odds, that after weeks of walking around the Wasteland, he falls right into the path of a herd of giant creatures that will stomp on him as though he isn't there?

Zeleng looks at me. I see the expression in his eyes, as though he's trying to say 'dude, I scraped my knee, serious injury'. I see the slight trace of panic and fear that is natural in this situation, but honestly, we have had so many close calls to death that this seems like an every other week occurrence—scary as heck, but not life-altering terror.

I run towards him with only enough time to say, "If I die Zeleng, I am going to kill you."

I charge forward. The treefs are now only feet away, closing in fast like a giant tidal wave of tusks, hooves, fur and death. I reach Zeleng in seconds and grab his hand, pulling him up without losing stride. The sound, the trumpeting and thundering of hooves, is so loud, my brain feels as though it's going to explode—and if ears had mouths, they would be saying some choice words right now. I spin around headed back to Auburn, pulling Zeleng behind me. Auburn is frantically waving us to move faster, as if he thinks I am not sprinting for my life. He's standing by a van with the back doors swung open. We reach the van and dive in—rolling into the surprisingly soft carpet of the interior—just as the wall of treefs crashes over the ground I had occupied seconds earlier. A wave of trash and wind that the treefs' hooves throw up in their wild charge whips my back. Auburn slams the doors behind us, giving me a look that only translates as a wow, you're not a dead face—not necessarily comforting, but good enough. The van is knocked around as treefs brush against it—however, brush isn't really a strong enough word. The treefs are more accurately slamming their entire weights into the poor van, shaking it and its unfortunate occupants.

The whole interior smells of mildew. All the windows are cracked, but this vehicle is a godsend. Even against a herd of giant beasts this place should provide enough protection from the onslaught to allow us to escape with only minor cuts and scrapes.

I crawl to the window so I can get a view of what is happening outside and, hopefully, figure out what to do next. However, I am rudely interrupted by a two-ton creature scraping up against the van's frame, which is suddenly not feeling as safe. I don't make it to my destination. The whole van shakes from a tremendous force, and a tusk pierces the metal, ripping into it as if it's paper. The tusk keeps coming, pushing through the metal right towards me.

I scuttle back, not wanting to get shish-kabobbed on the end of a six foot tusk, and press myself against the wall with so much force, that it must look as though I am trying to become one with the wall—but the point of the razor sharp tusk keeps coming. If it is sharp enough to cut through metal, I don't want to see what it can do to human flesh.

I suck in my breath, trying to become as small as I can. The tusk seems intent on stabbing me as it comes closer and closer to my unprotected stomach. The whole thing kind of reminds me of some of the cartoons I had scavenged. The characters almost always get stuck in rooms that have spiked walls that close in on them. That is exactly how it is now—nowhere to go, with a deadly point just inches from my body.

Either out of fear, or some other trauma-activated emotion, my mind sends insane images of a giant finger inching towards me, and a scary high-pitched voice screeching 'tickle, tickle'.

I put my hand around the not so sharp part of the tusk and push it back with all my might. It's about as productive as me trying to push a wagon by myself, but it's instinctive, and somehow comforting, to try to save myself. I vaguely hear the others shouting—then there's a blur of movement as Zeleng takes a swing at the tusk with his mace. Although that isn't number one on my list of how to make a treef stop killing you, it seems to work.

The tusk retracts with a horrible grinding noise. This would have been a good thing if I weren't still holding onto it. I am dragged several feet before the message from my brain travels through my nervous system to my hand, telling it to let go before I get pulled into a herd of creatures that would have no problem killing me. I let out a grunt, but continue to the window. I peer out. All around us, huge creatures, as large as the van we are hiding in, charge from every direction. Each one has thick white tusks as long as spears, but much more deadly. Where their mouths should be, a mass of small sharp teeth appears to rotate. It looks like a blender, but it's actually different muscles in the creatures' mouths that move individual rows of teeth back and forth so fast that it creates the illusion of spinning. This horrendous mouth is used for grinding up anything and everything that has the misfortune of being ingested by it.

Compared to the mouth of the treef, the rest of the body looks cute. The creatures are covered in long stringy fur from head to hideous three-toed hooves. The fur even covers its eyes, but the green glow of them still shines through. The fur offers just enough protection so that the unblinking eyes don't get sunburned or dry up, but still allows them to see excellently, even at night, which helps them greatly, because whatever the time, they can find food. Herds of these roam the unending Wasteland, devouring anything edible—and they do a good job eating up the rotting, molding scraps that no humans in their right minds would eat. They aren't usually hostile, but rampaging around isn't unusual for them—they do it to claim territory, and to protect themselves from volve attacks. I can't determine the exact reason for this particular parade of death, but I can tell they are moving away from us, and are now vanishing in the opposite horizon from which they had come. I let out a huge sigh of relief and breathe deeply.

"You got struck by some good karma. Had you not saved me, I wouldn't have been there to bash the heck out of that treef's ugly sideways fang." Zeleng offers a tightly clenched hand, as if asking for a fist bump. After what I just went through, I don't have the energy to return the gesture. Instead, I slide down the wall, slumping into a sitting position.

"It's called a tusk, and I am pretty sure that isn't karma. Besides, all I did was help you up when you fell," I say, fixing my eyes on Zeleng, and giving him my best serious look. I fold my arms and narrow my eyes for good measure.

"Pretty sure it was more like you sprinted back in front of a herd of raging beasts the size of our fat ancestors—not even caring about your own life—just to help me up from my certain death by enormous hooves." Zeleng is sure good. He manages to make his own act of saving me sound modest, while making fun of our ancestors, and making it very clear that since we are both even now, there will be no thanking each other. After all, we each had almost been killed. If that isn't impressive, I don't know what is.

Zeleng winces, suddenly remembering that his knee is torn open, and he collapses into the driver's seat—all thoughts of a celebratory fist bump gone. He picks pieces of glass and metal out of his leg—blood drips down from it. He seems to be more irritated than in actual pain.

"Out of all the places to fall, I had to fall into a pile of glass," sighs Zeleng, continuing to pull pieces of glass from his flesh like it is no big deal. That is one thing living in the Wasteland will do to someone. No matter how weak you start out, after a few years in the Wasteland, you become strong and tough. Pain becomes a daily occurrence and not something to cry about.

He wipes his forehead. Instead of making it cleaner, he

All in a Day's Work 43

manages to swipe a bloody streak across his hairline. "And it tore a hole in my pants." Zeleng lets out another sigh.

"I am pretty sure you already had a hole in that pair of pants in that exact spot," says Auburn, who seems to have escaped the near death situation unharmed, and is sitting in the passenger seat watching us.

"No way," replies Zeleng, but he doesn't seem sure.

The sound of the treefs has all but disappeared, and it leaves an eerie silence only broken by Zeleng's complaints. "Like this is going to leave some scars…"

Auburn interrupts him before he can go on. "Zeleng, I'm soooo sorry that you're perfectly unblemished skin has been scarred… but we get the point. You're hurt and you need to vent."

This doesn't do anything to shut him up, so I change the subject. "Are we just gonna sit around nursing our wounds and reflecting on our life threatening situation?"

"Yeah, that sounds nice, and we should pop open some of those fake beenies and weenies—they can't be too bad and it sure is comfy in here. I think I will take a nap and…"

Before Zeleng can finish, Auburn again cuts him off. "Zane is right, we should get a move on." After a few minutes and a lot more complaining from Zeleng, we have wrapped his knee, and only by promising him that we will go straight back to the wagon have we convinced him to walk. As we step out of the van, I keep an eye out for volves. Even though volves usually only show themselves at night, with the smell of Zeleng's blood in the air, I don't want to risk anything.

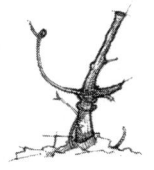

A Question-Raising Tug of War

When we arrive back at the wagons, the main room is nearly empty. In fact, except for Ham scuttling around preparing for dinner, the only other people in the room are Luke and Paul sitting at a table discussing who knows what—with them it really could be anything. Luke gives me an incredulous look as he sees us in the doorway. I don't blame him. Auburn, Zeleng and I are known for never ever returning to the wagon early. I, for one, like the effect that night has on the Wasteland. The whole Wasteland cools—everything grows dark, and you can almost imagine that you're not stuck on a planet covered in trash. Sure, it means risking a volve attack, but it is well worth the risk.

Luke nudges Paul and they beckon us over. Luke and Paul aren't like family to me as are Auburn and Zeleng, but I would classify them as friends that I mainly talk to because we are fellow walkers. Luke and Paul live in our wagon with their sister Arizon. I know they have parents, but they live in one of the other wagons. One of the things about living in a Nomad group the size of Leon's is that it is like having twenty different small communities tied together only by Leon's power. This means you can grow close to everyone in your particular wagon, but you only really 'know of' people in the other wagons. This also means that you can move to different wagons—it's almost like moving to a new place entirely. Luke, Paul and Arizon have moved away from their parents, either to become more independent, or to seek a different life with different people. I don't know which, and I usually forget that they even have parents because they have lived in our wagons for so long.

I take a seat next to Luke. Auburn and Zeleng sit opposite me next to Paul. Luke munches on a treef stick, one of the foods I like more than the others in the Wasteland. Made of dried treef and a few of the herbs we grow on the roof garden, treef sticks and volve jerky are probably my two favorite foods. Due to the treefs' massive size, which I had just experienced first hand, they are hard to kill, but when we do manage to kill one, we can make about a thousand treef sticks—we even replace the ground volve bone and oats for some ground tusk and oats, which really isn't an improvement.

"You won't believe what happened," starts Zeleng. Then seeming to consider it he says, "Actually, you will most definitely believe it, but that won't stop me from telling you anyway."

Even though Luke is only twenty, he has experienced about everything that you possibly could in the Wasteland and, more likely than not, being charged by treefs is probably something that Luke has purposely tried to do.

"Explain," says Luke, raising his eyebrows, as if trying to say, 'I bet whatever happened to you is lame and something I would do in my sleep'. Although his facial expressions do a good job, Luke isn't the kind of person who brags about what he has done. Instead, he exudes an attitude of yeah, what I did is cool, but I can do better. It is the kind of attitude that keeps him optimistic about escaping the Wasteland.

"Well, we were taking a very nice rest. Of course we didn't need the rest. We were prepared to run all day, no stopping, because we are that good—but that's not the point. We were interrupted by some treefs." Zeleng goes on to explain what had happened. To my surprise, Zeleng doesn't try to make himself sound like a hero, or say it was nothing. He talks about what happened, basically just the way it happened. When he comes to the part where I save him, he recounts just how dangerous the rescue had been. Luke doesn't look impressed, but I feel as though Zeleng is trying to thank me without having to suck up his pride and actually do it. I give him a grateful look—he returns it with only minor hesitation.

"Treefs, huh." Luke scratches his blonde stubble. He looks as though he is mildly interested in what Zeleng said, and he stares at his fingers as if in thought. It is never good when Luke starts thinking, so I change the subject.

"Why are you back so early from scavenging. Slacking much? I mean, shouldn't you be out there wrestling volves with your bare hands or trying to ride a treef?" I am being sarcastic, but Luke gives me a look that kind of makes me think I should've kept my mouth shut.

"I'll keep that in mind, but the reason I am here chilling instead of being out there risking my life," he pauses to gesture at the door where a strip of trash is slowly moving by, "is because Paul here is sick."

Paul just gives him a confused look. His short hair and pudgy face make him look about three years younger than he actually is.

"I said, Paul here is sick." Luke nudges Paul.

Paul grabs his head and starts groaning and coughing. I don't actually think they think we believe them, but they do know we won't tell anyone. If they want to skip work, it really won't matter. There is only so much that can be scavenged.

"Oh, wow, he really looks bad. Do you think he is going to be okay?" says Zeleng, in an emotionless voice.

"Doubt it, but that's okay. I mean we don't really need him. Isn't that right Paul," says Luke, playfully hitting Paul on the arm. Paul lets out another grunt and lays his face on the table.

Luke loves his brother more than he will ever admit, but that doesn't mean he can't also love making fun of him. He is kind of like a blonde Zeleng, but much more optimistic, brave and mature. He also doesn't complain, and despite what he makes you want to think, he is actually very responsible, and has basically put himself in charge of taking care of his younger siblings.

"What else is new?" asks Auburn. "I mean, I haven't talked to you in like two days—a lot can happen."

Luke gives us a smile. "Young Auburn, you see, we live in a world where we depend on other people's trash. Everything here is at least second hand, so no, I can't truthfully say that there is anything in my life that is 'new'."

Luke looks very proud of himself; as if after all the life threatening things he has done, this is by far the best one.

A Question-Raising Tug of War

Auburn doesn't look offended. "How has your life been going?" he asks, carefully.

"Um, south at about one mile per hour. Same as you and everyone else on the wagons," says Luke, with a devilish grin.

Auburn looks exasperatedly at no one in particular, and puts his head in his hands in mock frustration.

However, Zeleng is looking at Luke as though just seeing him for the first time.

"That sarcasm is impressive," says Zeleng, offering a hand across the table to Luke, "and I would formally like to congratulate you on your talent."

Luke takes Zeleng's hand and they shake vigorously. This is basically how all of our conversations go—ninety percent unproductive chatter and joking, and the occasional ten percent about stuff that actually matters.

Luke's smile fades. "In all seriousness, I have actually been meaning to talk to you guys."

Zeleng looks like he is going to let Luke taste some of his own sass, but decides not to when he sees Luke's serious expression.

"You want to come and hang out in my room? We can try to fix something or make something."

"Oh, I thought you were actually going to say something serious," I say, glancing at Luke and Paul. Luke looks at me as though I am crazy and starts to laugh.

"Do I look like someone who is actually serious?" He pauses to chuckle to himself. "Are you guys coming?"

Luke's room is almost directly opposite ours, and like ours, you have to take a narrow passage to get to it. However, instead of that path going by the engine, the path to get to Luke's room goes around the kitchen. It is such a tight fit that it's a miracle that Paul, who is by far the pudgiest of us, can fit. The whole passage smells of death, and I wonder if some of what Ham did in the kitchen found its way into this hallway.

Luke's room looks like a swimming pool for people who want to cut themselves on metal pieces. The whole room is overflowing with wires, gears, nails and tools. The only resemblance to an actual bedroom is the hammocks hanging in the corner and a couple of sleeping bags on the floor. Despite the horrible clutter, the room is surprisingly clean. No matter how hard I look, I can't see any dust or grime, and the place even smells half way decent. In the center of the room there is a big table, and besides a folding chair and a bean bag, it's the only piece of furniture in the room.

Despite really liking to destroy things, Luke also really likes to build things, whether that be a catapult that shoots trash at approaching volves (the one he built actually defends one of the other wagons), or a pulley system that brings him food from the kitchen right to his room. Everything he builds, no matter how impractical, is pretty amazing for only having trash to work with. Luke's imagination and his undying optimism of reaching the Clean World is more than enough incentive to build awesome things. Even if Luke never makes it to the Clean World, he will be able to find a nice job in Skumford working in a forge or a shop. I personally have no clue what I want to do with my life, and I can only see myself as a walker for the rest of time.

"So, what are we going to make?" I ask, moving across the room and plopping down into the beanbag.

"You're looking at me as though I am supposed to know," says Luke, smiling. "Let's just see what happens."

Seeing what happens is basically the daily life of a scavenger. You never really know what's going to happen, or what you're going to find among the trash. In the end being a scavenger is just being persistent, getting lucky and seeing what happens, because really, we have no control and nothing is guaranteed.

We mostly watch as Luke puts things together from his massive supply of small pieces from the mess of jars on his many shelves and in rows on his worktable. Occasionally, we hand him a tool or two when he asks for one, or hand him a piece that he can't reach, but nothing that takes much effort or brainpower. I sit in the beanbag waiting for the time to pass. I don't necessarily enjoy watching Luke work, but it gives me a way of burning time until dinner. Auburn, Zeleng, Paul and I talk, mostly more useless chatter and a few bad jokes, but I don't mind, as again it's a fun way of burning time until we get to stuff our faces. After several failed attempts, a few spurts of cursing, a fair amount of breaking things out of frustration, and about two hours later, Luke holds up the product of his labor.

"I call this the," Luke pauses for at least ten seconds, either as a dramatic pause, or more likely while he tries to think of a name, "The super cool bottle bomb." In his hands he holds an empty bottle with a mechanism on top. "You see, I have attached a match here so when impacted it strikes against this piece of wood and drops the flaming match into any flammable liquid I choose to put in the bottle—and then, boom."

"Save your explanations, Luke. Does it work?" asks

Zeleng, holding out his hand as if he wants Luke to let him test it.

"I never said it was going to work," says Luke. "But it's going to work."

"Yay, then let's go create a giant fire ball," says Zeleng, slightly more happily than he should.

"I am not wasting time. You never know when a fire grenade could come in handy," Luke replies, walking over to his scavenging backpack and slipping it in.

"Now, onto more important things, like dinner." No one disagrees with that, and we all head back to the main room, already smelling the scent of a lovely volve soup simmering away in the kitchen.

The main room is considerably more packed when we enter this time. People sit and stand everywhere, making a noise on a level with treef trumpeting. Besides being filled with many more people, the main room is also filled with a lot more stuff. Almost every walker has returned by now, all bringing the fruits of their long day out scavenging.

The tables are laden with stuff and larger things cover the ground. We all bring to dinner what we have found, and before we eat, we look through everything, keep what we need, sort it into its respective place—such as the canned food going to the kitchen and the metal scraps to our small forge—everything left over is free game for anyone who needs or wants it. We do a lot of bartering and trading to get stuff that we need from each other. We live as a community, like a single working machine with many unique parts. However, each person has hobbies and things he or she needs to thrive. We trade until everyone has what he or she wants, thus the whole machine continues to run smoothly. What is leftover is put into the main storage room where people can look for things later. Eventually everything that we don't use is burned for fuel or tossed back into the Wasteland. All in all, the wagon system is like a giant filter—we take in a lot of stuff, we filter out all the good things, and then toss out whatever remains. It's a good system and supplies us with almost everything we need. We take a seat back at the table where we were sitting before. It is already littered with an assortment of scavenged objects. I spot a blanket, a red hoodie and four books. The books interest me, but I really hadn't found anything I could trade to get them.

I am about to get up and start trying to barter my rusty knives for something, when shouts break through even the thickest negotiating and bartering. To my utter surprise it sounds like Leon's voice, deep and gruff, and in this case, very loud and demanding. Yelling sometimes happens when something good is on the line and more than one person wants it, but there is one problem here. Leon never yells. He is calm, reassuring and always thinking. The other voice is much higher pitched and definitely female. After several seconds of yelling, the main room grows quiet, for everyone recognizes that their calm, controlled leader is yelling—leaving everyone absolutely speechless. It is like hearing a mute man talk for the first time, completely foreign and strange.

I look around for Leon and the one he is yelling at. It doesn't take me long. I just follow the gazes of everyone else in the room. Sure enough, at the other side of the room I see Leon, his cheeks slightly red—his uncovered eye burning with desperation that I have only seen in the eyes of dying men and women, people clinging on to their lives with every bit of strength. He is definitely yelling at someone.

To my surprise, that someone is Arizon, Luke's red-haired sister. She is shorter than Luke, roughly the same height as Paul, but the resemblance to Paul ends there. Arizon is skinnier, her skin isn't blemished with acne, and she has a look of confidence that Paul doesn't have, seeing as he follows Luke around all day.

It is very clear what they are yelling about. They are fighting over a rectangular metal box about two feet long by one foot wide. It looks locked with a high tech lock, technology that here appears very out of place. It's strange that someone in the Clean World would throw away a locked box, especially one in such good condition, but what is even stranger is the way Leon is reacting. It makes absolutely no sense. Arizon's red hair whips Leon's face as she yells, "This is mine, seriously. I found it today. It's not in your power to just take it away." She sounds whiny, but I would too if my stuff were being taken away from me.

"I have every right to. I am in charge round here. I do as I please." His voice sounds different yelling. The calm tone it always has is gone, and it makes it sound almost crazed, and slightly insane. As a leader, you don't want to be thought of as crazy or insane. They strain against each other for several seconds, each trying to tear the box out of the other's hands. Despite Leon's obvious size advantage, Arizon is putting up a pretty good fight, which alone is surprising. Why is she fighting him so hard for it? Usually arguing with Leon is a bad idea, let alone all out engaging in a physical battle with him.

"Let go girl, you don't know what you're getting into." His voice is low as if he is only trying to let Arizon hear—however, in the silence of the main room, his voice carries. Arizon realizes she is fighting a losing battle. The desperation in Leon's face clearly says he's not giving up. Desperation and determination are very similar. Both power you to do amazing things that wouldn't have been possible otherwise, and right now, Leon has a good amount of each in his eyes.

With a final tug Leon pulls the package from Arizon's grip and storms off, pushing through the crowds of stunned people, through the door into his quarters. "Real smooth Leon, what the hell was that," Luke shouts after him. Talking that rudely to Leon, right after what had just happened, isn't on my top ten ways to get on Leon's good side—but then again, Arizon is Luke's little sister, so it's natural that he should feel protective of her. The second Leon slams the door shut everyone bursts into conversation.

Arizon just stands there stunned. Never has anyone seen Leon yell at someone, let alone use force like that. Without a doubt this is something to talk about, which everyone continues doing in hushed tones as if they think Leon is listening through his door.

"Arizon, what was that about?" Luke walks over to her, concern etched in every feature of his face.

"I honestly have no clue. I found that package today. I tried very hard to get it open, but it refused to budge—some kind of complicated locking mechanism. I thought I would bring it home and get some help opening it, and maybe trade whatever is inside for something. But the second Leon saw it, he came over, yelled at me, and ripped it out of my hands." I know Arizon is tough, almost everyone is nowadays, but she appears on the brink of crying. "Have I done something wrong?"

"Of course not. Leon is a strange guy. It doesn't make sense. Leon has to be hiding something," says Luke, trying to make his voice sound comforting as he puts his arm around her in a brotherly way.

"I agree. Leon is up to some not so funny, funny business," says Zeleng. I think about what Auburn heard Leon talking about to the weapon master. They had found something, and now Leon is taking possession of another found something. Are the two connected? What is Leon's interest in that package? Leon is acting suspiciously, but I find it difficult to accuse him of anything. He has never failed to do what is right for the wagons. He gave me a chance at a life I would never have had without him. He is a good guy, and maybe he is taking that package because it is best for the wagons. I have no way of knowing.

"Arizon, any idea what was in it?" asks Paul. Paul doesn't talk a lot, but his voice is friendly even if he mumbles a bit.

Arizon ponders for a little, a faraway look on her face. "Something heavy, but like I said, I was waiting till now to open it. It's strange—what kind of Clean World person would throw away a new unopened package?"

"Stunning use of description. But I honestly have no idea," says Auburn, laughing a little.

"Quit harping on Leon. He's our leader, so theoretically he has the power do whatever he wants—but he doesn't—he always puts us first. He just destroyed his reputation by taking that package. Unless it was insanely important he get that package, he would not have done that. Trust him," I find myself defending him. I just feel that I should. He is like an uncle to me, and no matter what, you always feel like you should defend members of your own family, no matter how much you like or dislike them.

"Okay then," says Auburn, with so much finality it concludes the conversation.

Later that night after dinner, which as expected is volve soup, and after much complaining from Zeleng and much talk of Leon's strange actions, we return to our room. We sit in our bunks, Auburn next to me and Zeleng sitting on the top bunk, his feet almost kicking me as he swings them back and forth. We agree to stop discussing Leon until we have more proof that he is hiding something. Zeleng argues that we have the proof we need, but in the end he also agrees. We have already discussed all there is to discuss, and he agrees to wait for more information before accusing Leon of something. We get into our bunks. I try to sleep, but the strange actions of Leon keep me up, pushing me back the moment I am on the edge of sleep.

Zeleng Is Not a Bird, but Has Flying Potential

I swing my stick towards Auburn's head, while using my other to fend off Zeleng's attacks. I back up, the two of them advancing. We finished breakfast minutes earlier, and the two of them thought it would be a funny idea to double-team me the second I climbed into the training room. I parry Zeleng's attacks with both my sticks, barely able to keep up with his rapid style. Auburn hits me on the knee with his stick. Pain flares up my leg, but I force myself not to fall—instead, I kick Zeleng over and use both my swords to knock Auburn to the floor. With them both down I run for safety. "Hey, get back here," yells Zeleng. He scrambles to his feet. I head for the other side of the room. Out of the corner of my eye I see that Auburn and Zeleng have gotten up and returned to their chase. I think about a way to beat both of them. I know I can't take them both on at once without being overwhelmed. I need to think of a way to separate them. The wall is coming up fast, and soon I will have nowhere to run. Sometimes I hate being confined to a room to train. Out in the Wasteland space is definitely not a problem.

I am forced to turn around, but at least now I have my back to a wall, which protects me from an unseen attack. Zeleng and Auburn are upon me in seconds. They attack together, and it's all I can do to deflect the onslaught. I can't keep this up for much longer. I swing at their legs, then juke, rolling to the side. It works somewhat, but my arm is still clipped by Auburn's stick as I dash away.

I raise my stick as I sprint full speed back the way I had come. I need to get some height on them. I spot the ladder that leads up to the jumble of rafters and support beams that hold up the crooked roof. Perfect. I sprint towards the ladder, taking a running jump and landing on the third or fourth rung. The impact slams my body into the ladder, but I keep climbing anyway. The sensation is terrifying, as I know the others will reach me at any moment. I am not even half way up when a hand grabs my foot. Somehow I manage to hang on. I start kicking wildly with my other foot. I hit something solid and the hand lets go. I scramble up the ladder. I look back and see Zeleng right behind me, Auburn still on the ground clutching a bloody nose. "Sorry bout that!" I yell, not feeling exceptionally sorry. They are the ones double-teaming me.

"Oh, I'll get ya for that. Don't you worry," Auburn yells back. I reach the rafters and swing on to one. I start to head across. Zeleng also reaches the top, and starts to follow me. I am about ten feet up. If I fall now, I'll probably break a bone, and I'm starting to regret coming up here. Zeleng seems to be kind of wary too, but it doesn't seem to stop him. I hold my sword out and face him. At least now it's a one to one fight and the odds are even. I don't even bother preparing to fight him, and I don't even have to.

Before he can reach me, I take a risk and jump wildly for the next rafter. I almost fall, but grasp it with only my fingertips. I use the upper body strength I have gained from climbing and lifting things to pull myself up. When I turn to look, Zeleng is standing, facing me from the other rafter, about a four- or five-foot gap separating us. He tries to jump to me, but trips and falls mid-jump. There is no slow motion flail of arms or desperate attempt to grab something; instead, he just falls like a rock, and before I know it, the moment is over and Zeleng is no longer in sight. Under different circumstances, perhaps if this happened to someone else, I would be laughing, but it happened to my good friend, and surprisingly enough, it isn't that funny.

"You okay?" I ask, which is an extremely stupid question to be asking the person who just fell ten feet.

To my surprise Zeleng answers, "Never been better." For a second I stand confused, but then I look over the rafter to see Auburn holding Zeleng in his arms.

"I caught him. I was just kind of standing here and all of a sudden here comes Zeleng flying right at me—I really had no other choice, so I caught him." I let out a huge sigh of relief.

"Maybe we shouldn't fight on the rafters anymore," says Zeleng, using some of his more advanced reasoning skills.

There's murmured agreement. Auburn sets Zeleng down and he brushes himself off as though nothing happened. "You hurt? Even if Auburn caught you, that is still kind of a long fall," I say, looking him over even as I am saying it, realizing he is fine.

"Only my pride. Can't even stay on my feet long enough to get to you. How's that for embarrassing?" He looks at the ground, but I can tell he really isn't upset. Zeleng loves drawing attention to himself—acting upset is a great way to do that, especially when people know you're faking it and can laugh about it. Anyone's first impression of Zeleng would be that he is kind of a self-centered jokester. The jokester part is definitely true—all Zeleng does is mess around, laugh a lot, and make anytime into a good time. However, the self-centered part is definitely not true. Zeleng is one of two kinds of people in the Wasteland. The first kind are the serious people, hardened from tough lives, intent on only helping themselves and making it to the next day—then there are people like Zeleng, who accept that their lives are rough and try to make the best of it. That might just be why I like him so much.

I can't help myself—the pudgy baby face Zeleng is making really doesn't work on Zeleng's teenager face. It is enough to make me laugh. Zeleng glares at me, muttering to himself 'Flying Zeleng'. Now Auburn also bursts into laughter. Eventually even Zeleng joins in. And we just laugh all the way to the main room.

Breakfast is the usual today. Ground volve bone and oats. No surprise there. I slowly chew it, pieces of bone crunch against my teeth, and when I swallow, it scratches against my throat.

"This stuff sucks. It feels as though I am trying to eat glass. Actually glass would probably taste better than this," says Zeleng, glaring at the glob of food.

Auburn sighs, giving me a look like 'we should really not eat with him'. "Zeleng, we get that you hate it. You don't need to remind us every day. Kinda weird, but I get as tired of your constant complaining as you do of eating volve," says Auburn, leaning back in his chair.

Zeleng seems to actually consider shutting up, but apparently decides otherwise. "You want to know what I hate more than volve? People who complain about my complaining." The comebacks are real.

"Seriously, you two, we could talk like normal people. You know, where you don't get mad at each other and talk about the weather, and then talk about the weather some more." They both look at me as though I have just taken off my skin and revealed that I am a volve in disguise—like I'm crazy.

"What is this 'normal' that you speak of?" asks Zeleng, jokingly, but it makes me think. Our lives aren't normal at all. We live in a world full of trash, with creatures that never should have existed. Who was I kidding? We aren't normal and can never be normal. Besides, would I miss the banter if we just had normal conversations? Life would get boring fast.

"I like the sun today. I also like the clouds. What do you like?" says Zeleng, contorting his face up into his impression of an old man, making his voice raspy. He laughs so hard, giggling uncontrollably. He's faking his laughter just to make fun of me. He pounds his head on the table, slaps his knees, smiles like a lunatic and generally looks like a complete fool. Let me rephrase that, he looks exactly like himself, the not normal Zeleng. People all around us look at him, food hanging halfway to their faces. Zeleng notices and stops so suddenly that the change of emotion on his face makes me laugh. Even if Zeleng loves attention, he doesn't like a whole wagon full of people staring at him thinking 'why did we let this kid into our wagons again?' We all laugh, I mean we couldn't help ourselves—once Zeleng starts laughing, his laughter is so contagious it spreads like a fire raging over the Wasteland.

We get off to a late start this morning to scavenge, which really isn't unusual for us—when we walk outside, the sun is already blazing in the sky. Today is the same as it was yesterday afternoon. Thanks to the pollution of our ancestors, most days in the summer are like this—sweltering hot, devoid of humidity, and lacking in any kind of breeze. It makes you want to run back to the wagon so fast that you couldn't even run faster if you were being chased by treefs. If my skin hadn't darkened from years of spending all day in these conditions, I would be fried beyond return. I ignore the heat and get into the zone of looking for things, and my eyes fly over the ground.

Immediately, I think I spot something. About ten feet away is a metal box, peeking out from under a pile of papers and a half dozen crushed soda cans. Nothing extremely exciting, but there is no harm in checking it out. I head over to it. It's not a big box—when I lift it up it is not heavy. I pry it open, revealing a pile of some awesomely amazing life-changing old toilet paper rolls. There isn't even any toilet paper, only cardboard cylinders. The feeling that fills me isn't disappointment—it's more of a sarcastic 'oh that's cool'.

"Yeah, well we probably don't need these. Who even saves up all their old toilet paper rolls in a box just to throw them away?" I say, kicking the box away in disgust.

"Um, probably people with a lot of toilet paper and metal boxes?" replies Zeleng, apparently not realizing it was a rhetorical question.

"Yeah, but I was expecting a little more, considering Leon's freakout over Arizon's amazing, totally not normal box," I say, massaging my toe that hadn't fared so well when I kicked the box and is now throbbing. Sure, my boots have metal plating on the bottom, but as far as the toes go, there is only a thin volve skin strip and my socks.

"Yeah, maybe her box had magic toilet paper rolls," says Zeleng, sarcastically. I get an image of floating toilet paper rolls flying around, and try to push the image out of my head. I have no need for any more toilet nightmares haunting me when I am alone in our small, dark, cramped bathroom back at the wagons. We move on, and within minutes we are all sweating and taking constant drinks of water just to counteract the water pouring from our pores. Heat shimmers on everything, and combined with the sun reflecting off anything shiny, makes an extremely bright haze that effectively makes looking at the ground almost impossible. I nearly burn myself on the hood of a car that I climb over, with only my fast reflexes stopping me from having some seriously toasted fingers. Some time later Zeleng says, "This is unsafe, we need shade." You better take something seriously when Zeleng does, because Zeleng is usually the last person to become serious about any problem. However, there's the small problem of not having any shade and absolutely nothing we can seek protection under.

"Sun, O Sun, weaken your rays. Spare us your holy frying. Use your heat for the common good and fry up some volves instead of us." Zeleng either thinks begging the Sun will work, or heat exhaustion is confusing him—he falls to his knees, hands stretched up towards the sky.

Then, as if on cue, a miracle—an absolutely massive shadow passes over us, and a loud humming noise vibrates the ground. Everything around us suddenly grows dark, as if day has gone on vacation, and night is getting an early start.

"That is one giant cloud. Oh wait, what?" Zeleng climbs to his feet, head so far back it looks as though it's about to fall off. I follow his gaze, slowly looking up into the sky.

Directly overhead is a huge circular disk of metal, propelled at regular intervals by high tech engines that are ablaze with uniform blue flames. The ship is as big as a— well nothing really compares to how big it is. It blots out the Sun as though it was never there. We all know what it is. A giant Trash Craft from the Clean World bringing a gift of garbage that is about to crush us into human pancakes. I know I should probably be scared, and should probably be running away screaming, but I find myself too stunned to move. I have never been this close to a Trash Craft (and oddly, I never have wanted to). There's a massive grinding noise as the bottom hatch of the ship starts to open. Trash begins falling from the direct center of the ship, but as the hatch opens wider, the radius of falling trash also widens. This shakes me from my daze and I break into a run, trying to get as far away from the ship as I can. Trash rains behind us, coming closer frightfully fast. The ship's hatch slowly opens wider still, but we manage to stay in front of the downpour of trash before the hatch can open fully. A vehicle crashes to the ground less than twenty feet behind us, spraying pieces of trash into the air. They slam into my back, but I am too pumped with adrenaline to feel anything. I sprint full speed, dodging the oncoming projectiles as best I can. Pieces of trash pelt me in the back, and I narrowly miss being crushed by a falling toilet. Is this just another way to die in the Wasteland—death by toilet? Then I think, this is my second near death experience in two days. This has to be some kind of a record. That leads my mind to think worse thoughts—perhaps this situation is not simply 'near death', but might be a 'real death' situation where I die. The realization isn't exactly comforting, but it does give motivation for my brain to scream at my legs to run faster. I know if something hits my head it will knock me out and I will be buried, drowned in junk with a crushed skull. I can see the edge of the ship's shadow now. Once we are out from under the massive ship we should be relatively safe. The edge is only a hundred feet away, and Auburn and Zeleng are sprinting ahead of me. No way am I going to die if they are going to survive. It makes me run faster—this sprint for our lives turns into a race for our lives. Our heavy metal boots don't make it easy to run, but without them, it would have been like scraping my feet on a cheese grater for a half-mile run. I pick up speed and leap into the light. It really isn't that significant, but I feel as though I have just lept from darkness and death into heaven. I look back and all I see is a wall of falling trash—but instead of pouring cats and dogs, it's pouring trash and garbage in a deadly rain of dangerous projectiles. The mind has a strange way of noticing obscure details in the face of death. This is something I realize in that moment. Instead of fearing solely for my life, my brain takes enough time to appreciate the intriguing effect of the descending trash: the large and heavy things falling to the ground, while the papers and plastic flutter down slowly on the wind.

I don't stop running until I'm a good fifty feet beyond the shadow. My chest feels as though it will explode, and my whole body shudders as I try to suck air into my empty lungs. I collapse on the ground and try to get my breathing under control. Auburn and Zeleng collapse beside me. My leg muscles are burning and sweat runs into my eyes. It doesn't matter to me. I'm just happy to be alive.

Eventually we recover enough to stand. The shock of this incident is much more vivid than yesterday's run-in with the treefs. Yesterday I was able to brush myself off and go on my way, but this time, for some reason, the shock doesn't wear off. The ship finishes emptying, and the deluge ceases. With the same grinding noise with which it had opened, it now closes. The blue flames of the engines grow large, blazing brighter as the ship gains speed and flies back up towards the blinding sun. It slowly gets smaller and smaller as it continues to gain altitude, oblivious to the humans it had almost killed.

"Well, we have something to scavenge now," Zeleng says, a little too matter of factly, as if we hadn't just about gotten killed by our new scavenging location. He surveys the fresh layer of trash.

"Is that Luke and Paul?" He gestures across the field of trash where two figures are standing.

"Without a doubt—one's short and fat and the other tall. If that's not them, I'm a idiot," says Auburn, squinting in the direction of the two figures, which are definitely, as Auburn described, one rather short and one taller.

"Are you saying you weren't already an idiot?" Zeleng asks. He says it so innocently that Auburn doesn't react for

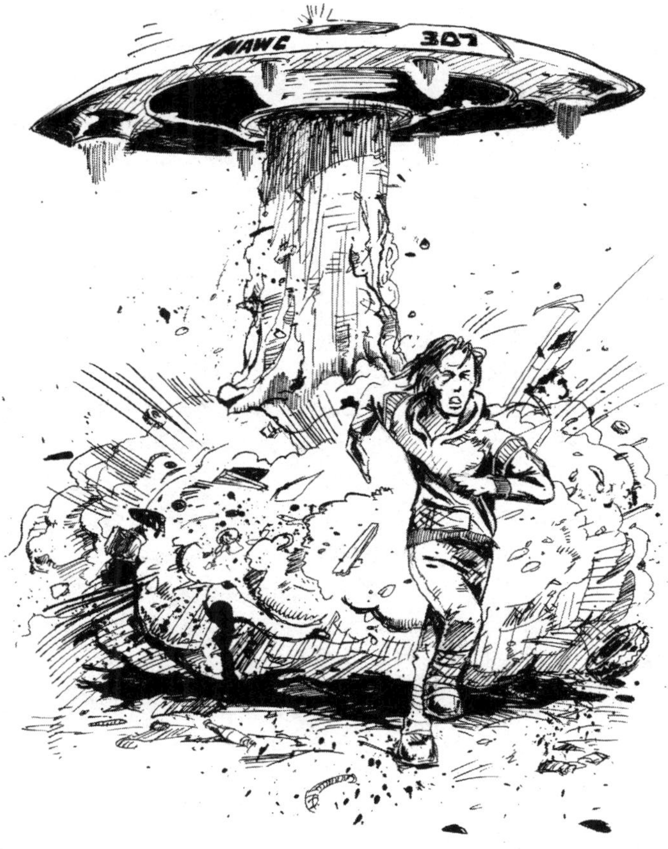
MAWC
307

several seconds. When he finally does, it's too late—Zeleng is running for his life for the second time in a few minutes, up the slight incline where Luke and Paul stand.

I follow and walk the distance to them in a few minutes. For now, Auburn and Zeleng seem to have forgotten about the heat, but I sure haven't. The ground is covered in fresh trash. (Can trash be fresh? I mean, it's a new layer of trash—not that trash is new because it's not—but it's a new layer of old thrown away stuff.) I'm still not over nearly dying, which I guess is normal, but like the treef incident yesterday, the memory of the near lethal storm is surreal. I guess that's what it's like with near death experiences—you never expect it will happen to you, so when it does, it is hard to swallow.

I have come close to dying countless times, but the one time that stands out the most happened when I was seven. I remember being very excited because Luke was going to take me scavenging with him. He was about fifteen at the time, and he was about the only person other than Leon and Ham who was nice to me. Everybody else seemed to see me as a nobody kid, whose sole purpose here was to annoy everyone and eat all the food. Up to that point I had spent almost my entire life inside that wagon, listening to the tales of others, the tales of volves and treefs and the Trash Crafts—but all I'd ever done was sit by one of the windows or stare longingly out of the main doors. I was a kid, and so I couldn't spend my life cooped up in this wagon all day. I felt I needed to prove to everyone that I was tough and not worthless, so I asked Luke to let me go with him to scavenge the next day. Luke agreed, even though he stressed how dangerous it was. I remember I was so excited all through my sleepless night.

The next day I got up bright and early like the walkers. All through breakfast Luke told me how to be safe, but I was way too excited to listen, even though it was dumb of me to feel that excited about spending a day walking around in trash. Finally it was time, and we stepped together into the Wasteland. The day went well, and we had no problems till we got lost right at sunset. It was my fault, as I hadn't listened to him when he had said, 'always make sure you can see the steam from the wagons'. I had run off—for what reason I can't recall. Luke had been too preoccupied with chasing me down to notice the steam either, and we had gotten lost. Luke got super mad and yelled at me, saying I was a stupid kid who didn't know anything, and that we were going to die because of me. At first I was too ashamed to be scared. That changed quickly when the volves attacked. Luke held them off by himself with his bow and spear even though I had a knife. We barely escaped the first pack—it was almost completely dark. We ran off, but I was so slow that Luke was forced to carry me. He had yelled at me again about how I was too young and stupid for anything. I can tell you, that night my self-esteem took a turn for the worse. We barely made it through the night, but somehow we did. We took refuge in a van much like Auburn, Zeleng and I had done yesterday. We lay there, huddled together. Volves attacked throughout the night, and Luke fought them off. By morning Luke didn't look good, as he had scratches and cuts all over and he was exhausted. We had eaten a little, then desperately looked for the wagon. We would have died, but a search party led by Leon (who wasn't the leader at that time) found us and took us back to the wagons. Luke was patched up, but my shame could never be patched. I had nearly gotten Luke killed, and then wasn't even able to defend myself, forcing Luke to save us both.

After that, I was determined to learn how to defend myself. I had to create a reputation for myself that was, at that point, lower than low. Every single day I would go to the training room and watch the older men and women train. I even fought them. Some took pity on me and taught me. When Zeleng and Auburn arrived, they were the only ones who would actually fight me without treating me like a little kid they had to go easy on. Looking at myself now, it's hard to believe I was that small little kid. Now I could take on a whole pack of volves if I had to, and with Auburn and Zeleng at my side, I feel unstoppable.

The pure terror of that night so long ago shaped me like nothing else could, and as much as I try to put the memory of that horrible night out of my head, I know that without it, I would not be where I am today. As I approach Luke, I realize that I owe him every moment I have had since that night. I know that without him, I would've died—but also without him, I would not have had that life-changing experience that made me the person I am today. It's just possible I might possibly owe Luke.

"Hey, hey did you guys see that Trash Craft?" yells Luke, waving his hands over his head as if he thinks we haven't spotted him yet.

"Psh. We did more than see it, we felt it," shouts Zeleng, who somehow had stopped running from Auburn and walked so slowly that I had managed to catch up with him before we reached Luke and Paul.

"What do you mean, felt it?" asks Luke. Then he raises his eyebrows. "Are you saying you were under it when the Trash Craft dropped its precious cargo?" He sounds a bit skeptical, and it makes me think we have done something he hasn't. But then again, what are the odds of being right under a Trash Craft when it dumps? This thought makes me think, that rather than Luke being too scared to try something like what we had just done, he just hasn't gotten the chance.

"I guess that is sorta impressive," Luke says. At that point we reach him and he pats each of us on the shoulder. "So, what are you waiting for? Tell me what happened."

Zeleng looks at me as though silently saying 'I told him about the treefs yesterday, so today is your turn'. I tell him what happened the best I can, ignoring Zeleng's frequent interruptions to try to make himself sound heroic. When I am done, Luke and Paul stare at me.

"So that is how it went down?" asks Luke.

"Yeah, pretty much," I say, moving to stand shoulder to shoulder with Luke, shielding my eyes as I scan the land. Where previously there had been a rather flat expanse, now towers a hill of trash.

"At least we have a new place to scavenge," says Luke, who apparently is thinking along the lines of what Zeleng had said earlier.

"Definitely more important than us narrowly avoiding death," says Zeleng, "but a good point none the less. Let's take a look." All five of us head over to the new hill and begin to climb up the gradual incline. We start scanning the ground—the first thing I see are some old shoes, which probably would have been pretty cool new, but with them ripped nearly to shreds, not so much anymore. There are a lot of broken plastic things. What's the point of building with materials that are so easily broken, that within a year you have to throw away what you have built? Wouldn't it be much smarter to build something with materials that last, so you don't have to replace it constantly—and also not to leave a massive amount of plastic debris that will never decompose and no longer serve any purpose? Clean World logic is no better than Old World logic.

I see a ripped up teddy bear, stuffing flowing from a rip across the mouth, so it looks like it's puking out its white fluffy insides. I most likely can get it fixed, and even if I don't, I can leave it in its regurgitating state, just for kicks. I pick it up and stow it in my bag. I decide I'll even give it to Zeleng to add to his neglected toy collection. We search for a good hour before meeting up again later. We have found half a dozen cans of food, several large pieces of metal plating (which are thin and perfect for adding onto the wagon) and some twine. Zeleng scavenged the most useful thing—a half-full tank of gas. Even in the Clean World gas is one of the rarest substances, because it has to be created biologically and it is illegal. I think back to Luke's empty bottle bomb that only needs this flammable substance to be deadly. The others laugh when I show them my teddy bear. "I think that is very manly. Don't listen to them, Zane," says Zeleng, obviously making fun of me.

"Actually, I was thinking you would want it," I say, grinning at him. He glances around to the others grinning nervously.

"I don't know what this guy is talking about. Why would I want a teddy bear with its insides hanging out of its mouth?" He holds his hands out in front of him, palms facing towards the sky in the classic questioning pose. For several seconds he seems to be having a silent battle with himself.

"Okay, I will take it," says Zeleng, snatching it away from me faster than I expected from someone taking a teddy bear. He shoves it into his bag, and does a good job of looking innocent—twiddling his fingers, whistling and glancing around at nothing in particular. We all know Zeleng is just putting on a show, so none of us feels bad when we laugh at his awkwardness.

* * *

The sun casts a golden glow over the Wasteland in the moments just before it completely disappears behind the horizon. It's almost as though the entire Wasteland has become ablaze with fire—frightening, but beautiful. With the setting sun comes the relief of the cool temperatures of night. We had spent the entire day scavenging the new trash, and what we found Luke and Paul had already taken back to the wagon. They wanted to get back for dinner, but Auburn, Zeleng and I didn't even bother discussing it. We all silently agreed to stay out for a late night dinner with the volves, trash and the food we had scavenged that day.

We throw down a metal sheet and build a small fire on it. We aren't taking any chances—igniting the Wasteland on fire is the last thing we want to do. We have about a dozen matches, and I am careful not to waste them. The fire blazes to life, burning through the incredibly dry paper and broken legs of a chair that I feed it. I pry open the cans of food with my knife, and set them next to the blaze to warm them. I have two cans of soup, one tomato and one corn chowder. Chowder is a weird name, and I have no clue what it is, but it smells good, and since it has corn in it, it must be good. I pull rock bread and volve jerky from my pack.

Rock bread is made from wheat that we buy in Skumford. The quality of the wheat, the lack of flavor, and our stone-age cooking techniques result in rock bread, not only tasting like a rock, but also having roughly the same consistency as one. Rock bread is basically Zeleng's worst enemy, and he groans as he sees it in my hand. We slurp up our soup and break our teeth on rock bread for about an hour, not talking much so that we can listen for any approaching volves that might try to kill us. At the conclusion of our meal we carefully stamp out the fire and gather our stuff. I keep an eye out for volves as we hurry back towards the wagon, but I see nothing.

Darkness has blanketed everything, and the impenetrable blackness makes it so I almost have to feel my way back to the wagon. Night is a scary time, the time of volve hunts and blindness, but it is the only time I feel truly good. Night is the time when I can almost imagine that I am not on a planet of trash, but in the Clean World. Night is also the time for sleep, which takes me away from the Wasteland in another way. It is the time when I dream, and those dreams of a better life might be the only thing that keeps me going as I plunge blindly back to the wagon with only the faint light of its fires and lit windows to guide me.

Hope From Soap

We climb the ladder up to the top of the wagon. The night watchman (a guy named Borkin) squints at us. We have a rotation of about five people who watch from different wagons each night—so it is only about every four nights that there is actually a night watchman on our wagon. He recognizes us and opens the hatch down into the wagon. We scramble down the inner ladder into the main room.

The main room is dirty, but relatively empty. Scavenged things, along with dirty dishes still cover the tables. Ham scurries around, piling the dishes into a towering stack in his arms. His twin daughters, Violet and Adalia, are piling the scavenged stuff into boxes and carrying them off to the junk room.

The junk room is off the main room, where all the stuff is stored that isn't claimed at dinner. The junk room is the go to place for just about anything you can think of. The cans of food are stacked in another box and taken to the kitchen to be locked away. We don't need anyone sneaking down here for a late night snack—still though, people sometimes sneak cans of food from dinner to take to their rooms, just in case hunger strikes during the night.

Ham spots us and nods a greeting—the movement nearly makes him drop his tower of dishes. He lets out a squeak and balances himself, moving back and forth until the dishes stop shaking. He quickly runs into the kitchen and deposits them. He scuffles back out towards us, his hands now free of breakable objects.

"I suppose you're not hungry," he says, noticing the empty soup cans Zeleng holds. "What a shame, I made up some delicious volve chops. I think I even used that volve you gave me two nights ago. If you want, you can have its stinky pelt and do whatever you want with it." He gestures with a thumb back towards the kitchen.

"Volve chops sound great," says Zeleng, somewhat forced. When Ham looks away, he mimes throwing up.

"Can I get some more of the volve jerky? I finished up the last of mine today," I say, opening my pouch and showing him that it is indeed empty.

"Yeah, I have loads. Don't know how dry it is—it's only been drying for a couple of days, but it tastes good," says Ham, beckoning us to follow him back into the kitchen.

I brace myself as I step through the kitchen doors, trying to hold my breath without looking like I am suffocating myself. As long as I don't sniff, the smell of dead volve isn't too bad. We weave ourselves around the many counters and volve carcasses to the back of the kitchen. The ceiling here is covered with strips of hanging meat, like an upside down fleshy forest extending from one side of the kitchen to the other. "You weren't kidding when you said loads," I say, admiring the freakishly huge amount of jerky. Ham smiles at me as he starts pulling the meat down and handing it to me. I stuff my pouch full of it.

"What's the status of our food supply?" I ask, taking strip after strip of jerky as Ham pulls it down, unwraps the string it was hanging from, and hands it to me.

"That's not even a question anymore, boy. We are pretty well off. Volves come in almost every day—same with the canned food—and we even caught a treef a few weeks ago. I am so busy I barely find time to sleep. I am struggling, but none of you boys is going to have to worry about getting fed." Ham exhales slightly as he finishes. It's not quite a sigh, but it definitely conveys some of his exhaustion.

I sort of admire Ham—for out of everyone in the wagons, he probably does the most work—cooking all day and cleaning well into the night. It's hard to believe he gets any sleep at all. I don't remember very well the early years of my life when I lived with Ham, and his wife took care of me, but I do remember there were some pretty good times, some of the only times I have ever felt loved. I owe it to Ham, and I want to repay him, but I feel as though I am just getting farther in my debt towards him. He feeds me, is nice to me, and always makes sure I have enough extra food, even though he is not really supposed to give it to me other than at meal times.

"We are a lot better off than most, even more than we used to be. It was only about six years ago people were starving. I would've killed to have this much food back then, but you know what they say, if there ain't a volve, there ain't no food," says Ham. I had never heard that saying before, and I half suspect Ham made it up on the spot—but I don't point it out, for I too remember the food shortage that left several people dead. Even in those times Ham had made sure I had just enough food to make do. I feel kind of guilty thinking about it. I owe Leon, I owe Luke and I owe Ham, but no one owes me. It makes me think that maybe I am just leeching off other people's labors. Ham passes me a final strip of jerky and I try to find space in my overflowing bag for it. He glances up at me.

"Thanks again, Ham—what would I do without you?" I say, trying to make my voice sound as grateful as humanly possible.

"You would starve to death," he says, smiling slightly. If anything, that phrase strengthens my determination to repay my debt to him so I no longer will feel so guilty.

"We will get out of your way—you probably have something important to do," says Zeleng, obviously eager to get out of the smelly kitchen and away from all the gore of Ham's everyday life.

"Yeah, gotta scrub these dishes, chop up three more volves and wipe down the tables," replies Ham, dejectedly. He rubs his hands together, wipes them on his blood-stained apron, and scurries off to begin his work. Since he obviously is busy, we thank him again and leave the kitchen.

Several minutes later, Auburn, Zeleng and I are all sitting on our respective bunks in our room. I run a finger through my choppy black hair. My hand comes away greasy and gross. I pull up the cloth of my shirt and smell it. That was definitely a mistake.

"I am taking a bath," I announce with slightly more excitement than you would expect from a sixteen-year-old considering his personal hygiene.

"Heck yeah, you are. If you don't, Ham is going to mistake you for a dead volve and make Zane soup out of your smelly body," Zeleng says. "And don't think I won't complain about eating you, because I will." I don't know if it's a threat, but it definitely reinforces that I need a bath.

Bathing is a luxury that really only we Nomads have. The water comes from the rain barrels, and occasionally one of the rivers. It's already heated to boiling temperature by the engine, leaving it relatively clean to bathe in. The CityFolk would never waste so much water cleaning themselves, and the Bargemen would never bathe in the dark polluted water they traverse. Even so, we only bathe monthly, not wanting to waste more water than we need to. "I'll bathe in like twenty minutes," I say. Typical me, always procrastinating even about enjoyable things.

"Sounds good," says Auburn, getting up from his bed.

"Hand me your bow and stuff. I'll put it away for ya." I pass him my bow, and Zeleng hands him his mace and shield. Auburn unlocks the chest, depositing our weapons, and then locks it tight. Our weapons are too valuable to risk losing, so we take no chances.

"Crack open the window. Zane really does smell," complains Zeleng. Auburn, who is already close to it from putting the weapons away, opens the circular window. A rather chilly breeze finds its way in. It's amazing how messed up the climate is nowadays. It goes from chilly to sweltering heat and back to cold again in a matter of days. I hear the howling of a volve carried on the wind. The sound makes me want to plug my ears and curl up into a ball. It isn't so much the howling as it is the prolonged high-pitched screech.

"Volves haven't attacked in a few nights now. Maybe they're finally getting it that they die when they do attack, and that maybe it's not the smartest idea," says Zeleng, now getting up to peer out the window.

"Don't see anything. Hopefully Borkin does though. We don't need him dead," says Auburn, rather matter of factly. "He's got eyes like a volve. He will see them before they see him—and Leon will be keeping an eye out with that lens of his," Auburn finishes, returning to his bunk. As he sits down, the rusty springs of his bunk screech almost as much as the howling volves.

"Yeah, the lens is sweet. I wish he had found more than one, cause I want one," Zeleng says.

We spend the next fifteen minutes talking about various things. We discuss the lens some more, then talk about roof gardens which we'll be harvesting this Thursday. I can't wait for some fresh food. It will be a great change and, oh man, that fresh food will taste so good. Ham can start making volve roasts with vegetables again. The thought makes my mouth water. The thought of water reminds me about my bath. "I'm headed out." I slip off my boots and socks and leave them by the door. My friends mutter some goodbyes, but I barely hear them because the door has already swung shut behind me.

I stroll back down the hallway for the second time that evening. I turn and drop down the ladder. As I descend, the air becomes thick with steam, and moisture starts forming on my exposed skin. I go down the steps and feel the temperature rising as I get closer to the bottom. There are three doors here—one to the engine, one to the baths and one to the fire room where trash is collected and burned

to keep the engines fueled. I push the bath door open—
of course, only after politely knocking to see if it's in use.
As I expected, it is not, because people really don't bathe
much. Inside it seems, if possible, even hotter and more
humid.

In the center of the room there is a single tub. Nothing
special, just an old rusty tub scavenged from a time before
most people were born, when the wagons were first built.
There are a few hissing pipes connected to the tub. Even
those are an odd assortment of welded pipes—in some
cases, held together with thick gray duct tape. The tub
is already filled halfway with slightly rippling water that
only needs to be heated. I walk over to the bath and turn
the handle with the large H on it in capital letters. Boiling
water spills into the tub. I am careful not to get too close
to the splattering, scalding liquid, so I go and sit on a small
ledge specifically made for people waiting for their tubs to
fill. Then I double-check the lock on the door, not wanting
some random person to barge in and find me naked.

I wish we had soap. I have only used it a few times when
we had the good luck of scavenging some. The wonderfully
smelling fragrance, something called lavender, had filled
my nose with a good refreshing aroma, and left my skin
feeling soft and clean. The soap was quickly used up, all
of us wanting a sample of its wonderfulness before it was
gone. When you are surrounded by a world of bad smelling
stuff, a little thing like soap is so wonderfully nice. People
in the Clean World probably have more soap than they can
possibly use. But I guess when you're surrounded with everything you need, you take stuff for granted. I think about
how escaping to the Clean World means I can have all the

soap I want. I am suddenly filled with an overwhelming urge to escape, or at least to try, for a world with soap is a world I want to be in

* * *

When I swing our refrigerator door open, I see Auburn and Zeleng dozing in their bunks. I have a ratty towel wrapped around my head and the same clothes on, minus my shirt—but I feel great. I'm clean and refreshed, nothing like these two tired dudes. They don't glance up as I walk in, for who else would be barreling half naked into their room? They have closed the window, and I don't blame them. The temperature has steadily dropped. I wouldn't be that surprised if there were snow on the ground tomorrow.

"Hey guys, long time no see," I joke, pulling off my towel turban to dry my hair. My long thick hair takes an incredibly long time to dry, but at least the drying stops my hair from dripping like a leaky faucet. I start working at the tangles with a comb (with at least half its teeth missing) that I grab from a shelf. It's a challenge, but now that my hair is rid of the rather impressive collection of grime, it is actually possible to detangle. I yank at my hair, which has become a tangled mess and almost looks like dreadlocks. My hair reminds me of a volve pelt, and about the only difference is that mine is now clean. I think back to the smelly pelt Ham offered me earlier. I had turned down the offering, but now I start to think that I might want it. I could use it for a number of things, or honestly, just as another blanket on my mildewing bed. There the dirty pelt would fit right in.

Eventually, after several minutes, my hair is combed and falls in uneven strands into my eyes. With all the usual grime, oiliness and tangles, it usually stays out of my face, but not so much now. I brush it aside, and chuck the comb back onto the shelf.

Now. On to more exciting things. It's time to get a fresh shirt. I actually have a lot of clothes organized carefully in a heap in the corner. The people of the Clean World seem to have no problem throwing out perfectly good clothes. I guess they outgrow them—they get stained or, even worse, they get tired of them, and throw them out to get something new. The reason doesn't really matter to me. I am sometimes thankful they are so wasteful, because my life basically depends on it.

I choose a new black shirt (my preferred color) and pull it over my head. I pick out a black hoodie and another black jacket and throw them into my 'wear tomorrow' heap. If I can, I only scavenge black clothing. This helps because black clothing always seems clean, no matter what kind of grime hides in its dark folds. I have a feeling it's going to be much colder tomorrow.

I move to where I left my boots before I took my bath. I pull out the socks that I had hastily stuffed into them. These socks are the only black clothing I hate. They are torn, so that they seem to have more holes than actual sock, and they smell worse than Ham's rotting volves. I gingerly pick them up, pinching them with my index finger and thumb. I use my other hand to shield my face, not only my nose, but also my eyes. I run to the window, swing it open, and chuck them out as fast as I can. Once the smell of the socks is gone, something possibly worse replaces it. A long cold rush of air forces itself through the small window, and hits me in the face with icy knuckles. It sends shivers down my spine, and I quickly slam shut the window. It's not freezing cold, but to me it feels like it is. Usually, in this climate, it is sweltering hot, and anything below that feels plain cold.

"Heck, if it's this cold now, tomorrow's going to be freezing," I say to no one in particular.

Zeleng answers anyway. "Maybe—or it could warm up, you never know, but better not get cold enough to kill the roof gardens. I will be mad—these vegetables are like the only edible fresh food we ever get." I'm glad for his optimism because I hate the cold. It forces me to bundle up, makes me clumsy, makes things slippery, and overall slows me down. I don't like being slowed down.

"Hopefully it does warm up. Cold sucks. I don't even have good gloves, and I don't want frostbite again," says Auburn, massaging his fingers.

Auburn had gotten frostbite several years ago in a random snow storm. He nearly lost his fingers. They almost became infected, and that would have been bad. We have a very small supply of medicine. Usually infection leads to loss of limbs or digits, and sometimes death. Auburn was lucky, and managed to keep all of his fingers—but ever since he has developed a very understandable fear of the cold. He is the most cryophobic scavenger I know.

Snow is rare, but is also a very bad thing. It covers the ground, making it nearly impossible to scavenge. However that isn't even the worst part. If it snows bad enough the wagon tracks don't have enough traction to keep moving and we come to a standstill until it melts. Luckily, the snow never lasts more than a few days, often melting the same day it falls and we can get moving again without a terrible delay.

Walkers always go to sleep early, since most of them like to get an early morning start. The exceptions are Zeleng, Auburn, and me—we like to sleep in and enjoy staying out later than the other walkers.

"Has anybody told Leon about the trash that nearly killed us? We should steer over that way so we don't have to walk as far to get there tomorrow," I say, looking at the others.

"Luke would've told him already. Unlike us, Luke's good about those things," says Auburn, laughing.

"Nah. We just know Luke will, so why do we also need to remember?" says Zeleng, perched high on his bunk. It makes me think back to 'flying Zeleng' in the training room. The thought makes me grin. Zeleng thinks I am grinning at him, and in a way I am. I am grinning at his past action, the one where he almost handicapped himself for life.

"I'm gonna try to sleep, getting kinda late and there's not much else to do." Zeleng and I agree with him. We each crawl into bed and I pull the chain. Darkness instantly takes its hold, welling up from its shady crevices and plunging the room into absolute blackness. I am pretty happy at the moment—it's dark, it's time to sleep, and I smell clean and fresh, almost like the soap that I so much like. Without further ado I let my mind take control and take me off to a better place. Tiredness envelopes me as has the dark, and I fall asleep.

Compared to our last few days, the next day is rather uneventful. There isn't a single close call or life-threatening experience, just a normal day for a scavenger. We start the day off with volve bone and oats, in all its globby grossness. After a few hurried fights in the training room, we are off to another day scavenging the Wasteland. It must be at least fifty degrees cooler today. Wind howls over the Wasteland, bringing the smell of slightly refrigerated trash, which is surprisingly not any better than regular trash odors. We bundle up in jackets and hats—the temperature is not freezing, but it is uncomfortably close to it. We scavenge next to nothing—our hopes are down, which is not helped by the cold rain that starts up at dusk. It comes down in icy sheets, soaking us within minutes, and basically making this day as miserable as possible. We never discuss it, but before we know it, we are running back to the wagons as fast as we can. When we finally get close enough to the wagon to clearly be able to make it out through the walls of rain, something seems slightly different about it. It is the same wagon, no doubt about it, but something seems different—it appears slightly bigger. I don't take the time to ask the others about it—instead we start the climb up the wagon. Usually the doors would be open, but because of the cold and the rain we are trying to keep as much warmth in and most of the cold and dampness out. I swing open the hatch and drop down the ladder. Rain pours in, but stops several seconds later when Zeleng pulls it shut on us and follows us down the ladder. I am still soaked and cold, but somehow I feel warmer now that I am no longer being pelted by rain.

The main room is packed. People are huddled in the corner by the fire. I spot walkers wrapped in blankets—all of them look soaked, and I am guessing their thoughts had been exactly the same as ours when the rain began. Ham stands by a table ladeling steaming liquid (some kind of tea) into cups and handing them out to the shivering walkers.

"I guess I missed out on the shower," says a voice. A moment later a blanket hits me in the face, momentarily blinding me. "Yes you did, Luke. What's your excuse for not being out there today?" asks Auburn. He sounds kind of accusatory. I pull the blanket off my head and see Luke standing next to Auburn. I wrap it around me and warmth starts to spread back throughout my body.

"Hey, Paul is actually sick today—just a cold we think. He's bundled up on a bunk, sipping tea. But that's also not the reason I am here. I don't know if you bothered to look, or if the rain was too thick or something, but we have added a new room to the wagon," says Luke. He looks at us in a half happy, half searching way.

"And...?" Auburn says it so that the word lasts for several seconds, drawing it out in a one-syllable question. Luke looks at Auburn as though it's obvious.

"Instead of spending my day out there freezing, Borken and I, plus a couple of other people, added a room onto this wagon," says Luke. "Let's go talk about it in your room." He says it as a question, but if anything, it's a suggestion that can't be argued with. We grab a couple mugs of warm tea and a big jar of volve soup and follow Luke to our room.

Our room isn't as empty as it should be. When I walk in I see a guy curled up in blankets on Zeleng's bunk.

"How's it going, sick boy?" asks Luke, addressing the obvious shape of Paul. Paul tries to grunt a response, but it's drowned out by Zeleng's indignant voice.

"Woah, woah, woah—why is he in my bunk? Now it's going to be infected." Zeleng curls over his bottom lip in a pouty face. "You do realize that we have four bunks and only three people. You could have used the empty one," says Zeleng, pointing to the empty bunk.

"Psh! No we couldn't. And about that room we added, it's cool." Luke tries to sound chill, but his attempt is rather defeated by the irregular sips of his less than manly tea.

"How'd you do it this time?" asks Zeleng, glaring at Paul, and going to sit on the empty bunk. I sip my warm tea as Luke begins to tell about it. My clothes are still wet and stick to me in an uncomfortable way, but I don't think this would be the most appropriate time to strip down and change.

"We got off easy today. I don't know if you saw that train car we passed this morning, but we used that for the new room. It took a dozen people and a makeshift pulley to get that thing into position, but when we did, we put up some supports and secured it on the side. We put up a layer of insulation; blankets, papers, the whole lot. I mean, you can see it if you want," says Luke. He summed it up to make it sound easy, but I am guessing it was much harder to build than he is letting on. Usually building a new room takes at least a day. It's not an exact science, and we just add on to it with boards, metal, tape, nails or whatever works. Eventually, after putting enough things together, we have, hopefully, a secure, waterproof room.

"Dude, we just brought food and drinks here. Why

didn't we just go there in the first place?" I ask, trying to sound somewhat reasonable.

"Good point. Tomorrow I will show it to you," says Luke. He goes over and sits next to Paul. Paul looks tired, but not too bad. He is a little flushed and his nose is a little runny, but besides that, he seems fine. "What's this new room for?" I ask, trying to keep the conversation going.

"Storage for now, and maybe housing later," explains Luke, without really informing me of anything I hadn't already suspected. Paul starts coughing.

"Pauly-Wallie, time to go. I wanted to stay, but man I don't need to get you all sick," says Luke. Paul grunts again, but doesn't move. Luke shakes his head a little, drains the last of his tea, and grasps Paul. With a grunt, from Luke this time, he heaves Paul over his shoulder, which alone is no small feat. Luke shakes a little bit, but manages to make his way to the door and kicks it open with his foot. He backs out slowly, barely fitting through the small door.

"We'll see you tomorrow," says Luke, waving with Paul's arm, and backing the rest of the way out of the room.

"Until then, farewell," says Zeleng. "I wish you the best of luck on your journey." Luke chuckles a little at that and lets the door swing shut. I also wish them luck on their journey. Carrying Paul that far through such tiny spaces isn't going to be easy, and Luke would never do something like that for anyone but Paul. I don't see why a cold has disabled Paul's legs, but I am not about to ask.

"He left his glass on purpose didn't he," says Zeleng staring at Luke's cup. "First he dirties my bed with Paul, and then he dirties our room with his dirty dishes. What a guy."

I change out of my soaked clothes, which is harder than you might think. After throwing on a new pair of dark jeans, I put on a fresh black shirt sporting the words 'Got Lactose Free Bos Primigenius Disambiguation Simulation'. I have no clue what the words mean, but I think it's some advertising logo for a company in the Clean World. I certainly wouldn't have bought this shirt if I were in the Clean World, but for a free black shirt, it's not too bad.

Even with new clothes I still feel rather chilled—I hope I am not getting sick like Paul.

Although epidemics are dangerous, they are more rare here than you might think. Because of the confined way scavengers live, should a contagious sickness occur to someone, that person is quarantined in a special room, where it can be more easily dealt with. Even if that is unsuccessful, the sickness usually never spreads from wagon to wagon. We usually don't have the medicine to cure most diseases, so isolation is the only way we are able to deal with disease. The sick person remains in that room until they heal, die or are banished.

Auburn sets the jar of soup down on a shelf. We had picked up enough soup for at least six people—a sort of silent challenge to us to see how much we can eat. I am hungry, seeing that my body spent extra energy to stay warm today. He hands out spoons and coffee tins to each of us—then we dip into the monstrously large amount of soup.

"Thanks, Auburn. You are totally the best," says Zeleng, flashing Auburn a grin. However, this time, instead of being a sarcastic grin, it looks more like the one he gave me after I saved him from the treefs—grateful and thankful.

"Yeah. Thank you," I say, feeling obliged to thank him, even though all he did was pass out eating utensils.

The soup is hot, but not tongue scorchingly hot, and more importantly, it tastes good and spreads warmth throughout the rest of my body. Usually volve meat is tough and chewy, but after soaking in broth for many hours, even the most gristly volve meat becomes tender. Sometimes I have to agree that hunger is the best spice. On days like this, when I am tired and cold and hungry, this soup is like liquid heaven—just looking at it makes me feel better. On any other day, it's blah and rather tasteless. Despite how hard Ham tries to make it taste good, it makes me want to complain right along with Zeleng.

I finish my bowl and help myself to seconds. In the past I would have felt guilty doing this, but in recent years we have been doing well, and we have plenty of food, so second servings are no longer sinful.

It takes a while, because I'm trying to ladle out as many chunks of volve meat as I can into my bowl, and as little of the plain broth as I can.

I pause before I start into my new bowl. "If it warms up tomorrow, which it probably will, cause snow never lasts, we should venture farther out." I look to see their expressions. They're blank so far, masks of puzzlement, though not exactly confusion. "We should leave some kind of trail that we can follow back, maybe drive rods into the ground every so often, hopefully something better than rock bread crumbs." They seem to be considering it. This is a spur of the moment decision, and the words seem to be leading me, rather than the other way around, pouring out of my mouth almost as though I am thinking aloud.

"I don't see why not. Is it worth the risk?" asks Auburn. Surprisingly, he looks to be very seriously considering the idea.

"We all know first hand how easy it is to get lost. It's not fun. So why do you want to, Zane?" asks Zeleng. He actually uses my name, something that he doesn't do very often, but it is also a sign that he, too, is considering the idea with more than his usual limited consideration.

"I don't really know; we are always going on the same loop. What if there's something just off our path that we are missing?"

I am referring to the wagon's almost reliable route. We go in a giant two hundred mile circle, stopping at the port city of Skumford during every rotation. Leon's logic is that we would always be close enough to Skumford to reach it in about a week if anything serious would happen. We never run out of stuff to scavenge because Leon plans it so that we are always in a place with a relatively new drop of trash.

Skumford is a giant city by Wasteland standards. The population is around ten thousand. No one has ever counted, but just by looking at it, you can tell there is a ton of people in Skumford. Skumford is a mass of shambled together buildings built atop the shallow water of a dirty lifeless lagoon. The city is split into sections by canals that serve as roads for Bargemen, and everyone else is forced to use the web of bridges, walkways and zip lines that connect the roofs.

Skumford, hence its name, is a dark dirty place, but is surrounded on all sides by high, thick walls. Living in a city is rough, and sickness and food shortages are common—but at least you're guaranteed safety from volves, treefs and bandits.

The CityFolk farm on the roofs of the buildings, as well as on the water, itself. They use buckets, plastic boxes and anything else that can float to set up makeshift hydrofarms. They connect them with long ropes, and when it is time to harvest, they reel them all in. This is one of the most ingenious things done by anyone in the Wasteland, and it manages to supply the city with enough food to survive. The water keeps the temperature mild, and there's nothing to block the sun. The farms also don't need soil, or at least not as much, and this saves valuable time, because the CityFolk don't have to spend as much time digging deep down to reach the soil. The CityFolk call the farms bobbers, because they bob up and down in the soft motion of the water. Skumford also houses the biggest forges, the only place to get a new wagon or a repair, and the best place to get blades and guns. We have small forges in a few of the wagons, including ours, mainly for welding and sometimes for making small parts that we aren't able to find. But for the best quality stuff we always buy from the Skumford forges and metal shops. On our stops to Skumford we trade volve meat, volve skins, canned food, rare parts, gas (like Zeleng found), and large amounts of scrap metal. In return we get dried fish (from the Bargemen who trade with them in the city's large bustling port), repairs to our engines, clothing, vegetables and weapons. I get my thoughts back on track.

"I think there may be something out there—where there has been enough time to build up a collection of things untouched by any other Nomad group. They haven't been scavenged in years, and the Clean World must have thrown away loads of stuff since then," I say, thinking of all the possibilities that might lie just out of sight, over a crest of trash that we have never seen.

"Yeah, but there are tons of other Nomad groups. I accept that there's land with undiscovered stuff, but why do you think we will find something great?" asks Auburn. He tries to be reasonable, but I don't even really listen.

"Because, why can't we? Why can't it be us who get lucky? It's always someone else who takes the risk, and it's always someone else who finds something great." They don't have a reply to that, and really, why can't it be us who find something amazing? What do those other people have that we don't? The answer is—nothing; and nothing is what we will find if we don't take a risk. If we play it safe our whole life, nothing is ever going to change. I go to sleep that night feeling inspired.

We Find a Buried Person (Kind of)

The next day pays off. The morning passes much like yesterday's—volve bone and oats, Zeleng complaining, and some battles in the training room. We walk into the Wasteland ready for whatever this world can throw at us. Last night, in the long minutes before sleep had overtaken me, I had been restlessly forming a plan—almost subconsciously spitting up ideas, until finally I had come up with a plan I found suitable. Once having done that, I thought so much that I felt I had every detail planned out. I start to tell Auburn and Zeleng about the plan as we walk alongside the wagon. The remains of yesterday's cold rain are drying up, returning the Wasteland to its usual state.

"We set up a trail of 'breadcrumbs' that we can follow back to the wagon. We won't use actual bread, for obvious reasons, such as the bread we have available requires, at minimum, a large sledge hammer to break it into crumb sized pieces. Additionally, throwing crumbs into a landscape half filled with crumbs anyway and hoping for it to serve navigational purposes is just plain idiotic. Instead, we will put up poles, rods, broom handles, and anything else that will be visible from a distance, as a sort of trail we can follow back." The others don't look very impressed, but they just haven't yet heard the good part.

"And if something happens to these markers? What—are we just gonna run around till we find our way back?" asks Zeleng. It's a valid question, but I don't even hesitate before answering—I have thought out everything.

"We just continue in a straight line till we can find a marker that remains intact. Each one is in the same straight line, so even if we are missing one, we can head in the same direction and eventually we will find another," I reply. My voice sounds rather smug. "And if we get lost, Ham gave me enough rock bread and volve jerky, and I brought enough water to last at least a couple of nights. And I packed extra ammo for your gun, Zeleng, so hopefully we would be able to defend ourselves throughout the night."

"Sounds like you have this all planned out," says Auburn, in a flat voice.

"That's because I have." I laugh a little. Just thinking of my master plan makes me smile. "Follow me—I will explain what I am doing as we go." The others exchange silent conversations, questioning how much they trust me—and they seem to agree, because they join me as I trudge out in front of the wagon.

The temperature has warmed up considerably, hopping fifty degrees back up to a good hot blaze. The rain has dampened everything, and the smell of rot and trash are even worse than usual. It smells like a mixture of wet dog, or more accurately, wet volve mixed with trash and human waste. Not a pleasant smell, but my nose is used to it, and

We Find a Buried Person (Kind of)

I only gag a few times. The only sound is the crunch of the wagon's tracks, slowly growing fainter behind us.

I have done the math. The wagons move at one mile per hour (slow and steady wins the race), but as determined walkers, walking briskly, we can move at a good five miles per hour. If we walk for two hours, we will be about eight miles ahead of the wagon. If the wagon were stationary, we would be ten miles ahead of it, but with its movement, we lose two miles of that from the time it takes us to walk this far.

At this point we can branch off without the worry of finding the wagon eight miles ahead of us when we follow our trail back, and this maneuver should give us a good eight hours to explore the new region before the wagon meets back up at the start of the 'bread crumb' trail. I explain this to the others—they seem genuinely stunned.

"Yep, you definitely have thought this out—but you're still an idiot," says Zeleng, who would never admit that he is actually impressed.

"Yeah, a smart idiot," agrees Auburn. I know they don't really believe it, but they have a reputation to uphold, and being impressed doesn't strengthen it.

We spend the next two hours walking out in front of the wagon, following the plan. We are moving too fast to actually take into consideration scavenging the trash. Hopefully, what we find on our little excursion will make up for that. Once we are eight miles ahead, we can no longer see the steam of the wagon. I feel as though I am lost in an endless expanse, with no comforting wagon as a beacon of safety. The only thing that keeps me from panicking is the thought of my plan. If my calculations are right—if we stay in this exact spot for the next eight hours—hopefully we would be right in the path to be 'crushed' by the wagon when it catches up.

"We put up our first marker roughly a mile to the right from here—about at the point where the wagon usually goes out of sight if it were right here." I point to the trash under my feet. "On our return trip, in about eight hours, the wagon should be in a place where we can see it from a mile out.

I judge that we take roughly twelve minutes to reach the location of the first marker. We can only roughly judge how far a mile is by how long it takes—but in this case, it shouldn't matter how precise we are. We just have to hope we will be close enough to see the wagon from this point.

We drive our first marker into the trash, which easily gives way when we push the pipe down into it. Once its tip is buried and secured, the pipe stands a good seven feet into the air—a marker that can be seen from quite far away on the rather flat surface of this trash covered land.

"I haven't decided how often to place markers. If we place them every twenty feet, as I suggested earlier, we will be using two hundred and eleven per mile. And now that I reconsider it, that's too many. So let's just see how long it takes for us to barely be able to see the previous marker, before placing another one," I say. I am somewhat surprised at how logical I sound, almost as though I am reading the speculations from some book entitled *Scavenging for Dummies* maybe.

"Sounds good. Let's just count our steps. I take about a three foot stride, so we can like do math and stuff and figure it out," says Zeleng, trying to contribute his own intellect to the conversation.

I had been going to say that, but instead I say, "Yep, exactly, twenty-five seems way too small, now that I am actually out here looking at it for real."

We walk on, counting our steps as best we can. When only the top of the metal pipe of our first marker is faintly visible in the distance, we decide to place the next marker.

I'm the only one who hasn't lost count. Eighty-three strides—two hundred forty nine feet between markers—almost ten times what I had originally been planning. So much for my plan being so well calculated and thought out. I hope it doesn't matter, but I start to get somewhat wary. I don't voice my worries—the worst thing I can do is to let Auburn and Zeleng think that we are lost. Staying calm and following through with the plan is our best option.

Auburn seems to have come to the same conclusion about our calculations. "So we use around twenty markers a mile—that's a lot, but it's better than two hundred and eleven," Auburn says, finishing his wowing display of math. I sometimes forget—Auburn and Zeleng aren't that smart. Let me rephrase that, they have the potential, they can use logical thought processes to make decisions, but they weren't taught to read, write and do math until they joined our wagon when they were eight. So technically, education-wise, I'm four years ahead of them. It's not often I get to display my superior knowledge, but now I can't help but rub it in despite my thoughts of miscalculations and their effects.

"Figured that out all by yourself, did you?" I ask, immediately regretting it because I sound like a jerk. But don't

I like sounding like a jerk? Auburn doesn't look offended in the slightest, and I realize I probably owe him an insult or two.

"Yep, I figured it out all by myself." He gives me a mockingly proud smile so that he looks like a puppy waiting for a treat. (By the way, that's a volve puppy.)

We continue on, marking our place at regular intervals of eighty-three strides, or whenever the marker goes out of sight. We use sticks, standing house lamps, and even a full sized lamppost as markers. After that large marker, we wait four hundred feet before placing a new one. It's hours before we place our fortieth marker, two miles from our first marker, and roughly three miles away from the wagon's designated spot. It's also the farthest away from a wagon anyone of us has ever been. I feel alone out here, cut off from everything. I try to distract myself by searching the trash, and keeping my eyes on the marker.

We start keeping an eye out for useful things. We are now in a land that has never been scavenged, as far as we know. At first it's not the heavenly jackpot I had imagined, but we do find some things.

Best of all, we find soap. The box is rectangular, discolored by age or grime—I can't tell. I can tell from a clear plastic opening that there are twelve bars. When I first spotted it, I let out a cry of joy, rushing to it, falling to my knees and cradling it in my hands. And no, I was not over-reacting at all, not even a little. Other than the soap, we also found an intact bottle of wine, encased in styrofoam in a cardboard case. The two other bottles in the half empty case had been cracked, spilling their contents everywhere, like a wine covered crime scene. Sad, because

We Find a Buried Person (Kind of) 103

this stuff was more valuable than oil in the Wasteland. I personally didn't want it or like it, but richer people in the city would pay loads for a bottle of the real stuff. The city does make alcohol, crude nasty stuff mixed with their water to kill germs, and definitely not brewed for taste. This wine is carefully grown in the Clean World, and perfectly aged only for enjoyment. More than likely we will manage to sell this bottle for a load of necessities. Everything else we find is barely worth mentioning—four cans of food, a sealed package of dried fruit, a couple of rusty dishes, and a flashlight with at least a few hours of battery life remaining.

We stop for a very late lunch, warming the jar of volve soup left over from last night, and dipping into it with rock bread and a couple strips of jerky. I stare over the expanse of trash. It's surprising how foreign this place looks. You would be amazed that you can grow familiar with certain patches of trash, but you can, and these are definitely patches of trash I am not familiar with.

After our hasty lunch is when we find it—that thing that gets better and better. We walk in the same manner we had been doing all day, when I noticed something protruding from the ground—so far away I can't tell what it is. At first panic rushes over me—I think I am seeing one of my markers, and that means I have gotten my direction mixed up, which means that we are almost certainly lost. Then I look again. The thing gleams green in the sunlight, and it looks to be at least twenty feet tall, bigger than any of the markers we placed. I don't waste time feeling relieved—instead, I rush towards it.

"What do you reckon that is?" I ask, pointing to the

horizon where the thing stands.

"Dunno, tip of some buried skyscraper?" says Auburn, squinting at the thing.

"I don't think so. It's too lumpy, not uniform enough to be a building." We hurry forward with excitement, almost forgetting to place our marker. It takes five minutes at a steady jog to make out what it is. We all come to a stop, looking at the thing in amazement. Several seconds pass, maybe a full minute, while we stare in awe at the thing.

Poking out of the trash is a twelve-foot tall green hand, carrying a large torch of discolored greenish metal. I shiver, something that shouldn't happen in this heat.

I did not know it then, but we had just discovered the Statue of Liberty, buried beneath five hundred years of trash. The beacon that had once stood for hope for so many years for so many people, now buried in trash, all its former glory banished—a buried remnant of the glorious nation that thrived here before hope was lost—and this treasure was abandoned, signifying the loss of hope for this world as well as the ending of it.

But believe it or not, that wasn't going to be the most amazing thing we found there.

"Do you see that?" asks Zeleng, wide-eyed. His mouth falls open and his jaw drops until it seems to rest on his folded arms.

"No, I am just standing in front of it, totally ignoring it. Of course I see it," says Auburn, without taking his eyes off the carefully crafted curling flames of the giant torch.

"Thats not what I meant. Look!" I follow Zeleng's pointing finger to a ledge just below the flames.

Sitting on the ledge is a package nearly identical to the

one Leon took away from Arizon a few nights earlier. The metal package has the same locking mechanism I had seen on Arizon's, and the same high-tech look that doesn't fit in with the rest of the Wasteland's junk.

We stand there stunned for several more seconds. It isn't enough that we found a mysterious green hand sticking out of the ground, but we may also have found the answer to the mystery about the packages. I shout and run towards the hand, filled with a sudden desire to reach the package. That desire comes to a sudden stop when I realize I have no way to get up to the box perched at the top of the torch towering above me. The others also come to a stop next to me, realizing the problem.

"We could chuck stuff at it and try to knock it down. It doesn't look too secure," says Auburn, scanning the ground as if looking for throwable things.

"No way. Something inside could break—I'm not risking that," I say.

"That means we gotta get someone up there," suggests Zeleng. I barely hear Zeleng. My mind is racing—what could these identical packages mean? If I am not mistaken, Leon already has two, and I doubt that three identical packages are any kind of coincidence—so what could they be? Despite my mind's racing, it comes up short, not generating any ideas that seem probable.

It takes forever to finally reach it. At some point, I don't know exactly when, the other two silently volunteered me for the job of climbing the hand. Auburn and Zeleng hoist me up as far as they can, which is barely to the first giant green digit. They aid me slightly, pushing at my feet, and, combined with my own upper body strength, I manage to place my feet on the first finger while desperately clinging to the index finger with both of my hands—a task made more difficult by the curve of the finger and the greenish metal's lack of grip.

I am now directly below the circular base of the torch. There is no way to get over this barrier from where I am now, unless I do something stupid, something dangerous, and something that could kill me. I move my feet up two fingers so I only crouch on the top two. I prepare myself, taking deep breaths and moving my limbs into position. I move one leg and rest my foot on the thumb that curls around the torch until it rests just above the index finger. I take several more deep breaths and push off. I fling myself outwards, off my perch on the hand, trying with all my concentration to direct myself at a slightly upward angle. I am airborne for a fraction of a second, but it feels much longer. Thoughts flash through my head—most prominent of them is the thought of why in the heck am I doing this for a stupid package that might only contain some more worthless toilet paper rolls?

Then with one hand I feel the edge of the base of the torch. I desperately flail out for it. I grab it with one hand, and for a moment I hang there. With a grunt, I will my other hand to reach up and grab the base. While still maintaining my grip with the other, I steady myself from the momentum swinging me back and forth.

I have the top two joints of my eight fingers grasping the ledge, and even those are slipping. My heart beats fast and sweat runs down my forehead—a droplet falls off my chin and drops to the ground below. The distinct smell of copper mixes with my sweat. I hear the others yelling at

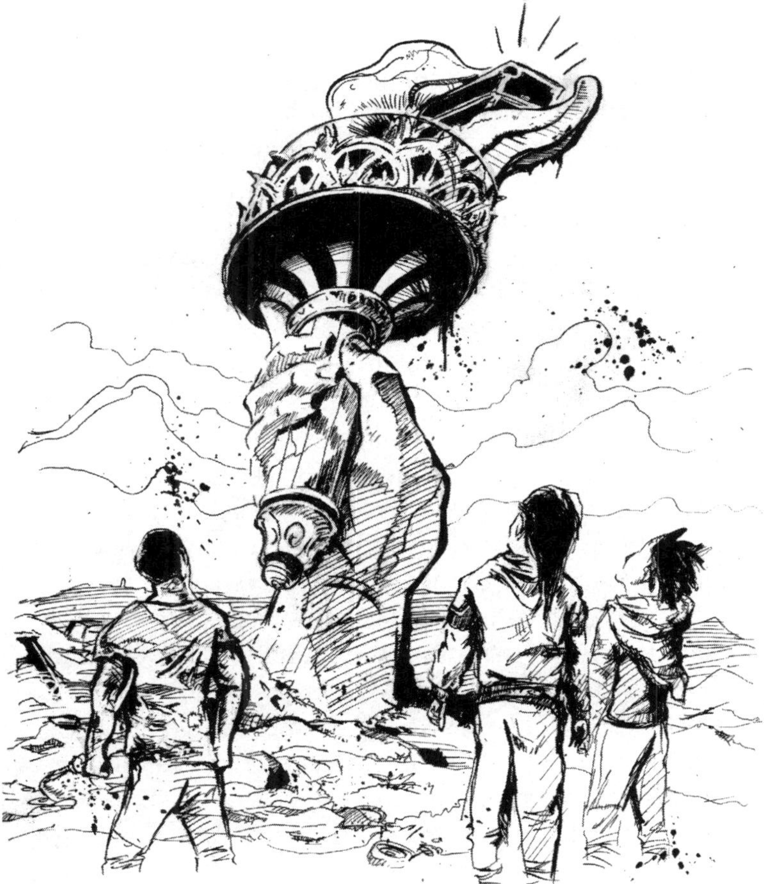

me—I can't tell if it's encouragement, chastisement, or just them yelling how stupid I am. If I hadn't spent years doing pullups on the bar in the training room, I would never have been able to pull myself up. Even with that practice, it is still a struggle. My muscles shake and I have to jerk my legs, kicking at the air to move myself up. I pull myself up and over the next railing into the circular room that contains the metal flame. There, on top of the flame, wedged in the individual flames, is the package.

I just want to collapse and rest. I am breathing hard and my heart thuds in machine gun suggestion. But I have come this far, and I am going to finish my job. I clamber to the box and tug it free. I rest it on the metal platform and examine it. There's a metal locking hatch. When I put my hand on it, I hear a click, and the box and the hatch swing open, revealing stuff I had only dreamed of.

I stare at the contents, not believing what I am seeing. I don't think I can ever look away, but I close the box, my mind going crazy. What I had found was more valuable than anything I have ever seen.

After a few minutes of discussion, and of my bossing Auburn and Zeleng around, they stand directly below, Zeleng's volve skin coat stretched between them as a makeshift landing pad. I almost whimper as I let the package drop down to them. I really don't want to drop the package—its contents are so valuable that I don't even want to let it out of my sight. As planned, the package drops safely into the coat. The others surround it.

"Go ahead and look inside—you won't believe me if I told you. It should just open," I say, peering down at them.

They try everything to open it, but they can't. They

We Find a Buried Person (Kind of) 109

touch and tap every part of it, looking for hidden latches, buttons and levers. When that fails, they try opening it by force, just plain yanking at it with all their might.

"Not opening," yells up Zeleng, as if it isn't obvious. It doesn't make sense—why would this package open so easily for me but not for my friends?

I lift myself back over the railing, and let myself fall back into the eight finger hanging position I had been in earlier. With my feet hanging down like this, it's not such a horrible drop. I let go and fall to the ground. The impact jars my body, but isn't too painful. I move to where the others stand over the package.

"Show us your magic. I don't know why we can't open it—just too dumb probably," says Zeleng, examining me closely as I walk to the box and lay exactly one finger on it. When it swings open, they let out stunned gasps, first, because I had opened it, and then again when they see the contents.

The chest was stocked with treasures; batteries, lights, soap, two bottles of aspirin, painkillers, bandages, a first-aid kit, salt, perfume, and a curious device—a disk of metal with a small projector at its center. It looks high tech and not exactly safe. It has a blue circle at the middle that seems to glow slightly.

"Holy Crap. We are rich!" says Zeleng, slowly pausing between words.

"No kidding. This is everything we need, but that doesn't solve the question of why the heck are we finding this in a bunch of trash? Why would anyone have thrown away a package with so many new useful things that don't have any reason to be thrown out? And why would it be locked?" asks Auburn, looking around in disbelief and confusion.

The question is answered when the small disk lets out a beep, and emanating from the glowing blue circle is a glowing blue light. The light takes the shape of a man about two feet tall. Despite the hologram's size, he appears tall. Something about him seems very familiar. "Hello, Zane," the hologram message says, "My name is Zenith, and I am your father."

Reunions and Confusion

At first I don't believe him and don't want to. My father—I guess his name is Zenith, seems to be expecting this reaction, because he continues, "I know you probably don't believe me, but hear me out. If you have gotten any of my previous packages, this is a repeat of my message." He has a sad expression on his face, one of loneliness and regret.

"What do you mean? My father is dead, and I never knew him," I say. My voice sounds angry, but my emotions are much more complicated than that. How could this man, this random stranger in the box, be my father? The hologram doesn't reply, and I realize this message is recorded. That realization shuts me up, for he can't hear anything I say. Auburn and Zeleng give me confused, incredulous looks, and I can't do anything but return them.

"Fifteen years ago, back when you were barely one year of age, I came into some trouble with the government. I had information that they wanted. You see, I was a hacker for NAWC, the government born from the crisis on Earth. I won't go into detail, but when you arrive at the Clean

World, you will understand. Like I said, I was a hacker, so I had access to some of NAWC's top-secret files. I was never supposed to ever look at them, but one day I did. I looked into them, snooped a little, and hacked deeper into their past, finding out information I don't want to ever repeat, and for the sake of the story it isn't important." The hologram of Zenith states the last part with distaste.

"I guess I left traces of my investigation behind and NAWC found out. NAWC didn't want anyone to know this information, and I don't blame them. I knew I was in trouble. I wanted to flee, but NAWC was my whole life, my employer, and the only reason I had a home. I didn't have anywhere to go. I expected them to torture me, or just kill me to eliminate the risk that I might spread the information. What they did was oh so much worse." True sadness crosses his face, and even in the hologram's flickering images I think I see tears welling up in his eyes.

"They took you, Zane—they took you, and I never saw you again. You don't know how hard it was for me. I can't say I was ever truly happy again after they took you from me. I gave NAWC all the information they wanted and let them lock me up. I did anything and everything to spare you. They did let you go, but not to a safe place. They sent you to Earth, to the Wasteland, the dumps, the trash pit, the junk hole, just to make me pay for what I did in a more painful way than death."

My thoughts are reeling like a bucking treef from his words, my emotions are scrambled even more than before, and I can't think straight. According to Zenith I was born in the Clean World, presumably into a loving family with plenty of money and food. "I guess it was just my bad luck.

I blame myself everyday. Everyday I think about all I could have done differently. If I had just not hacked that file, or done a better job covering my trail, then I would still have my son. I bet I could have saved you from a whole lot of suffering and hardship."

My brain blames Zenith and curses him, but in my heart I feel a connection to this man who is my father. That is, if I believe him—which I do—for who would lie about something like this, or set up an elaborate way of getting this message to me if it's not true? I even see the resemblance—we have the same dark hair and eyes, and something about his expression reminds me of, well, me.

"NAWC released me, whether because they didn't want to pay for my imprisonment or what, I don't know. They gave me a job as a factory worker making weapon parts for their military, a job far from any computer. I despised the fact that I was helping defend the nation that took you, but I had no choice. At first, I was overcome with sadness and was constantly depressed. I struggled to see happiness in a world that I felt had none with you gone." The expression on his face tells me that he is remembering bad times—very bad times.

"It took years, almost a decade, in fact, before I pulled myself together. When I did, I realized I couldn't stay working this factory job. I ran away, barely survived and joined the rebels. Ever since then, I have monitored the GPS chip I had installed in your arm at your birth. I have always known where you were, but until very recently I felt there was nothing I could do. Without funding and an interstellar spaceship I had always thought it was impossible to come and get you. Two months ago though, I realized I didn't have to come. You can find your own way back. All you need is help." The hologram finally smiles, and a small ray of hope crosses his face. "Two months ago I sent the first package, or rather, I threw away the package. I made sure it ended up on a Trash Craft headed for your general area. I have been sending one every week since then, and I programmed each box so that it can be opened only when your GPS chip is within a five foot radius of it."

It finally hits me. Leon has the other packages, and if what Zenith says is true, that means he hasn't yet opened them. Leon could have found at least seven other boxes if he had collected all of the boxes Zenith had sent.

"In my first package I sent a grenade, the most powerful electro magnetic grenade I could get my hands on. The grenade has the power to shut down any Trash Craft for thirty minutes, hopefully enough time for you to board the ship. I have no way of knowing if you have received and opened my other packages. But when you do find them, if you haven't already, I hope it gives you the chance you need to escape back to your home in the Clean World and back to me." We all gasp in unison.

Zenith has just given us a chance, a hope of escaping to the Clean World. As much as I wanted to, I didn't agree with Zenith. The Clean World was not my home. No matter how crappy the Wasteland is, it will always be the place where I grew up, the place I call home.

"In the second package I included guns and weapons to help you past any obstacles there might be on the Trash Craft. I gave you ammo in the next package, and every single one after that contains supplies to help you have a good life if you decide to never undertake the journey back to me. I bid you farewell and good luck, son, on anything you choose to do." With that the 3D image of Zenith abruptly blips out of existence, leaving a silence that lasts for several seconds.

"Holy shit man," says Zeleng, slowly looking at me. Auburn does the same, both looking at me expectantly. I shrug, returning a look of stunned confusion.

"Guys, I know about as much as you do." My voice is shaky, and as I reclose the package, my hands are trembling. "I just don't know. And I don't understand," I say, putting my head in my hands.

"Sounds to me like you have a long lost father trying to help you get back to the Clean World. Do you know what this means? We now have a chance, a real god damn chance." Auburn talks with more and more enthusiasm, his voice getting louder and louder. Auburn manages to sum up the physical happenings pretty easily, but I don't know if I will ever be able to understand my emotions.

"Leon has the other packages—we saw him take one in front of our eyes, but why? Did he somehow know what was inside? From what your dad said, only you can open them, which means Leon hasn't been able to get in. So if we convince Leon to open them, we can get all the other things. I don't know about you, but an electromagnetic grenade sounds pretty awesome," says Zeleng.

"He's right—we have to have a word with Leon first thing when we get back," says Auburn, with absolute certainty in his tone.

Despite all my worried doubts, we have no trouble on our return journey. The markers we left work perfectly, and before we know it, we are back at the first pipe marker.

We don't wait for the wagon to catch up with us. Instead, we rush back to meet it. It takes about an hour, as the wagon is still a few miles back. We have time to discuss everything that we found in the box, and everything Zenith had said. I am still not ready to call him dad or father yet. The shock has worn off faster than expected, and I guess it's because I feel a connection to him, as though a conscious memory of him hovers at the edge of my consciousness, only close enough to know that, indeed, he is my father. Despite the connection I don't feel close to him, which is understandable because he is millions of miles away, a stranger, like a distant star. It's odd, suddenly realizing someone has been concerned about you without you ever knowing. It's almost comforting to realize that no matter how alone I have felt, I never truly was. Thoughts like these, deep and philosophical, fly unrestrained through my mind. Before I know it, the outline of the wagon appears in front of me, and for the first time I realize how hard I had been thinking, my mind being so consumed in thought that time flew and my legs walked me along by themselves.

It's almost six, so the main doors are still open, at least for a while. We climb up the ramp, our metal boots clanging against metal, a comforting sound. The sound always signifies that we have returned home to the wagon and to its safety. Although I now know my father is out there, home is still here.

Auburn and Zeleng carry the heavy package between them, trying their best not to be noticed—however, it really doesn't work. We avoid the shouted questions and ignore the surprised looks. We aren't the only ones to realize this package is identical to the one Leon had stolen from Arizon.

Once we make it through the crowd, we have one destination in mind—Leon's quarters. It's convenient for us since his room is right off the main room, so we don't have to heave the package up a ladder. I raise my hand to the door to knock, but it opens before I can, and Leon's grim face greets us.

"Get in here now." His voice isn't mean or angry, but it does have a distinct air of command. "We need to talk," I say, crossing my arms as I cross the threshold.

"Believe me, I know. Sit over there." Leon's tone surprises me, as he gestures to a gray couch positioned in front of his magnificent oak desk. The desk is the most amazing piece of furniture I have ever seen. The wood is a pale, heavily grained polished masterpiece. A piece of furniture passed down from the early years of the Nomads, when a desk like this was still possible to make. It reminds me very quickly that Leon is a person of importance, the person in charge. It makes me feel a little small.

As Leon told us to do, we take a seat, but only after Leon himself also sits. He fixes his eyes on us—one a normal emerald colored green eye, and the other a shiny green lens. The colors work so well together you would think Leon was born with that lens on his face.

"I have been untruthful with everyone, and I hope you will forgive me. As you have probably guessed, I have found three packages, identical in shape, but not weight." He looks expectantly at me.

"And you haven't been able to open them," I say. I know I am right, the look on Leon's face, one of frustration, reveals it.

"Yes," Leon says with a little sigh, "But now I believe I have found the key. I saw you coming with that box, and the look in your eyes revealed that without a doubt you knew what was inside. With you having that information, I can no longer try to hide it. I will tell you everything, just as long as you tell me how to open the others."

His eyes haven't once moved from us. He looks at each of us in turn, and I feel every time his eyes rest on me that the lens is drilling into me, revealing all my secrets.

"Zane is the key. His dad said if he is close to one of the packages, it can be opened," explains Zeleng, not, however, doing a very good job.

"What do you mean, his father? Zane has been an orphan since we found him." Leon just looks at me and his stare bores into me.

I return his stare almost helplessly. "I can't explain it to you, but I can show you. Now, where do you keep the other boxes?" I ask, already bracing myself for what I might find inside.

※ ※ ※

I stare down at the three packages. Leon pulls them from a secret compartment under his desk, which now seems even more magnificent to me. I slowly move my hand to the first box. There is a small click, and the lid of the box pops up. It is instantly clear that this is not the first or second package, for it does not contain a grenade or a weapon of any kind. Instead, it's filled with much the same content of the package we had found today—batteries, light bulbs, first aid supplies, medicine, soaps, shampoos, and a hologram disk. However, this box also includes a digital screen, which, when tapped, displays little colored images with titles. I realize they're book covers, and that this is some kind of a digital reader like the Kindle of over five hundred years ago, maybe slightly better.

"So much for the electromagnetic grenade—this seems so much cooler," says Zeleng, flipping through the titles with the swipe of a finger.

"It's for reading books," I explain, tapping one of the titles and watching as it expands into the title page of a book.

"Never mind, an electromagnetic grenade is much cooler."

It quickly is apparent that as we browse the device's content, that it contains thousands of books on modern weapons, Trash Craft history and atlases of Earth today, all incredible to us. Our small supply of outdated books suddenly becomes obsolete. When I activate the hologram this time, it repeats much of the same story as the one we had listened to previously that day.

"I can't say that I am not truly amazed that your father has been able to communicate with you, and does make sense. I doubt anyone has told you the story of how we found you, or am I wrong?" Leon runs a hand through the well-trimmed stubble that rings his mouth.

"No. I don't know it. I never thought about it. This place is my whole life, or so I thought until today. I didn't know I wasn't always here," I answer, nodding at him to continue.

Leon looks at me with his full attention and I get slightly uneasy. "It's not an exceptionally exciting story, but it does line up with what your father said." Everytime someone mentions my father, it sends a new tingle of shock down my spine as though each time one repeats it, I am reliving just a little of the shock of when I first found out.

"You were an unexpected surprise. The night we found you was a cold, dark one. Around seven we started getting pelted by trash. It's not often we have the misfortune of being directly under one of those ships, but we were. Spirits were down—no one was looking forward to having to dig our way out the next morning. We sent out a few scouts, Borken and a few others, and when they returned, they had a baby. I didn't know how it was possible. People rumored that the Clean World now considered babies trash and threw them away. That's how we got you, so I suppose in a way they were right."

"Wait. I came in a Trash Craft, and they dropped me? How could I survive that? I was only one year old." I try to imagine how it could have been. I am suddenly grateful that we can't remember the early years of our lives, because I wouldn't want to remember mine.

"From my understanding, they sent you here as a punishment for your dad. They wouldn't risk killing you, because they wanted to always let your father have just that small little hope, while feeling the pain of knowing he's not there for you, as you survive in this horrible Wasteland," says Leon. Even now, he is trying to logically explain NAWC's actions. I want to be mad at him for that, but I realize that is just the way Leon is—and even if it seems uncaring, I can still hear the sympathy in his voice, even if it's hidden under many layers of thoughts.

"Let's keep moving," says Zeleng.

We move on to the next package. When I open this

one with my magic hand, I immediately realize this is the first package. Inside, surrounded by a foam casing, rests a sleek metal sphere. The grenade is as big as my head. Zenith wasn't kidding when he said he sent the most powerful one he could get his hands on. On one side, there's a control panel with a mass of buttons. Zenith explains how it works in the hologram message, which is, I realize, the first one he ever recorded. His exact words are, "The grenade, when activated, will lock on to the nearest Trash Craft it senses. It will fly up to the ship, detonate and wipe out all the ship's computers on board. It will give you thirty minutes at most to board and take on the guards if you have to."

"That's pretty cool," expresses Zeleng. "All we must do is take out the ship, board, and there we go—a free ride to paradise."

Leon looks much less enthusiastic. "This is what I expected. When I saw the first package, my lens picked up on the high tech tracker in the lock. Immediately I assumed it was some sort of top secret weapon, which lost its way somewhere along the line, and ended up thrown away. So, naturally, I hid it away, for I had failed to open it even though I tried everything," Leon continues, "and when the second was found, I knew something was up. Then I had to take that one away from Arizon. Three high-tech packages in such close proximity and close succession is no coincidence—I had no more success opening these two boxes either. These boxes are lined with titanium and they self-destruct if opened by force."

"Wow. My Dad really only wanted me to have this." It makes me feel good to know that someone cares enough about me to try so hard to send me these packages.

"Cool, cool, but let's move on," says Zeleng, obviously impatient to explore the next package.

The last box is not the second package sent by Zenith, because it contains no guns or weapons either. In this box there are only rows and rows of ammo clips—compared to our crude guns, these clips look as though they belong to alien weapons. In a funny way they do, since they are from another planet.

"Quite unfortunate. This package went with the second, the one containing the guns. Won't be very helpful till we have the contents of the second package," says Leon, taking one of the clips and examining it closely with his lens. "These are bronze and copper, a little better than our crude bullets, but not that much different. Still, these clips won't fit into our guns, and the bullets are too slim." He sighs a little at that and closes the lid. He sits back down at his desk chair and faces us. "I owe you more of an explanation than that."

"Yes you do," says Zeleng—then realizing his rudeness, he quickly adds, "sir." Leon doesn't look it, but I can tell he's struggling to find the right words.

"I don't know how to say this any other way. I am not a good leader," Leon says, an expression of regret crossing his face.

"Woah, no, what do you mean?" argues Auburn immediately.

"He's right, we have never had a better leader," I add.

"Sit down. I will explain myself. As you know, when I found the first package I kept it secret, but not for the safety of the wagons. I kept it because I was afraid…" He pauses, thinking again for the right words.

Zeleng takes this opportunity to say, "Afraid of what? You are the bravest person I know." Leon gives him a sad look.

"This isn't a question of my bravery, you see. I am terrified to lose my power. When I first saw that package, I thought it was some kind of weapon, something that would give people hope for an escape. I was right. I know that now, but if we ever make it back to the Clean World, who is going to listen to me? Who am I going to lead? So I selfishly kept the box all to myself, trying in vain to open it. I chose myself over my people. What kind of leader does that?"

I can't see why this is such a big deal to Leon. I don't blame him at all for keeping the packages a secret. It was the right choice no matter what his incentive was.

"There is no such thing as a perfect leader. With power comes selfishness—it's unavoidable—and I think you're wrong. People always need a leader." I don't know if I'm trying to comfort him, or deny what he's saying.

"That's nice of you to say. But I was just selfish. There's nothing worse than a selfish leader. It hurt my confidence, I never know anymore if I am making the right decision. It is scary for me when I don't know what to do, because my decisions can mean life and death for the wagons."

I don't know why Leon is spilling his secrets to us. Maybe it is because we have helped him open the packages, or maybe he just couldn't hold it in anymore. "I am considering resigning." His face droops and his features sag.

"No. You can't and you won't. You made one bad decision—thinking of resigning after making one mistake shows how much you strive to be a flawless leader," Auburn argues. Leon doesn't seem convinced. "Just think about what would happen without you. You can't do that to us."

It takes much more talking before we finally convince him that one mistake isn't the end of the world. He apologises for his lack of control and his mistake.

"Don't mention it. I have made a heck of a lot more mistakes than you, and I'm not even half your age," ends Zeleng. With that we bid him farewell and leave the room. Leon even gives us a smile before we go. I don't know why I am not worried that our glorious leader seems so unstable. Maybe because I know Leon is stronger than this—or am I just making a terrible mistake?

King of Garbage

I can't sleep that night. Everytime I try, images of Zenith and Leon and the grenade pop into my head, driving me crazy. I toss and turn so wildly that I know I must be keeping Zeleng and Auburn awake, not as if they could have slept either. I should be exhausted. We walked nearly fourteen miles today, but somehow I'm more restless than ever. I count sheep, but I can't get past ten before the sheep morph into Zenith or a Trash Craft. When I finally fall asleep, I am assailed with dreams of everything that happened that day. I wake repeatedly, and each time it takes me longer to fall back to sleep. Once the sun rises and shines through the window, I get up. My clothes and hair stick to my skin, damp from the sweat.

I look in the mirror nailed into the wall at the side of my bunk bed. A crack runs down the middle, cutting my reflection in two. I look awful—my black eyes are bloodshot and bags hang for miles under them. I need to cut my hair—it hangs in mats and sticks up. My lips are chapped and cracked in places where I had bitten them last night. I am a wreck. I go to the bathroom, that is, the room with the toilet, not the one where I had taken my bath only a day earlier. So much had happened since then—too much to even grasp. It all seemed surreal and hard to believe. I have a father. Those four words had been floating around in my head all night, nudging me whenever I was on the verge of falling asleep. Once in the bathroom I splash water on my face. The sink is hooked up to rain barrels on the roof. It's heated with only the sun, so the water is cool and feels good. It doesn't do much to wake me up, but I no longer want to go to sleep. I lift the toilet seat—I can see the ground from here. The toilet dumps its contents right onto the ground. Interestingly, we dump into a dump.

When I return to the room, I find Zeleng and Auburn sitting up in bed. They don't look much better than I do.

"Sleep well?" asks Auburn hoarsely.

"Haha, good one. I slept like crap," I reply, rubbing my eyes for at least the tenth time that morning.

"Yeah, we heard ya thrashing around all night," says Zeleng. "Kept me up, but I still think I slept better than you." With that he collapses back into his bed. "So what's up, daddy's boy? Wonder if your dad will spoil you with anymore presents today?" The remark isn't really mean and since it's actually quite accurate, I laugh. The laughter makes me feel good, brings me back down to earth, so to speak, and makes my crazy life feel normal again.

"Yesterday I woke up thinking about eating volve bones and oats—today, I wake up thinking about stuff that's so different it doesn't even compare. It's just now hitting me how much has changed so fast," I say. It's not usual for me to be sharing my thoughts, mainly because I have never been good at it—but today I feel as though life is different, so maybe I should start by being different.

"Yeah, it's probably even harder for you now that you got a daddy," says Auburn. I think about what he says. I have a dad—those four words again. He is my dad even though I don't know him and have never seen him as far as I can remember. What about my mom? I must've had a mom, right, so who is she? That thought opens up a whole new world.

· · ·

At breakfast that day Leon walks up to us. He looks better than yesterday, at least less hopeless and slightly more cheerful, but still serious. "Finish up quickly, then come with me," orders Leon. We stuff our faces so fast that even a treef would be impressed—then we push our chairs out and follow him to his quarters.

When we are all standing inside his room, he locks the door behind us, hopefully because he doesn't want anyone to disturb us, and not for any other reason.

"Have you guys made any plans?" The question confuses me.

"What? No," I answer, taking a seat where I had sat yesterday.

Leon looks relieved. "Good, because you aren't going to, at least not yet. I will reconsider it when we have collected all the packages."

"Clarify, please?" says Zeleng.

"I don't know if you have been too shocked to think about it or what, but you have been delivered the chance of a lifetime on a silver platter—weapons and a way of getting transportation to the Clean World. This is real—you could make it to the Clean World." He looks as though he is going to go on, but I cut him off.

"But you're not going to let us go, are you?" I look at him, asking silently, for as Zeleng had put it, more clarification.

"The time isn't right. And honestly, guys, do you want to risk everything? You're fed here, you have shelter and protection—why do you want to attempt an extremely dangerous trip to an unknown world that might not even be the paradise you guys all believe it is?" I guess I had never thought about it that way. We do have all those things Leon had listed and more. This is our home. I wonder if this was what the Pilgrims had felt. They had made this exact decision almost eight hundred years ago. I knew about the Pilgrims from the history books we have in our library. It isn't big, but it contains a lot of random books and a whole ton of outdated textbooks.

"Zane needs to get back to his father—that's why we have to go," says Zeleng, bringing me back into the conversation. I am not sure if I liked Zeleng saying what I need and don't need, but it seems to convince Leon to reconsider a bit, for he takes time to think before he replies.

"Zane's home is here, and so is yours and mine." What Leon says just reinforces my own thoughts of where my home really is. I must say, Leon is right. He is always right, no matter what he might think about himself. "Zane, your father might be alive, but how much of a father has he really been? Zane, you don't even know him, and he's never been there for you." I disagree that my father has never been there for me. He took a job in a factory for ten years just to make money so he could help me now. He always

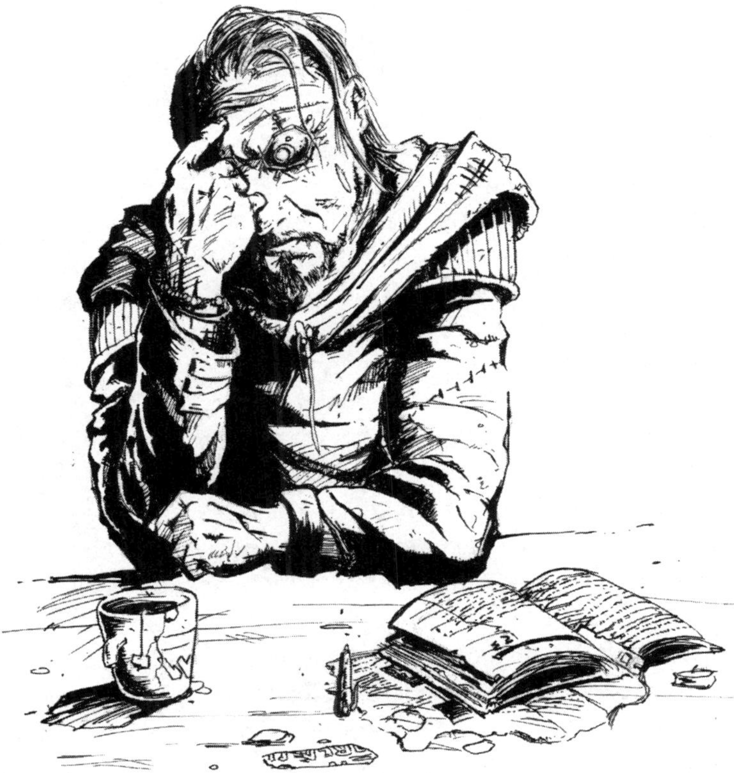

watched over me, tracked me with the GPS tracker in my hand, and always has thought about me. What Leon says puts an angry edge on my voice, and when I speak, the sharpness of my own words surprises me.

"So you're suggesting we just give up, play it safe, never take a risk. You want to know something? If I did that, I would never have found that package and you would never have known that I was able to open these packages. They would sit there till the end of time," I say, pointing to Leon's desk, where underneath I knew the packages were hidden. "I have played it safe my whole life, sat around and waited for something to happen, and it only ever did when I took that risk yesterday and went farther out than I had ever gone." Leon doesn't even blink an eye. He stares at me exactly the way he had before, listening and calmly calculating.

"We don't know what lies out there; we have this once in a lifetime chance, and we can't just waste it, go unprepared and fail. We have to have a well thought-out plan, and at a minimum, find the other packages before we try anything. And if guards await us at the Trash Craft, we can't kill them without becoming fugitives in the Clean World—and if we don't kill them, we won't get the Trash Craft to get there. We will be demons in heaven. You see, we can't go blundering off to the Clean World until a possible alternative shows itself." It's a valid point, one I hadn't ever considered. Leon always seemed to be able to see the entire situation. His calculating mind always thought about every eventuality. I think that is what makes him such a good and fair leader.

"We could, uh...," Zeleng trails off, "never mind, you are

right." Zeleng and Auburn look defeated. Leon must see this because he continues, "I said we weren't going to try until we had all the packages. You forget we don't have the stash of weapons from the second package yet. Once we have them, I will consider it, because it might make this impossible journey somewhat more possible."

"Then you should tell everyone to look for these boxes, and tell them why too. There won't be a single person who won't want to help in some way," I say, already thinking that with over one hundred walkers searching, how fast we could find all the other packages.

"No. I can't give everyone false hopes like that. Once we find all the packages, everyone will want to go to the Clean World, but not everyone will be able to. Do you see now? Trying to keep everyone happy and everything fair means sacrificing some good things because we can't all have all of them. The second I promise some things to some people, I will have destroyed the entire foundation on which I have built my leadership. This is part of the reason I kept the packages hidden."

I can tell he's struggling to make the right decisions. If we tell everyone, it will get out of control. This is the only way to keep order. "You're right again, this is our only shot, and if we screw it up, we probably won't get another. Better to wait. We need time to prepare and plan."

Leon looks relieved. "I am glad you understand. Now on to other matters. Zane, you can read the best out of all of us, so you will get the reading tablet. Read every night—figure out about the Clean World and its weapons. Read everything and anything that could help us." He is changing the subject on purpose as if to say, 'case closed'. He hands me the sleek shiny screen. "How am I supposed to read everything? It would take years," I say, slightly overwhelmed that he is entrusting this huge job to me, on top of everything else. For all I know, there are thousands of books on this tablet.

"Prioritize, read the stuff that can benefit us first," explains Leon. I take the tablet into my hands and marvel how incredibly light it is. He also hands me a long cord that I assume is a charger. "I hope we have an outlet this high-tech," I say, examining the cord's plug-in.

"Good luck to you guys. I do hope you get to the Clean World someday." We all look up at him. "You say that as if you aren't coming," I say, slightly perplexed.

"Oh, I would never leave this place. This is my kingdom."

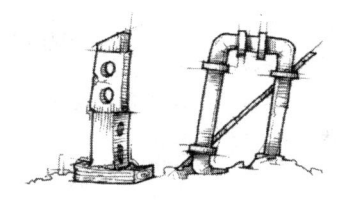

The Only Place Where People Love Their Vegetables

Today is harvesting day—all walkers have the option of staying to help harvest, but Auburn, Zeleng and I are too preoccupied with finding the other packages to even consider it. So when most of the others get up and start climbing the ladders to the roof, we head down the ramp. Today the sky is filled with dark polluted clouds, and it still hasn't warmed up completely since that icy rain. I wrap a scarf around my face and pull my hood up, partially to keep myself warm, and partially to block out the stench of garbage. I look like some kind of second-hand ninja.

I left the electronic tablet with Leon, not wanting to risk damaging the device that held so much priceless information. We trek alongside the wagon for a while, and hand stuff into the engine room to be burned. It's one of my least favorite jobs, and includes a lot of heavy lifting and lack of fun. The only reason we are doing this job is the fellows who usually do this task are up harvesting the roof gardens. I find a long board and pass it to Borkin, who is standing on the wagon. Borkin then throws it into a chute where it slides down to a pile in the engine room.

With all the soap we have found in the two packages, bathing from now on would be a heck of a lot better. I wonder what Leon is going to do with all the loot we have found? It would be rather suspicious if fifty bars of soap and containers of shampoo appeared in the bathroom, but it would be selfish if Leon kept it all to himself. Leon sure did have to make some pretty hard decisions. And all those light bulbs—we had almost none of them, for when we do find them they are either shattered or burnt out. I guess Leon will just have to cycle in this loot slowly so no one notices the sudden increase.

At noon, most of the harvesting is done and we are free to start scavenging. Since we are so near the wagon, we decide to join the others for lunch instead of our usual on-the-go meal we eat scavenging. No one can wait for a taste of fresh vegetables. Just thinking about all of it makes my mouth water.

Everyone sits around the tables, even most of the walkers. Everyone is very eager to see what wonderful dish Ham has made from the produce. People in the Clean World would find us crazy for being this excited about vegetables, of all things, well, at least they probably would. What Leon had said is right. We don't know anything about the Clean World. Hopefully, that will change when I start reading. Maybe, like Leon had said, the Clean World isn't a paradise, but maybe it is. I sit at a table with Paul, Luke, Zeleng, Auburn and Arizon. There's already a mixed assortment of plates, pans and silverware, including chopsticks (if they count) on the table.

With so many of my other friends around, it's hard to keep everything that has happened to myself. My life has changed so much, but nothing is different for anyone else. Except for Zeleng, Auburn and Leon, life is just as normal as usual. Just another day. Everyone else seems just as eager to eat the fresh food as I am. "I can't wait," says Zeleng, confirming my assumption.

"Zeleng, that's a first. I haven't heard an ounce of complaining," says Auburn.

"Nah, the first time I couldn't wait for Ham's cooking was the last time we harvested the roof gardens." He smiles at me, grabs a fork and a dull knife, and pounds them on the table in anticipation.

"Yeah, sure. What do you think Ham's gonna make?" wonders Auburn.

"Won't matter; it will still be delicious," I say, looking towards the kitchen where I can hear the muffled sounds of Ham clanging dishes and muttering to himself.

At that moment the kitchen door swings open and out strides Ham, pushing a cart laden with so much food you can barely see the short man behind it. On the cart is one of my favorites, roast volve stuffed with vegetables. The volve is complete with head and limbs hanging down off the cart. The meat glistens; the volve is so stuffed with vegetables that it looks fat. Trailing behind Ham are his two twins pushing trays laden with rock bread and vegetable soup. Everyone cheers. The three of them bustle around doing their best to pass out the food as fast as they can. Ham slams a slab of meat onto my plate and blankets it with vegetables. The twins hand me a bowl of soup along with several slices of bread. I soak the bread in my soup with the hope of making it more chewable, and start on my roast. The meat is tough, but that's to be expected from the flesh of such a muscled predator, but it has soaked up all the vegetable flavors and comes out as a chewy delight. When I take the first bite of a carrot, it almost melts in my mouth. The room has grown amazingly silent; everyone's head is buried in this feast. Then one by one they let out exclamations of satisfaction. Ham rushes back into the kitchen as I would have if I were the cook. I never know how to respond to praise and thanks.

We are all in a good mood, and the conversations are loud and full of laughter. When my plate and bowl are empty, and all that remains are a few crumbs, I finally speak. "That. Was. Good," I say. I feel as if my stomach is going to explode. I didn't mean to eat so much, but once I started, I couldn't stop until every bit was gone.

"That's an understatement. That's the best food I have had in a very long time," Auburn insists. We can't seem to stop praising the food. All I want to do is sleep, but I force myself to get up and walk back outside.

At first we walk slowly, seemingly weighed down by our packed stomachs, but we scavenge all day. We find absolutely nothing; not one package, nor anything else of use, not even a single can of food. Disappointed, we return early, even before dinner, which is very unusual for us. We find Ham in the main room still cleaning up from lunch.

"You guys, get in the kitchen. We need help canning the vegetables," says Ham, pushing us toward the kitchen. He drags us inside. Hopefully, this will be a way to do something a little more productive than the rest of my day has been. Inside there's a row of people—each person seems to have his or her own job—like a production line.

"We got some amateurs over here. Put them on cutting

duty," yells Ham's wife. It's kind of weird to see her work in the kitchen. She's working at the fire, stirring a huge pot of steaming vegetables. I know Ham's wife well—she took care of me when I was young. However, since I moved into my new room, I don't see much of her. I still remember what she looks like. She's not much taller than Ham, but her presence seems greater than her size would suggest. She bustles around, ordering people to do this and that. She used to be almost like a mom to me, so when she directs us towards a cutting table, I don't refuse.

"Yeah, perfect. I am good with sharp objects," chuckles Zeleng, already following Ham's wife, Rosemary, over to a counter where several people are cutting. I stand beside him and start to cut the steady stream of peeled vegetables that comes from the peeling station to our right.

We can vegetables for the rest of the afternoon. The stack of jars in the corner of the kitchen steadily grows, and I feel a small sadness because we no longer have any fresh vegetables.

Our roof gardens aren't very big at all—they produce barely enough food for one meal and about a hundred jars. We can get vegetables in the city, Skumford, but they're pricey and we don't often trade for them. There's always a next time, I think to myself. Now that all the vegetables are in the jars, we finally quit. It wasn't very hard work, but it was repetitive and slow, and left me extremely restless. At dinner that night we are served a few vegetables in our volve soup, but I am really not hungry after that lunch, and so I mindlessly stir my food, staring at it more than actually eating it.

"I am going to the training room tomorrow. It's been a

while since I have, and I need to get some of that fighting out of my system," says Auburn, cracking his knuckles.

"Nah, we gotta go look for the packages," says Zeleng a little too loud, and we get a few odd looks.

"Keep it down. No one else knows, remember," I warn, almost whispering.

"We should still practice—we might have to fight the guards if we make it to the Trash Craft. Have you forgotten that?" asks Auburn.

"True, I guess we should, can't hurt, can it? And it's not that likely we would find another package in the hour we spend practicing instead of searching," I reason.

"I guess that's settled," says Zeleng.

"Okay, sounds good," I reply. I gulp down a few more bites of soup before we return to our room. I really want to discuss the packages and everything else that has happened, but there's something else I want to do more—read the tablet, and figure out the truth about the world of my dreams.

When I am sitting comfortably on my bed with my pillows pushed against the wall, I turn on the tablet with a small button. The screen blazes to life and the book covers appear on the screen again. I select a first title, *The Brief History of the New World*. This looks good. The picture on the front shows a fleet of human transport ships. They remind me of the Trash Crafts, therefore I don't think much of them.

I don't exactly know what I am doing, but after a few tries I tap the book, and it expands to fill my screen. I slide my finger along it and turn from the cover, through the table of contents, to the first page.

Introduction
A Story of Before

New Earth was born from a dying world. Humans destroyed it. They used everything up, ruined everything, and then just left it. I am not here to criticize the actions of our ancestors, but they were foolish. No one could accept the problems of overpopulation and global warming until it was too late, and the world was nothing more than a sphere in the universe, devoid of everything but starving humans. Something had to change, and it did. We moved on from the Planet we had ruined, using all the remaining resources to build the fleet, the fleet known as the Exodus, that took almost all the people from that planet to New Earth. We were unimaginably lucky, for only ten years before we had made the choice to leave, to find a new planet, a place where we could have a second chance. And so we left the planet that had housed life for billions of years, and which humans had destroyed in only a few hundred, and traveled to our new home. New Earth is nearly three times the size of Earth, with four habitable moons. It also is home to many new undiscovered species. No intelligent beings, at least none on the same level as humans, were discovered. We started mining asteroids and have built a great new empire on this new planet. But the most important thing was that the human race had learned a lesson. This new planet has no oil or natural gas so we are forced to use green energy. At the formation of New Earth, NAWC vowed to never let anything like what happened to Earth ever happen again.

I had heard this story before, but not in such a complete way. I enjoyed reading it immensely. I read the rest of the early history, but stopped when I found the part where they had added a new set of rules called the Commandments of the New World. The new rules were these.

Commandments of the New World

Each family can have no more than two children—violators will be fined two hundred and fifty thousand dollars. If there is a break in the family, the person is not allowed to have more children with any other person.

The use of anything but green renewable energy will result in a fine of one thousand dollars—it is also a federal offence. Continued abuse will result in imprisonment and increasing fines.

The rules went on and on, and all of them made me happy. They all had one purpose—to never let what happened to Earth happen again. Why couldn't the governments have had the power to make these rules on Earth before everything went downhill? I spend the rest of the evening reading. I quickly master the tablet, and within the first hour have categorized the titles into how helpful reading them would be. I search for keywords in the books to find which ones contain information I want. I also set up a reading list and search each one for what chapters I will read. I haven't read much yet, but from what I have read, I am amazed. I have already learned about the formation of the New Earth, and the many problems NAWC faced, including lack of materials, lack of knowledge of the new planet, and lack of immunity to loads of new diseases.

It took nearly ten years to set up New Earth as a habitable place, and that's when they started sending trash to Earth, desperate to keep their new home as pristine as they could. Present day New Earth contains forests of wind turbines, multi-level farms, and massive underwater hydroelectric turbines. Cities now have limits to how much they can expand, and the population is controlled completely. The information all points to one conclusion—that NAWC has set up a great new world on New Earth and that everything is controlled and calculated for the greatest possible outcome. If so, what did my father find in their files that made NAWC tear apart his life and send me down to exile on Earth? How could a government that sounds so good do something so evil to keep some dark secrets from tarnishing its image? My dad would not have sent me a tablet full of books of lies, so most of this information must be accurate. I find it hard to know what to believe. I feel resentment towards NAWC, but at the same time, I want to love them for all the positives steps they have taken on this New Earth. My mind is too tired and confused to benefit from reading anymore, so I force myself to stop and try to sleep.

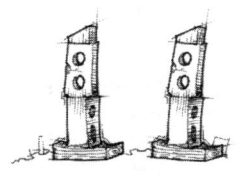

Caught Red-Handed by a Volve

At breakfast the next day I try to explain to Auburn and Zeleng everything I had learned, but I had neither the words nor the time. When we finish and head to the training room, I feel as though all I have done is to thoroughly confuse them. We climb the ladder up to the training room, and when we swing ourselves up this time, there are lots of people already there.

"Okay, I want to fight Zane one-on-one. Lately we have either left him out or ganged up on him. I want to take you on," challenges Zeleng, grabbing a sparring stick and swinging it around.

"If you wanna die," I agree, and we step into the ring. Auburn hands me my wooden weapons, and we each strike defensive poses. I am pretty confident that I can beat Zeleng. I usually do, as I have size and speed on my side. He may be a little faster, but if I play defensive and strike while he's distracted, I should be good. I look around to get my bearings. The room is large, one of the largest in the wagon. The walls are a mass of metal and boards held together with large amounts of duct tape. At one point, someone had put up a metal rigging and some supports, and that is probably the only reason this place has not collapsed. I bring my stick up to guard my chest and face, feeling the cool wood under my fingers. I wait for Zeleng to strike first—it doesn't take long. All of a sudden Zeleng lashes out, lunging forward and striking rapidly. I dodge and deflect the best I can, but he catches me off guard with a fake that allows him to hit me in the ribs. Pain shoots up my chest and my arm reacts almost reflexively. I hit his sword away and pin it to the ground. He spins around me, trying to get behind my back, but I turn as he goes. He attempts rolling to the right, but I put my weapon in his path, and he bashes his head into it, sprawling out on the metal floor. I try to attack him when he's down, but he scrambles to his feet too fast and strikes out. He nearly catches me in the neck, and I am suddenly glad we aren't using real swords. I glance around. I can see Auburn and a few others watching us with mild interest. We fight each other for minutes, and in this time Zeleng only connects with my body twice—I have hit him four times. You can tell I am wearing Zeleng down.

The problem with Zeleng's strategy is, that if he can't beat his enemy quickly, he will wear himself out. I notice his heavy breathing and decide to take the opportunity. I dive forward, jumping as far as I can. My stick goes straight for his head. He manages to block it, but the blow knocks his stick out of his hand and my strike carries me into him. I decide to go with it and tackle him to the floor, punching as I go. I don't punch him hard enough to do lasting damage, but it still hurts him, and he yells, "Okay. Okay, you win."

I let go of him and climb to my feet. The fight has been relatively short, compared to the usual. Either Zeleng was having a bad day, or I am getting way too good. I help Zeleng to his feet.

"Woah, dude, at least give me a chance, really." He wipes the hair and sweat off his face.

"I am going to fight Luke now, okay?" Auburn asks, looking over to the hatch where Luke is just now clambering through with Paul.

"You want a butt kicking too?" laughs Zeleng. Luke is one of the best sparrers in all of the wagons. He's better than I am, and definitely better than Auburn.

"Good luck, and don't die on me," I say. Auburn beckons Luke over and tells him the plan. They both position themselves in the red circle and Zeleng counts down.

It takes exactly thirty seconds for Luke to disarm Auburn and push him to the ground. Auburn pushes himself back up and faces Luke. Again, Luke disarms him and pushes him to the ground within a minute. It continues like this—Luke letting Auburn get up just so he can repeat the technique that he changes slightly each time so that Auburn can never be prepared. I have to admire Auburn for being so tough and persevering, but Paul, Zeleng and I can't help but laugh. If we ever get a chance to board one of the Trash Crafts, I want Luke with me to kick some Clean World butt.

We each fight a few more times before setting out for scavenging. Luke and Paul come with us. I want to tell Luke and Paul about the packages and everything that happened, but I know I can't. Our feet crunch over broken glass and papers. The sun is warm today. The gentle rays reflect off Luke's sword as we cross the expanse. I look around—there are a few other walkers headed out in other directions. I look down at the ground now, and start searching for stuff, only finding lots of plastic and paper. The wind picks up and papers swirl—a plastic bag flies by and catches Zeleng in the face. I find a broken shovel and use it to overturn trash to see what's below. I don't find anything. I turn over a cardboard box, and still nothing. "Why do we need to scavenge more? We have everything. We have a decade's worth of scavenged stuff in our wagons," Zeleng complains.

The wagons are stocked pretty well—the Nomads have been collecting trash for hundreds of years. True, we lack some necessities, but if it weren't for the thoughts of the packages, I would agree with Zeleng. I want to remind him, but I can't in front of Paul and Luke. The rest of the day passes slowly—we scavenge some canned food, string, a roll of twine and a half used roll of duct tape.

※ ● ※

It's not till later that night that things happen. We are walking along, admiring the sunset, which is brilliant orange, a sight rarely seen. The wind stirs the trash and sends shivers down my back. We make our way back to the wagons. The sun sinks lower until it completely disappears and darkness envelops us. We follow the lights from the wagons, hurrying now. That's when I hear the snarl. I stiffen—all around me the others do the same, raising their weapons. I pull my bow off my back and ready an arrow. I point it into the darkness, from where I thought I heard the sound come. More snarls break the silence; the sound now comes from every direction.

Sweat trickles down my face even though it's cold now that the sun is down. I am not usually this scared of volves, but it sounds like there are so many. We form a circle. I stand in the middle with my bow. The others keep their weapons pointed in each direction: Luke and Auburn their swords; Zeleng his mace and shield; and Paul with his axe. We look threatening standing together like this, but we don't even compare to the pack of volves surrounding us. The seconds tick on and my heart beats faster and faster. The howling gets louder until it cuts into my ears like a knife. I now see shadows crawling over the trash towards us—so many of them that the ground seems to be rippling like a wave—a very scary, dark, evil wave. Yellow eyes surround us like the lights of the wagons—volves, at least forty of the fanged brutes. They claw the ground with their four-inch claws and saliva drips from their open mouths in anticipation of the tasty treats they see before them. Their long narrow bodies are arched and they are crouched in a pouncing position, head down and back up. Then all at once they charge, flying towards us. The others yell and I let loose arrow after arrow.

The first arrow strikes a volve in its head and the arrow sticks there. When the beast falls, another comes up to take its place. I shoot so rapidly that I run out of arrows in a matter of seconds. My hands shake so badly—I can barely draw my sword, fumbling with its scabbard. All around me I see my friends battling. Zeleng swings his mace swirling through the volves, blocking them with his shield. He smacks one in the face and its neck snaps back with a sickening crack. He slams another with his shield and it tumbles backwards towards Luke, who quickly stabs it. Luke barely has time to wrench the sword free before another volve pounces on him. Paul stands close to Luke, hacking the volves to pieces with his axe. He slams the axe into a volve's head—it sinks into its skull, but unlike Luke, he can't pull it free. I rush forward to help him. I stab and slash my way through the sea of volves. I am amazed I stay alive long enough to reach Paul. I fend off the volves long enough for Paul to yank his axe from the depths of the volve's head. Then Auburn sprints towards us, trailed by at least six volves. Before he can reach us, one lunges at his back. Auburn snatches it out of the air and grips its jaw before it can collide with him. Using one hand to pull the top of the jaw, and the other for the bottom, he pulls the mouth, opening it so wide that I feel as though I can stare down into the volve's insides. The volve's jaw breaks and Auburn slams the bottom of the jaw back up into the roof of its mouth. It is a stomach-churning sound, and the volve falls limp to the ground, its own teeth poking out of its skull.

Auburn reaches us, and together we fend off the seemingly ceaseless surge of volves. The air is charged with shouts, howls and whimpers and the smell of blood. Luke joins us and we form the circle again. I am panicking too much to think straight, but I feel as though someone's missing. Every time a volve lunges, one of us would slice it to pieces. A pile of dead carcasses starts to grow around us till the volves are literally clambering up a mountain of dead bodies, then jumping at our heads.

The waves of volves slowly weaken—volves are attacking less and less often and in fewer numbers. I slash a

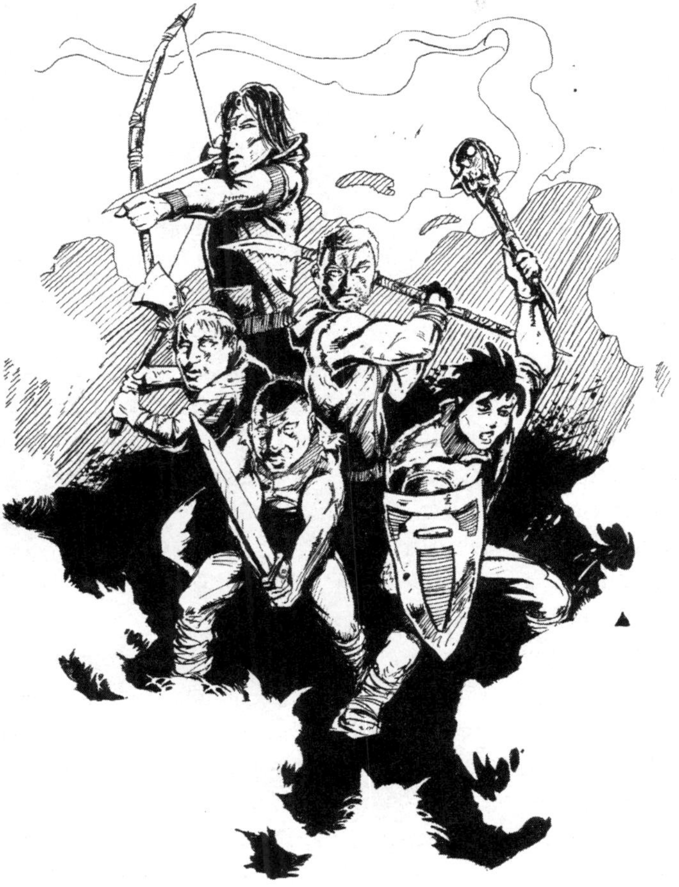

giant monster of a volve across its neck, and it drops to the ground, spurting droplets of blood in a scarlet cascade. A final volve jumps at us. Auburn knocks it out of the air in mid-leap, his sword nearly slicing through its whole body. The volve rolls into a lifeless heap. I look around—dead volves are lying everywhere, practically drowning in their own blood. I let out an incredulous laugh and then a strangled cheer. The hysteria is clear, but the joy of being alive, the rush of victory are clearer.

Then we hear the scream, and all thoughts of triumph vanish. "Where the hell is Zeleng?" I yell, suddenly realizing that Zeleng isn't among us. I hadn't been wrong about someone missing!

"Holy shit, he's not here! Zeleng, you better not be dead, you better not be dead," I yell at the top of my lungs. We sprint towards the sound, recharged with adrenaline. I slip and slide from the blood of the volves which covers the ground in puddles. The remaining volves that challenge us now are soon reduced to a pile of organs and blood, joining their dead brethren. The screaming continues. The sound is painful just to listen to, and I find myself covering my ears as I run. I sprint faster, now charging through the night like a bullet. Then I spot him. Time seems to slow down. Zeleng is lying there in a pool of blood. A volve looms over him ready to crunch down on his neck with its bloodied fangs. Zeleng tries to push it away, and that's when I realize Zeleng only has one hand. Something explodes within me, something terrible, something painful, but something powerful. I scream with rage and horror, unthinkingly flinging my sword at the volve. The sword swerves mid-flight and clatters out of sight, but I don't stop running.

Caught Red-Handed by a Volve

I launch myself forward and tackle the volve, carrying it off Zeleng. My hands find the creature's front claws, and I bend them back as hard as I can. When they snap I punch the thing until it becomes a lifeless heap on the ground. My knuckles are bruised and torn. My whole body is so overcome with numbness that I don't feel the pain, nor the rough fur of the volve, nor the warm flowing blood. The creature lies victim to my rage and anger. When I am certain every ounce of life has been beaten out of it, I rush to Zeleng—the others already surround him. The volve attack seems to have ended, but Zeleng is dying. I can barely bring myself to look at the stump where his hand should be. When I do, I let out a long-held shuddering breath. His arm is a mass of torn flesh and bones. Blood squirts out at an alarming pace, drenching his shirt. For seconds no one does anything, no one moves, no one breathes, no one acts. Then Paul drops to his knees, his face contorted with horror and clenched-back agony. Tearing off his belt he wraps it around the wound just above the section of ripped tissue. He strains to pull it as tight as he can. Zeleng's face is deathly white, his eyes are rolled back in his head, and his breathing is shallow, with blood streaking his face. Paul seems to know what he's doing because the flow of blood has been all but stopped, leaving just a slow trickling.

"Oh my god, oh god, oh god," repeats Auburn over and over again.

"Help me. Grab his legs. We have to get him back to the wagon fast," yells the panicked Paul.

His words tear me from my shock and I rush to help, hoisting Zeleng over my shoulder. Then I sprint full speed towards the wagons. I no longer care about myself. My only thoughts are about getting Zeleng back to the wagon. I run faster than I ever have before. My legs burn, but I barely feel it—my whole body still feels numb. I feel Zeleng's blood dripping down my back, but I ignore it and run faster. Auburn sprints up to me, pulls Zeleng from me and drapes him over his shoulder. He sprints ahead of me faster than I could ever believe. At this pace it takes us five minutes to get to the wagon, but it feels like years. Auburn reaches the wagon, trailing Zeleng's blood as he goes. He catapults himself into the wagon and I follow, screaming for help at the top of my lungs. We charge into the main room. People are there for dinner, the healthy den of conversation and clattering dishes abruptly stops. The silence left in its wake is the eery kind that precedes an earthquake. Auburn shoves people out of the way, even knocking one or two to the floor. When he reaches the table, he swipes his arm across it, knocking everything off. Then he sets Zeleng on the bare surface, lying exposed for everyone to see. The earthquake hits, foot steps, shouts and screams shake the wagon, but I just stand there at my friend's side, helpless and terrified by what must inevitably soon be a loss. The loss of a friend, of a brother, of one of us.

"Get Rosemary. Rosemary. He needs. He needs..." My words weakly die. Something unidentifiable makes my head spin, and I can't believe the pure horror that fills me when I look at Zeleng sprawled out on the table so pale that he already looks dead.

Rosemary, besides her full time job as Ham's wife, is also our medic. She rushes forward, a blank look on her face. This reminds me so much of the times when I was young and Rosemary would rush up to me when I got a scrape or a cut and would bandaged me up. The memory is too much for me and I sink into a chair. No matter how much we bandage up Zeleng, he is never going to heal. An injury like this never turns out well, but injuries like this aren't supposed to happen to me, or my friends. They happen to other people, in other places, in other times. Even through all our close calls, I never actually accepted the idea that one of us could get seriously hurt or die, but that belief has changed. I was just another victim of nature's not giving a shit.

Someone brings bandages and supplies, and Rosemary dumps alcohol onto the wound. Zeleng spasms—his whole body arching in a painful jerk. I know I should be with Zeleng right now, helping, or at least comforting him, but right now I am paralyzed by fear. The thought of losing him scares me more than volves, more than treefs, more than my own death.

Rosemary works speedily, wrapping the arm in the cleanest cloth that we have. The injury is hidden behind cloth, but the act of hiding it away unveils more agony from inside me. I slide off the chair and onto my knees, my mouth opening, silent at first. Then a sound echos up from deep inside, a sound I had never heard before, a sound so loud and so concentrated with pain that I forget everything. I scream until I can't feel my throat and I am taking long gasping breaths. My mind is now completely blank for I don't have the faintest idea as to how I am supposed to feel. Strong hands grip me—Leon's, pulling me to my feet, half-dragging me to his office.

"What happened," shouts Leon into my face, spittle flying. I explain the attack in a calm monotone and somehow by speaking in this way I can hold back the emotion and stop myself from reliving it. Tears trickle down my face as I talk, but I don't feel them, they are just droplets of water and the source is unknown. I am telling a story and a boring one at that. This water on my face is rain, the blood on my shirt just a bad dye job. Everything is normal, everything is fine, my breathing steadies, my mind stays empty. Leon puts his head in his hands, and I can't understand why, for this is just a story.

"He was a good kid and he didn't deserve this. Even if he lives, that wound will never heal without getting infected. We don't have any antibiotics," says Leon, putting his hands on my shoulder. He shakes me and his touch and his words shatter my weak resolve, my pitiful act. Everything was real and I was going to have to believe it. The only thing I could do was hope. Hope would get me through this, for if I were certain of better times to come, I could outlast these, because these would end and the times would be better again. The only constant is change. Things would change and I hope they'd change for the better.

"He isn't going to die. Let's take him to the city. Get him help. Leon, we can save him. It is just an arm." I pull away from him and feel tears welling up in my eyes, but I blink them back. I turn away. I don't want to break down or cry anymore. Through my entire life I convinced myself that crying is useless, that being sad is useless and doesn't solve anything—but tonight I know I am wrong. I had needed to scream and cry and let all the terror and shock and sadness go, but it had clung on.

"No, Zane," says Leon, "You have to understand that there is nothing we can do for him." I want to attack him when he finishes. I want to scream at him that he's wrong, but I don't have the energy—maybe there's a shred of truth to his words. Zeleng might not make it, but that doesn't mean I am not going to try everything in my power to save him.

Leon doesn't try to comfort me, for that isn't his job—instead, he rushes back out of the room, and I am glad for the solitude. I don't know how long I lay in his room, tears running down my face and teeth gritted with new resolve. When I finally stop, I know it must be some time later. I pick myself up with effort and walk towards the door. I wipe the tears from my face and try to take deep breaths. I ball my hands into fists, holding back all the emotion, and push the door open.

In the main room Auburn, Paul and Luke are sitting at a table. Auburn has his head face down on the table. Paul and Luke just sit there staring into space. Zeleng has already been moved to a bed in another room.

"This is my fault—I could've of helped him, but I ran off to you guys," Auburn says, his voice cracking, and his words muffled by the table.

"No, it's not our fault: it's the fault of the Clean World. They created those beasts," consoles Luke. His face is such a mask of misery that it is almost scary. He is the closest of all of us to adulthood, the one who braved more, worked and cared more than anyone else. But even he is broken. It is like having your keystone crumble, and it is just a matter of time before we all will follow, crashing down, never to be built back up.

The next few hours are a blur. I stay up with Zeleng all night—not caring that I am soaked with blood and exhausted. This is my friend and he will not die.

> Darkness is the shrouder. The veil that hides. But when light does come darkness cannot fight. A shadow is all a blind man sees, but even he can believe.

It is a bit of poetry from one of my old books and I have been repeating it to myself all night. I do not accept the foolish hopes that believing will help Zeleng through this, but damn, there is nothing I wouldn't give for it to help.

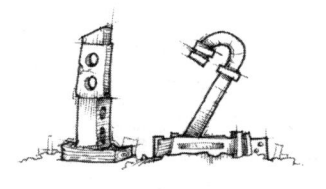

The Feels

Zeleng's arm is soon likely to become infected, a side effect of the volve's bacteria-laden saliva. By the next day we know there is little hope for him, there is no medicine to stop an infection, which, if not treated, will run rampant through his bloodstream.

"Let's take him to Skumford—come on Leon," I beg, and even though I am exhausted, I still sound determined. Through the long hours of the night it had finally sunk in, and I am now fully able to accept what happened.

"They can do nothing for him, and it's out of the way—it will be a waste of time." His words are so matter of fact, nothing like they had been the night before. We sit on two stools in front of Zeleng's bed. A few feet in front of us Zeleng lies on a large bed in the room usually used to quarantine ill people. Zeleng is still frighteningly pale, and I hope with all my heart that he has enough blood left to feed his vital organs. His hand, or what should be his hand, is wrapped in clean bandages. They have changed him out of his blood soaked clothes into a new white shirt and pants. His head is propped up on the pillow, but still lolling to the side.

"There has to be something we can do," I plead. Leon looks up from staring at the ground. His face is blank and as calculating as ever.

"I am afraid there's not, Zane, unless we have the kind of medicine that can only be found in the Clean World. We can't do anything for him," Leon shrugs. He doesn't keep his voice down. Zeleng is out cold, drugged with painkillers to the point where I doubt if anything makes sense to him.

"Then I am going to the Clean World." I don't know when I decided, or perhaps I always had known it in my mind, but now I know that this is what I am going to do, and nothing is going to stop me. Since Leon doesn't blink at my words, I guess he was expecting my reply and also my determination.

"I won't stop you, but I won't be helping you. I have twenty wagons under my command. Don't get me wrong, I am horribly distraught, but I can't put one person's welfare above that of everyone else. I am sorry." He fixes his lens on me, and crosses his hands in his lap. He doesn't look distraught, but I know under his cool calculated look he most likely is, and is only controlling his emotions with his mental strength.

Although one of his own is dying, he still has the willpower to put the greater good over any of his emotions. This is what makes him such a good leader, but also at times makes him seem cold and heartless. We are different in this way. My emotions are pulling me, giving me strength to try the impossible to save Zeleng.

"Fine! Give me the grenade and some supplies and I will

be on my way," I say, trying to verbally commit myself before I lose conviction. Leon looks at me sadly.

"This is not what I want for you. You will die, and even if you do get to the Clean World, you won't be able to make it in time. You don't have to throw away your life like this." He sounds genuinely sad. "Like I said, I am not going to stop you—but just think about what you're doing. Think! Okay?"

"I will do anything for my friend, including dying," I say, hoping it's true.

"I never doubted you would. You have a good heart." He doesn't elaborate—instead, he stands up, brushes himself off and strides out the door.

I am now alone in the room with my dying friend. Instead of looking at him, I stare at the ground. I just sit where I am on my stool somewhat stunned. I am finally going to start making my way to the Clean World. Leon is actually going to let me do this. I don't care that I probably am going to die. I am going to try to save Zeleng even if it is the last thing I do. I couldn't bear sitting around letting him die. I have to do something. I look up from the ground now and look around trying to distract myself.

The room is barely big enough for the two small wooden stools and the bed. The walls are of solid metal sheets. This is part of the original wagon. The walls are bare—I assume that makes it easier to clean after a sick person gets better or dies. It's several minutes before Leon returns with a backpack and hands it to me. He gives me another sad look, his eyes downcast and his mouth tilted down slightly. "Goodbye, Zane, I do hope your attempt isn't in vain. The grenade is in here along with some basic supplies. I don't know how you are going to carry it all and Zeleng, but you are going to have to."

"I will have help. Auburn will want to come—and Luke and Arizon and Paul too."

"If they are willing to do this, they can also go with you. I do love all of you guys, but if I didn't let you go, you would hate me for it, and I couldn't live with that. So like I said, goodbye." With that I stand up and stride to the door, but before I can leave, Leon says, "Please try your hardest to make it, and don't die on me. This is the best chance you will ever get."

"Don't you worry, I probably won't mess everything up," I say, and finally walk out of the room.

* * *

We are all seated in Auburn's and my room, and I guess Zeleng's also, but he will most likely never return to it. Luke and Paul sit on Zeleng's bed and Auburn sits on his. Arizon sits cross-legged on the floor. Four sets of eyes are on me as I explain everything, starting with the packages and the reunions with my dad. They are surprised about it, but it's masked by the thoughts of Zeleng and of what has to be done next.

"So that was what I found in the package, a grenade powerful enough to wipe out a Trash Craft. If I had known that I would have been more careful with it," says Arizon, with a wry smile. She brushes her red hair from her face. "Tug of war with a bomb was what I was doing—could have blown this place to smithereens."

"Actually, I think it only short circuits computers- that's why it will stop the Trash Craft because they are completely driven by computers. My dad is sure it will work, whatever way it does," I say, trying to reassure myself more than anyone else.

"I'm in. Wouldn't miss an opportunity like this. It's always been my dream to get to the Clean World, and if we can help Zeleng at the same time, all the better," says Luke. Luke should be much more excited, but Zeleng's injury hangs over us like a dark veil, smothering us as soon as we feel the slightest bit of happiness.

I pull out the grenade. Everyone crowds in closer to examine it, apparently eager to get close to an explosive object.

"I have to activate it for it do anything, and I am pretty sure it only detonates when a Trash Craft is near," I explain, hoping I am right.

"I see a problem—how can we get up to the Trash Craft once the grenade detonates," asks Paul, being his usual questioning self.

"I don't know—hopefully the ship falls to the ground when it's disabled or something. If not, we will just have to figure it out," I reply, suddenly seeing how many cracks there are in my cobbled together plan.

"And...," continues Paul, "how are we supposed to know how to be in just the right place to detonate that grenade when a Trash Craft drops in?

"We walk to the city, looking for Trash Crafts as we go—if we find one and can detonate this grenade, great. If we don't, we will reach the city and see what can be done for Zeleng there. We can check out the Trash Craft prediction charts that they keep there, and position ourselves accordingly. Zeleng is not going to die if I can help it. We don't have time to come up with an elaborate, well thought out plan, so unless you have a better idea, just go with it." I sound more forceful and commanding than I mean to, but it is probably a good thing. If I am going to take charge and lead us on this journey, I need to have their confidence.

"That sounds dangerous—how are we going to survive three nights in the Wasteland, if Zeleng got hurt in one?" asks Luke. His eyes are full of anticipation, but also more worry than I have ever seen on his features.

"I have no clue, but we are doing this for Zeleng. I know I am in, no matter what dangers await," I say, trying to sound confident even as I let them know I have no clue whether this plan is going to work.

Paul shakes his head and then says, "Well, if Luke is in, I am too." Luke slaps his brother on the back.

"Good man," says Luke. Paul almost looks happy to be embarking on a deadly mission.

"Same for me. I wouldn't let my brothers run off without me," agrees Arizon, slowly nodding. Luke and Paul both look at her. Several very tense seconds pass as they exchange what seems to be an entire silent story, with hand gestures, facial expressions and head movements as their pens.

"You can't come," says Luke, finally breaking the silence. "I am not letting my little sister risk her life for this. We have enough people, and who is going to stay here if you don't? We need someone to stay at the wagons—we can't all ditch mom and dad." I had been too caught up in Zeleng's injury to even consider what this quest would do to Luke's family. I am headed towards my parents, and Zeleng and Auburn have none, so I didn't even consider that this journey would tear Luke's family apart.

Arizon looks to be in a struggle as to whether or not she was going to argue with Luke and leave their parents distraught and childless, or to stay watching her brothers go off to a place where they would never see each other again, even if Luke and Paul survived the journey to that place.

She sits there, staring at her knees for the longest time. "Fine, I'll stay." She says it so quietly, so submissively, that it almost breaks my heart. Luke seems to just be realizing what he is saying. By doing this he is saying goodbye to his little sister forever—the little sister he had always watched after, cared for, and ultimately raised is to be left behind with her parents. The pain on Luke's face while making this decision is almost equal to Zeleng's screams of agony.

"I only want what is best for you and mom and dad. You can grow up happy and safe. We don't have that much chance of succeeding, and if I die, it will be knowing you are safe, which will be a success beyond anything." A statement with that much emotion and feeling is not commonly heard from anyone, especially a tough, twenty-year old who has faced the worst terrors of the Wasteland.

The seconds pass by—we might have been sitting there for minutes—no one speaking a word. The plan, the journey and even Zeleng are almost forgotten as we all think of the implication this separation has. I feel bad to break this silence, but when I do, it shatters like glass falling from a Trash Craft.

"As for plans, we will never be returning here, so bring everything you have, well, at least the important stuff. Zeleng has the only gun." Just saying his name fills me with sadness, but also determination, "...so he would want one of us to use it." We go from the sad thoughts of Luke, Paul and Arizon's separation to the thoughts of Zeleng's horrific injury, which now doesn't seem that different. It's the separation of a brother and sister and the separation of a hand and arm. Sure, I am not bursting into tears and screaming, but just trying to have empathy with Luke and Paul and Arizon fills me with so much sadness that I feel that once again I must cry, letting it out before it consumes me. I hold back, but the lump that forms in my throat is so bad that I fear talking will bring the tears.

"Well, I'll ask Ham for food and water for you," suggests Arizon. She, like all of us, looks sad, eyes downcast, but her mouth set in determination. Just by offering her help, it shows that she understands that the best place for her is to stay, and if she wants to help her brothers, the best way will be not to argue on and on, but to help prepare them for what they might face. No one says anything as Arizon stands up and exits slowly.

"I've got weapons covered," says Luke. I can tell he is trying to be strong, and to continue forward. "Paul, come help me." They also exit. I would never voice it aloud, but I am slightly glad they are leaving. I had felt out of place witnessing the whole thing, and my chest lightens slightly as they leave, but it doesn't last long, and even as the door slams shut behind them, thoughts of Zeleng drag me back down.

Auburn and I start to pack. I am going to have to carry the backpack Leon gave me, so I choose a smaller bag, more like a purse. I don't bother packing any clothes except some gloves, a scarf and a hat. I get out my hoodie and a coat to wear when we leave. In my bag I place the tablet and a few extra batteries for it. I also pack some stuff we might need, such as string, matches, a lighter and most importantly, duct tape. Auburn packs a much bigger backpack with clothes and various other things. We pack in silence, each too preoccupied with our tasks and thoughts to talk. I walk over to our weapon chest for what I realize is the final time. I unlock it. I first grab my knife and then pick out Zeleng's gun. Auburn and I had spent several months secretly saving valuables so that we could buy this for Zeleng's birthday. We don't actually know Zeleng's exact birth date, but once a year we always give him a present. Just thinking about those happier times makes me feel better. If Zeleng dies, he would die knowing he had a pretty full life for a sixteen-year-old.

The metal gun is long and engraved with designs. It has no scope and has to be reloaded after each shot. I attach a strap to the gun and sling it over my back. Then I reach down inside to the chest again and feel around for the bullets that are scattered along the bottom. One by one I find them and put them into one of the bigger pockets of my pouch. I grab a few pocket knives and close the now empty chest. I strap my sword at my belt. My sword is long but narrow, much like the sticks we fight with in the training room. I had wrapped duct tape around the hilt until it fit my hand comfortably. I sling my bow over my shoulder and strap the empty quiver to my back. I hadn't yet gone back to get the arrows from where they stick out from dead volves. I don't know why I even bother taking my bow, if I am so arrowless. When I have finished strapping all my weapons to me, I weigh about sixty pounds more than before. If I weren't a walker, it would be a heavy load to carry.

I put the backpack and pouch on now. Before I do that though, I look in the backpack to see what is in it. The grenade is in there, of course. The backpack is also stocked with lots of stuff from the other packages—light bulbs (wrapped in layers of cloth), batteries, and medicine. I guess Leon thought they would be good for trading if we made it to the city on our journey. When I am completely finished, I go stand by the door waiting for Auburn. I look around for the last time at the room that has been my home for so many years.

It is so small for three people, but it had been the place where I had spent so much of my time hanging out with Auburn and Zeleng. The place holds so many memories that leaving it seems as though I am letting a part of me go. When Auburn finishes packing, he too strides to the door. We both look around the room a bit longer before heading out. The refrigerator door then slams for the last time.

We meet the others in the main room. Arizon is returning from the kitchen, laden with bags of jerky and rock bread. She also holds several jugs, canteens and bottles of water. Luke and Paul also have large bags filled with their own stuff and, hopefully, the weapons they talked about.

"I guess this is it," I say—the implication of that is just hitting me. I am actually going to leave this place that I have called home for so many years. "One last thing, we need to get Zeleng." I head towards Zeleng's room, which is down a small hallway. When we enter the quarantine room, Zeleng lies just where he had been this morning. Auburn hoists him up over his shoulder—Zeleng doesn't move, and for the first time I realize he doesn't know about any of this. We have concocted this journey just to save him, yet we never once consulted him. I don't look at Zeleng as Auburn carries him to the door, but I don't have to. He will be no better than this morning—pale and limp, almost fragile.

The only ones who see us off are Ham, Leon, Arizon and Arizon's mother and father. Only five people out of the five hundred under Leon's command care enough about us to say goodbye. It's sad, but almost a relief that we don't have to break more peoples' hearts by leaving them.

Luke and Paul's parents approach their sons. This is the first time I have ever seen them. They look like good people—there is just something about them makes me trust them. Maybe it's because they have produced such loving, caring kids that have good enough hearts to risk their lives for one of their buddies. They move away from us and do whatever you do when saying goodbye to your kids forever. Hugging, talking, and crying were among them. I watch them with a mix of emotion, happiness and sadness clashing together to such an extent that I don't know how to feel.

I look back at Leon and Ham. Their faces mimic my feelings. They look happy for us, but saddened for having to say goodbye.

Ham looks at us with as much affection as an animal slaughterer can. "Don't die and let all that food I have fed you over the years go to waste," says Ham, trying to lighten the mood. Ham stands there, the whole four feet eleven inches of him, and smiles at us. Ham is as close to a father as I have ever had. Maybe my emotions aren't quite as strong as Luke's with his parents, but they are still there.

I feel terrible for leaving him. Even after I moved out of his care, he always fed me. To leave him now makes me sad. I try not to let thoughts of how I will never see him again fill my head, but somehow they find a way in. I almost have to crouch as I hug him, but I do. I smell blood on his apron and the slightly unusual smell that reminds me of my childhood, which no longer can be if I undertake this journey. Once I step out into the Wasteland, I have to become a leader, and not one to be led. I break free, and while I am still crouched, I take a moment to stare into his eyes. Those few seconds convey more feelings than any words could. When I look away, I feel like he has given me something that no one else can, and that is, his belief in me that I can pull this off—that I can save Zeleng.

"Good luck out there," Leon finally says, gesturing up at the ceiling—I guess to signify our travels out of this atmosphere.

"Bye Leon..." I had almost said 'see you later', but stopped myself. Instead of having to crouch down, I stand on the tips of my toes to hug Leon. He squeezes me back, and it makes me think of how good of a leader Leon is. For a leader to show individual affection for each one of his people, just signifies that he cares about us. I don't hug him long, but like the eye contact with Ham, this gesture conveys more than anything else can. I turn away from him feeling stronger. I have two people who believe I can save Zeleng. That is as good as a kick in the rear to start me on my way.

"Get going guys, Zeleng doesn't have much time." Zeleng lets out a small moan. The others say their goodbyes and we step out of the wagon for the last time. I look back to see Leon and Ham staring at us from the doorway of the wagon. It might just be the sun, but Leon's eye looks as though it has tears in it.

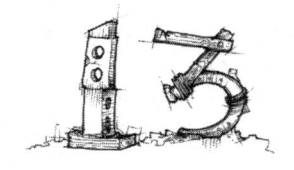

We Go on a Small Walk

As Auburn walks, Zeleng's head bumps up and down on his limp neck. The sun shines down on us—it makes Zeleng's face, if possible, appear even paler. The wagons disappear behind a drift of trash and the sight of my home is gone. I don't feel a longing to go back—the people whom I care about are either with me, or have expressed their confidence in me. The last thing I want to do is turn back and let everyone down.

The five of us crunch along in the trail made by the tracks of the wagons. The trash is flattened here, so much that it is not much different from a trench. There are two rows of these trenches running parallel next to each other and we are able to walk on relatively flat ground with decent protection from the wind. Our plan to make our way towards the city, in hopes of spotting a Trash Craft, is under way. It's strange, that after so many years of staring at the ground, we now search the skies. It's a change that reminds me that my days as a scavenger are over, one way or another. It makes me feel free, but I also feel a loss. Scavenging was my entire way of life—to lose that makes me feel almost lost—but rather than being lost, I just have a new goal, and a new goal means a new journey.

If we don't encounter a Trash Craft on our way to the city, we will examine the detailed maps and charts of Trash Craft appearances (which can be predicted, since they follow a pattern that repeats itself every couple of years) in order to find a Trash Craft to grenade. The Clean World does this to evenly distribute the trash and not just pile it up in one place.

All that can be seen of Luke and Paul are their heads sticking out from the opposite trench. We move much faster than the wagon, and, hopefully, if nothing goes wrong, we can reach the city within three days. Auburn strides determinedly out in front, carrying Zeleng on his back. Zeleng's head rests on Auburn's shoulder, his black hair falling limply. I see the sweat on the back of Auburn's neck and the shuddering rise and fall of his shoulders.

"I can't carry him much longer. We need to switch off. I am going to die if I have to carry him the entire way," shouts back Auburn, pausing in his march.

"We need some kind of stretcher that can be carried by two people, so we can better balance him and distribute his weight more efficiently," I suggest, my mind already spinning with thoughts of how we might create a stretcher. My scavenging days just might not yet be over.

I yell to the others to hurry up so we can discuss the idea. Luke and Paul scramble out of the trench wall and jog to join us. "Auburn can't carry Zeleng the whole time. We need to make some kind of a stretcher."

"I could be of some assistance here, I think," assures Luke, "We need a large flat surface and something to use as hand holds. I am sure you guys can handle that." We set to looking. I find a board about six feet long, lightweight, but sturdy. Paul kicks apart a chair and hands the four chair legs to Luke, who attaches them to each end with string and duct tape as makeshift handholds. I hand him a black sock and sheet. Luke throws the sock back at me, but tears the sheet into strips and wraps them tightly around the handles.

After several minutes and quick working, the stretcher is finished. Auburn begins to lower Zeleng onto it.

"Hold up," mutters Luke, putting up a finger, "before we strap Zeleng to this at least let's make it comfortable. Grab some papers, he can have my blanket." It doesn't take us long to gather a large pile of paper. Luke pushes it onto the board, and then wraps it in a blanket he whips from his pack. It's not much, but it serves as a decent cushion. Auburn lowers him down onto the stretcher. He takes more strips of the sheet and ties Zeleng down to such an extent that he resembles a mummy. I push that thought from my head. Zeleng is alive. A mummy is not.

Auburn rubs his shoulders and stretches his arms. I bend down and take the front of the stretcher, facing forward with hands out behind me, gripping the stretcher so I don't have to see what Zeleng has been reduced to.

Together Luke and I pick up Zeleng and start to walk again in the direction of the city. I stumble at first, taking some time to get used to holding the stretcher. The chair legs make good handholds, but they're a little too wide, so my hands don't quite fit around them.

We follow the blazing sun so we don't get lost in the never-ending landscape of trash. It is very easy to get lost because there are no landmarks on which to base our location and direction. Sure, there are cars and other things, but nothing really memorable enough for a landmark. So the sun, what's left of the moon, and the ruts of the wagon are our only guides. As we walk, I realize how terrible our plan is. How are we going to survive the nights with the volves, and how are we going to have enough food?

We stop for lunch. I pull volve meat out of my backpack and put it between two wrapped pieces of rock bread. The others gather around and do the same, each of us making a sandwich. Luke and Paul set down Zeleng, whom they have been carrying. Zeleng mumbles for the first time, but doesn't open his eyes. His face seems to have recovered some of its former color, but not much. I reach into the backpack Leon had given me, and pull out the bottles of medicine, aspirin and painkillers. I pull a pill out of each, and kneel down at Zeleng's side. I don't know how he is going to swallow these when he's unconscious, but I have to try. I pry open his mouth and drop in the pills. I then remove my canteen and drizzle water into his mouth. Zeleng splutters and squirms, which might be a good sign, but I don't know.

He mutters something like "Bye bye hand." Then he opens his eyes.

For the first time since the accident I see something on my friend's face other than pain and the blankness of sleeping. I see him again, peeking out from his mutilated body. Zeleng again closes his eyes, wincing. He seems to have swallowed the pills because they are no longer there when he speaks. "I feel as though my hand should hurt, but strangely, I can't feel it." His speech is surprisingly clear. I had expected a drawling slur.

"That would be because you have no hand," says Auburn, surprisingly warmly for delivering such horrific news, but I guess it is probably wise to let him know the facts before he realizes them by himself and freaks out.

"That wasn't exactly subtle," I say, staring at Zeleng's face for his reaction.

"Yeah, I remember now. I got my hand bit off. I guess I was having a bad day." His voice is slightly singsong and I am starting to think this has something to do with the painkillers. "You want to hear a joke?" Zeleng's voice is higher pitched than usual, and it was really starting to freak me out. "What did the volve say to the treef?" He pauses, but no one has the heart to go along with his madness. "Pass the salt—oh wait, we have none." He lets out a painful chuckle. Yeah, I am definitely scared now. Is it a good sign or not to be so positive when you have such an injury?

"Are you okay?" I ask worriedly, hoping that his answer will reassure me somewhat.

"Oh yeah, I feel great, except I am missing a hand, but oh well, right?" At that Zeleng lifts his severed stump of a hand in front of his face and waves it back and forth. That should have caused him excruciating pain. These painkillers are good, but without the natural warning sign, he could unwittingly be causing much more damage to himself.

"Right now I should be moving my fingers—it's weird—I can feel them moving, but they're just not there." Zeleng stares at the air right above his arm with unrelenting concentration.

"Don't do that—you are going to damage something. Just because the painkillers are working doesn't mean you won't cause more damage to your arm," I say, expressing my thoughts to Zeleng, but also to the others, who in silence are watching the events play out.

I look to the others to back me up. Paul, standing a few feet away, nods in agreement. "He's right—just take it easy."

Zeleng laughs at that. "Just like the volve took my hand—easy." Zeleng sets his arm down again and closes his eyes. "As long as you guys are carrying me, I will take a nap."

"No. Wait. You have to eat first. Here, have this," I say, pulling a single strip of volve jerky from my pocket. He reaches towards it with his bandaged stump. I don't know why, but it was one of the most pathetic and sad things I have ever seen. I just stick the jerky in his mouth instead. Zeleng chews slowly, "At least I get to eat one of that damn volve's pack," he says through a mouthful of jerky. With that he closes his eyes with a smile." I will just get some sleep. Nighty night." I don't really know if I am reassured with Zeleng's state of mind, but at least he doesn't seem to be in horrible pain.

The others hadn't said much during the ordeal, choosing to stand back and let me do all the work. I don't really mind – any way I can help Zeleng is what I want to do. Despite his good mood and his apparent improvement, I can tell he is not any better. The drugs make him feel better, but in the end he can be nothing but worse. A single strip of volve jerky is not enough to fuel his body as it desperately fights off infection and attempts to heal the wound as best it can. I get back on my feet with new determination—we need to hurry if we want to have any chance of saving Zeleng from the grasp of bacteria. I refer to it as bacteria, because that is manageable in my mind. The grasp of death is impossible to escape. Thinking of Zeleng in the clutches of death would mean he is incurably gone.

※ ● ※

We stop again later that evening. The hardest part of our journey will shortly begin—surviving the night. We start out by building a fire. It may attract more volves—but now that the sun is down, Zeleng needs the warmth. His face is no longer white, but a shade of gray, flushed with the red of fever. I walk to his place on the ground and nudge him. He slowly opens his eyes. "You have to drink something. I think you are getting a fever." He accepts the canteen I offer to him, but doesn't say anything. He uses his good hand to pour some water into his mouth. He seems to have difficulty swallowing, but that may just be because he's lying down. He drinks for a while which, hopefully, is a good sign. Auburn and the others come up to us too. Auburn walks up and stands over Zeleng.

"How are you feeling?" he asks, looking down into Zeleng's face. Zeleng grimaces.

"Not so hot anymore. I think that medicine wore off and the temperature's dropping," mutters Zeleng, giggling to himself. This horrible joke reminds me that Zeleng is still alive—not just in a physical clinging-to-life way—but where his personality is not yet lost to pain or trauma. Zeleng must be ungodly strong to remain himself through all of this.

I reach into my backpack for the small bottle of painkillers. When I find it, I offer Zeleng a pill, which he takes gratefully and swallows with more water.

"That will take a little time to take effect," informs Paul, who stands several feet away, surveying the whole scene.

"I know a little about this kind of stuff from an old medical book. Lucky for you I do, or you would probably have bled to death." I don't know when we became so blatantly harsh, but Zeleng takes it so well.

"Yeah, thanks. I enjoy having blood," says Zeleng, trying to lift his head to look at Paul. I am amazed at how positive Zeleng is, and I think it might be more than just the painkillers. He is truly trying to make this easier for us. He lost a hand, but not once has he been thinking about himself. I silently thank my dad, the guardian angel, for the painkillers that have been my only way of returning Zeleng's favor and making this easier for him.

We move Zeleng closer to the fire. All of us huddle around it except Luke, who is on the lookout for volves. We eat volve jerky and rock bread again. At this rate we will run out in a few days and will have to start scavenging. It's time to get ready to sleep, but there's no way I can sleep on this uncomfortable, glass-covered ground. The others can just put their sleeping mats down, but I had not thought to bring one, so I was going to have to go Zeleng style and sleep on a board. It doesn't take me long to find a board and drag it back near the fire. I check it for any nails that might skewer me, and then pull my blanket from my pack where I had stuffed it this morning. I lie down on the board to test it out, and, as I thought, it is extremely uncomfortable—but it's better than being cut to shreds lying on broken glass shards. I use my backpack as a pillow. When I rest my head on it, I feel the spherical shape of the grenade pressing into my skull.

This should do. I pull myself back up into a sitting position and look at the others. Our fire sends sparks high into the air before they flicker out. The stars are barely visible with all the pollution, but I occasionally glimpse one of them peeking out at me from behind the dark veil. The wind brings the odor of smoke, which smells like burning plastic. The smoke gets into my eyes, making them sting and water. The heat of the fire makes up for all that, however, and I am glad for the extra heat as the cold of night settles in. I pull my blanket over my shoulders. I can barely see Auburn through the fire, but he is sitting there next to Paul, and is warming his hands by the fire. I bring a can of food out of my pack and set it near the fire to heat. This reminds me of so many nights where Auburn, Zeleng and I ate late night meals out in the Wasteland. This can never be again, even if Zeleng survives, because we will be in the Clean World, so far away from this place. I savor these moments because they might be my last. I know I should conserve food, but we can get more in the city. Hopefully, we will have enough until then.

Luke stands on the raised ground between the trenches. From his height he will be able to see volves coming from far off. The moon lights the land with an eerie glow, but he should have no problem seeing volves approaching. "We should get some sleep. Big day tomorrow," I tell the others.

Auburn looks up. "I am kind of afraid to sleep out in the open like this after what happened to Zeleng. A volve can just crunch our necks while we are asleep," Auburn says warily.

"Luke's got us covered. He will sound the alarm if they attack," reasons Paul, looking at me through the fire.

"Still, just to put down my guard and sleep is going to be hard," says Auburn. I start to unstrap my bags and weapons and lay them next to my makeshift sleeping mat. Then I drape my blanket onto it. The blanket makes the board more comfortable, and the fire will keep me warm. I settle back, but then remember my can warming by the fire. I retrieve it and crack open the can. Steam pours out and the smell of spices and beans wafts into my nose. I scoop out the sizzling food with my fingers and shovel it into my mouth.

"Hey, gimme some," complains Auburn. I pass the can to him.

"Sure, don't eat it all," I say, uselessly. Auburn proceeds to eat it all. I put my head back onto my backpack and close my eyes.

"Night guys." I turn over and cover my head with my hands. I try to slow my breathing. The sounds of the crackling fire and the quiet of the others' conversation is the last thing I hear before I fall asleep.

I feel as though I have been asleep for only a few minutes before I am shaken awake. "Dude, we gotta move!" Auburn's face looms above me. I rub my eyes. All around me it's still dark.

"Why, what's happening?" I ask, glancing around to see if I can glean anything for myself.

"Luke spotted a pack of volves. We are going to try to outrun them." That gets me going. I get up and hastily start to collect my stuff. The others seem to have already done this, and are working on putting out the fire. Luke jumps into the trench.

"Yeah, they are definitely coming our way. We need to get out of here. I think they are only about a mile out." Luke looks tired, with bags under his eyes and under his arms, for he is carrying all of his stuff. His blonde hair is streaked with dirt and its usually spiky shape is all but gone—it falls into a dirty blonde pile on his head. I sling the backpack onto my back.

"Okay. Let's move." I go to Zeleng, who is still sleeping.

"Paul, get the other side." Together we lift Zeleng. I notice that, since Paul is short, the stretcher tilts down towards his end. We start to jog, which isn't an easy thing to do while carrying a stretcher. Auburn trots to the left while Luke brings up the rear.

"How many were there, Luke?" I ask through breaths.

"Sixteen. It looked like a large pack. I don't want to risk another Zeleng incident, and it's easier just to get out of the range of their noses," says Luke, running up to us now. Our feet pound over the flattened ground. We jog for minutes. The wind blows my hair into my face, and since I am carrying the stretcher, I can't even push it from my eyes. I can barely see, so if it hadn't been for Auburn, I would have plunged right into the river that suddenly appears out of nowhere. Auburn grips my arm, steadying me. In front of us is one of the rivers. If the moon's reflection weren't clearly shining on the river, I wouldn't have been able to see the slowly moving black water at all. Rivers are unpredictable, often carving new paths when Trash Crafts block their flow—and this river is no different.

"Son of a...." Luke cuts Auburn off.

"How in the world are we supposed to cross?"

I had been thinking the exact same thing. The river is at least fifty feet wide and filled with plastic bottles, pieces of wood and a fair number of chemicals.

"I doubt if it's shallow, and besides, I am not wading through that. Who knows how stocked it is, full of acid, oil and gas. It could be radioactive for all we know," I say, voicing my concern while surveying the river with distaste. The only things that could survive these waters are the genetically modified fish created to feed the population when the world was desperately overpopulated—no other fish had adapted to live in the polluted waters.

"The volves will catch up with us if we don't do something pronto," says Luke. His voice has not yet lost its calm edge, but it's close. He pulls something out of his pocket, but in the darkness I can't make out what it is. "So we prepare to fight."

"That's heroic and all, but it doesn't help us get across this damn river," says Auburn, even as he pulls his sword from his back sheath. The wind howls and sends trash into the river, making it ripple. The wind, however, isn't the only thing that howls. Like the screech of some dying animal, come the sounds of volves howling for blood.

"Not this again," I whisper, as I set Zeleng down and swing his gun from my back. I slip a bullet into the chamber and point it into the darkness. Only last night we had defended ourselves in much the same way, forming a circle. Tonight, we form the circle in front of Zeleng with our backs to the water. The howls grow louder, and so does the roaring in my chest to avenge Zeleng. I tighten my grip on his gun and imagine the sound when I pull the trigger—the blast, the whistle of air, and then the thud of the bullet striking a volve. I imagine that sound to fill me with a sense of accomplishment, but that is all wrong. Slaughtering these beasts would not make anything better, no matter what my heart is screaming at me to do. My old sense of loss when I kill a volve tries to break through my cold reasoned resolve.

The first volve comes into sight, sprinting over the trash, chasing its prey—chasing us. More follow from the darkness, running after their leader towards us in a feral race. I take aim at one and apply pressure to the trigger, ready to shoot it down when it gets within range. But all of a sudden there is a shout, a whistle of air as something flies through it, and a shattering of glass twenty feet in front of us. For mere seconds I am confused, but then a blazing fire billows up from where I heard the glass break. It expands outwards burning the trash. I am stunned, dropping the unfired gun to my side. Throughout my entire life I have dreaded a Wasteland fire, and now one blazes in front of my face, burning towards me. The volves skid to a stop on the other side of the wall of flame, searching for a way in. The heat of the fire grows—sweat trickles down my forehead.

"Now that is why I call it the super cool bottle bomb," yells Luke, pumping a fist into the air. The crackling of the fire almost drowns out the volve's howls, but somehow Auburn's voice can be heard above the noise.

"Cool as in you just trapped us to be burned to death or jump into the acidified water." Auburn looks around. The volves whimper as the flame expands on the other side towards them. I too want to whimper. The fire now is only a few feet away. We may be safe from volves, but I would rather fight a volve any day instead of a fire.

Then a flickering light appears on the river, one that comes from a flame in a lamp, rather than the flames of the blaze in front of us.

"What's that?" I yell, squinting into the darkness, my eyes taking a moment to adjust. The light grows closer. Could this be happening? Were we getting lucky for the first time?

"I think it's a boat," yells Auburn. He is half right, but as the thing draws closer, I realize it is a barge instead. The fire comes closer, the heat is almost unbearable and I take a step closer to the water.

"Nooooo. I thought it was a Trash Craft," says Luke agitatedly.

"What's a barge doing sailing up the river?" I ask, confused. Usually barges stay in the ocean unless they are transporting goods, and usually then the Nomads just did the moving.

"Hey, over here," shouts Luke, waving his hands over his head.

"What are you doing? They could be evil," I hiss at Luke.

"Have a better Idea? Either this or we get burned to death." Luke is right, and I begin shouting along with him. The large metal barge seems to have spotted us, or at least the figures trapped so close to the blazing flame, because it sails over to the side from the middle of the river.

The barge pulls up to the side where we are. A man stands on one of the decks, yelling and waving at us to jump on. I take in the ship in a glance. It is about a fourth the size of a wagon, but still very big. It is made of wood and metal sheeting, but it has the same look as the wagons—as though it had been added onto many times—except the additions to the barge seemed more thought out and symmetrical, probably so one side didn't get too heavy and tip the ship over. The man is tall, his skin is tan, almost an orange color, and he wears a long beard and an eye patch. He holds a giant sword and wears a dark cloak. His nose has a ring piercing, but that's not my main concern—the fire blazing behind me reminds me every second of its approach with a new wave of heat.

The barge lowers a ramp that clangs on the trash at the river's edge. I am first to spring onto the ship, pulling Zeleng's stretcher. The others follow as fast as they can. Less than a second after the rest of us jump onto the barge, the flames claim the place where we had been standing, engulfed now in a fire that would have fried us in a matter of seconds. Once on deck I am met by the man's one-eyed stare. Sweat pours down my face from exertion, stress and the heat. The barge pulls away from the burning shore before the flame takes its hold on the ship.

"Evening, the name's Marty. How did your friend get hurt? And may I ask why there is a giant fire burning out of control?" The man is staring with concern at Zeleng on the stretcher, but glances at the flame that still lights up the night even as we move away from it.

"To make a long story short, he got his hand ripped off by a volve. It is most likely infected and we were trying to prevent another such incident with a wall of fire to keep the volves out," I explain as briefly as I can. Marty winces.

"I am sorry to hear that. I will get you to the city. It's the least I can do." The man beckons us to follow him through a metal door with a cylindrical window into a room at the center of the deck.

"Thank you so much," I say, looking over the well-lit room, which contains a few couches and chairs.

"No problem. I have plenty of space, but it would be greatly appreciated if you could pay me a little," says the man, grinning at us.

"Sure. We have light bulbs, batteries, and food. What do you need?" I ask. The man raises his eyebrows.

"Really? That's rare stuff you got there." I pull the light bulbs out of my backpack and show him.

"Sweet. I will take all of them," the man says, laughing. He seems to be a nice guy.

"Yeah, sure," I say, handing him one light bulb after another as I pull them out. I also hand him the bottle of wine we had found.

"Oh, wow, thanks kid. That's even better." Marty is all smiles. The others come into the room—Luke and Auburn bring Zeleng in.

"I am Marty, in case you didn't hear. I am captain round here. Much of my crew is asleep, but you may have spotted one or two of them doing their duties. These are my quarters. Make yourself at home." I should have been more concerned about hitching a ride with a stranger, but Marty seems nice and trustworthy. I look at his eye patch—it must be a requirement that leaders lack at least one eye. Maybe it is this symbol of sacrifice that gets them their positions in the first place.

"Thanks again," I say, taking a seat on one of the couches. The room is small and although being damp, it is still warm. The walls are a mass of boards. A fire burns in a metal hearth and shelves jut out in random places. Marty goes to stow the light bulbs and wine in a cupboard, while the rest join me on the couch—except Zeleng, Zeleng we place on the floor.

"You sure this is good idea?" whispers Auburn, nervously.

"It's our only idea. There is no other way to cross the river." Marty strides back up to us. In the few seconds it takes him to cross the length of the room, I have time to truly look him over. He is a large man in both height and width. His face peeks out from a mane of curly hair. His nose is large, but not lumpy or crooked. The eye not covered by his eye patch is as black as the water on which he sails, and it seems to have the same rippling effect that the water does, so that it is impossible to stare into it for any length of time. His beard is so massive that it covers his entire neck—it is impossible to know where his head meets his neck and where his neck meets his shoulders. His right arm hangs at his side—the sleeve of his massive cloak falls over the end of the arm so I can't see it. I do notice that as he walks, it doesn't swing back and forth as does his left arm. He walks with a limp, not very noticeable, but every couple of strides I detect a slight give in his leg, as it buckles just a slight bit. His cloak falls to just above his knees, revealing massive feet covered fully with massive boots, which more than likely have a massive stench. I observe this, and more, in the time he crosses the room and stands in front of us. Even as he does, I notice that he favors his right foot, and puts much of his giant weight on it.

"Can I get you anything—fish, a drink?" he says warmly.

His voice is smooth and low, and it's apparent he is an accomplished speaker. I don't know when I became so perceptive, but I hear something in his voice that sounds like something I heard in my dad's voice. The way he pronounces and enunciates, and even the way he pauses, reminds me of my father. It may be an accent, I can't tell. After taking apart the way he speaks, I actually focus on the meaning of his words. Did I want fish or a drink?

"No thanks...," I say, but before I can finish, Zeleng speaks up.

"Sounds great—bring on the feast." We all stare at Zeleng, who, lying on his stretcher on the floor, we didn't even think was awake.

"Okay. I'll go get that. Take the poor kid off that board and get him onto a couch. You will be with me for about two days until we reach the city. He needs tending to." The man limps off and I get up to untie Zeleng. I pull the string away, and with the help of Auburn, hoist him onto the couch.

"Thanks, guys," mutters Zeleng, gratefully. I find a pillow and put it under his head.

"No problem," I say. Once he's comfortable, Zeleng again closes his eyes.

At this point Marty returns, holding a tray of small whole fish—complete with heads and eyeballs—in his left hand. I notice that his right arm still rests, unmoving, at his side. After Zeleng's arm injury I am curious to know what is wrong with this man's arm. If I were not a guest on the Marty ship, I would have asked him, but I choose not to upset him with prying questions.

"You guys Nomads?" asks Marty, pushing some things

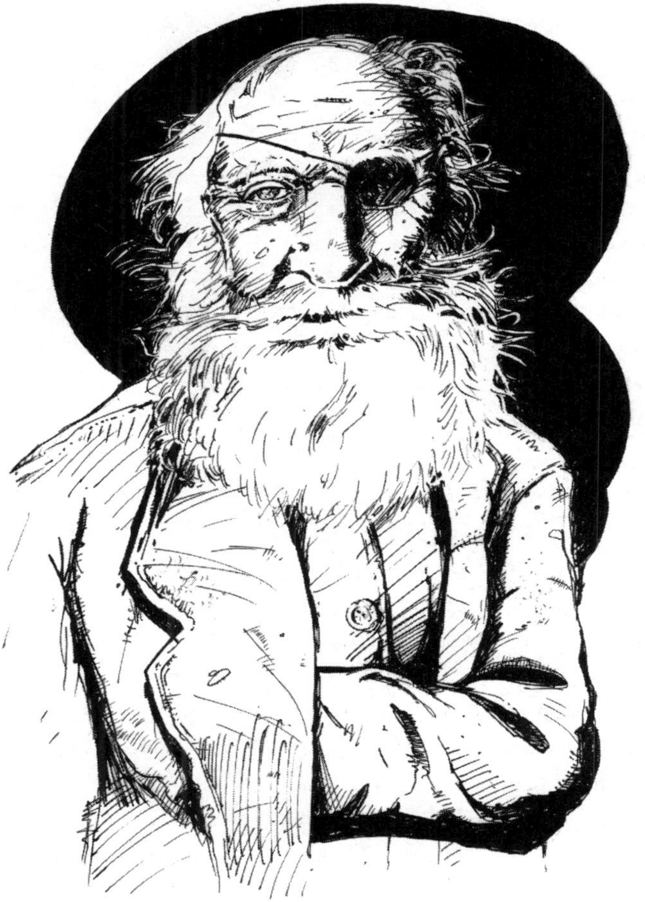

off a side table to make space for the tray of fish.

"Yeah, why?" I say, watching him take a seat, slowly lowering himself as the movement pains him. He doesn't look old, fifty at the most, but he appears to have the achy joints of a much older person. Once he has relaxed back into his chair, he looks at me. I don't know if I am honored or scared to have his entire attention focused on me.

"You probably have never done this before—it's a Bargemen's tradition. Just take one of these," he says, picking up a long metal stick with a pointed end. "Then skewer the fish like so." He stabs the fish in its open mouth until the metal rod protrudes out the other side. Gory, yes, but nothing compared to skewering living volves, which I had been forced to do with the point of my sword on numerous occasions.

"Now just roast it on the fire." He looks as though he is regretting ever sitting down as he pushes himself to his feet again, using only his left arm. He walks over to the fireplace and sticks it into the fire. I get up and get my own fish—then I get a skewer and do the same, shish-kabobbing the fish through its open mouth. The fish is slimy and slippery, and I nearly drop it as I push the skewer into its body. I join Marty at the fire. He is whistling as he rotates his fish over the small crackling flames, contained only by the metal frame of the fireplace.

"Why are you helping us?" I ask, once I am at his side and my fish is roasting in the fire, sending up a fishy smell.

"I try to do good things. There aren't a lot of people who do good things any more, ya know." He looks at me with a grin that doesn't quite reach his rippling eyes. I try to ignore his features and concentrate on what he is

We Go on a Small Walk

saying. Of the two kinds of people in the Wasteland, Marty is definitely the type who tries to make the best of things. It is apparent that Marty is in pain from numerous injuries throughout the years, but he still has the goodness of heart to smile at me and help us on our journey.

"And besides, did you not give me light bulbs and a bottle of wine? That's as valuable as anything." I turn my fish over slowly. The others come and Marty and I are forced to scoot over to give them space.

"Well, thanks again, Marty," I say, using his name in the hope that its meaning will be greater.

"You can stop thanking me. I am just doing the humane thing." Marty takes his fish off the fire. The humane thing to do, I think. The meaning of humane has changed over the last five hundred years, since our instincts have reverted back to more primal behavior in order to help us survive in a harsher time. The more our instincts take over, the more we lose some of what makes us human—the ability to control our instincts. In effect, as humans changed, in a way, so did the 'humane thing'. For Marty to be offering us food and shelter, and overall saving us from a fried future, is the most humane thing that a stranger has ever done for me.

"Okay, once the fish is cooked well like this, we dip it in salt and spices." Marty walks back to the tray, which contains a silver-colored tin, and removes its lid. He shoves the fish into the tin. When he brings it back up, it's covered with little salt flakes. I remove my fish from the fire and do the same.

"Try it. It's good," insists Marty. I don't doubt it, but I am wary of eating such a thing.

"Do I just bite into it? What about the bones and scales?" He smiles at me.

"Stop worrying so much and start enjoying," says Marty. I don't think Marty meant for those words to sound wise, but they do. I have been so worked up and stressed out these past few days, that if I just stopped worrying and started enjoying—just the tiniest bit—I might find the relaxation I need to make the journey mentally accomplishable. I take a bite of the fish. I chew. I can't believe the fish is so good.

"You like?" asks Marty. I just nod, a nod that doesn't do the fish justice. I fill my mouth with more fish. The others finish cooking theirs, season them, and also try them. Just like the vegetables on harvesting day; no one seems able to get enough.

"This is a small step above rock bread," says Luke.

"I could live off this stuff," agrees Paul.

"I do live on this stuff," says Marty, licking the fingers on his hand. I notice how massive his fingers are.

After we all finish, we settle back onto the couches. The light and warmth make me feel cozy and almost at home. The couch is comfortable and decently clean—it envelops me. Marty takes a seat in a red armchair and looks expectantly at us.

"What is your story? You have to fill me in." I look at the others. They nod as if to say go ahead.

"I wonder where to start," I say, wracking my brain for a good place to begin.

"How about the day when this kid got injured? And don't forget to introduce me to everyone." So I start to tell him. I don't lie to him, seeing that he asked me to start on the day Zeleng got hurt, so I can easily leave out any part about our journey to the Clean World. I am careful not to mention the packages or anything to do with them. I told him that we are trying to get to the city, how we had been pursued by volves and got stuck at the river, and how we started the fire that he spotted. It takes several minutes, but Marty is a good listener and never interrupts. When I am finished, he sits there in silence. There's a pause while Marty swallows the information and continues to digest it.

"Woah. You were attacked by a pack of more than forty volves and the only injury was a hand? I doubt half my crew could accomplish a feat like that."

I wasn't expecting praise, so I react with a blank look and a safe reply.

"Yeah." I eat the fish until all that's left are some bones and the odd organ. "How 'bout we sing?" asks Marty enthusiastically.

"How about we don't?" Auburn starts to say, but it's too late. Marty bursts into song.

> A-fishing at the black sea with only your barge and crew.
> You never know what you will see or what you have to do.

The verses continue to get more and more ridiculous. I start to have trouble even understanding what the song is trying to convey. I have never heard very much singing, so I am not sure if it is normal for songs to really have no purpose other than to cheer you up. If this is the purpose, I hope it helps Zeleng to grow more cheerful as his voice floats loud and off key from the general direction of his comfortable couch. Much like previously that day, I start to wonder about the benefits of using these painkillers if they are leaving Zeleng loopy enough to join in song with a 'pirate captain', singing a song in which he knows neither the words nor the tune.

No one else joins in, and as the verses start to get even more outlandish than I thought possible, Zeleng spouts random words, not helping my futile attempt to make sense of the poetic garble. Marty doesn't seem to mind. If all Bargemen are like this, I can't believe the difference between them and the Nomads. Marty is cheerful, helpful and kind. Nomads are much more serious and business-like. They also are nowhere nearly as friendly. I find it strange that this is the first Bargeman I have met. Since all the trading is done through the city, Nomads and Bargemen never have the need to meet face to face to do trading. Some time later Marty finally stops singing.

"I will leave you with that lovely lullaby. You guys probably need some sleep. You can have these couches and I will bring you some blankets." Marty gets up and starts to move to the door where we came in.

Once he is out of earshot Auburn mutters, "That was a lullaby? Sounded like a baby listing all the words he knows in a way that happens to occasionally rhyme."

Auburn says it quietly, but Marty doesn't seem like a guy who would take serious offence from Auburn's criticism. He walks with a commanding attitude that doesn't fit him at all, but fits the captain he is. His robes are tattered—as if they had been worn for many generations—and made of leather, which is incredibly rare. As he strolls out the door, I get up to give Zeleng another pill. When he swallows it he says, "Should we trust this guy? I mean, we don't even know him."

"We have no other choice, and he serves great food,"

Zeleng blinks. "Speaking of that, I didn't get any." I look at him. His face is pale and he is sweating. Blood has soaked through the bandages by now and I realize we are going to have to change them. "I'll cook you up one after we change your bandages." Zeleng sighs and looks at his mangled arm.

"Yeah, okay." I call Paul and Auburn over to help me, not wanting to do this alone.

"I am not going to watch." Zeleng closes his eyes and puts out his arm as though offering it as a sacrifice. Paul reaches for it gingerly. "Well, if this has gotten badly infected I am not sure if I even want to look." Paul starts to gently unwrap the bandages. I pull out the clean bandages and get ready to hand them to Paul. Slowly the mass of bandages falls away and a horrific sight meets my eyes. Zeleng's wrist is swollen and red. A few crunched bones poke out from flesh, and pus oozes from everywhere. Dead skin and tissue peel in discolored sheets, starting at the end and moving their way up his arm. I nearly gag and turn away.

"I'll be darned, I haven't seen anything like this in twenty years," says Marty. Something about the way he says it makes me think. He sounds almost sad, as if he is remembering worse times, almost as though he can relate to Zeleng's situation. Marty had been so quiet I hadn't heard him approaching.

"That's not pretty. I might have something that can help, though." Marty sets down the pile of blankets he had been carrying and hurries to one of the cupboards.

He returns with a small tube of antibiotic ointment. "Not much for a wound like that, but it might help." He hands me the tube.

"Thanks again," I say for at least the fifth time since meeting this man, yet this one I mean the most. Marty smiles and I hand Paul the ointment.

"Maybe this will help around the edges, and possibly slow it down," says Paul, unscrewing the lid and squeezing the entire tube onto Zeleng's wound. Paul winces as he slowly starts to rub and spread the ointment around. Even though Zeleng is like a brother to me, I don't think I would ever be able to rub ointment into a wound of this scale. The mangled flesh almost gives way under Paul's ointment covered fingers, almost as though it's peeling from the bone. I look away.

"Okay. I need the bandages now." I hand them over. Paul starts to rewrap Zeleng's arm with a new clean bandage. I sigh with relief as the injury is hidden from sight. Somehow, with the injury wrapped it is less horrifying. I don't know exactly why, maybe it's because I can imagine it otherwise, without the actual sight of it bringing me back to reality.

"You almost done?" asks Zeleng, his eyes still closed. I am amazed at how controlled he is. I think this must hurt him, but he remains still, letting Paul work.

"Yeah, just about," says Paul, finishing to wrap the remainder of the bandage into place.

"Okay, all better," says Paul, even though nothing is better.

Zeleng opens his eyes. "Looks better, I guess."

I ask Marty a question that had been nagging at me. "Do

you know where we could find the schedule of Trash Craft ships?" Marty, who stands a few feet away, stares at me curiously with his one eye.

"Yeah. They're kept at the head honcho's place. Just ask one of the guards there. Why do you need to see them anyway," he says, suspiciously. I glance around nervously, looking at any of them for help.

"We are trying desperately to find some antibiotics for Zeleng, and if we know where new loads of trash are coming to, we might have a better chance," says Auburn, saving me from giving away our secret plan. Marty doesn't look convinced, but he doesn't push the matter.

"I do hope you find some." He turns around. "I will be in my room on the second floor. Just stop in if you need anything." He limps out of the door, pushing it open with his left arm.

"Guys, let's get some sleep," I suggest. The others nod and we collect blankets from the stack. We each take a couch.

"I need to get some rest," says Luke, rubbing his eyes. I settle down on the couch, pulling my blanket from the bag. Roughly a second after lying down on the couch, I realize that it's much more comfortable than the board I had attempted sleeping on earlier that night. I fall asleep, even before I have completely sunk into the cushions of the couch.

When I awake the next morning, I am alive, which is a good sign. If Marty had wanted to harm us, he would have done it while we were asleep. The sounds of voices outside the room woke me up. Already it sounds as though every Bargeman on the ship is up and working. I glance around the dark room—the fire has burned down to a few orange embers. The rest of my group is still asleep, so I quietly get to my feet and tiptoe to the door. I slowly open it and slip out, trying to let the least amount of light into the room as possible.

The decks are bustling with Bargemen. All wear an assortment of clothes, eye patches and bandanas. The barge is split into three decks stacked on top of each other—each one becoming smaller, like a stepped pyramid. The door I came from is on the first deck, and I see a ladder that seems to ascend to the second. The boat slowly moves down the river, seemingly propelled by the current of the river alone.

"Greetings, what are you up to?" asks a large balding man with curly white hair clinging to the skin above his ears as if for dear life. He wears strange boots. I guess they only appear strange to me because I am used to everyone wearing boots with metal protective plating. "Just looking around," I say, my voice sounding rather small with all the noise that surrounds us. The man nods in understanding.

"Welcome aboard," says the man, hurrying off to continue his work. No one else speaks to me as I walk along the first deck. No one even looks at me weirdly and, like the man had said, I feel welcome and not like an intruder at whom everyone stares. The barge cuts through the water faster than a wagon, but still relatively slowly. Water laps at the sides of the boat causing ripples. The crew works non-stop, mopping the decks and raising the sail that I didn't even know existed. I walk to the ladder and climb the rungs to the second deck. This deck is slightly smaller and only has a few doors leading into the rooms. I don't know which one is Marty's, so I climb to the next deck.

This one is smaller than the last. There are two long pole masts for the sails. Men bustle around them pulling on chains to raise them from within the boat. It looks as if the masts are retractable into the body of the ship. When they are raised, the sails billow and the boat picks up speed. The sails are made of old sheets, blankets, rugs and clothes all sewn together into a huge sheet. It also looks as though the barge has a steam engine because pipes and chimneys stick out of the roof seemingly at random. I look from the ship to the outside. The river snakes its way for miles, curving in many places. Pileups of trash in the river occasionally cause small hills of trash, and the ship has to push its way through them. If there are fish in the river, I can't see them, for it is too clouded and polluted.

"Hey kid." says a voice that I already can identify as Marty's. I look to see Marty poking his head up from the ladder.

"Oh, there you are," I say, walking over to him.

"If you're looking for something to spend your time on other than gawking around, we could sure use a bit of help fishing, mopping, the whole lot."

"Sure, but how exactly do I fish?" I ask, completely new to this endeavor.

Marty makes a gesture for me to follow him. "It's not difficult. I'll show ya. Right this way." Marty leads the way down to the bottom deck—a distance of about twenty-five feet. On the way down we run into a sailor who is climbing up. The sailor, seeing the captain, hops down immediately and salutes him with a flat hand to the forehead. We move to the edge of the bottom deck, where a line of sailors with long fishing rods stands, casting poles into the river.

"You see, usually we use a net, but since we are sailing, the river is too shallow to use such a thing," explains Marty, grabbing two fishing rods from a barrel near the edge. "Why are you traveling the river anyway? Don't Bargemen stick to the ocean?" I ask.

Marty pauses for a second. "Just business, you know. So take the rod," he says, changing the subject and throwing the rod to me.

"See this here? It's the bobber—when you see it go under that means a fish has taken the bait. It really isn't very difficult."

"And what's the bait?" I ask, curiously.

"I was getting to that. Fish round here will eat just about anything, but they love flesh, so just hook a little piece on like so." He takes a piece of what looks like fish out of a container and attaches it to the hook. Apparently these fish are also cannibals. The other Bargemen reel in fish like crazy. A disheveled looking man in a blood soaked apron runs up to collect the fish and sprints back to the kitchen—the Bargeman equivalent to Ham. Just before the door swings closed, I spot an army of people swinging around large knives. The cutting crew, I figure.

"You even paying attention?" asks Marty, following my gaze towards the kitchen door.

"Yeah, we put the bait on the hook," I relay to him.

"Very good—now just toss in the bobber." Marty flings the bobber along with hook and bait into the rippling black water, the string trailing behind. The bobber zigzags around in the current of the river, but Marty still manages to reel in a fish in a matter of seconds. "These fish were bred to reproduce like crazy. I'd be darned if there aren't half a million of these little buggers in this single river," says Marty, pulling the fish off the hook and letting it join the others in the flopping pile.

"Seems like it—can I try?" I ask, holding my hands out for the rod.

"Yeah, just do what I showed you. I have some important captain stuff to do." He smiles at me and hurries off up the ladder, which I now notice he struggles doing with a single hand what usually requires two.

Now it's my turn. I repeat the steps Marty had shown me. It's quickly apparent that I am no good at fishing. I nearly impale my thumb trying to get the bait on. I finally get the bait on only to have it fall off. After several more times, and much more frustration, I succeed. I fling my bobber into the water, narrowly avoiding whipping a Bargeman next to me. The Bargeman doesn't even blink—as though he's used to such a thing—and continues fishing. I watch my bobber carefully. The other Bargemen continue to catch fish after fish.

"What you up to?" sounds Auburn's voice from behind me. "Aren't you supposed to reel the fish up when the bobber is down?" Auburn comes to stand next to me.

"Yeah, why? ... Oh." I had just looked back to the water where my bobber had just popped up from being underwater. "Darn, this is hard. You try."

Auburn is wearing a different set of clothes today. A black shirt that says: Call of Duty 11 Battle of Stars. The shirt has a picture of a man with dual laser pistols, with a background of starfleet ships. I have no clue what the shirt meant, but it was cool. He also has on a pair of dark black jeans. Auburn takes the fishing rod and gives it a try, throwing the bobber back into the river with a fresh piece of bait. "This can't be that hard." He watches the bobber intently.

"Where are the others?" I ask. "They are taking care of Zeleng and other stuff. Mostly other stuff," replies Auburn, not even taking his eyes off the bobber.

"Oh well." I am cut off by Auburn's happy shout. He madly reels in his bobber. When he pulls it up onto the deck there is a large fish about twelve inches long. The fish is covered with black scales. Its fins look sharp and its mouth hangs open, revealing sharp teeth. Its pupil-less round eyes bulge from their sockets, and a mangle of weird tentacles spreads out from below the mouth like a slimy beard. It doesn't look like the one Marty had caught, or even the ones we had eaten last night. This fish is scary and definitely does not look edible. If anything, this fish looks like a mutant predator.

"Nice job," I say, in a disgusted voice.

"Nah, this thing looks creepy as heck, definitely not good eating," says Auburn, poking the fish with a finger. He drops it down onto the deck.

One of the Bargemen glances over and grunts. "You caught yourself a little shadow, so you have. If I was you, I would kill it and throw it back into the water—let the fish chew it right up."

Auburn looks at the man. "Why, though?" he asks, suddenly looking at his prize with less enthusiasm than before.

The man scratches his wispy beard. "They aren't right, those ones—they pop up every now and then. Some say it is bad luck—don't believe it myself—but cast it back in, will ya?" Auburn picks the fish off the deck where it had fallen, and after a slight pause, throws it back into the water.

Spray from the river hits me in the face as the barge suddenly lurches and I am thrown off balance, nearly falling to my doom into a pile of stinking fish. There's a horrible grinding sound of metal, and the barge comes to a stop.

"What was that?" asks Auburn, getting to his feet, because he had fallen and his fishing rod had dropped out of his hands.

"I'd be questioning my own thinking—that shadow has caused us some trouble. We've hit a spot of trash we can't push through," calls the Bargeman with the wispy beard, rushing to a ladder that descends into the ship's lower hull. Other Bargemen follow him, shouting things such as "do we have a leak?" and "How bad are we stuck?" People rush down from higher decks. I spot Marty, who is calmly descending a ladder.

"Why is it shallow here?" I ask when Marty comes closer.

"Number of reasons, Trash Craft dropped a load and caused the river floor to rise, or there's been an underwater build up of trash. It happens more than you would think. It's not serious if we haven't sprung a leak. Speaking of that, I need to go check it out," says Marty, rushing off again with his cloak swirling. There's noise all round as Bargemen rush about even faster than before—the pile of fish forgotten for now.

Many of the Bargemen nearly slip on them as they rush

by, all dropping down to the inner barge. Without the steady movement of the barge, which I had already grown used to, there is a strange feeling of homesickness. The movement had been so comforting, like the movement of the wagons, which reminded me of home. The Bargemen now start filing back onto the deck.

"No leaks. Let's get this thing moving," yells one of the Bargemen.

"How are they going to do that?" I mutter. Auburn shrugs.

"Don't know." We both look around.

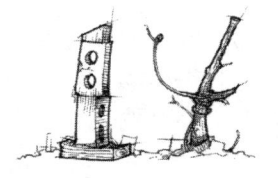

A Helping Hand

Marty leads Auburn, Luke and me to a room in the hull of the ship where rows of tables with benches are laid out in neat lines. Paul continues to stay at Marty's quarters, taking care of Zeleng, who isn't improving. This room is lit with the odd candle and a fire that blazes in a hearth made of metal. The flickering light makes our shadows dance on the walls behind us. "I don't know how you Nomads eat, but round here we eat together," says Marty, gesturing around with a wave of his hand.

"Yeah, this is pretty much how we eat," I explain. "Why is there no one here?"

"It's not time to eat, boy, I brought you here to work," says Marty, a strange twinkle in his eyes. "Oh great," adds Auburn, his face a mask of disappointment. "I would definitely love to help," he continues with hidden sarcasm.

"That's good." Marty moves on from the doorway and further into the room. He stops in front of a cabinet. "One of you mops the floor, the other cleans the table and the last one cooks fish." Marty opens the cupboard and pulls out first, a mop. It is discolored with grime and looks as though it's about to fall apart. He holds it out to Luke, who takes it gingerly.

"Oh, okay, but I am more interested in making things. You know, building and fixing. I don't..." continues Luke. Marty stares at him—his one eye seems enough to put Luke in his place. "Do I use anything else?" Luke looks curiously at the mop. Marty answers, plunking a metal bucket over Luke's head.

"Fill up the bucket over there," says Marty, gesturing to a faucet. "Then mop the floor."

Marty makes it sound easy. "Now you get the tables, and Zane, I will teach you how to cook fish. He pushes a rag into Auburn's hand and escorts me away.

"Good luck," I call back to them. Luke just stands there—the bucket over his eyes—and Auburn moves the rag from hand to hand. Marty pushes open a door at the far end of the room. The second the door opens I am hit with the smell of smoke, spices and cooking fish. The room on one side has a row of fires with grills above them, and the other has a row of counters. There are two people in the room—an elderly man with a white mustache, and a large round man.

White mustache guy speaks first, "This that rascal you picked up? At least you're putting him to good use, I see." I already don't like this man very much and the feeling seems to be mutual, as the man scowls at me. This proves me wrong—all Bargemen aren't as nice as Marty.

"Yes he is, and I would like you to teach him how to cook fish," Marty says, staring down the white mustached man.

"Aye, aye captain," says the other man who grins at me.

"Let Otis have the kid. I don't want him slowing me down," says the white mustached man, looking back down to where he is filleting fish.

"Sure thing. What's your name, boy?" questions the round man whose name is Otis.

"Zane. Nice to meet ... " I start to say, but before I can finish, Otis walks up to me, gives me a big hug and says, "It's great to meet ya. Name's Otis." I found it odd that Otis introduced himself with a hug, but it might be some Bargemen tradition. The old white mustached man would never hug me—so maybe not.

"Okay, let's get down business—you staying, captain?" asks Otis. "No. I better get going. I've got important captain stuff to do—evening," Marty replies, striding to the door. They reply with their own farewells. Otis wobbles over to the grill where a row of fish is sizzling.

"First thing you need to know about cooking fish is how to cut them thinly. I suppose Smith will cut them for today." Smith, being the old scowling man, looks as though he has a large fluffy caterpillar above his lip. I don't need the description, for Smith is the only other person in the room. "And ... sorry about Smith, he doesn't much like other people, especially other new people," says Otis, lowering his voice.

"I can see that," I reply. "So I just put thinly cut pieces of fish on the grill and let em cook?" Otis shakes his head at me and starts to explain the fine art of grilling fish. By the time he's finished sometime later, I feel like a masterchef. I can already flip fish like a pro, and I only occasionally burn one. Otis and I each man a grill, cooking fish up a storm. The trays of cooked fish grow larger and more numerous.

"Throw in a bit more kindling. You're a fast learner," remarks Otis, flipping three fish at once with his metal spatula.

"Yeah, I suppose," I say, attempting to match Otis' triple flip. I fail miserably, and two of the fish nearly fall to the floor. Otis laughs and I can't help but join in. I cross the room and grab an armful of assorted flammable scraps and pile them in Otis' grill and then mine. Smith glares at me as I return to my work, but continues slicing fish. His hands move like lightning, the knife slashing so fast I can barely see it. The two of us have a hard time keeping up with the flow of scaled and cut fish. Otis sprinkles thyme and rosemary onto his sizzling meat.

"Where do you get the seasoning?" I ask, taking some and sprinkling my fish in the same manner.

"The city, fifty fish for a bag of spices—steep price but, as you can tell, we have plenty of fish," explains Otis.

"Yeah, makes sense. Nomads just eat volves and canned food." I think back to all those meals of volve soup. I never thought I would miss them.

"I have never had volve meat before. Is it good?" asks Otis, curiously.

"Depends, I guess. I got pretty sick of it. If you would like, you can taste some volve jerky. Should still have some in my pack," I say, somewhat surprised that Otis had never had the meat that I had eaten everyday for my entire life—but then again, I never really had fish, except the dry tasteless stuff we traded for.

"I would love to try some," exclaimed Otis, taking the last of his fish off the grill. "I think we have cooked enough fish by now. Thanks for your help."

"No problem—glad I could help," I say, and I was really glad to help. Otis is as kind and friendly as Marty. "Can I leave now?" I ask.

"Sure, unless you want to help us serve the food," says Otis.

"I'm good. I guess I'll see ya around." I start to head for the door.

"I would hug ya but since I am up to my knees in fish oil, I'll spare ya," says Otis, waving at me with his spatula. When I push the door open sound hits me. Laughter, loud voices, and conversation meet my ears, along with the clang of dishes and silverware. The room is filled with Bargemen all seated expectantly at the tables. There are at least sixty people in the room, some tall, some small, some young, some old, some kids and some adults. The only thing they have in common is their clothes, which are all dark. They look up when they hear me open the kitchen door and walk in. There are some disappointed groans when they see I am not here to serve them their dinner. I spot Auburn and Luke in a corner. Luke is holding the mop, which somehow he had snapped in two, and Auburn still holds his rag. When I approach, Luke says, "That was not very enjoyable." Both of them look exhausted.

"Do you know how hard it is to mop an entire room?" asks Luke, talking loudly to be heard over the clammer.

"No, actually, because I was busy having a blast cooking fish with the cook." I don't mean to sound so smug.

"Yeah, he gave you the fun job, scrubbing all the tables in this place isn't easy," complains Auburn, massaging his hands, which are wrinkled from the water he used to clean.

At that moment Marty strides into the room and it falls

silent almost instantly. "Take your seats everyone." I can tell he isn't trying to call us three out, but everyone looks at us because we are the only ones standing. We hurry to a table and sit down, Auburn on my right side and Luke across the table. I glance around at the others at our table, all of whom are complete strangers.

"Let's pray," Marty's voice carries well over the silent room. The fire light flickers and Marty begins his prayer. Everyone bows his or her head and clasps his or her hands. "God, whether it be your will or conditions out of your control we accept our fate. We may have been abandoned but we are never alone, for you watch over us. I must ask though. Why must the sick so often die sick? I know you will oversee our guests in the times to come." I had never prayed before since Nomads do not pray. Our reasoning is that you shouldn't hope for some extraterrestrial being to help you—that you should help yourself and make your own life. We believe you don't pray to god when you have problems, but you solve them yourself. It is a new experience, a new outlook on the world, and it makes me wonder—is this why so many of the Bargemen are so kind? They believe they have a god that is watching over them, protecting them, but also influencing them to be a force of good in a world that truly lacks it.

"We thank you for the food before us even when times are rough, and pray to never go hungry again." With that he ends the prayer and the whole crowd murmurs 'Amen'.

The voices start up again and Marty makes his way over to us. I am surprised. Shouldn't the captain have some throne at the front of the room where he looks down on everyone? Instead, though, he comes to sit with us.

"Hey guys, how did you like your work?" Marty takes a seat across from me and looks directly at me—not down at me—directly at me, as equals would do.

"Hated it," both Auburn and Luke say in unison. Marty starts to laugh.

"Not half bad," I say, looking towards Marty. Marty beams down at me.

"The day's half good, then—Smith didn't give you any trouble?"

"If you don't count glowering and mentally projected anger as trouble, then yes."

At that point the food is brought in and served. Otis places a tray of fish and bread in front of us all. The tray is made of wood, and so is the table. I take a bite of the fish—it is almost better than the fish we had last night. One of the few similarities I could make between the Nomads and the Bargemen is that we both love our food, and when served, the whole room gets quiet. I devour my fish, and then shove the bread into my mouth. I feel as though I should be more polite, but when I glance around, the others, even Marty, are also stuffing their faces. "Wait. Zeleng and Paul aren't here," I say, noticing for the first time.

"If it comforts you, I had someone take them some fish already. They are most likely enjoying this meal right now," says Marty, absentmindedly ripping a piece of his bread and eating it.

"Good. I haven't checked in on Zeleng. I hope he is still okay," I say. Thoughts of the mangled swollen mass of his arm float to the forefront of my mind. I am suddenly very unhungry, and with a sinking feeling I realize my full stomach isn't the only reason.

"The boy needs antibiotics badly. I fear he will not last another week without them. We will get to the city in one night and two days," Marty says sadly.

I take a drink of water and try to clear my head of those thoughts. Zeleng would make it because he can't not make it—he just can't. I put my glass down and look to the others, who are still silent.

"He's going to get his antibiotics even if it's the last thing I do. I am getting him to the Clean World." The words rush out of me in a flow of emotion before I can stop them. I clamp my hand over my mouth, but the damage is done.

"What do you mean get to the Clean World," says Marty, not taking his eyes off me. For the longest time I just sit there. I can't lie to him because he would know I am lying—but I can't tell him the truth. Sweat beads on my forehead. Auburn shakes his head at me. "I ... I meant we are get..."

Marty interrupts my stumbled ramblings. "I understand what you are trying to do, but you are going to fail. Getting to the Clean World is impossible." His voice is quiet, but stern. He is sitting straight up in his chair, staring at us one by one.

"If you understand so well then you understand we have no other choice," says Auburn. I search Marty's face, trying to understand. The grin that I have already grown used to, has now been replaced with a line that allows his beard to fall over his mouth—out of sight. There is a slight slant to his mouth that I can barely see, and his bushy eyebrows are furrowed.

"I know what you guys are going through. I know the feeling of desperately trying to save a loved one who is slipping away from you. You do crazy things without thinking." Marty lowers his voice so the others at the table wouldn't hear them. I have no clue what to say.

"Come with me, we need to talk in private without the others." Marty stands up slowly, as if it pains him. I do the same and follow him out of the room. There are a few odd stares from the Bargemen, but no one says anything. Once we are in the hall, the door swings shut behind us.

The hall is suddenly silent and Marty starts to talk. "About twenty years ago I was going through exactly what you are. My wife had gotten very ill. I was desperate to help her. I took her to the city just like you. The CityFolk said there was nothing they could do for her, but I couldn't give up that easily. I gave her all the medicine I could find or afford."

His words leave us speechless—for what is the appropriate response to such a tale? I am not the type to empathize or give comfort or say sorry, but I am also not cold and heartless about it either. Not knowing what to do or say, I take the safe route and say nothing. We follow Marty, climbing the ladder to the first deck. Our feet clang on the metal rungs.

"When nothing helped, I became desperate. I thought the only chance was to take her to the Clean World. So I tried by attacking a Trash Craft—this is all I got out of it," says Marty, pointing to his eyepatch. I think about his limp, the arm he never moves, and wonder if those are also from the same incident.

"I nearly died and I didn't make it. Then my wife died, and I was left without a wife and without an eye. I am telling you it's not worth trying." Marty pushes his way into his quarters. Paul is sprawled out on a couch, eating his way through a fish. I assume it was one of those I had cooked.

Zeleng lies unconscious where we left him. Paul looks up as we walk in. An expression crosses his grease-covered face, and his second fish pauses on its journey to his mouth.

"Dinners must be quick around here," says Paul. Then he sees Marty's face. "Uh oh, something happened."

"Zane accidentally mentioned that we were on our way to the Clean World," says Auburn, tilting his head and staring daggers at me.

"Oh wow. Not good," Paul says, basically summing up the state of the situation in two words.

"That's right," says Marty, his voice cool. "Getting to the Clean World is impossible. It's been hundreds of years, and not a soul has made it half the way. Forget it. I care for your friend, I do, but getting yourselves all killed is not going to do him one darned bit of good." He waves his one good hand in front of his face.

"Marty, you don't completely understand the entire situation." I walk to my backpack where the grenade is and pull it out, brandishing it the air. Carelessly waving around explosive items isn't number one on my list of safe things to do, but it is pretty high on my list of convincing people of the possibility of getting to the Clean World.

"What is that?" asks Marty. His face had been a mask of sadness as he told about his wife, but now his eyebrows rise and his mouth opens slightly in the image of curiosity. Limping to my side, he puts his hand out to the grenade, feeling it under his massive fingers.

"It's a grenade. It disables Trash Crafts, and that's why we will be the first to make it to the Clean World and save Zeleng," I tell him, saying the words with a confident air that I have learned to use on occasions involving desperate quests to other planets.

"Mother of God, I have never seen anything like this before," says Marty, staring in awe at the grenade with his good eye. "Where on this darned planet did you get such a thing?"

"Long story—really long story," I say, and it is. It had only been a couple of days, but the things that have happened are unbelievable. "The point is, we have a chance with this, and we must take it to save Zeleng."

"This changes everything," mutters Marty, his hand disappearing into his curly beard as he strokes his chin, deeply in thought. "You have got to let me come with you."

"What?" I burst out, before I can stop myself. I seem to have made randomly bursting out something of a habit.

Marty sighs. "I am coming with you," he says, with conviction. He strides back across the room—and then walks back again.

"You're captain of a ship. You can't just run off with us." I try to reason, but my voice sounds weak.

"I know. I know. But I can't give up an opportunity like this. I failed once and this is my chance to succeed. I have nothing left on this planet. Sure, I am captain of this ship, but it's just a matter of time before sickness hits, this barge sinks, or the numerous other things that might ruin my life come into play, and I am left with nothing. If I can escape that before it ever happens, it will be a miracle in itself. Oh, and I have other reasons," he ends, without further specification or explanation—it makes me wonder what possibly might be his other reasons. He sounds desperate and I can tell he's barely holding it together. His emotion seems out of place. He has such a stable life here. Why isn't he clinging to his power like Leon—too scared to take a chance just because it puts his power at risk? I look at Marty, and any questions I have die in my throat. Marty's beard quivers and his large frame seems to lose some of its stature as his shoulders slump.

I look at Paul, who is sitting on an arm of a couch swinging his legs. He looks confused and uncertain about what to do. I look to Auburn who still stands in the doorway. I look to the others. All of them just stand there as if they're waiting for me to speak.

"I don't know, I barely know you. How can I trust you enough to let you come with us?" I finally say.

Marty just sighs. "You can't, but you have to. I must go with you." Marty stands in the center of the room now. The small fire casts his hulking shadow on the side of the wall and onto the ceiling.

"If you are to come, let's start by being completely honest with each other. Trust is going to be key on this journey, so you can start by telling us what is up with your arm. Why do you never use it, never even move it?" I ask, but it's more of a demand than anything else. Marty's eyes get wide for a second—he takes a step backward. He looks like a cornered animal, a giant hairy cornered animal. But he recovers quickly, his face returning to normal. He takes a deep breath. In one fluid movement he moves his right arm for the first time, thrusting it upwards, simultaneously using his other hand to pull down his sleeve. I immediately think my eyes are deceiving me—the room's only light is flickering, and I think I must be imagining things. I had thought Zeleng's injury was so awful, that it could never happen to anyone else, but here, in front of my eyes, it has. Marty's arm ends just above the wrist, giving way to a rounded stump. It's an old injury, that much is clear, years, maybe decades old. In this case time doesn't seem to have healed all things, and this injury is nearly as gruesome as Zeleng's. For the second time that night Marty leaves us speechless.

"Is that a good enough explanation for you? I want to get to the Clean World so they can fix my arm as well as your friend's." He lets his arm drop back to his side, allowing his sleeve to cover it once again.

"How did your arm not get infected? Zeleng's did within days. How did you survive an injury like that without the medicines of the Clean World?" I ask a series of questions, leaving Marty no time to answer.

"That, we will never know," answers Marty. I want to question him so that I may be able to better help Zeleng, but I can't. That single statement avoided all further discussion of the issue. I know there is something he isn't telling us—something about the way he phrased it makes me feel uneasy. However, he is being honest, even if he is holding something back, so I can't call him out on that either.

It's hard to get the image of his stub of an arm out of my mind, but I work on it because Marty is coming with us. I have decided that he will. I can compare this to Zeleng's injury, and if he wants to help himself as much as I want to help Zeleng, then I can't stop him no matter what. If he has anywhere near the determination that I do to save Zeleng, then he won't rest until he accomplishes it.

"I don't see the problem. I mean, we could use extra help, and this guy is probably a heck of a lot smarter than we are. We could use his help." I hadn't expected Zeleng to answer—I had thought he was sleeping. He sits up almost straight, his back supported by pillows. He looks bad. His hair is damp with sweat. When he speaks again, his voice is a hoarse rasp, "Bring him along for me." Despite it all, Zeleng gives us a pouty baby face.

"I agree with Zeleng—we are trying the impossible. Bringing him along can do nothing but increase our chances," Luke says, leaning, arms crossed, against the wall by the fire.

"Amen," says Marty. "Does this mean I am in?" Marty almost smiles—his eye twinkles with hope. Everyone looks at me as if it's my decision whether he goes or not. Already having made my decision, I voice it.

"He can go." I know those three words have a life-changing effect on Marty, which is shown by his returning smile, which is even wider than before. A grin that spreads to the corners of his face, nearly separating the top of his head from his bearded chin. His eye is full of tears, and I realize I am seeing tears of joy, a sight I thought I would never see until Zeleng was better and we were in the Clean World. The sight fills me with good omens. My simple decision has made Marty happier than he most likely has ever been before.

"I will get packing then." He heads for the door without another word. He practically runs out the door, for now, the pain in his legs forgotten, and his limp almost not visible.

"He's a good guy. We will need him," says Paul, getting up from the couch and walking over to feel Zeleng's forehead. "You're burning up. Let's get some wet cloths on your head and get you some medicine."

"Actually, I am pretty sure your hands are just freezing," he grimaces, but I think he's trying to smile. "About that medicine though." Paul smiles and brings him the painkillers. Paul finds some rags, wets them in a bucket, and lays them on Zeleng's forehead. I am glad Paul has taken over doctor duty. I was no good at it. Water drips into Zeleng's eyes. Zeleng doesn't bother to move even his good hand to wipe it away. When I look at him I can barely contain my fear for him. This was one of my only friends, and he is dying in front of me. I want to help him, but there is really nothing I can do for him until we reach the city.

Luke, who had been sitting by the fire, speaks up. "We should be reaching the city the day after tomorrow, right?"

"Yeah, then we have to get moving fast..." I would have said more, but I am not about to say to his face, "We have to move fast because you're dying, Zeleng," no matter how true it is.

* * *

The sun sets outside, casting an orange glow through the window into the room. The barge slides along. The sounds of voices echo up through the walls as the Bargemen prepare for the night. Zeleng lies conked out on his couch, his neck curved at an uncomfortable angle. His bandages already have blood streaks soaking through. Everyone else is already on his couch as I move to the one they have left for me in the far corner. I get onto the couch and pull off my metal boots, not even bothering to untie them. I run a hand through my dirty hair and lie back, resting my head on a pillow. The sounds of Luke's snoring fill the room. I close my eyes and try to clear my mind. Should I have let Marty come along? I am not so sure anymore. There is no one to give me advice, and no one to lead us—we have only ourselves to answer our questions. Then the door swings open, spilling light into the room. In marches Marty with a single backpack slung over his shoulder. Twenty years as a captain, and all his belongings fit into one bag? That's how it is to be a leader in the Wasteland. You have no valuables but your own people.

"I'm packed, guys." Marty looks around at the silent room. "Oh, there is no one awake, whoops." It's too dark to tell, but I think he's embarrassed. "I'll just set this stuff here," he mutters to himself, placing it next to the door. He walks back out of the room. When the door shuts behind him, the room is cast back into darkness. I get the reading tablet from my backpack and switch it on. The screen casts a white light around the room. I reopen the book I had been previously reading and flip to the new chapter.

Weapons

Weapons have advanced dramatically in recent years due to newly discovered metals and natural resources found on New Earth. The advances can also be credited to the increased funding for the military. NAWC has become increasingly protective and has focused taxpayer money on international security. Therefore, weapon advances, such as those in gun technology, biological weapons, and weapons of mass destruction have made life both safer and more dangerous at the same time. All these things have made the alliances of NAWC fragile. The individual parts of the great NAWC alliance are afraid that a so-called ally will come in and wipe them out with one weapon. The structure of the New Earth is all about having allies and never provoking other countries, because if there were a full scale world war, New Earth would be destroyed in a matter of days, and the last chance for human survival would be gone.

I am interested, but scared in what I am reading. If what is written is true, we have next to no chance of overcoming the guards on the Trash Craft. And by the sound of it, not all is right on New Earth with this alliance called NAWC. I read the rest of the chapter on weapons, which includes detailed descriptions and pictures of some of the more widely used weapons. I flip through pages until I come to a new section.

The Rise of NAWC

The power lies in those who strive for better lives for everyone. Economic equality is necessary and a dominant controlling government power is indispensable if we are to keep greed from ravaging this new planet. NAWC, founded in an attempt to save the human race, unified nations, for it promised hope in a time of fear. The Exodus fleet cost NAWC nearly $75 trillion dollars and a majority of the remaining resources on Earth. This kind of money leaves a lasting debt, and is now the duty of all to pay it back.

A doctor still makes more than a fast food worker, but taxes equal out their actual incomes. Once the debt is paid off, those who have worked the hardest in these times of economic equality will see a pay raise and those who don't will not. It is a temporary form of communism if you will, and people still strive to do their best and create the best products simply because they know they will be rewarded for it. In the meantime many of the resources are still being rationed and a socialist regime does remain. President Mo Sestka, called the savior of human existence for his successful migration from Earth and the efficient settlement of New Earth, in his final years nominated Zoe Frazer as his replacement.

Zoe's parents, Bar and Telkine Frazer, best known for their work on the Celestial Messis and for their mega company Frazer Industries, would later contribute large amounts of money to the election. Zoe Frazer, fueled by this wealth and the loss of her husband and one year old son, rose to power as council woman of the Cal Commision, which decided what steps to take in further exploration of New Earth. Mo Sestka said, "Never have I met a woman who seeks the welfare of all as Zoe Fraser does." President Zoe Frazer won a landslide election in 2488, where she promised to continue to uphold the ideals of the Mo Sestka administration.

The page starts to dim, and my eyes start to close on their own. I want to stay awake and read more, but my body has other ideas. Why did Zoe Frazer feel so familiar? Where had I heard this name before? I slip the tablet back into my pack and close my eyes.

The next two days are among the slowest of my life. Zeleng worsens to a point where it worries me almost constantly, yet I spend my days mopping and helping out on the barge. I feel so helpless not to be able to do anything. My friend is dying, and all I can do is watch and mop a few floors. The fish that tasted so good on the first day grow old, and I start wishing more and more for volve. With the revelation of Marty's injury, he no longer tries to hide it, and bustles around whistling and being his usual smiling self.

Marty joins us everyday to talk about the plan, but we seem to get nowhere, everything is so up in the air. I don't feel as if I can depend on anything going right, but I do feel almost everything will come down to luck and the little skill Marty can provide. I sleep worse and worse, as Zeleng wakes me often with his agonized moaning. He is often no longer coherent, and the painkillers only help with the physical pain, but do nothing to keep away the nightmares that seem to haunt him every night. When he isn't sleeping, he seems to be able to make it without pain, but I know the medicine is doing nothing to stop his fevers or the infection that is surely spreading throughout his body. Each day I read more from the tablet's library. I like to think that I am better preparing myself, but if anything, it makes me doubt if this journey is actually possible.

The thing that keeps me going is Marty's positive attitude as well as the man himself. The sheer fact that he survived a similar injury is the only thing that gives me hope that maybe somehow Zeleng will also survive. It feels that a week has gone by in the two days we ride the river—but when that day finally arrives, it catches us unprepared.

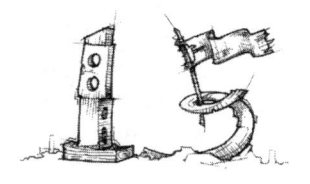

'Bout That City Life

"City up ahead," yells Otis from his perch on the top deck. I scramble up the ladder to join him. Sure enough, right on the horizon lies a barely visible row of buildings bordering the ocean. Below me, Auburn and Luke scramble up the ladder. Wind whips at our hair and clothes, and I cling to the railing so that I am not blown right off. We continue to float towards the city.

"We are finally here," says Auburn. I can see on his face how relieved he is. I am relieved too—on the barge there was nothing I could do for Zeleng, but now that we are arriving at Skumford, it's time to get moving again. The river starts to curve and I see we are now heading for the ocean, parallel to the city. After several minutes we pull into one of the ports. Walls of brick, wood and concrete loom above us on each side. The port extends into the city like a river. Above us is a web of bridges and walkways bustling with people.

"Here we are. Time to get off." Otis gestures to a bridge that extends at the level of the third deck. Once we are lined up with it, we walk off. Luke hurries up, bringing

Zeleng on his back, but most of our stuff is carried by Marty, who follows several paces behind Luke. I cross the bridge first and step onto steady ground for the first time in three days. Around me bustle men, women and children carrying everything from fish to guns. Marty hurries off the bridge after us.

"Okay, now follow me." Marty starts walking quickly down a path of wooden planks. Doors open out of the walls, and several have open windows through which people are trading goods. Right on our left above an open window reads a sign that says *Volve and Fish Shop*. The small man inside is nearly hidden behind piles of meat. As I watch, another man walks up and shows the seller a handful of bullets. After a little discussion, the man walks away with a bag full of fish.

I turn my eyes back to Marty, who is dodging and darting around the crowds of people, making it hard for us to keep up, especially Luke, who is carrying Zeleng along on his back. No one gives us odd looks, so I guess they see a lot of handless people. A barge sails by in the canal to our right, and I already start to miss the security of the barge. Out here we are in the open, with thousands of people who could harm us.

The wooden path we walk is slippery from the water that splashes onto it. If I lose my footing I will plunge into the dark water of the canal where I will either be poisoned by the polluted water or get run over by an oncoming barge. Neither of those things sounds very appealing, so I am increasingly careful as I run along. Marty is slightly taller than the people around him, so I can just see his head bobbing through the crowds in front of me, as though a hairy

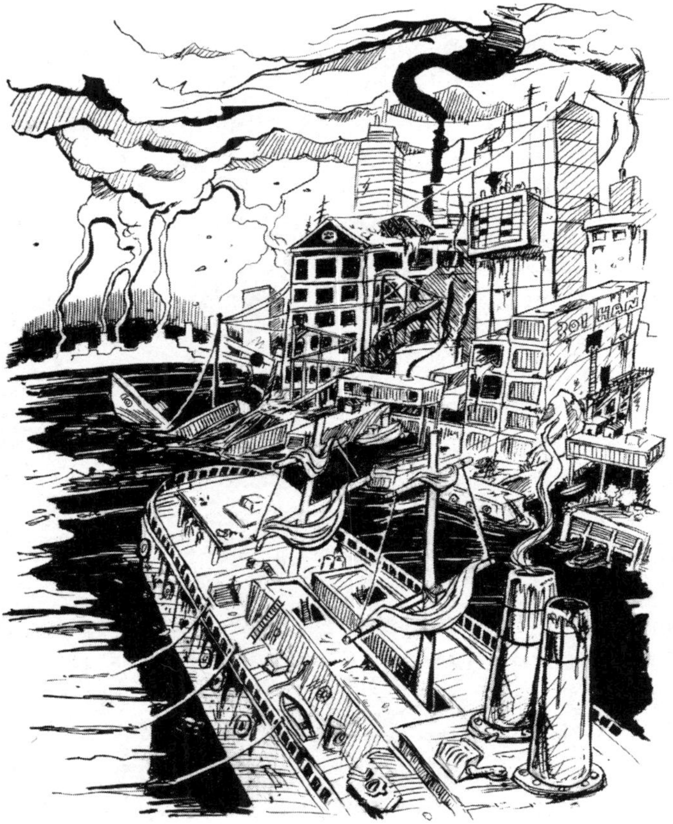

301 HAN

nest leads my way.

"I have never entered the city through the ports. This is crazy," says Paul, walking to my right just on the edge of the canal.

"Me neither—nothing like what I expected. I have never gone this far into the city before," I reply. We turn a corner—I am hit by the smell of rotting fish, garbage and sewage. I gasp and bury my nose into my shirt. Luke, whose arms are full with Zeleng, looks like he is about to die. In front of us is a barge filled with trash. As we watch, people continue to throw things onto the barge from windows in the walls on either side. By the looks of it, the barge is completely hollow, and trash is overflowing over the edges—some of it falls into the canal.

We walk for several minutes before Marty stops. "Here we are." Marty is pointing to a set of double doors set into the wall.

"This is what?" I asked, confused.

"The government building. What else would it be?" Marty says it like it's obvious, but I had been expecting something a little grander for the most important building in town. Marty pushes the thick doors open and we step inside. The room is furnished with some chairs and a desk. Behind the desk is a woman dressed all in black. There is a guard in each corner, and two flanking a set of stairs leading up. The guards are also dressed all in black, with volve leather masks and assorted metal armor. Each guard holds a deadly looking spear. When the double doors slam behind us, the woman in black looks up.

"May I help you?" she asks, as she stares placidly at us.

"Yes, we need to see the Trash Craft records," explains

Marty, towering over the seated woman and casting a shadow upon her.

In a monotone voice the women in black says, "First door on your left." She gestures at the stairs. Marty heads towards them and we file up the rather narrow flight. The wood creaks beneath us, and I feel as if the stairs are going to collapse under my weight. I am surprised how run down the place is. In front of me Marty pushes open the door and steps inside.

"Yep, this is the right place," he calls. I follow him in. The room is surprisingly large—the walls are made of bricks, but they can barely be seen because they are thoroughly covered with what looks like hand-drawn maps, each one dotted with pins. Several tables placed around the room are also covered with stacks of maps. I move to the closest table, and when I look closely at the pins, I see that each one has a little tag—on each tag reads:

Last date: January 12th, 2501
Predicted Date: January 12th, 2505

Apparently this particular site is scheduled to receive a load of trash in roughly one year, a full four years since the last dump. The others spread out searching the walls. I move on to the next map, looking for one that has the city marked on it. I don't find it on the next map, or the next. I think to myself that they must have some sort of system, but I can't decipher it.

"Got it. Right here." It's Paul who speaks. Luke hurries over first with Zeleng still on his back. I walk over. The map indeed has a little square label THE CITY in capital letters. I lean forward. According to the pin, the last time the city had gotten trash dumped on it was four months ago.

"Yeah, this is good," I say, scanning the other pins near the city. "We need to find one that has a predicted dumping time within a few days, but is still near the city." Marty arrives at my side and we scour the maps.

"Right here, about a mile west of the city, there's a predicted dumping in three days." Marty points triumphantly to a little red pin located about eight inches from the city.

"Not good enough," says Luke, who is standing back watching. "Zeleng might not have that much time." He is right—even now Zeleng doesn't look good. His face is white and his eyes are closed. His hair and clothes are damp with sweat, and his hurt arm hangs limply over Luke's shoulder. I turn back to the map, if anything, more determined than ever. It's several minutes before someone speaks again.

"This one dumps tomorrow, but it doesn't have the exact hour—so are we going to camp out there all day?" asks Paul, his finger on a pin about a foot away from the city. "If that's the earliest, then we will go there and wait. Keep looking though," I say. After almost ten more minutes of searching we have scanned every pin within a four-foot radius of the city. The tag Paul found is still the earliest.

"I guess tomorrow we will head there and wait," says Luke.

"Sounds like a good plan," I agree.

※ ● ※

We cram ourselves into a tiny room, all seven of us in one bedroom at a dumpy old inn. The man, who rented the room to us, gave us a skeptical look when we said we would like only one room. We traded the bottle of wine for it.

Zeleng gets the only bed, and since there is only a single shabby chair in the room, everyone but Marty sits on the floor. The room is old and smells like mold and mildew. The walls are made of bricks, and the whole place feels cold and unwelcoming—yet still it is better than nothing.

"We still have no idea what we are doing tomorrow," I say, sitting with my back against the cold stone wall.

"We have no plan. We don't know how to overpower the guards, and we don't know how to drive the ship even if we do make it aboard."

The others sit in silence a bit. "The only viable choice I see is to sneak on and hide without them noticing. Last time when I tried to fight the guards, it wasn't pretty," says Marty.

"Like they're not going to notice that someone used a grenade to knock out their computers?" asks Paul. He stands to my right towering above me. "They will search the entire craft."

"They might think it's a glitch when they don't find us—or something, I don't know," Luke suggests. "We have no idea what it's going to be like. Zane, have you found anything useful on the tablet?"

"No. I will read tonight and hopefully find something," I say, moving to the backpack so I can get the device.

"Hold up, what's the tablet?" asks Marty, watching me as I unzip my pouch.

"Got it along with the grenade—has books from the Clean World on it," I say, standing up, tablet in hand. I cover the short distance to Marty in a few hurried strides and hold it out to him. He examines it with the interest of a caveman who doesn't yet know the thin rectangular "rock" he holds contains more information than he could ever paint on meager cave walls. However, something in his expression looks forced, almost fake.

"I'm not saying I understand this ruddy piece of gadgetry, but why did you never tell me about these devices?" Marty gives the tablet back to me and I return to my spot. I choose to ignore his question.

"I should get an early start on reading, as Luke said. I don't know how long it will take to find the right information," I say. The others just nod. I flip on the tablet—then, with my back pushed uncomfortably against the wall, I begin to read. What I read changes everything.

After several hours I stop reading. I go to the others and tell them what I have learned. They all stare at me, unbelieving. With the new information we make a plan, the best plan. So tomorrow we are going to set out to accomplish this, and tomorrow we are going to succeed.

When dinnertime comes, we, minus Zeleng and Paul, whom we leave behind, walk from the inn and go in search of food. Marty leads us down the walkways and across bridges until he stops outside a door. The place is called the... I can't decipher the name because the sign is so dirty and hangs at an odd angle from one screw. Inside, it's crowded with people sitting around tables and at a wall-to-wall counter. A small man in a badly stained apron, moves towards us.

"Welcome. You need a table?" asks the man. "We got a free one over there." The man points a dirty finger at a round table in the far corner.

"Yeah, that works. Thanks." Marty follows the man to the table. I follow, dodging people and chairs. There are so many people in the small building, everyone talking loudly. With it all blended together, the sound is quite deafening. We get to the table and sit down.

"I have never gone somewhere to eat before," I say loudly, in order to be heard over the crowds. "It doesn't seem that different, though. Loud, lots of people, and a small little man in a badly stained apron."

"No. It's not different except you can pick what you want to eat," Marty says, pointing to the wall where words have been carved. "You can get volve, fish, and bread with vegetables. Or try some other stuff." Marty scans the menu.

"Vegetables, as in the ones you grow. Possibly delicious green ones?" asks Auburn. He licks his lips.

"Those are the ones," answers Marty.

"How are we paying for this? Vegetables are pricey," I ask, looking at Marty, who doesn't appear to be carrying anything tradeable.

"Don't worry about that, we dropped off some of the fish we caught earlier. We have been doing this now for a couple of years. We give them fish in exchange for a couple of meals a year," Marty says, smiling at me.

At that point, the small man scurries back up.

"What are you guys having?" asks the man, with a bored voice.

"I would like volve soup with vegetables," orders Marty. I nearly burst out laughing—Marty is ordering the meal that all of us had gotten so tired off.

"What?" asks Marty, defensively.

"With the Nomads we have volve soup for almost every

meal, and I got kind of sick of it. Just kind of weird having you order it," I say, realizing it had sounded a lot funnier in my head, because no one else laughs. Maybe they're just thinking how Zeleng always complained about the volve soup, and how now he couldn't even eat.

The rest of us order. Just to switch it up, I order fish soup with vegetables. I also order some kind of drink. I have no clue what it is, but Marty assures me it's delicious. We sit in silence, and I spend time looking around. The table we sit at is made of some kind of light wood, but it is chipped and stained in so many places that it looks dark. There are no windows in the room, and the only light comes from crude wax candles in the center of the table that have burned down to stumps. The smell of cooking meat and vegetables fills the room. It reminds me of the few times I was in for dinner and waited for Ham to serve us.

The food comes within a matter of minutes. The small man slams a bowl of soup and a glass of amber liquid in front of each of us. I try a sip. It's the sweetest thing I have ever tasted—the flavor is completely new.

"How are you liking your apple cider?" asks Marty. I know Marty already knows the answer because he is watching me slurp it down as fast as I can.

"It's great," I finally say, once I set down my half empty glass.

"Glad you like it. Now try some soup." I had nearly forgotten about my soup even though it sat in a metal bowl right in front of me. I use the spoon to try a mouthful. It tastes almost the same as volve soup, but the fish gives it a slightly different flavor.

"Let's talk about Zeleng—while he's not here," says

Luke. "Paul rewrapped his bandage this morning on the barge before we set out. It doesn't look good. It's all swollen and..."

"No need to describe it while we are eating," interrupts Auburn.

"Right—well it's bad—I don't know how much longer he can make it. If we fail tomorrow, he dies."

"That's why we are not going to fail. Zeleng is going to live," I say, clenching my hands into fists under the table.

"I know, but we can't afford to mess this up tomorrow, is all I am saying," says Luke, half-heartedly stirring his soup—pushing it around more than actually eating it.

"Let's discuss our plan one more time. Okay?" suggests Marty, in a voice so soft that we can barely hear it—making sure that possible eavesdroppers from other tables have no chance of overhearing what we are saying.

We spend the next half hour eating and discussing the plan over and over again until we know it by heart.

We leave the dingy eatery with parts of the plan swirling through our heads, and food swirling through our stomachs. The canal path is bustling with Bargemen and City-Folk alike, all busy at work, trading and unloading barges. We head up some stairs to one of the walkways that goes above the canals, so that we can take a direct path back to the inn. We cross bridge after bridge until we make it back to the inn, where we take the stairs down into our room, which is at water level.

Marty pushes the door open and I rush past him to check on Zeleng. He seems bad, but he's stable. He's lying on the bed asleep, just as we had left him. His arm, I notice, now has fresh bandages on it. He is still sweating. I move to his side and pull a small bottle that I had them fill with apple cider for Zeleng. I nudge him. He groans, but doesn't open his eyes.

"Drink," I prompt, "but first try to sit up." Zeleng slowly opens his eyes, as if the movement pains him.

"I'm not thirsty…" His voice is so quiet and weak that I nearly cry.

"You have to drink. Guys, help me get him up." Auburn moves to the other side, and together, very gently, we push him into a sitting position. Zeleng's body feels hot and limp in my arms. I put the bottle of cider to his lips and hold it for him. As much apple juice trickles out of his mouth as goes in, but he seems to be swallowing because his throat is moving.

"You feeling okay?" I ask. I know it's a stupid question, but I have to hear it from him.

"Not so great," he mumbles. He closes his eyes again. "I'm dying, aren't I?"

His words send a shiver down my spine. I had always known the truth, but until then I had been able to shove it to the back of my mind. I try to hold myself together.

"Goddamn it Zeleng. You can't die and you won't." My eyes sting and my throat constricts so that my next words come out almost as a whisper. "I couldn't live without you. I can't explain it, but you fill a hole in my life that would kill me not to have."

"You were never much of a swearer," replies Zeleng, his eyelids closing. "But it's an honor to have been your symbolical life plug." Zeleng almost smiles. I fight back tears. Zeleng has started using past tense, as though he is already gone.

"Hang in there, man," I whisper, turning away. I move across the room and sit on the floor in the cold corner. The atmosphere in the room perfectly matches my mood—damp, dreary and dark. I wrap those feelings around me, tightly surrounding myself with them, in an attempt to smother them. My throat aches with the pain of clenching back the sadness that threatens to break through the little resolve I still have. I put my head in my hands and rest them on my knee, again choking back the sobs that want so desperately to escape. Why me? I think to myself. Why did my friend have to be the one to lose a hand, and why did it have to be my responsibility for saving his life? I remind myself it could be a lot worse. I could be watching Zeleng die in front of me, helpless to do anything. At least I am lucky enough to know I am trying to help him. A lot of people don't even have that feeling.

Auburn comes and sits beside me. "You know it's just as hard for me. I am as much Zeleng's best friend as you are." I hadn't actually ever thought about that. It doesn't exactly make me feel better, but at least I am not alone on this journey. I have people like Auburn here, helping me hold the other side of the stretcher—helping to lessen the load emotionally as much as physically. I pause for a while, afraid that when I open my mouth I might let loose the tears.

"Yeah, it is just hard now that Zeleng's getting so bad. It's up to us to save his life, and I don't know if I am up for that," I say.

"You have to be for Zeleng's sake. We have no other choice." Auburn and I sit there in silence. Where had our peaceful Nomad life gone, where our biggest worries were getting back to the wagons for food and sleep? That life would never be again. My new life would be in the Clean World millions of miles away. I slouch my shoulders and pull my hood over my head so that it flaps down over my eyes.

"So, what will be the first thing you do when we get to the Clean World?" I ask, on a different, more positive note, but I don't quite register what I am saying. My voice seems to belong to a different person, for how could I be trying to have a conversation in such a situation.

"I don't know—even though it has always been my dream to get there, I guess I haven't actually thought I would ever be on this journey, so I have never thought about what I would do when I get there—probably take a bath, eat some new foods, and watch some movies that aren't five centuries old."

The part of me that I can't quite control smiles, and I feel guilty that I can have such expressions at a time like this. "We could try the meats of all the animals that became extinct on Earth." I keep the conversation up, but my my thoughts are still on Zeleng.

"Oh yeah, food. Beef and pork and ham and all that." Auburn smiles. His teeth are so white, even though he never cleans them.

"Yeah, they will just grow Zeleng's arm back. It will all be okay," Auburn says, rising up to brush himself off.

"Yeah." I say, and I hope with all my heart it's true, for I would be empty without Zeleng plugging my metaphorical leak.

Grenades and Demon Turtles

The hours pass agonizingly slowly. Every minute feels like a millenium. I sit there, staring at the wall, thinking about nothing for more than a few minutes at a time. Zeleng sleeps fitfully on the bed and each time he moves, it reminds me, with increasing strength, of his suffering. No one talks in the room, but I know each of us is feeling what I am feeling. I don't even know what I am feeling— something like nervousness, anticipation, dread, with a little bit of grief and sadness thrown in for good measure. I find myself thinking about my whole life so far. I haven't really done anything. If I die tomorrow, almost everyone who knew me will die with me, and I will be forgotten forever. If I succeed tomorrow, my life hopefully will get a heck of a lot better.

I don't know when I drift off, but all of a sudden I find myself in a very different place. I am back in the wagons, sitting on a pile of rags and blankets. Right above my head is a cardboard roof. I look out through an opening into a room I know well. It is Ham's room, the one he shared with me, his wife and daughters until I was eight, when

I moved into the room with Auburn and Zeleng. It is also the room in which I had spent so many of my early years. The only difference is Ham isn't in the room—instead it is Zenith, my dad. He is made of flickering blue light just like the hologram when I had first seen him. He sits on the bed looking at something in his hand. I can't tell what it is from my minimal view from my box hideout. I slowly crawl out, and as I do, I see my hands, toddler hands, small and pudgy. I try to stand, but I fall over and hit the ground with a thud. It doesn't hurt, but Zenith looks at me with a smile. His mouth moves, but I hear nothing except my own breathing. I crawl towards him, but before I can reach him, he flickers out of existence, leaving nothing behind but a small roll of paper.

I crawl to the bed and pull myself into a standing position. My eyes peek over the side of the bed. There is the paper right in front of me. I reach for it—my short arms barely reaching the paper—but I somehow manage to grab it. I plop down on my bottom, fumbling to unroll the paper. When I do, I see a picture of Marty. It takes up most of the top half of the page. Below it are lines of text. I try to read them, but I can't. The words look like lines. It is like trying to read English that's written in the alphabet of another language. I look back to the picture of Marty. He looks younger, much younger, in his early twenties or thirties—his beard is short and well cut, with fewer gray hairs. He stares expressionless at the camera. I don't understand why my dad was looking at this. I close my eyes, and when I open them, I am back to reality.

I don't know what time it is because there's no window. Auburn is asleep on the hard floor. Marty sits with his chair facing away, so I can't tell whether or not he's sleeping. Paul sits with his back resting against the bed. Although he's awake, he doesn't seem to register anything he's seeing. His eyes have a faraway look and I can tell he's in deep thought. He rests his head on his hand and his wrist is bent, palm supporting his chin. Paul's short army haircut has started to grow out some and is curling slightly around the ears. I stand up and move around to Marty's chair and see that he is indeed sleeping. I look to the bedside table, which seems to have been built from cardboard, and a music stand. Resting on it is a crude wax candle and two bottles. One is filled with water and the other with the rest of the apple juice.

You would never have thought this would have been a hard decision. I should leave the apple juice for Zeleng and drink water, but that apple juice is so good. With an act of extreme self-control, I reach for the water. I lift it to my lips and take a long swig. I set the bottle back on the table, looking Zeleng over. He lies there motionless, except for a soft rise and fall in his chest.

"You only have to hang on a little while longer." I repeat the words several more times. "You're not going to die." I say this to reassure myself more than Zeleng, who's asleep and doesn't even hear me.

The door of the room creaks open behind me and I spin around so fast I nearly fall. Standing in the doorway is Luke, holding a box in his hand.

"Oh, it's just you," I say.

"Yeah, just me," agrees Luke. "Wake the others. We gotta get moving. Oh, and I brought breakfast." Luke brandishes the box at me. "They're some kind of bread thing.

Try one. They're okay."

I take one of the golden brown rolls.

"Do I smell food?" asks a voice. Paul materializes at my side and grabs a handful of rolls. "Oh yeah, I am starving," says Paul through mouthfuls. I can't eat. I am too nervous.

"It's almost eleven. We should get going."

"Wait. What? Is it still yesterday?" asks Paul, taking another roll.

"Yeah, we have to be out there before midnight. It can dump anytime tomorrow, including the early morning," Luke explains.

"I never thought of that," I say, kind of sheepishly. How could I have I overlooked something like that?

"Good thing you have such a smart friend—but anyway, wake up the others."

It doesn't take long to wake everyone because no one had been sleeping that soundly in the first place. We all try to eat because we don't know when our next meal might be. However, like me, no one else has much of an appetite except Paul, who downs at least half of the rolls. Finally, everyone's awake and ready. Paul has his large axe strapped to his back so the blade is scarily close to his head. I have Zeleng's gun and my bow slung over my shoulder, and my sword and knife strapped to my belt right next to each other.

"Time to roll. Am I right?" asks Paul, who apparently thinks his pun is extremely funny and starts laughing at himself. I had never seen Paul like this, so I guess it might just be his way of dealing with stress.

"Yeah, time to go," says Marty, much more seriously. Marty has on his long cloak. His five-foot broadsword nearly scrapes against the ground as he moves towards the door.

Luke, who seems to have become the official Zeleng carrier, hoists Zeleng onto his back. Luke carries his sword on his belt, but I don't know how useful it's going to be without his hands free. Marty is the first to leave the room with me right behind him. We climb the stairs at a brisk pace and channel out of the inn into the dark streets of the midnight city. The streets are lit by an occasional window, but even most of those are dimmed by shutters.

We start our trek through the silent city, which, as we walk, reveals itself to not be so quiet. The sounds of hammered anvils clanging from multiple buildings mingle with shouts of men and women working. The city is different at night—not bustling with as many people—but the people who do bustle are not intent on friendly trading or bartering, but on darker activities. I hear the occasional scream, but try to block out the noise. I have enough problems on my own without trying to figure out other people's problems. I spot a man lying on the ground, huddled in blankets, clothes torn and hair matted with grime. The man repulses me and I step away as we walk, but he notices our passing by and lets out a croak.

"Help me, please." He rolls over so he is facing us, and his face is a sight I don't want to ever have to look upon again. In the fraction of a second before I turn away, I take in rotten, broken teeth, sunken cheeks and eyes that speak of pain and misery. I glance back at the pathetic man. He is such a hollow shell of one, that I barely consider him human. A second look into the man's eyes changes this. His eyes are so full of suffering that I can't pass him and do nothing. To pass another creature to whom you can easily give help is unacceptable no matter who you are. I pull a piece of rock bread from my pack and throw it to the man. One way or another, I no longer need this food. Tonight, I either am going to escape the Wasteland or die trying. In any case I can spare this food. The man reaches for the bread, cradling it in his hand as if it's the most beautiful thing he has ever seen. A crooked, toothless smile crosses his face.

"Thank you," he whispers. Even as we move on, I hope that the poor man with his rotted teeth is able to break the impenetrable crust of the rock bread, so that he may satiate his hunger. I also hope the food will help him and not just prolong his suffering.

We walk up a set of stairs. I can now see the wall that rings the city. Fires and guards are dotted along the walls at uneven intervals, protecting the city from outsiders, but doing nothing to help the many hurting citizens who live inside their walls.

"Will the guards let us leave?" I ask Marty, who is making his way across a walkway.

"They couldn't care less about stupid suicidal people who want to walk into the wilderness in the middle of the night and get eaten by volves. What they care about are people coming in." That didn't necessarily reassure me. We move on, our feet thundering on the wooden walkways in the silence. When we arrive at the wall we are met by a thick gate made of assorted metal pieces, wood and plastic. Above the gate is a small tower about the size of an outhouse. Flickering candlelight shines through the window, illuminating a masked face. There is a click and the man slides open a grate. He calls down to us.

"What is the meaning of this—an old man strolling along with a bunch of kids headed for a gate out of the city in the middle of the night? Are you crazy?" The man watches us through the eyeholes in his mask. "And you have a cripple," he says, noticing Zeleng whom Luke still carries. If Marty was offended by the old man's insult, he concealed it perfectly, and when he spoke, he didn't sound the slightest bit angry. "Just let us out of the city."

"Bossy, bossy." The man opens a door and exits the tower, walking along the top of the wall, which is quite thick, like a large sidewalk. He is dressed in a soldier's uniform with a volve leather mask and armored leather garments. He has a bow that is nearly as long as he is tall slung over his shoulder. It is so large—I wonder how it is possible that it had even fit into the small tower.

"Once I unlock it, you guys will have to help me push the door open," says the man, descending a ladder. When he reaches the bottom, he moves to a mound of latches and padlocks that secure the door. It takes him several minutes of cursing to find the right keys from his belt and unlock the door. When he does, he beckons to us to help him. Together we slide the massive door open. I get my sword ready, just in case, and we step out into the darkness. Would kind of suck to have come this far just to be assassinated by a volve the second we leave the city.

"I would wish you good luck, but there won't be any. See you later. Oh, but I guess I won't, because you're going to die," shouts the guard as we leave. On that positive note we move into the darkness of the night. It takes almost forty-five minutes to walk the two miles to the location that is roughly indicated for the Trash Craft's descent. I don't know if it is luck, but we don't encounter any volves or anything else that might want to kill us. If we have calculated correctly, we should be at the right place. The ground here is littered with trash, just like anywhere else. We build a fire and set up a ring of stakes in a very large circle around us. We attach assorted old food and soda cans, along with bottles and eating utensils, so when they are touched, they rattle, alerting us of an impending volve attack.

"I just thought of something," I say, "Won't we be right under the Trash Craft, and won't we get crushed?" It's an honest question, but the others laugh.

"Don't worry, I made sure that won't happen," says Marty, taking a seat on the ground by the fire. "Time to play the waiting game."

The rest of us sit around the fire. I pull the grenade out of the backpack and examine it. "It would really suck to have come this far and not even know how to use this thing, so I am going to try to figure that out right now."

"Don't accidently blow us all up, please," says Luke, moving away from me.

"I'll try not to." I look at the small screen on the metal sphere. The weapon is sleek and looks high-tech, even though it's just a sphere, like a demon turtle hiding in its shell, waiting to strike. That is probably one of the best analogies I have ever made. "On second thought, I am not risking it. If I accidently set it off now.... either it will kill me, or you guys will kill me."

And then I went blind. Light shines out of the sky so suddenly that I stumble back and heroically fall on my backside. I am glad it's too bright for anyone to see me.

I squint into the blinding glare. Above us, silhouetted against the dark sky, is a giant disk of metal—a Trash Craft.

"Zane, Zane, *the grenade now!*" shouts Luke, running towards Zeleng and hoisting him onto his back. The ship is silent, thanks to high-tech engine mufflers, but looms over us like a UFO.

"On it," I yell, jabbing my finger into the large button on the grenade. The screen blazes to life, but I can barely see it through the blinding glare of the light. I push another button and my heart sinks—no, my heart dies. The words

> **ENTER PASS CODE TO ACTIVATE TRACKING MODE AND DETONATION SEQUENCE**

appear across the screen in capital letters. Right below are seven blank boxes. This is not happening, I tell myself. There was no way I had come this far just to be missing a passcode for the grenade. This couldn't be happening. No matter how many times I deny it, the words still don't go away. I drop the grenade in defeat and let it roll away—it clatters to a stop several feet away. "You have to be kidding," I scream so loudly that my voice echoes through the land—the back of my throat is raw. Paul runs up to me. He looks first at me, then to the fallen grenade, and he seems to get the point. "What's wrong with it?" says Paul, talking so fast that he's almost incomprehensible.

"Passcode," I answer, and that one word seems to explain everything.

"No, no, no. We aren't going to make it. We aren't going to flippin make it." His words drive a spike into my heart. What he meant was that Zeleng wasn't going to make it.

The rest of us would live, but Zeleng wouldn't. All the hard work of the last few days, all the sacrifices we have made are all going to end in failure. The ship starts dropping its rain of garbage and it clatters to the ground in front of us.

Paul runs to the grenade and starts frantically entering codes, with no luck.

"It's useless, Paul, the keypad has letters and numbers and it's a seven digit long code. There are millions of possibilities." I am giving up and I know it. The others huddle around the grenade shouting at each other, but I just sit there on my butt where I had fallen, helpless to do anything. The Trash Craft finishes dumping and the ship's bottom panel closes with a hiss. Steam pours out of its engine as it slowly starts to ascend back into the sky, only foot by foot until it accelerates fully.

"A weapon so small probably wouldn't of worked anyway." My voice is thick with defeat. Laden with failure. Filled with sadness.

"There has to be a way," shouts Luke, running his hands through his hair. "Why didn't we think something like this might happen?"

"You guys screwed up—you massively screwed up," says Marty, slowly backing up from the grenade which Paul holds in his arms, still attempting passcodes. "I have come so far a second time just to have my hopes and dreams crushed again."

"Forget you!" yells Auburn. "Zeleng's dying and all you can do is think about yourself. I don't know why we even let you come along in the first place." I know Auburn isn't thinking about what he's saying. No one is—everyone is too panicked.

"Oh yeah, kid, you know how much I care about you and your little friends," says Marty. His face is twisted in rage. "I couldn't care less about what happens to you—I just need a ride out of here so I can continue my work in the Clean World." In the light of the ascending Trash Craft Marty's grin looks demonic and freakishly evil.

"What do you mean, your work in the Clean World?" I ask.

"I mean, I was placed on this land because I am a bloody criminal. When I was convicted, instead of putting my butt in jail, they sent me here to think about my actions. And you know what I did? I thought very hard about them—and all I could think was I must continue them."

"What exactly were you convicted of?" I ask. I am not about to admit it, but I am scared out of my mind. I had no clue what was happening, and all I could think about was how Zeleng was now going to die.

"Treason, supporting the revolution, fighting with the rebels, the whole list. I was helping the good side win, and you see where it got me." The grinning cheerful Marty I thought I knew was gone, replaced with a wild raging side that was so well concealed. "It's hell up there," says Marty, pointing a gnarled finger to the sky where the Trash Craft was receding, "and it's hell down here. Humans have a knack of damn'in themselves into a hole wherever they go, and it is just a matter of choosing between hell of the Clean World and the inferno of Earth. Up there is not the paradise you guys think it is—it's a dystopia." I can't think straight. My mind is muddled and doesn't want to believe what it's hearing.

"Sure—they have some good things up there—instant

communication, food surpluses, advanced medicine, blah blah blah. But just think—a society that is so corrupt they leave millions of people behind on this dump and never come back for them." The others are listening with a mixture of fascination and horror. I feel only the latter.

"What do you mean?" I ask, even though Marty is being one hundred percent clear. Marty's sword is drawn and he swings it back and forth carelessly. Paul stares dumbstruck at Marty, the grenade in his hand apparently forgotten.

"And now you guys have failed me—you were supposed to get me to the Clean World so I can continue the revolution started so many years ago."

"So, that whole thing about your wife was just a lie?" I ask, glaring at Marty. I back away from him as he moves towards me, sword drawn. I clutch the soft volve leather hilt of my sword so tightly that my knuckles turn white. My breath comes in short breaths and vision is turning red at the edges. All my combat training might just come in handy.

"No, it wasn't, and that's the worst part, they sent me here with my wife who already was ill, just so I could watch helplessly as she died. That's the kind of government that's up there—corrupt and evil. A bunch of power hungry tyrants." I don't want to believe him, but I find myself believing every word.

"My dad said that he worked for the NAWC—and my dad's a good person. He would never side with a government that is as evil as you say." I try to plug the ship that is my heart, so it won't sink any further, or, like the Trash Craft, fly away.

"NAWC is a joke—communism with a dictator tyrant

that is said to be 'elected' every four years, but actually shoots his way in with military power. And if your dad works for NAWC, then your dad is as evil as they get."

"My dad is not evil. He sent these packages to save my life, not exactly something an evil person would do," I argue. "Why would my dad send me the keys to reverse his punishment that was dealt out by NAWC if he thought they were so good?"

"His punishment?" Marty raises an eyebrow. "You say your dad was punished? For what?"

"Hacking NAWC. They sent me here as punishment for him." Marty looks at me curiously.

Your dad is lying ... unless he actually doesn't work for NAWC. Unless he works for the rebels, which would actually make sense." Marty appears deep in thought. "What is your dad's name?"

"Zenith," I answer. Marty's eye widens—he leans on his sword, either for support or out of habit, I can't tell.

"You mean the Zenith, notorious hacker for the rebel force. Also the one who stole valuable files on secret executions carried out by NAWC and made them public."

"What are you talking about? My dad would never work with you, and why would he lie to me about everything?" I think I hear the sound of feet or claws running across the trash. The last thing I need now is a volve attack, but then again maybe a quick end would not be so bad right now. At least I wouldn't have to watch Zeleng slowly die.

"Well, all Trash Crafts belong to NAWC. He might have been trying to protect you, so that you didn't think NAWC was the enemy when you boarded one of their ships." Marty fixes me with his contemplating stare.

"Guys, what you're talking about is revolutionary and all, but the Trash Craft is leaving," shouts Paul, who continues his work at the grenade. Sure enough the Trash Craft had risen another fifty feet, and it is not slowing down, but rather speeding up as the engine's blaze grows ever more intense, shining an even more brilliant blue. It isn't long now before the Trash Craft will blast up, accelerating so that it can exit Earth's atmosphere and be gone from this place forever. When that happens it will mean only one thing. Zeleng isn't going to get help and he isn't going to make it. I start to break down. I run to Zeleng. Luke stands next to Paul, but Zeleng lies in a heap on the ground, apparently where Luke had dropped him to help Paul. However, before I can reach them there's a shout and I turn around.

Running towards us from the darkness is a set of robes—a very familiar man with shoulder length black hair and a green lens covering one eye.

"Oh my god. It's Leon," says Luke in a stunned voice. Sure enough, Leon is sprinting towards us getting closer by the second, yelling and waving his hands above his head. I had never expected ever to see Leon again—one way or another—but here he is running through the wilderness towards us. "Missing something?" he shouts waving a small piece of paper over his head. "Need a passcode, possibly?" Hope surges through me and I shout with uncontained joy. Leon looks tired and sweaty but he doesn't stop running until he reaches Paul.

"Type it in!" I yell, rushing towards them. Leon hands me the sheet of the paper—written across it in a scrawling handwriting is:

Zane—the grenade has a passcode so that only military personnel can use it. The code is 9091231.

"How do you even have this," I ask, frantically punching in the code. My hands are shaking so bad it's a miracle I enter it correctly.

"That doesn't matter right now. I will explain later," he says through heavy breathing. "I just ran like two miles, couldn't talk well anyway."

With a final jab I enter the last number and the words

AUTHENTICATION SUCCESSFUL

flash across the screen. I had done it. No, we had done it. Immediately the grenade shoots into the air and off into the sky, propelled by thrusters that spew out blue fire. The grenade shot itself up into the sky. Fifty feet, then a hundred, then a hundred and fifty until it was just a speck racing towards the massive hull of the Trash Craft, which had risen another fifty feet. Then it collides and for a horrifying second nothing happens. Then there is the explosion, an explosion that contains no fire, only a storm of electric blue lights that dance over the ship's hull.

The arcs of energy dissipate, and for a second time nothing happens. And then the sound of an engine slowly powering off comes from the sky and the ship starts to sink slowly back down to earth as the engines try to operate without their computers to keep the ship aloft.

"Heads up," yells Luke, already sprinting away, with Zeleng on his back. Not wanting to be crushed, I run after him. There is a sound like an enormous boot crunching down as the Trash Craft touches down. It is not the loud explosive crash I had imagined. The engines had slowly powered off, perhaps a security feature, and in any case the ship had eased its way down before the engines had completely died and it came to rest on the ground. I turn around slowly. On the ground before me is the metal shape of the giant Trash Craft.

I let out a cheer and run back towards it. The ship doesn't appear to be damaged, just disabled. The lights inside the craft are out, and it sits there like a dead animal. The ship is so large I can't take it all in with one glance, or even a thousand, but what I can take in is a wall of metal that rises up in front of me like a massive tidal wave.

After each one of us returns from running for our lives in different directions from the falling metal ship, we meet back up for our final council in the Wasteland. Leon stands there quietly, but he looks as though he is on the edge of speaking. Knowing our time is limited I prod him.

"What's up, Leon," I say, looking him straight in the eye.

"I just think you should know. Arizon saved you, Luke. Your little sister discovered that essential piece of paper you overlooked in the package and left behind. Somehow she managed to convince me that I should chase after you with it. I was about 7 hours behind you the whole time. I took a direct route to city in hopes of catching up with you, but no such luck. I went to the map room and did exactly what you must of done. I only had twenty minutes to get here once I discovered this location, and I took the gamble that this was the Trash Craft that you had picked to ambush. I sprinted, and when I spotted you guys with my lens from a mile off, I could already see the Trash Craft coming down from the sky. According to my lens I ran a five minute and thirty-eight second mile getting to you guys. Not bad for an old guy I guess, but the true hero is your sister, never forget that," explains Leon. Luke looks as though he is about to crumble, and Paul doesn't look that much better. For the first time, I really appreciate what they have done to save Zeleng, and what Arizon has done to make it possible.

"I didn't want to leave her, you know," says Luke, "It was just for the best."

"I know," says Leon, "She didn't want to let you leave, but it was necessary for the final outcome of this mission. I will tell her you miss her, when I return. Time is short—the effects of the grenade will only last so long." Leon's calculating look is back.

Luke and Paul remain silent. "I never thought I would have to say a second goodbye to you, Leon, but here I am repeating it," I say.

"Agreed," answers Leon, and much like we had the first time, he first embraces me, and then Auburn and Paul. Then he turns to Luke and embraces him, with Zeleng still on his back. "Get this boy some help," says Leon, touching Zeleng's face. I never expected that those words would be the ones that would inspire me, but they do, and I turn back to the Trash Craft where, hopefully, that help resides.

"Well, I better be off. Who knows what the wagons have been up to. When I return it will have been six days. Who knows, they could have replaced me for all I know." With that, Leon turns and begins to walk away, back over the trash he earlier had sprinted on to reach us. I am about to turn away when Luke speaks up -

"Tell Arizon she's our heroine. Tell her that I love her

and that she's made her big brother proud. And Leon, take care of her and be there when I can't." Luke's voice cracks before he breaks down completely. His face sinks like the Trash Craft falling to earth. Leon gives a little nod in reply, a nod that Luke never saw.

※ ● ※

We initiate the plan that we had devised after I had read a small section that included a 3D model of a Trash Craft and all its moving parts. I had discovered a secret hatch that opened on the side of the Trash Craft from the outside and the inside. It was put in as a precaution to let stranded soldiers into the Trash Craft in case such a scenario came to play. It wasn't exactly top secret and the book did nothing to try to hide it, but in reality NAWC really didn't have to hide because before us no Scavenger had the means to access such information.

It takes five out of the thirty minutes we have to find the precise location of the hatch. Like the model on the tablet had said it opens even from the outside, revealing a door that seems to enter into the main body of the ship which is the part that holds the trash. From here a ladder leads up to the main body of the ship, but the ladder is a struggle. Luke, ever since hearing the news of Arizon's discovery and her ultimate salvation of our efforts, has resumed a hard resolve and unbreakable determination. He ties Zeleng to his back with all of our remaining rope and grits his teeth and begins to climb the forty foot ladder with an extra hundred and seventy-five pounds of dead weight, a feat I don't think I could have done. At the top of the ladder we push through another hatch and we enter a passageway.

Once inside the passageway, we walk single file down a narrow, low-ceilinged hallway, with barely enough room for our arms and legs. Rows of light strips snake across the ceiling, casting such a dim light that we can barely see. We have done it! We are on the ship! Now all we have to do is lie low until we get to the Clean World. In front of us there is a door, an airlock, I think, with a handle that looks like a steering wheel.

Marty puts his ear to the door and whispers. "Can't hear anything—that's possibly reassuring—but probably an ambush." For two reasons I had decided to trust Marty, even if he were a criminal. First, he is working with the same group as my dad, which would increase our chance of finding him. Marty would know where to go. Second, because, as usual, there is no other choice.

"We need to get through that airlock. Being on the wrong side of an airlock doesn't sound exactly healthy," I suggest in a whisper. The others nod, and I slide my hand across the wall as I move closer to the door. The metal is cold and hard—it sends tingles up my fingers. I raise Zeleng's gun, aiming it at the door. Marty turns the handle, apparently effortlessly. There is a small hiss, then the door swings open, revealing another set of corridors that seems much the same. It looks empty, but I take no chances and keep my gun aimed. Marty steps forward. He holds a dagger—about nine inches of deadly sharp steel, finished off with a hilt of leather that Marty wraps his fingers around. His sword is too large and bulky to unsheath, something that we quickly discovered once we had entered the hallways. Marty points his dagger forward, signaling us to follow as he steps into the next room. Luke, carrying Zeleng, follows me into the room, and Auburn and Paul bring up the rear. The only difference between this room and the last is a ventilation duct hanging from the already low ceiling. I hear the muffled click of Paul shutting the door behind us. We continue on. Every time someone's weapon clangs against the wall, or someone takes a loud step, I wince and silently shush them by bringing a finger to my mouth in the literally universal sign for silence. At that moment the light strips suddenly shine bright as they switch from emergency power from the back up generators to the bright glow of full power. Coming from somewhere at the center of the massive ship, the humming of an engine begins.

"Here we go," whispers Luke. I can't feel it, but I know we must be rising into the air. I am going back to the Clean World after almost fifteen years. I am headed not home, but to my new home, which is also my old home, or something like that.

"I never actually thought we would make it this far. We have actually done it," says Auburn, incredulously. I rest my back against the wall.

"I owe you guys an apology," says Marty, also resting against the wall. "I was blinded by anger. I didn't mean what I said. I do care about Zeleng. Just when I saw the Trash Craft flying off. It was too much to have come so far just to be thwarted once again by something as simple as a passcode."

"Dude. Don't worry about it. The important thing is that we made it," says Auburn.

All of sudden there is metallic click and the door at the

end of the narrow hallway swings open, revealing a man in an armored suit. I don't have time to get a very good look at him before he pulls out a sleek rifle and opens fire. I dive for the ground, expecting the sound of bullets to fill the air, but the only sounds I hear are hisses followed by thuds. I hear my friends yelling and scrambling around for their weapons. Unfortunately, the hallway is too narrow and cramped to put up much of a fight. I hear the muffled groans and the thunks as my friends drop. Marty, who is closest to the man, throws up his arms, shielding the rest of us. He is immediately hit first in the chest, then in the shoulder with long skinny darts. For a second Marty yells in pain, but his call is abruptly cut off as his eyes roll into the back of his head and he collapses to the ground. I hear darts whistling over my head and I devise the only possible plan I can think of. I crawl as inconspicuously as I can, which is hard to do because I am right under the soldier's nose. Somehow, I reach Marty's side undetected. I immediately reach for the dart in Marty's chest. I move my hand so slowly it appears my hand is frozen in midair. When my fingers finally close around the dart I pull it free. It takes all my willpower not to just yank the dart from his skin. Instead, I slowly pull the dart free, trying to ignore the sickening squelching sound of the dart leaving the skin. I roll over slowly—even as I do, I hear Auburn shout, followed by the sound of a falling body against metal. I ignore the urge to run and help the others. I raise the dart, hoping that my hunch is right and plunge it into my own arm. The sharp pain of the needle stings, but I don't remove it. Instead I pretend to go limp, the dart still hanging out of my arm. I hear another person fall, then another. Finally there is no sound at all.

"Mission Sedate is successful. Can I get the clean up crew in aisle nine?" The soldier's voice sounds muffled, and I know without looking that he is wearing some kind of a mask.

"They are already on their way," says a second female voice that sounds as though it's coming from a speaker. It's frustratingly hard to keep my eyes closed and my breath steady, but somehow I manage. All I can hear is the sound of my own breath and the soft footsteps as the soldier moves down the hall.

"Yep, they are all sleeping like logs, or babies rather," says the man.

"That easy? Hmmm," comes the female voice over the speaker again. I can hear the man right above me as he says, "Roger that, they were lined up and everything—all I did was knock them down." I feel the man stepping over me. I hold my breath—then remembering that I should be out cold and breathing steadily as though I am sleeping, I let out a long breath. A huge long, deep sigh rather. The man's footsteps stop.

"Hold on, I might have missed one," I hear the voice looming down towards me. Then, I feel a hand on my shoulder. I feel myself being dragged over onto my back. I try to control my breathing and remain limp. Several long, very tense seconds pass. I can almost feel the soldier's eyes boring into me. Then the hand lets go of my shoulder.

"False alarm. He is tagged in the arm." The footsteps move on down the hall. After about ten more seconds, other footsteps join his, and the sound of other voices fills the hallways. They sound relaxed, nothing like strict military personnel.

"The clean up group has arrived," announces a low voice. "Gather them up, take them to the control room and tie them up." More hands touch me and I feel myself being lifted off the ground. I let my head droop and my arms fall limp at my sides. I am not sure, but I think I feel the muscular shoulder of the soldier under my stomach. I feel the soldier moving and I bump up and down with his movement.

"Oh my, this one's missing a hand," says a voice that doesn't sound the least bit concerned. I risk a glance through my eyelashes. We are moving up a narrow staircase. I can feel the rise and fall of the man's breath beneath me—from the feel of it the man is quite large. After several minutes of silent walking he stops. I feel him take one hand off me. Several seconds later, there is a beep, and then the hiss of sliding doors opening. I hear more footsteps following us up the stairs. The room we enter is full of electronic beeps and the whirring of machinery. I feel myself being set down in a hard metal chair, and feel something smooth and sleek bind my hands and feet together, and then to the chair. I don't know if it's safe to open my eyes yet, so I pretend to still be unconscious.

"They're only kids," says the female voice, but this time it lacks the slight buzzing, so I assume this time it's her in person.

"Not all of them," answers the voice of the person who is carrying me. Unexpectedly, I feel my bound hands being wrenched up and the dart being yanked from my arm. The person who does it isn't exactly gentle—I feel my flesh tear slightly when it catches.

"We will have to stop for refueling on the moon station—engine is running low after that grenade explosion. Messed up the computers, maybe even busted a hole in the fuel tank." It's the woman's voice again. Her voice is clear, well enunciated, and sounds very professional, but there's something about it that I can't put my finger on, the same thing I heard in my father's voice and also Marty's. And about the moon station—I thought when the moon was nuked, that nothing had been rebuilt there. Apparently I was wrong.

"Yeah, but what are we going to do about these?" There is a brief pause. "Prisoners," he finally says.

"Keep them hidden and deliver them to the rebels," the women whispers. "These people didn't do anything wrong and I am sure as heck not giving them over to NAWC. They would probably be tortured for fun there." These people work on a NAWC Trash Craft, I think to myself, so why aren't they hurting us, and why wouldn't they turn us in? Questions like these bubble up inside me, clawing to get out, and it's all I can do to remain silent.

"GET OFF ME!" comes a shout from the other side of the room, followed by the sound of scuffling. That voice can only be Marty's. Well, if he's awake again, I can stop pretending to be knocked out. I open my eyes slowly and look around.

The room is large with walls that are cleaner and smoother than anything I have ever seen. On one side is a line of computer screens and control pads, all beeping and glowing. I have never seen technology of this quantity or this advanced—the site is almost overwhelming. I glance to the side and see the others. They are all slumped in chairs held up only by the restraints that bind their shoulders. Their eyes are closed and Auburn's tongue hangs out of his mouth, but the most amazing view is above the computers, where a large window dominates most of the wall. Outside is a dark void, peppered with tiny stars, and for the first time I understand the reality of the situation. We have escaped the Wasteland into the endless darkness that is space.

The sound of a beep makes me look towards the corner of the room where Zeleng lies on a gurney, tubes and IVs sticking out of his arm. He has a mask over his mouth. A soldier wearing a lens—somewhat like Leon's, but slightly slimmer, as though it is a newer model—stands over him, examining his arm.

"Is he going to be ok?" I ask, before I can stop myself. Every soldier in the room looks at me, but thankfully no one raises a weapon. The woman who spoke earlier—well I think that's who it is, because she is the only woman in the room—stands in front of me. She is dressed like the other soldiers in white body armor. Glowing strands of light flow like blood vessels all over the suit. She holds a sleek silver pistol with a cylinder clip that looks as though it contains some kind of blue plasma. When she speaks, her voice sounds stern.

"I don't know, our medic is trying to stabilize him right now, but we will need better equipment if we are going to save him."

"Where is this better equipment? He needs to live." I had hoped beyond hope that we could get him help immediately, but as it turned out, Zeleng is still not safe.

"At the moon station," explains the medic, who is

standing over Zeleng. "I put him on life support, and I am feeding him antibiotics and painkillers, but this arm needs surgery immediately. Why didn't you give him antibiotics earlier?" The man addresses me, looking me over with his glowing lens.

"Because, we don't have any antibiotics where I come from. Down there, if you get an infection, you die." My voice sounds much harsher than I had meant, but now that I have started I can't stop.

"Just because you have everything you need doesn't mean everybody does. Do you see him? He got his arm ripped off—he got it ripped clean off by creatures that you created." I point an accusing finger at the man, who stands there silently. "And ..." But before I can go on the women speaks again.

"We are aware of this, kid." The way she says kid, as though I am somehow lower than she, annoys me, and that condescending smirk that seems to be her trademark doesn't raise my opinion of her. "We know about the horrid conditions down there, and we can empathise with the dangers and hardships of life down there."

I nearly burst out laughing. "I can tell you totally care."

"May I remind you that we used darts instead of bullets? I could've ordered you to be killed, and I could have cast your bodies out into space and that would have been the end, but I didn't—so you better start showing me the respect the commander of this ship deserves." Her voice is calm, but irritates me more than anything. I want to walk over to her and punch her right in the face, and I would have, if I hadn't been securely bound to my chair.

"And ...," she continues, "Am I not trying to save your

friend? It looks as though he wouldn't have lasted much longer without my intervention."

I want to reply with a withering remark, but I realize she's right. "Okay, fine, why didn't you kill me, ma'am?" I nearly choke on the last word.

"If you know anything about NAWC, and I am guessing you don't, then you would know NAWC isn't the glorious, free country that it claims to be."

"I actually do know this. I was a rebel exiled to the Wasteland," says Marty, coolly. I had almost forgotten that Marty has been sitting two seats down this entire time. "I know how darned corrupt they are, believe me, but for Zane's sake, explain it all." He attempts to gesture towards me without the use of his bound hands. The effect is some kind of facial spasm mixed with a nod.

"I knew there was something about you. Exiled eh? I am also a rebel, secretly working for the government. I'll explain when they wake up," she says, looking at the others, who were still snoring in their seats.

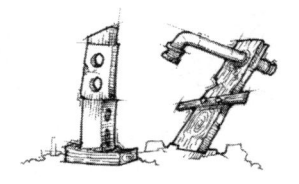

Thanks for Clearing That Up

It is about ten minutes later before the others come to. I sit in silence, staring off at the stars, literally spaced out. It's not much different than gazing at the night sky from the Wasteland, except that my old home is among the view, a dark sphere discolored with trash that I imagine had once been a beautiful green. No one speaks except the commander, who occasionally whispers things into her headset, 'commanding' people around. When everyone is sitting up straight in their chairs, she mutes the headset and turns her attention to her off-world guests.

"The corruption of the Earth's governments started long before we ever migrated to the Clean World. It was in a time of panic. Everyone was too blind to the reality of global warming and the scarcity of natural resources to ever be prepared for what happened. The Government had no idea what to do when the inevitable shortages of oil and natural gas occurred. People starved, blackouts covered huge sections of the world, and civil war broke out in almost every country. World leaders were desperate and helpless to reverse course. They formed the National

Alliance of World Crisis or NAWC. All funds and resources were redirected to space travel research and used to build an enormous fleet of escape ships called The Exodus—fifty thousand ships capable of holding nearly six billion people. The human population on earth at that time was 9.4 billion, despite the government's strict population control laws, leaving the weakest third to fend for themselves on a dying planet. NAWC didn't waste any more time or money building ships. Sixty percent of humans left Earth that year on their voyage to New Earth and the rest were left to die."

"Really? So NAWC just happened to have a perfectly habitable, back up planet to run to?" asks Auburn, clearly dubious. Up until then everyone had been listening silently, giving the commander their full attention.

"This planet had been discovered ten years before the world crisis, and ships had been sent out to explore it, but had only arrived four years previously to the Exodus fleets' departure, and once it was declared habitable and the signal had time to travel back to our ears, we began the fastest assemblance of the largest fleet of ships of any kind ever. Four years is all it took the world working together to build 50,000 ships. Imagine if we could have come together before things got so bad. Imagine if great progress and unity did not only arise when faced with such disastrous problems. We could have saved Earth, but now it is too late. Much too late." She paused a moment to let that sink in. I glance at the ceiling to avoid having to look into the commander's eyes. They blaze with such passion that they are hard to meet.

"Something doesn't add up. Are you saying you travel

interstellarly, to take out the trash?" I ask.

"The first and the last journey of the Exodus fleet took twelve years. To put that into perspective, nine million babies were born during this first fleet, and about twenty-five million elderly died of old age during it. However, that's not the case anymore. Recently, after arriving on New Earth, scientists discovered a worm hole that linked New Earth and Earth almost perfectly."

"What's a wormhole?" asks Luke, eyebrows raised, arched like miniature blonde rainbows above his eyes.

"It's two different places that are linked by bending space, first theorized by Albert Einstein. It now takes roughly forty-eight hours to reach New Earth," she explains, as though she had rehearsed this before, or had to repeat it on a regular basis, which seemed a little odd.

"Small time improvement, I guess," says Paul.

"For my entire life I have asked myself why the Clean World dumped its trash on Earth instead of just incinerating it in the sun or another star. Why bring it all the way to Earth?" asks Paul.

"Earth is a storage facility. We bring trash not only to dispose of it and keep New Earth spotless, but also to store the thousands of tons of scrap metal, and assorted resources that could one day be needed by New Earth. It is very likely we will never need the resources, but NAWC is being overly cautious and rightfully so. They are already responsible for enough horrible things, so they don't need to destroy the resources that might save us one day. Also, it is just more convenient to drop the trash on Earth. It's closer to the wormhole entrance. At times we also transport rebel prisoners to Earth where we can store them, without fear of them taking revenge." She gives a more detailed explanation than I expected, but no one points this out—instead, we continue listening.

"Anyway, the point is, NAWC abandoned over three billion people on Earth. When was the last time a good government condemned that many people to starve to death on a forsaken planet? But it doesn't end there. When we settled New Earth, NAWC set up a new form of government called the New Republic. This government was based around the idea of preventing anything like what happened to Earth ever happening to New Earth. In truth, it was a communist dictatorship. Sure, this new government has some good things; population control, guaranteed jobs, food and housing, but this government controls everything, and the citizens are turned into government-owned people, not that much better than slaves. Thinking for yourself and actually enjoying life are things of the past. This government treats people like batteries, for powering the machine they believe is the road to the absolute efficiency of a government that is desired. Can you now understand why I didn't kill you?"

"You don't seem much like a happiness-deprived battery slave," counters Auburn.

"I have it better off than most people. I spend almost all my time billions of miles away from government control. I don't know how to explain this to you without showing you. You will just have to believe me. I am a government commander with a high position, but I still believe NAWC is horrible. I don't know what more proof you need."

"She is right. It is horrible up there, and worst of all, most people don't even care. They do what they are told," says Marty. With Marty backing her up, I can't doubt the truthfulness of what she's saying.

"So, what are you going to do with us?" asks Paul.

"First, we are going to have to refuel on the moon station, where we will be arriving in a few minutes. Then we will enter the wormhole and head for New Earth. We will sneak you off to the rebels when we arrive." The plan didn't seem exactly thought out in detail, but did seem rather fool proof.

"Did I mention Zane's dad is Zenith," says Marty. He has a sneaky smile on his face, and a glint in his eyes. The commander stops in mid-sentence. She looks over to me wide-eyed, dark hair framing her face.

"What, why are you just now telling me this? That changes things. Guards. Unbind them." Four guards step forward from their posts and unquestioningly move towards us. The one that approaches me whips out a long army knife and brings it towards me in a long arcing motion. For a second I think he is going to run me through, but his arm is directed at the plastic ties that bind my hands. With a few quick slices the bindings fall away. I massage my wrists and stretch my arms for the first time in what seems like a very long time.

"So my dad is big stuff? His being my father is an instant respect boost." I realize I sound kind of stupid after I say it, but the commander just nods.

"He brought us closer to victory against NAWC than we had ever been before. I am not about to get on his bad side by imprisoning his son." She walks a few steps closer to the pilot, who still sits obediently in his chair.

"How?" I ask. My nose had started to itch really badly,

and it is a relief to finally scratch it.

"How what?" She gives me a questioningly look, and I quickly explain. "How did my dad make it possible for you to almost win?"

"The rebels were and still are a very small, underfunded group, but your dad changed that. He used to work for NAWC as a hacker. He was one of the government's most respected people. Of course, that was until he uncovered NAWC's darkest secrets while he was snooping around their database. He was horrified that he had ever helped NAWC. He immediately took the information to the rebels and we made it public as fast as we could. When people started to hear about it, revolution was in the air. Thousands and thousands of people instantly joined the rebels and millions more turned their backs on the government. The war lasted barely a month. Government troops slaughtered us rebels with secret biological weapons that, unfortunately, your dad hadn't uncovered."

"I thought you said that was the closest time you had ever come to victory. Sounds more like you got destroyed." It's Luke who speaks. Even though he is unbound, he still sits slumped in his chair.

"It was the first time the rebels actually took action. Before that we were all hidden away in bunkers and safe havens, too scared to show our heads in the fear we would get them blown off." She keeps talking, but her eyes are far away, staring at something none of us can see.

"Your dad brought us hope. He sparked the fire that will one day burn down the evil NAWC."

* * *

We have a good view from the window when the moon station comes into sight a few minutes later. It is an enormous metal structure against the impenetrable darkness. As we near it, I make out a ring of identical landing pads. Each landing pad looks like a tiny circle next to the massiveness of the tower, but judging that a giant Trash Craft can land on each one makes me finally realize how insanely large the station is. The station looks to be made of some kind of metal painted white that blends almost perfectly with the cratered moon rock that can be seen for miles on either side. It's sleek and high-tech like the Trash Craft we travel in, and makes me feel as though I have skipped hundreds of years into the future in a matter of hours. It takes us another minute to reach the station and to slowly land. The engine gently hums, and then comes to a complete stop. There is a small thud as the landing gear hits the landing pad. The second we land the commander looks at us, her face back to its emotionless mask.

"You guys don't have to move. We are only having a damage inspection and a refueling. And we are going to bring better medical equipment." I want to protest, but before I can say anything, she strides out of the room, her black hair flying behind her. Four of the guards follow her in single file, marching in unison out the door. It hisses shut.

Not one of us speaks—instead, we continue to stare out the window where a tunnel is snaking towards the ship. It gets smaller as it goes—each new segment emerges like a radio antenna. I expect to hear some kind of thud when the tunnel connects with the ship, but I hear nothing. I glance around the room and see that there are still three guards and the doctor in the room. Images of me attacking the guards and escaping into the moon station fill my thoughts.

I feel a hand on my shoulder. I look to the side where Marty is giving me what I can only imagine is a serious smile. "Don't try anything—these people are most likely good." I don't know if he read my thoughts, and I definitely don't know if it is reassuring.

"I know," I reply, raising a hand and prying Marty's hand from my shoulder. I walk to where Zeleng is. I am still wearing my metal boots and they clang loudly as I walk. I almost die with relief when I see Zeleng. His face seems to have regained some color and his arm doesn't look even close to as raw and swollen as before. It's a small improvement, but that was still an improvement. Since his injury, it had all been downhill, but now the tides have shifted. Zeleng just might be okay.

I can definitely tell this is not a state of the art medical facility. What I thought was a bed is actually a table, and the only medical supplies seem to come from a large first-aid crate. The crate is ajar and several tubes are coming out of it and into an IV in Zeleng's uninjured arm. Zeleng's injured arm is encased completely in some kind of high-tech cylinder that seems to be sterilizing and analyzing the wound. Auburn joins me at Zeleng's bedside, or tableside rather, and I see him let out a big grin. We stand there in silence looking down at our friend, who I had thought, surely, had no chance of making it.

* * *

The wormhole is literally a hole in space. We approach

it, and it as if looking through a window into a far off part of space that is trillions of miles closer than it physically should be. It is by far the most amazing thing I have ever seen in my life—it is so mind-blowing that the second after passing into it my mind seems to have forgotten how it looked when I entered it—as though the sight was so inconceivable that my mind didn't want to remember an event that seems so fundamentally impossible. For the first time I felt truly lost.

Being on a spacecraft should be fun—zooming through darkness at almost the speed of light through galaxies and stars. It's the experience people dream of having, but if the truth be told, it totally sucks, and after a while it's scary. I am one hundred percent trapped in a metal box and I am scared of colliding with an asteroid or losing oxygen and succumbing to a horrible death where my internal organs could explode and float off into space, scattered through the stars in a not so milky, milkyway.

Besides that, I am also unimaginably bored, I feel as though I am back on the barge, helpless to do anything until we arrive at our destination, and, in fact, helpless to do anything at all. I find myself sitting the hours away in my chair, staring at the wall, trying in vain to amuse myself.

Another problem—the walls are white metal, without a single flaw, mark, scratch or imperfection of any kind. Stupid of me, but I am already feeling homesick for my cluttered mess of a room back in the wagon, where life in the Wasteland is so interesting, so unique. I start to see the truth in what the commander said about thinking for one's self. Being creative now appears to be a thing of the past. I am already struggling with it—I mean, how are you supposed to find creativity in an almost empty room with blank white walls. Not that I am a doctor, but I diagnosed myself with homesickness, spacecraft sickness and deprivation of anything that is not uniformly manufactured.

Don't get me wrong. I am happy to be on my way to the Clean World, but also a small part of me wants to go back to the wagons and the life I am used to—the Zane way of life. Also, I don't like the commander either—sure she's a rebel and sure, she is on our side, but come on, humans are supposed to have more than one emotion and more than one tone of voice. However, the commander makes do with only one of each. She speaks with authority, but not a good authority. She is a commander, but that doesn't make everyone else of lesser value than she. What I am trying to say is, I will sure be happy when the last day of my journey on the Trash Craft comes.

I wake up to the pain in my back from the supposedly comfortable gel padded memory foam bunks. My blankets, sensing that I am awake, retract off my body—an annoying feature that leaves you almost no choice but to roll out of bed when you awaken. I push myself into a sitting position, legs dangling off the bed. Motion active sensors sense this movement and the lights flick on. Well, they don't actually flick on—instead they slowly grow brighter, allowing my eyes to adjust. Despite my homesickness for my room back in the wagon, there are some seriously cool things that I already couldn't do without.

The first of these is my shower unit. It's a floor to ceiling cylinder, equipped with water jets and self-scrubbing arms. It also acts as a self-doctor. In less than ten seconds it could take a painless blood sample, heart rate, and identify almost any sickness. When I had first used the shower I thought I had died and gone to heaven. Compared to the metal bucket I used for my baths back at the wagons, this thing is paradise. All you have to do is stand in it, and it will automatically clean you with massaging jets of perfectly heated water and soap. And the biggest thing is, there is soap in what seemed like an endless supply. The first thing I did when I had figured out the shower setting was to turn the soap settings from thorough coating to death by soap. I had been using so much soap that I even programmed in a rinse of lotion solution into my daily shower routine, just to counteract my rapidly drying out skin.

I feel as though I have been cheated my whole life. This is too easy. Life here is too easy. And from what the guards have said, this is low-tech military housing on a Trash Craft. If that is true, I can't even fathom what luxury living is. When I finish showering today, I move towards my 'washing machine'. Until I had first used it on that first day, I had no idea what it even was. It cleans my clothes for me, mends tears and damaged parts and folds them. Back at the wagons we don't fold clothes. We shove them into dressers and wash them a couple times a year, if at all. Again, I feel as though I am cheating, like this is somehow too easy. It's stupid, but life doesn't feel as rewarding when all your day's work can be accomplished by pushing a few buttons.

After retrieving my clothes and putting them on, I move towards the door. I grip the handle and slide it open. No automatic door for me. One of the guards had shown me a diagram of the Trash Craft and now I can easily navigate the ship. The ship has a very small number of actual human quarters. About ninety-seven percent of the ship is the massive 'trash can' as they called it. I start to pull myself up a ladder, but before I can climb more than a few rungs, there's a small beep in my ear, alerting me that I have a new message. The ear chip is so small and compact that I usually forget about it. The commander issued me one because it is ship protocol, or something. I hadn't been listening. I found myself doing that a lot, not listening to the commander. I use a voice command and the message starts to play in my ear.

"Zane, I suggest you get your butt up here. You won't believe what's just happened." The voice is clear and loud in my ear, and I recognize it as Auburn's voice. Auburn never used his ear chip, so I know it must be something big.

"Locate Auburn Muldrow," I say, not even bothering to enunciate clearly. The device already has a library of my pronunciations of words stored on its microchip that it has gathered from listening to my conversations over the last two days. Again, I am amazed at how fast I have adapted to this new way of life.

"Room 221," the voice says. "Would you like me to give you directions?" Another cool feature of the ear chip is that it has an automatic location reporting system like a GPS that is not limited to a single planet—another word that I hadn't even known existed until a few days ago, but was now a common acronym in my vocabulary. When I asked my ear chip to give me instructions to get back to the Wasteland on a particularly homesick day, it suggested that I use the nearest off-ship exit and take a right and continue that direction for nine billion miles.

I tell the ear chip that no, I do not need instructions, but thanks for asking. Then I make my way towards room 221. The number system in this place doesn't make sense to me, as there are only a few dozen rooms on the ship, but oh well.

When I arrive outside the room, Luke and Paul are already there. "Did Auburn message you too? I wonder what's up."

Luke and Paul are wearing matching metallic gray jumpsuits with the NAWC logo on them, an eagle with its claws eagerly wrapped around a planet and the ring of moons circling its head. Their hair is neatly cut and combed, a style that I had never seen on either of them until yesterday. I haven't got my haircut or new clothes, and I am not planning on it.

"Yeah, I got the message too," I answer, looking at the door in front of me. As if on cue, the door slides open and Auburn's face appears.

"You guys have got to see this." His voice is excited and he beckons us to follow him into his room. I don't immediately notice what Auburn's so excited about. His room is identical to mine with a bed, shower unit and blank white walls. Then I see him. Sitting in the pod chair in the corner, Zeleng, with his jagged black hair, his tan colored skin and his expression of joking confusion and sarcastic smirking that he used to have, now appears again. The only thing missing is his volve skin cloak, replaced by a hospital gown, and, of course, his hand and the lower section of his arm, which looks so much better.

It's been surgically cut at the elbow, removing the

horrible mess of bone and torn apart skin. Where his forearm should be, there is a metal socket, which looks as if a prosthetic arm could be attached to it. However, the most surprising thing is, that he is not only sitting up in a chair, but his eyes are open—something I haven't seen in days. I stand in the doorway for several seconds, too surprised to move. Zeleng slowly raises his head towards me and we lock eyes. He lets out a wide smile, and I do the same.

"Oh my god," comes Luke's voice from over my shoulder.

"Is there something in my teeth or something? This much staring is starting to make me uncomfortable," says Zeleng, with a grin. I want to burst out laughing or maybe crying, but I can't decide which one to do. So I just walk over to the bed and sit down right across from him. He is still grinning at me, but I notice now how his smile never reaches his eyes. His eyes are those of someone who has just gone through something traumatic—not quite focused, but full of pain. Not physical pain, because he is drugged with painkillers, but more of an emotional pain. I try to look past it and be happy, that, against all odds, Zeleng is alive and improving, but I just can't quite do it.

"You good?" I ask.

"Do you understand why that is quite literally the dumbest question you could of asked?" He speaks to me in a joking, slightly mocking tone, but there's nothing mean about it.

"Oh! I have no clue. Would you like to enlighten me?" I say, mimicking his tone.

"Let's see, I believe I got my bloody arm ripped to pieces by a volve and..."

"It's kind of a given that when an arm is getting ripped off, that it might be bloody." Wow, I am clever, I think. Zeleng just shakes his head at the floor, trying to hide his exasperated expression.

"Like I was saying." He throws his words at me and gives me an accusing look. "After I got my arm ripped off, my half dead body was dragged across trash and..."

"You weren't half dead, you were only missing an arm, that's more like one-eighth dead. Get it right," I say. This conversation feels good, it makes me feel somewhat normal again, I guess, because it is almost identical to the ones we had had back in the wagons when life wasn't so difficult. Correcting Zeleng had been a favorite pastime of mine, because it was usually easy to do.

Zeleng just ignores the comment. "I was dragged all over the place on a board and halfway through the universe, all the while being about this close to death." He holds up his thumb and index finger, holding them about a fourth of an inch apart. I am about to correct Zeleng, explaining how death happens to your body, so technically you can't be any physical distance away from it, but before I can, the door slides open and the commander walks in.

"Ahhhh! What graces us with the presence of the all glorious commander on this fine morning?" asks Zeleng, who is smart enough not to use a mocking tone with the commander, but it is basically implied. So, I guess she had met with Zeleng before we had, and explained exactly where his place on this ship was, which was smack down at the bottom—and she had most likely explained that even if she had saved his life, she would still have no regrets about chucking him into space if he annoyed her too much.

"I am just checking up on you guys, and informing you that we are going to be arriving early to New Earth." She gives Zeleng a withering glare, silently telling him to show her more respect. If anything, this only fuels Zeleng even more.

"Why not send one of your guards to talk to people as lowly as we are?" Yep, Zeleng definitely has a death wish.

"You were more tolerable when you were unconscious and not a constant annoyance. But no matter, I am trying to inform you of our plan."

"What plan?" asks a confused Auburn. He hasn't done much more than chuckle since I have started talking to Zeleng, so I assume he has already had a lengthy conversation with Zeleng before he had sent me the message.

"You didn't seriously think, that after all you have heard about NAWC, that you could just waltz off a Trash Craft that you weren't authorized to be on—undocumented human beings from another planet, one that we are forbidden to even have contact with, and then be free to roam around our planet unvaccinated without anyone raising an eyebrow?" She definitely had worked out that line before coming to talk to them, her smug smile giving it away. Technically it wasn't a smile, because from what I have seen, it was physically impossible for the commander to smile, but it is as close to one as I have ever seen on her face.

"Oh," is Auburn's only response.

"The plan is a simple one. Guard." At her command a guard steps into the room with an arm full of neatly folded gray soldier uniforms. The guard is tall with a bald head so shiny that even the dim blue light of Auburn's room reflects off it. He reminds me of a butler and I can already see why this was the commander's favorite guard.

"As you see here," she said, palms outstretched to the guard. "We are going to disguise you as guards and escort you to a rebel bunker."

"That seems just a bit simple. Will it work?" I ask, walking over to get my own uniform. When the Guard drops the smooth fabric into my hand, I feel how light it is.

"I should be able to program your fingerprints and retinal scans into the security system so you don't throw up red flags at the first security checkpoint, but they will quickly find the breach, so we are going to have to hurry." She stares at us, one by one as we take our uniforms, except for Luke, who also grabs one for Zeleng.

"How will we know where to go or what to do? This is a completely different planet than what I am used to, and have you told Marty yet?" I already knew the answer to the last question. Marty had been spending huge amounts of time in the control room discussing things with the commander and her guards. I don't understand why Marty actually chooses to talk to the commander, but I guess it's because she treats him more like an equal than anyone else. The whole fellow rebel thing must help.

"I will come with you and lead you to the safe haven."

"Wait, won't you lose your job? Or at least get deranked? You're willing to do that for us?" I ask, kind of surprised that she would be willing to do anything for, as Zeleng said, lowly folk like us.

"Please, quit with the questions and let me explain," says the commander. Did the commander just say please, and that look on her face, is it lacking the usual stern glare?

Is it possible that I was completely wrong about her?

"Cease your nonsensical inquiries and just listen." Never mind, it is still the commander I know—false alarm.

It's a surprise the commander doesn't bore us to death in the ten minutes it takes her to describe the plan. Even in her boring monotone, the plan is exciting enough to keep us on the edge of our seats and, in my case, edge of the bed. She doesn't even bother to stress how dangerous it is going to be, but by the time she is finished, I am scared out of my mind. I shouldn't be scared after all the things I have been through. All the times I have fought volves, all the times I nearly died and all the other dangerous things I had been forced to do on my trip to the Clean World, but somehow this plan seems even more dangerous. I think it's because it is life-threateningly dangerous every step of the way.

* * *

The uniform fits me perfectly and I wonder how the commander knew what size to get me. The entire thing is skin tight and made of some kind of flexible plastic. Like Luke and Paul's jump suits, it has the NAWC crest threaded into the chest with golden threads. I haven't had a chance to look closely at it before this point. The eagle sits, perched on New Earth, its claws wrapped around it to a point where it is almost piercing the planet. The meaning to me is clear. We destroyed one planet but we have another in our clutches and at our disposal. The eagle's neck curves down towards the planet, its head surrounded with the moons. The symbolism is clear. We also have a belt of moons at our fingertips, or in this case, beak tip. I don't know why the crest bothers me so much. I shouldn't mind that it's scrawled across my chest, but I do.

The arms and legs of my uniform are a slightly darker gray than the rest of it, except for a dark, almost black gray that runs in two lines down each side of my chest. The uniform doesn't appear to have any armor or kevlar padding in it. For the plan tomorrow, I wish it did. After examining every inch of my new clothing, I go to the gel pod and sit down. Anytime now a voice will ring in my ear informing me of our arrival and the beginning of the plan. I start feeling nervous, so many things could go wrong, and our entire journey could come to an end before we even reach the end. I sit there, thoughts whirling through my head, and for the first time since stepping foot on the Trash Craft, I am not having trouble creatively imagining things, even if those things are the many ways I might die in the next few hours.

We stand in a semi-circle. I am the farthest to the left, almost crammed against the wall. Everyone else is here—Luke, Marty, Paul and Auburn, and even Zeleng, who has healed enough to stand with the help of Auburn. They all have expressions of anticipation or fear, except Zeleng, who, in spite of himself, has a somewhat forced grin on his face, showing that, of course, he is happy to go into a potential fire fight with one arm. The commander stands cross-armed in the middle of the circle, staring at each of us in turn. She wears a uniform similar to ours, but hers definitely looks as though it belongs to someone with important status, or at least status more important than ours. It has more stripes and is a lighter color. She speaks, "Listen up, you guys are going to have to act like soldiers.

Just don't say anything stupid and definitely don't call attention to yourselves. We don't have much time before people notice that our group is six too large. What I am trying to say is, don't screw it up for yourselves."

"Another positive pep talk from the almighty speaker of truth. Oh how enlightening it was," says Zeleng, who seems to have no fear of the commander's wrath.

"That's exactly what I don't want you doing. A soldier disrespecting a commander will not go unnoticed," counters the commander, who, like always, has thought this out before hand.

"Oh," says Zeleng, not embarrassed at all.

"You're going to want to get a gun and some armor. We don't need you guys getting blown to pieces." She sounds as though she almost cares, but almost isn't good enough. I, myself, definitely care. I am all for anything that gives me a better chance of survival. I rush forward to get my firearms. The guns are laid out in a neat row on the table that Zeleng had occupied that first day. I reach down for a gun and wrap my hand around the handle's rubber gripping. The gun is short and kind of stocky, like a mix of a pistol and an automatic rifle. A blue cylinder pokes out of the bottom like all the other clips I have seen on modern guns. When I lift the gun off the table, it's heavy enough that I have control, but not so heavy that I have to drag it behind me like so many of the guns from the Wasteland.

I swing the gun up into a firing position and point it at a blank wall. I am already getting a feel for this high-tech death machine, even though it's nothing like my bow.

"We do not have the time to train you into master sharpshooters, or to train you at all. The guns are mainly to symbolize that you guys are true soldiers, and not a group of kids hitchhiking from one planet to another, but I wouldn't be surprised if you actually have to use them."

The commander says it matter of factly, but her words make the gun in my hand feel different. I am going to use this gun to kill people, real living people. I had had a hard enough time killing volves, but to kill a human being seems out of the question.

"It better not come to that," I say, but even as I do, I know that it will. I am going to have to kill people no matter if I want to or not.

Next I pull on the armor vest. The vest is arranged in an octagonal theme, with two octagonal chest plates, and octogonal shoulder armor. It's light enough, but I still feel weighed down and constricted by it. I pull on some arm and shin guards. When I am done I step back and let the others access the table. I watch them pull on their own armor—their faces don't show their thoughts and I wonder if anyone of them is having thoughts similar to mine. No one, not Auburn, not Zeleng, had ever had as much of a volve killing problem as I did. Are they thinking of the people that they might have to slaughter as feral genetically modified killing machines? To them are they just another volve?

I notice Zeleng struggling to get his vest on with one hand. I notice how unsteady on his feet he still is. When I move over to him he looks to me with a grateful expression.

"I wish I had a shank or something I could replace my arm with so it's not totally useless." He laughs a little at that and looks at his metal stump. Apparently the commander had overheard him, because she walks over to us with a long blade in her hand.

In usual circumstances, if the commander was coming at me with a blade in hand, I would run away screaming, but when she approaches, I stand there at Zeleng's side.

"Luckily I was thinking about you and had a guard make you this." She holds up the blade—nine inches of razor sharp steel finished off with a modified handle that looks as though it will fit into the socket in Zeleng's arm. Zeleng gives the commander an incredulous look, as if trying to say 'after all my annoyingness, you would do something like this for me'? However, the expression doesn't last long. He adopts one of his sarcastic faces again and takes the knife. The commander is holding the knife by the handle, so when Zeleng reaches for it, let's just say he nearly lost his other hand. After some tricky hand maneuvering Zeleng holds the blade. After a few more seconds there's a small click, and all of a sudden Zeleng has a dangerously long knife for a hand.

"Let's just hope I don't forget and try to pick my nose with this," says Zeleng. I chuckle, and Zeleng bursts out laughing as he fakes stabbing a sword through his face.

Zeleng walks overs to Luke and Paul, who stand a little bit away, clad in gear with guns in hand. Zeleng walks right up to Luke and holds out a hand. "Good morning Luke." It takes a few moments for Luke to realize what's going on, but when he does, he starts laughing along with the rest of us.

"Luke, it is polite to shake hands when someone greets you. You don't want to be impolite, do you?" Zeleng pushes.

"Which would I rather do, be impolite or have my hand slashed to ribbons? Let me think." He scratches his head. We can't help it. By now everyone is laughing. It's so good to have Zeleng back that I just take a moment to soak it all in and be happy.

The commander brings us back to reality with a commanding voice. "We are arriving now. Start to act like soldiers." That shuts us up pretty quickly because it reminds us of what's to come.

Outside the window I can see New Earth, an enormous sphere of green and blue. I have seen maps of Earth from scavenged science books and atlases that we had in the wagon's small library. From what I can recall, Earth looks very similar to New Earth. I guess all planets that can sustain life must look somewhat alike. They all have to have certain things such as water and vegetation. The planet that is before me is an almost solid planet of green dotted by a number of lakes. Unlike Earth, there seems to be no massive bodies of water, no oceans or seas, but only tons of lakes. Rivers scattered like veins stretch across the whole planet.

I stand admiringly, my face almost pressed against the glass. The planet grows larger as we get closer until it takes up the entire window. It takes no more than a minute before we are descending through bright fluffy clouds. They are so clean, compared to the ones back on Earth, that I want to reach out and touch them. We break through the clouds. A bright clean light streams through the window, and I get my first closeup view of New Earth.

Sprawled below us is a gigantic city bordering an even bigger lake. Skyscrapers rise into the sky—from this height they look like the spikes on some enormous beast. After another minute we are close enough that I notice that we are heading to the center of the city where a giant building stands. The building is split into quadrants—in three out of the four of those quadrants is a neatly parked Trash Craft. An unexplainable feeling overcomes me as we near the landing platform. It hadn't really struck me until that moment that we are actually about to land on another planet—the heavenly paradise that so many generations of scavengers had only ever dreamed of reaching. The feeling is exhilarating and I press my face even closer to the glass. The landing pad below us is all I can see out the window now. Like on the moon station, there is a loud thud as we touch down. However, unlike the moon station, no moving tunnel comes to get us. Instead a ramp descends from the entrance.

"Ready?" asks the commander, who is standing in the open door. "Form ranks and let's move." We all form two lines of six and start to briskly exit the ship. The first thing I notice as I step off the ramp is the rush of air that rustles my hair. The air is so clean, so fresh, and so sweet, that I stop for a moment, just to breathe some in. Never in my life have I smelled air so sweet. I guess that's not saying much coming from a kid who grew up in air that always held the smell of rot and other horrible things. Even on the Trash Craft on the way here it hadn't been this amazing. This air was truly clean and oh, is it nice. Marty is the only one of us who doesn't seem affected by the air. I guess because he has experienced it before.

The commander glares at us until we start moving. I see a door about one hundred feet in front of us. I have no clue what we are doing, but I do know that door is our first destination. So far I haven't seen a soul, not even a soldier, but I know that will change once we get inside. I look to the others, dressed in their soldier uniforms, all looking professional, that is, except Marty. Marty is just a tad too wide to pass as an athletically fit soldier. I start to get nervous. What if someone notices him and runs a search on the fake file the commander had made of him? I can only hope no one does until we are far away.

Zeleng smiles at me, but even I can tell it's a struggle. The door is only twenty feet away now. I try to control my breathing because I am starting to lose my breath to fear. I am out in the open, trying to hide from all of my enemies right in the middle of their own base. I let out a deep breath. From behind me comes a giant crash, followed by smaller clings and clangs and the fresh air is replaced by a much more familiar smell. Trash. The sound reverberates off the building and the metal landing pad and the sound is almost excruciatingly loud. A memory sparks in my mind of Zeleng, Auburn and me running just ahead of a storm of trash. Had that really only happened a few days ago? I am about to look around when the commander whispers.

"They're refilling the Trash Craft, don't look around. Remember you're supposed to have seen this a million times, soldier." I think about what she said. Did regular soldiers feel good right now? Were they happy to be back on solid ground? Did they feel like voyagers returning from a voyage into space? Surely they didn't feel as I do as I walk towards that door, scared, exposed and lost. We reach the door and the commander swipes a card to open it.

The door slides open and I notice, with a gasp, that

it's almost a foot thick. No breaking this thing down. The commander steps inside and I have no choice but to follow. I take yet another deep breath, and step through the door. When we are all inside the door slowly slides shut behind us with an ominous thud. A pit begins forming in my throat, sinking into my stomach, burning a fiery trail as it goes. I have just been trapped inside a glorified cage with people who would kill me if they figured out who I am. I feel as though I am stuck in a cage with a pack of volves just waiting to be spotted and torn to bits. This place is definitely somewhere I don't want to be. I gulp and look around.

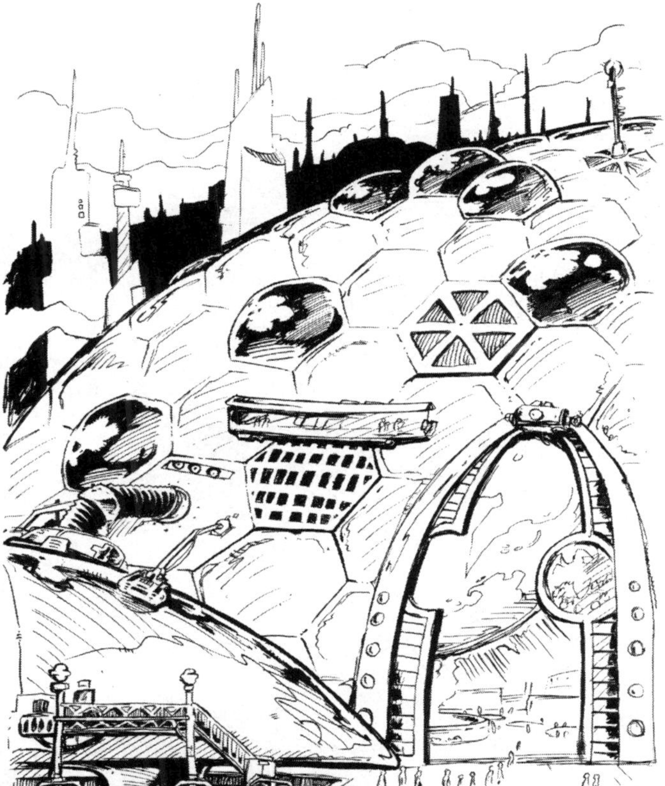

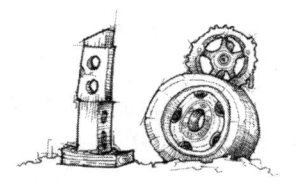

Volve Cage Rage

The room we stand in is enormous. The ceiling soars above us, curving towards the center in a giant dome. So much for being stuck in a cage, I am stuck in an egg. We are standing on some type of overhang that runs the entire length of the wall and looks down into the center of the buildings where curved rows of computers sit on tables. In the dead center of the room is a holographic globe. People are crowded around it, spinning it and zooming in on it—some type of super high-tech 3D map of New Earth, I guess. In normal circumstances I might have been intrigued by this, but these are definitely not normal circumstances, and I don't spend long thinking about it. Instead, I continue to look around the room.

Above us light shines through giant skylights that curve with the building's dome shape. Windows are something I have never appreciated before. Back in the Wasteland, windows are made of melted glass fragments and are almost always impossible to see through. They don't have much more purpose than to seal a hole in the wall. However, these windows are so perfect I feel as though they are not there at all.

"Welcome back," says a low, but controlled voice from somewhere close by. I glance around almost frantically for the person who spoke. I remind myself to play it cool. We just have to get out of this building and then we will be safe.

"Thank you. It's good to be back and it is good to see you, Pierre," comes the commander's polite voice. Seeing as she is being polite, this Pierre fellow must be her captain or something. I get my first glimpse of the man walking up the curved stairs towards us. His booted footsteps ricochet off the walls and echo into the depths of the massive room. For the first time it hits me how quiet it is. Besides a few hushed conversations from the people standing around the globe, there is no sound at all.

Pierre wears a uniform that is very similar to the commander's, but his has even more stripes and some official looking badges. The man is about six feet tall with a fair complexion. His hair is perfectly slicked back under an important looking flat topped hat—the type captains wear. I decide to refer to him as Captain Pierre. He stops a few feet away from us. For a moment all he does is stare at us contemplatingly. His expression is unreadable, but there is definitely a questioning rise in his eyebrows. Beads of sweat form on my head. I have to remind myself to breathe.

"Just thought you should know the refueling crew wants to inform you that your soap usage has been exceptionally high this trip." He gives the commander a smug smile. The commander takes just enough time to glare at me before answering. "How odd, maybe there was a leak or something," she says, with an almost undetectable hint of sarcasm. Captain Pierre's smile changes into more of a line than anything.

"I highly doubt that, but I will inform the crew to run a scan." I can hear the suspicion in his voice now and I can see it in his eyes. The real question is if he is suspicious about the soap or us, or is he putting two and two together, and slowly figuring us out. The way he looks at Auburn and Marty makes my skin crawl.

"Well, if you can excuse us, we are going to go get a bite of fresh food to eat. Tired of that trashy food, you know." Her voice wavers a bit as she tells the excuse, but it's almost undetectable.

Captain Pierre's suspicious look is clearer than ever, but he just walks away. I let out a breath I didn't know I was holding.

"Let's move, he won't let this rest." The commander leads us down a set of curving stairs off the overhang and onto the flat stretch in the middle. I glance around—a couple of soldiers salute the commander. Friendly enough, but I can't help glancing at their pistols, holstered on their hips or sitting on their desks. I rest my hand reassuringly on my gun. I have never shot a gun like this before, and I don't like my chances in a firefight, but I am glad that at least I am not defenseless.

We come to a door in the wall. Again the commander swipes her card and the door slides open. The room that is revealed is absolutely tiny compared to the one we had just been in. Before I can figure out what's going on, I am crammed into the room by Auburn who is being pushed in by one of the guards. The doors shut, enclosing us inside. Why the heck are we being locked into a room that we can barely fit in? That thought is just passing through my head when the floor drops. I clutch the walls.

"What the heck is going on? Zeleng, be careful with that arm. I prefer not to be impaled," says Auburn who, like me, is clutching the wall. The descent continues.

"We are riding an elevator. That is all." The commander's tone suggests that it should be obvious.

"And what exactly is that?" asks Zeleng.

The commander lets out a little exasperated sigh. "Mental note—take stairs next time." She gives no further explanation. The thing called an elevator comes to a stop and, with a beep, the doors slide open, revealing another giant room. Counters run the entire length, manned by an army of men and women in white suits. If all this place is, is a garbage disposal building, why is it swarming with people wearing casual attire. We start our considerably long walk to the doors at the far end of the room. A new round of nerves strikes me, and I try to calm myself. We have almost done it. All we have to do is get to that door undetected. The crowd is thick, but not impermeable, and I follow the commander. She walks at a brisk pace, but every part of me wants to go faster. I want to break into a run and sprint towards the door, but somehow I just keep walking.

People brush against us. A man wearing a pair of thick glasses, that he controls with voice commands to display different images in the air in front of him, steps on my foot, but upon seeing I am a soldier, he quickly apologizes. The door isn't far now, and a familiar feeling overcomes me. And no—it isn't fear—it is the same feeling I felt when I first stepped on the Trash Craft and the first time I had stepped off it. It is the feeling of accomplishment. I tell myself that we haven't done it yet; there is still ten feet to the door. Things could still go horribly wrong.

It happens when the sunlight streaming through the doors hits my face, and an orange warmth spreads through my body. However, it's short-lived, as a shrill wail cuts through the quiet den of talking. At first I am disoriented, standing half dazed, trying to figure out where the ear-grating noise is coming from. It doesn't last long, and just like the warmth I had felt seconds earlier, it vanishes before I can really think. The commander and her guards break into a full sprint, and without thinking I follow. The commander shoves people out of the way and I follow the path she creates through the crowd.

Two guards in matching uniforms, with matching pistols, stand blocking the exit, listening intently to their headsets. One is much taller than the other, with black hair and dark gray eyes. The other has blonde hair cut short, and bright blue eyes. Their appearance is the least of my worries right now. Thoughts that this is the end swirl through my head, blocking out everything else. The guards are going to stop us, or we will have to fight them. Best-case scenario—we kill the guards without injuring ourselves. I prepare myself to fight, finger on the trigger of my gun. I see the commander and her guards also raise their weapons, and I see the determination in their eyes. I take a deep breath to get ready for whatever I might have to do.

Apparently I was wrong about the best-case scenario, because an even better one emerges. As we cover the last few feet to the door, the guards give us a confused look and just wave us past. They must not know yet what the alarm is for, and they might even think we do, and are rushing off to the cause—and technically they are right, because we are the cause. I am grateful for that, but I keep running so fast I barely register my surroundings. The gray of stone and metal, the glint of light reflections off giant glass buildings, large vehicles, and the occasional patch of green are all I glimpse out of the corner of my vision. The rest of my sight is on the commander, who charges ahead to a vehicle. It's a large truck with armored plating and the NAWC logo painted across its side. It has at least twenty massive wheels and looks like it could run over an entire pack of volves—no problem. A guard sprints for the driver's seat and opens the door with a fingerprint scanner.

"In here," shouts the commander and I notice the others filing into the rear of the truck through the back doors. I move to them and help Zeleng, who is having trouble getting in without the full use of both hands. I start to climb in when the first gunshot goes off. The sound isn't like any of the guns I had fired in the Wasteland. Those sounded like mini-explosions, but this gunshot is much more controlled, and much more calculated, the sound of an accurate killing machine.

The gunshot shocks me into reality. I am being shot at. Any second now I am going to feel the pain of what I imagine a shot from one of the guns feels like, and I am going to drop to the ground. It is simple, really, so why am I still so confused? The massive truck starts to move and I run behind it. Strong arms grab me and pull me into the truck as the door slams shut.

The sounds of bullets slamming into the door, a fraction

of a second after it shuts, creates an almost constant barrage of ear-splitting noise. I slump against a wall and gasp for breath. Sweat runs down my face, but I find myself shivering. The truck picks up speed, but it does nothing to lessen the rain of bullets clattering against the armor of the truck. I am very thankful to be protected by its armor. A screen positioned on the wall shows the view from a camera on the rear bumper. When I look I see we are being pursued by at least four other identical trucks. On top of each truck is a mounted gun, each looking capable of shooting down a Trash Craft. The trucks take turns firing at us.

"What the hell! Why am I risking my life for a group of kids," shouts the commander. Sweat pours down her face and she is breathing hard.

"The better question is why they are sending four military armed trucks through a public area to stop a bunch of kids," counters Marty, his one good eye locked on the screen, a look of furious thinking furrowing his brow.

"It's NAWC—they're in charge of this entire planet. They can do whatever they want and they ...," the commander trails off as though she had just thought of something horrible.

"And," shouts Zeleng, "Speak, woman!" The commander doesn't even react to Zeleng's frantic words or the unintentional rudeness they carry. After losing an arm, traveling millions of miles with an infected wound, and to top it off, being shot at, let's just say he isn't holding together too well.

"They can shut us down." The commander's voice is soft, almost inaudible over the gunshots. She continues to stare at the screen, but she doesn't seem to actually be looking at it.

"Shut us down? What do you mean?" asks Auburn, who is sitting in one of the benches, rubbing his eyes. He seems to be holding together much better than Zeleng or me. His voice is calm and controlled, with only the smallest hint of panic.

"Once they pinpoint what truck we are driving, all they have to do is disable manual control and drive us back to them. It's a safety mechanism in case something like this ever happens." Her voice is soft, but it causes much more fear than shouting ever could.

"Oh shit, then we gotta get out of here before we are zooming back to them." says Luke, pointing at the doors with his gun.

"Thanks. I didn't figure that out for myself." Either some of Zeleng's sarcasm has rubbed off on the commander, or it is a side we have never seen before. "And, as a bonus, we can get blown to pieces."

"Shut up. Everyone shut up." I am surprised at how loud my voice is. Either out of surprise or fear, everyone shuts up. And all the eyes, whether they are the hardened ones of the commander and her guards, or the fearful ones of the rest of us, turn to stare at me. I would have felt self-conscious under normal circumstances, but fear is the only emotion I seem to have today.

"We determined we only have one choice, so what's there to argue about. Let's do what we have to! I haven't come this far to die." I don't know if what I am saying is helping, or if I am just reinforcing the obvious, but I continue on. "Let's back up into a building and make a run for it through the buildings, where we will have some cover." I haven't really thought out the plan but I don't see any other options.

"That's genius. They will have no way to shoot at us, commander." Marty looks at the commander for approval.

"Let's do it! Quick!" Her voice carries through the entire truck. The bullets continue their barrage on our vehicle as the commander relays the plan to the driver.

"Sure. We have some big ass guns and we have revenge on our side, but we also know how to run like hell when we need to. I feel like we are no match for NAWC, so get ready to run like hell," says Luke.

The seconds pass slowly and I find myself holding my breath. Any second the driver could lose control of this vehicle and we will lose every chance of escape. The truck is moving so fast and so crazily that standing up is hard to do without falling over. Suddenly there is a skid of brakes, and I am thrown against the wall as we make a giant turn. Just as I am sliding down the wall there is a colossal crash of stone cracking and metal grinding. For a panicked moment I think that it has happened, that they have taken control of our truck and that everything is lost.

Then the commander shouts and flings open the doors. After climbing to my feet, I run after her, gun raised, I see that we are in some kind of parking ramp. Support beams about two feet wide fill the room like trees, with just enough room between for cars to park, or a scared felon to sprint through. I look back at the truck as I sprint after the commander. Poking into the building from a hole in the wall is the back of the truck. Bricks are scattered everywhere.

"This has bought us a little time, but we have to get from building to building before NAWC barricades the exits. The rebel bunker is close now," shouts the commander through gasps. No one replies—the only sounds are our pounding feet.

We arrive at a set of stairs and begin to scramble down them, five at a time, falling more than anything else. The sounds of shouting and a new group of footsteps can be heard close on our heels. Bullets ring out as we reach the first floor. I am glad for the many support beams, which make a clear shot almost impossible. The commander returns fire as we push through the doors at the bottom of the ramp. We return the fire. We are in a firefight, and someone is going to die, either us or them. I am not sure which I would prefer. Yes, I want to live, but would I kill for it?

We emerge into an alleyway for only a second before pushing into the next building. The group of NAWC guards is definitely gaining on us. Sirens wail from outside and I gasp for breath so hard that my chest aches. We have burst into some kind of long hallway with doors every ten feet or so. Panic clenches me. When the guards follow us in here, they will have a clear shot at us down the straight hallway. We better be out of here before that happens. The thought makes me run faster even though my legs burn and my vision is obscured with exhaustion and sweat.

At the end of the hallway there is only a large square window, but no door. Without breaking stride the commander raises her gun and lets out a quick succession of bullets that shatters the window into a cascade of glittering glass. The commander dives through it, closely followed by her guards. Just as I reach the window, I again hear gunfire, but this time it isn't from the commander or anyone in our group. Bullets fly by my head, narrowly missing multiple times, creating a whistling of air so close to my ears that I nearly scream. I dive through the window. The jagged edges of glass would have ripped me to shreds without the armored vest. I land on my back and fling myself up. I take a sharp left, following the others. We are now in some kind of courtyard, well tended, with beautiful flowers that in the Wasteland we could only dream of— whites and reds and purples—colors that are rarely seen in the brown desolate landscape of the Wasteland. It doesn't take much looking around to see that the only exit is a metal staircase that wraps its way up the building to the top floor about hundred feet above.

"Climb," shouts Marty somewhat needlessly, but no one points that out, most likely because everyone is breathing too hard to utter anything but panting gibberish. The commander sprints up the stairs directly in front of me and I follow. The feeling that fills me is utterly terrifying. Any second now the NAWC guards could reach the courtyard and begin picking us off. All I want to do is look behind me and see if they have, but I can't, without slowing down and breaking my stride. Instead, I look at the steps flying by under me, waiting for the sound of a bullet or the sharp pain of a bullet piercing my skin.

I climb and climb and climb. Powered by my fear and adrenaline, I scale the stairs faster than I could ever have done otherwise. The top of the building is only one flight away, when the expected sound of bullets clang against the metal stairs below. So far our group has managed to stay ahead just enough to always be around the corner in front of the NAWC guards—the same thing is true now.

I climb onto the roof just before the guards can get a clear shot, and for a little while, at least, we are safe from them. However, now we are stuck on top of a building with no place to hide and no way down, but the staircase we just ascended. The fear that filled me earlier seems to have toned down or at least been pushed to the back of my mind. My mind, apparently accepting the fact that being scared isn't doing a darned thing to help me survive the situation, allows me to calm down enough to think, but the commander has already thought for us.

"Come on," shouts the commander sprinting towards the edge of the building. Is she committing suicide? Has she run all this way just to end her life? I think this in the split second before she flings herself off the building. She soars through the air and drops out of sight. Her guards follow right behind her, each of them throwing themselves off the building as though it's the most normal thing they have done all day. Now there is a level a loyalty I don't see often. I don't know if I would have followed Leon off a building just because he said so, but these guards didn't even hesitate. Before I can stop myself, I am also plunging off the building. For a fraction of a second I can see the view of the street almost twenty stories below. Wind whips at my clothing and I frantically flail my arms, attempting to slow my fall. However, it only makes me look like an idiot as I plummet to what must be my certain death.

Then, much sooner than I expected, I crash into something very hard, almost blacking out. Crazy thoughts fly through my head just as fast as I had been flying when I jumped. I think to myself, how on earth, or how on New Earth have I fallen twenty stories so fast? And then I have an even more disturbing thought. Why am I not dead? Surely a twenty-story fall should break every bone in my body and make my blood burst out of its veins, or something else equally painful.

I barely have enough time to think about that when, for the second time that day, strong hands pull me up and start to drag me along. Although my body refuses, and every muscle in my body screams at me to stop, I pull away from the guard who helped me up and I run. I have the tiniest amount of time to take in my surroundings. Instead of the asphalt of a road, I stand on the metal plating of a flat roof—the roof of the adjacent building. All I had done was jump from one building to the next like some hero in a movie. Unlike that hero, I didn't do this maneuver as gracefully as a staged actor carrying out his staged action. I did no controlled soaring, and I didn't even land on my feet. I had flailed my arms and landed on my side in a painful pile. In the end it doesn't matter. The plunge, no matter how it was carried out, seems to have bought us seconds of time and rewards us with an escape from certain death, trapped on a rooftop.

Ahead of me the commander and one of her guards are already working their hardest to kick in a roof entrance. It doesn't take long, and for the third time in a matter of minutes we forcefully charge uninvited into another building.

I sprint inside, climbing over the fallen door as I go. I just about trip as I am met by a staircase, but somehow I manage to keep my balance and keep running down.

One of the guards stays behind—mumbling something about blowing up the entrance to delay pursuers. I don't think about it too much. My head spins from exhaustion and pain, and I am so glad that at least the commander is thinking about what we have to do.

My footsteps join the others as we thunder down the stairs. I notice dimly how nice the red carpet lining the stairs is before I hear a giant explosion and a wave of hot air pushes me faster down the stairs. Just as we climb the stairs in the adjacent building, it takes us only a few minutes to reach the bottom.

"We have to take the street the rest of the way. We won't have cover for a couple of blocks. Kill everything you see," shouts the commander, slamming through yet another door, and yet again out into an alley. The commander takes a right and begins to run. Our footsteps echo through the deserted alley. I hoist my gun—although my thoughts are a bit fuzzy, kill everything is a pretty clear order. I let my finger rest on the trigger. The gun feels cold and sleek in my sweaty palms.

The alley is scattered with dumpsters that will only slightly help cover us for this final sprint. I don't know how long it takes. Is it seconds, minutes, hours? Time is meaningless. I can only think of putting one foot in front of the other as fast as I can—knowing only that by the time we reach the end of the first block, I hear the NAWC guards burst into the street behind us and open fire. The sound echos a hundred times louder than our footsteps—to the point that it sounds like a thunderstorm meeting a megaphone. For at least the tenth time that day bullets fly past me. They clang against dumpsters and the ground just behind me.

The world doesn't go into slow motion. I don't whip out any incredible back flip, wall-running bullet dodges, use my fists to deflect the bullets, or do anything even slightly heroic. Instead, I sprint as fast as humanly possible, terrified to the point that my mind starts to question if what is happening is actually happening. These things are not supposed to happen to me. I am a sixteen-year-old kid from the Wasteland. I am not supposed to travel through space and I am definitely not supposed to be running as fast I can from bullets, with every ounce of my body revolting from the strain of running so hard for so long, under so much stress. But being shot to death is much less favorable than running through the pain, so I keep going.

Miraculously, I am not hit. Bullets come so close to my head I wouldn't be surprised if after this I have no hair left, that is, if there is an after this. Then I notice something is wrong. The commander is no longer running ahead of me. Instead, only her guards lead the way. I look around searching for her. I spot her as she walks calmly back the way we came, a loaded assault rifle in each hand.

"You guys are going to make it. It's just at the end of this alley." Her voice is loud, stern, commanding and calm, but can be barely heard above the enemy fire. It is also not the voice of someone who is walking single-handedly back into a group of enemy soldiers, outnumbering us at least twenty to one. I now see the NAWC guards charging behind us, dressed in black armored suits with face masks and guns. They swarm towards us like ants, and more file in from other alleys. I think I hear the sound of helicopters whirling above, circling us like volves circling their prey.

The guards fire.

The commander lets out a yell of curse words, something about flaming female dogs dying and raises her weapons, shooting before the NAWC guards can react.

The recoil of trying to shoot two massive assault rifles at once shakes her entire frame. So much for me not doing anything heroic—the commander more than makes up for that. The sound of her bullets join the enemy's in an explosion of noise. I sprint on, not fully understanding what is going on. Is the commander, with all her sarcastic remarks, and in all of her high-flying superiority, actually going to sacrifice herself just to save a group of kids from another planet?

The commander screams a high-pitched shriek of pain, and I take just enough time to see her body being pushed back by a torrent of bullets. They shred her body, seeming to puncture every part of it. Blood sprays everywhere, but somehow, with a shout of determined resolve, she remains upright, guns pointed at the NAWC soldiers. I don't take the time to look, but I hear the shouts of guard after guard yelling and falling to the ground. The alleyway ahead of us ends in a single door, and I think to myself that must be the entrance to the rebel bunker. I put every bit of energy into sprinting this last stretch to safety.

I take a final glance back. The bodies of the NAWC soldiers lie everywhere. The only person who remains standing is the commander, staggering around, about to collapse. She turns her head as she falls, and for the first time I see the commander smile, a truly genuine smile. Life leaves her eyes even before she hits the ground—only a smile remains for another second on her lifeless face before that too dissolves into the clutches of death. Tears and sweat mix together and fall off my face in sheets. I hadn't liked the commander, and as far I knew, she didn't like any of us. But for some unexplainable reason she had given her life for us. Emotion beyond anything I have ever felt threatens to bring me to my knees. Never, not even when Zeleng got his hand torn off, have I ever been hit by such a wave of wretched sadness. I am alive because of the commander and I am going to have to live with that debt that I can never repay.

We thunder on. Tears stream down my face and I don't try to hold them back. The door is so close now. Fifteen feet. Fourteen feet. We were going to make it. Ahead of us soldiers flow into our path from an adjacent alley. They seem to have been taken by surprise at how close we were, barely having time to raise their guns before we crash into them. I pull my sword from my belt and slash, catching a soldier in the shooting arm. Screaming, he drops his gun. Shouts of pain, the clang of weapons on armor and every now and then a burst of bullets. The soldier whose arm I had cut leaps towards me, attempting to bring the heavy gun up with his unhurt arm. A spray of bullets barely misses me as I jump to the side. I dart back and tackle the soldier, driving my sword into the synthetic material below his helmet and above his armored shoulders. The man goes limp, his shout reduced to gurgling as blood fills his throat.

I think back to the volve I had shot so long ago. The volve that would have choked on its blood if the arrow hadn't killed him. This was not a volve. This was a human. I had ended another life for my own. I pull my blade free, stumbling and ready to pass out. The clattering din continues around me. I see Auburn kill a man, by slashing his head clean off. Zeleng shanks another and Marty swings his massive sword killing more. Realizing something for the first time, I feel an out-of-place twinge of happiness, but it is choked down by the smell of blood and the horror of the murder. The only reason we were not dead was that we had short range weapons that we had mastered and these soldiers were only skilled with guns. The hours of training had paid off. The hours of training had saved us. They feebly try to block my friend's furiously desperate swipes and stabs with short daggers pulled from their belts, but they have no chance. I stumble again. Most of the soldiers are dead and we return to our flight. I am in the lead and I run as much for my life as to get as far away from the man I killed as possible.

At the end of alley the door opens, revealing a man with a pistol. He beckons frantically for us to hurry, as though we could go any faster.

I hear more soldiers burst into the alleyway behind me and I know with absolute certainty that they are raising their guns and pointing them at our exposed backs. They would shred Auburn first, then as he fell and Zeleng was exposed, the bullets would find him and he would follow Auburn to the pavement. Luke would go next. Then Paul. Then Marty. Then I. We would all die in that order. It would be worst for me. I would hear the screams of pain as one after one my friends fall and I hear Marty yell, thudding to the ground, and I will know that I have only seconds to live. I will have the longest time to dread what is coming, I will have the most hopelessness and I will die with

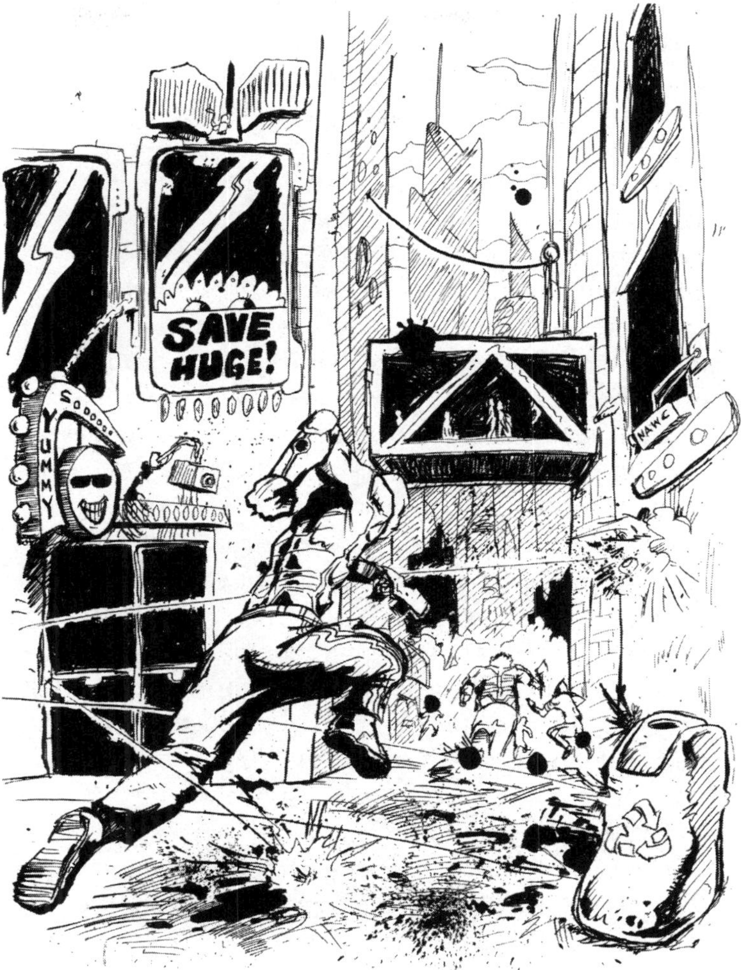
SAVE HUGE!
SOOOOOO
YUMMY
NAWC

a chorus of my friend's screams echoing in my head. Bullets will pierce my body and the pain will end it. End this flight. End this journey. End my life. With hope all gone, something changes inside me. I no longer can cling to existence, because I have no belief anymore that a better place waits if I keep pushing on. It wouldn't be giving up. It would simply be an end to the madness. I longed for my safe wagon home. If only I closed my eyes I could be there again for a few moments. If only I let the darkness be my only reality I could dream I was in a better place, even if it was never to be. I had lost my will to go on. To collapse now would be bliss. My legs started to seize up and my eyes were closing slowly when I hear the shout, Marty's shout. It sounded far off. As if at the end of a long alley.

"God damnit Zane. Keep going." Why does his voice sound so distant, why does it seem to be the echo of it that I am hearing and not the direct sound? Then I realize. Looking behind me I already know what I am going to see. Marty is catapulting his way out of a dumpster, directly behind the soldier's firing squad. In one ferocious swipe he slams his blade into the line sending the soldiers sprawling and redirecting their guns so that bullets barrage the wall, sending shards of stone flying. Marty had hidden, calculating what would happen. He had positioned himself perfectly to save us.

The soldiers turn on him and Marty wades through them, stabbing and slicing. They retaliate with thrusts from their own daggers and bullets from their guns. Marty deflects as many daggers as he can, but there are just too many. I focus my attention back on reaching the door with new hope and energy. With every fiber of my being I want to reach the door so that Marty's sacrifice is not in vain.

"For a moment in that dumpster I thought I was home," comes Marty's voice.

Tears roll down my face, knowing that those would be the last words he ever uttered. A rapid burst of machine gun fire signals the end.

We push past the man into the building, all five of us. The man points his pistol out the door and lets off a few rounds before slamming it shut. A clattering of bullets collides with the shut door seconds later.

I don't look very closely at him. He is tall and bearded, wearing a sleek black jacket. Every other part of him is shrouded by the darkness of the room. He pushes open another door and we start descending more stairs.

"What the hell happened?" asks the man. He follows that question with a string of curse words that even Zeleng would have been proud of. We move farther into the building and down a set of stairs. The man struggles to push shut a massive metal door, and then turns to a switch on the wall.

"There might be a thud." Then he pulls the lever and a massive explosion knocks me to the ground. Dust rains down from the ceiling. It was obvious what the man had done. He had blown the entrance.

"You're safe now. They can't follow you in here now. We will get on the railroad and get you out of here," the man explains. The only word that registers with me is safe. And a relieved feeling washes over me. We enter a tunnel.

"You can walk now." says the man, lowering another thick door into place, blocking off the entrance to the tunnel and plunging us into complete darkness. There is another massive explosion, but I am ready for it this time and stay on my feet. Tears run down my face and I am glad of the darkness. We had lost the Commander and we had lost Marty. I had known Marty for less than a week and the Commander for only three days, so why am I so distraught? Why do their deaths cause me so much grief? I know the answer. It is because I am to blame. They sacrificed themselves for me and for my friends. I think back to Marty when I first met him. Eternally cheerful, kind and generous was his facade. A facade that came crumbling down when he talked about his dying wife or his true intentions as a returning rebel to the frontier of battle. He had shown that he was capable of selfishness when the the Trash Craft was flying away and he thought that he had failed to return once again. He had apologized, but had that event tormented him? Had that led him to this sacrifice or had this been an on-the-spot decision? We will never know. We can never know. I thought of his last words.

"For a moment in that dumpster I thought I was home." Had that just been a parting joke or was it deeper. Had Marty changed his mind? Had he decided that the Wasteland truly was his home? Had he sacrificed himself to escape the hell he promised us the Clean World was? Or was it that he wanted to escape the Hell? Marty believed in God. Was this selfless act a desperate attempt for repentance? We had gained and lost friends on this journey. The original five remain and we stumble down the tunnel in total darkness. I don't try to imagine that I am in a better place, for this place is the place I would have imagined. I am in the Clean World, safe now from harm and this is what I had always wanted.

It takes roughly an hour. We only talk in order to explain to the man, who reveals his name to be Jaharr, about all the things that had occurred. When we finally see the light at the end of the tunnel, everyone is exhausted. I feel as though my legs will give out at any moment. Zeleng is having an even worse time. He hadn't fully recovered when we started, and I have no clue how he is still going on if I barely can. I put my arm around him and help him along. Auburn takes his other side and together we limp towards the door that swings open when we are a few feet away. Inside are more men and women with guns, all talking excitedly. We pay them no attention as we walk past them and into the room. I want to look around to see what is going on, but when I try to lift my head, black spots blur my vision, and the next thing I know, the ground is rushing up to meet me. I black out with the thought, we have made it. Zeleng has survived. We have managed the impossible. We have made it to the Clean World.

The Story Tale Ending

I guess my brain is too tired to plague me with nightmares, because I sleep deep and long. When I finally wake up, I slowly open my eyes. I am lying in a bed, and for a second I think that I am back in my bed in the wagon. The bed is run down, made of wood and smells bad, exactly like mine back at the wagon. A mass of blankets is thrown over me—just like back at the wagons, it's a mix-match of random blankets.

"How are you?" asks a strangely familiar voice. I try to place it. I turn my head to look at the person who spoke. I must be dreaming still. I blink and rub my eyes. The man next to me is me. He has the same longer style black hair and the same black eyes that always greet me when I look into the mirror. The only difference is this man has wrinkles around his eyes and he has a well-trimmed beard ringing his mouth.

"I came when I heard you made it, however you did it," says the man, scratching his eye the way I always do when I am nervous or want to avoid making eye contact.

"Seeing as you are here, I assume you had a safe

journey," I say. The words come out of my mouth without my thinking—most likely a side effect of my exhaustion.

The man chuckles—"Relatively safe—but how about your journey. I think it's just a little more interesting than mine. What did you do after I spoke to you?"

This man spoke to me? That explains why his voice seems so familiar and why he looks so much like me. Even in my exhausted state I put two and two together.

"Dad?" The way I say it sounds as though it is a question, but I already know without a doubt this man is my father. He smiles a little at that.

"Son." After a slight pause he repeats his first question to me. "How are you?"

"I guess I am doing good now." But is that the truth? Zeleng has lost his arm, the commander is dead, and Marty is dead. I have left my only true home and most of the people who are like family to me. Am I really good now?

"Let me rephrase that. How have you been? We've had fifteen years apart, and I think some catching up is overdue." His eyes twinkle at me, and I can see he is genuinely happy to have me back. I know I should share his happiness—this is the kind of fairytale reunion that only happens in stories, but truth is, this guy is still a stranger to me. I have no more feeling towards him than I have towards Marty. I feel guilty about these feelings, or rather, the lack of them, so instead of telling him about my feelings, I begin to tell him my story.

I start with my first memories of being raised by Ham and his family, and about the time Luke and I had gotten lost at night and nearly died. I tell him of the day Auburn and Zeleng stumbled upon the wagon, half starved and terrified, and how we took them in. I tell him about first finding the packages he sent. And last of all, I tell him what happened this past week as we made our way to the Clean World.

When I finish, there is a painfully long silence, and I don't blame him. It is a lot to take in. Learning the entire life of your child in a half hour really could leave you speechless. Finally, I break the silence—the sound of my voice is almost painful after such a long pause in speaking.

"Did you know Marty?" I pause, trying to think of his last name with no luck. I didn't even know his last name, yet we had done so much together and he had died to save us.

"Martius Varallo," my dad supplies. "Yeah, I know him or knew him rather. Haven't seen him for twenty years or so, but... why do you ask?" Zenith leans forward in his chair.

"He was a good guy. The best I ever knew." I am surprised at how shaky my voice is. I needed to tell someone this. I needed someone to understand this.

"I know." The silence lengthens and all I can see is Marty jumping from that dumpster and the Commander screaming as she is torn to shreds.

"She was a good person too. She might not have shown it until the end, but she was." Her rank has been lost with death and I didn't have a name to call her, but my dad seemed to understand.

"I know." Another long silence, only interrupted by the sound of running water through a pipe on the ceiling.

"Marty told me you were a hacker and a pretty good one at that." I haven't taken my eyes off him since learning he is my father, and for the first time an expression of distaste crosses his face.

"I am glad you said were. All hacking ever brought me was loss. First it was you, then your mom, and then all the people who tried to fight in the first revolution. All are dead or gone, and now that I have you back, I am never risking you again. My hacking days are over." His sudden anger and resentment stun me, and out of everything he says, only one word actually registers—that word is mom.

"My mom—what happened to her?" I say, sitting up straight in my bed. The strangest expressions cross over his face—sadness, anger, betrayal, or maybe all three. I definitely see tears welling up in his eyes, but his eyebrows are furrowed in anger, and that line of his mouth can only mean one thing—lack of understanding. Not so much about what happened, more likely why.

"No," is all he says as he gets to his feet, being careful to let his hair cover his face and to keep it tilted away from me. He turns around and walks briskly to the door. He stops in the threshold and briefly glances back, and I see the faintest etch of a tear rolling down his face. Without another word he walks out of the room, and I am alone in this strange place with only my thoughts of my mom, and the sadness of the deaths to keep me company.

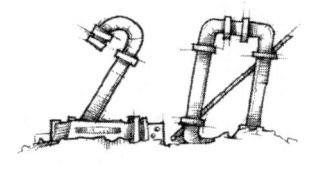

That Is Life

The bunker in which we had collapsed the previous day is damp, cold and severely run down, but I absolutely love it. It reminds me so much of the wagons. It's cluttered, smelling slightly of mildew and definitely nothing like the Trash Craft's blank boringness.

The rebels, I soon learn, conduct most of their work underground. It's about the only place safe for them, but it came with having to live in sewers and cramped underground rooms. However, this doesn't really bother me. For my entire life I shared a small room with two other guys. If anything, it's comforting, and for the first time since leaving the wagons, I don't feel homesick.

When I first arrived, I collapsed immediately—then I slept for a very long time—then I had a conversation with my long lost dad, and now I am hungry. The last of that list is on a level of significance with the rest of the list.

I find Auburn, Luke, Zeleng and Paul sitting at a table when I arrive in the main room of the bunker. I can almost imagine I am back in the wagon, coming down to the main room to get some volve bone and oats, and maybe some canned fruit—but for the first time those thoughts don't make me homesick, and I start to think. I could really live here and be happy. The room is a neat square with only enough room for three tables and a handful of chairs. On three out of four of the walls are floor to ceiling cabinets, packed with colorful cans and boxes. A row of what I am guessing are refrigerators lines the entire left wall. A light hangs from the ceiling, casting a dim light onto the room. For a world that has all this technology, this place looks like something you could find back on the Wasteland.

"Ayyy, Zane. How's it going?" Zeleng grins at me. He's cleaned himself up since I last saw him. His hair is combed as neatly as possible, and at least it looks clean. He's also changed clothes. I am glad he is out of that soldier uniform—it really didn't suit him, or any of us, for that matter. He wears jeans and a cloak, just the way he did back at the wagons, but I have a feeling this one isn't made of volve hides.

"Food?" I mutter. Zeleng flashes another smile my way.

"You won't believe this food." He holds out a red box speared on his knife arm. In neon letters across the front of the box is spelled R-A-I-N-B-O-W-O's.

"This stuff is called cereal. And can you believe this?" Zeleng holds up a large container of white liquid with his good hand.

"Apparently they squeeze this stuff out of cows. Real live cows, can you imagine that?" Zeleng has a disgusted look on his face, but he still looks as though he's about to explode with excitement—as if drinking cow fluid is the coolest thing he's ever done.

"So this stuff is cow juice," I say, taking the glass Zeleng offers me.

"Actually, it's called milk," explains the oh-so-knowledgeable Auburn. I don't notice until then that he is reading—like one would read a book—a giant black and white paper.

"What are you doing?" I ask, finally taking a seat, milk in one hand, cereal in the other.

"Reading a newspaper," says Auburn, not even looking up from it. "Oh, so what does this piece of paper say?" I ask, starting to open the box of Rainbow-Os.

"Surprisingly, nothing about us. Not a single mention of why there was a military chase through the city." He turns a page.

I finally get the box open, wondering why they make these things so hard to open, when I notice that inside the cereal box there is a bag that actually holds the multicolored cereal.

"This is honestly the stupidest thing I have ever seen. Why do they have to put it in a box and a bag? Wouldn't a box be enough?" I hold up the bag in exasperation.

Zeleng, seeing a chance to make use of his knife arm, slashes the bag open for me.

Turns out it is worth all the trouble getting the cereal open, because it is literally heaven in the shape of little rainbow-colored rings. After living off meat and expired canned food my entire life, with the best thing I ever ate being vegetables, this box of cereal makes me want to dance—and that's saying something, because I never want to dance. I take a moment just to savor a few in my mouth. The sweetness of them only compares to the apple juice I drank back in the city—and not even that.

"Not bad? Hmm?" asks Luke, who has been silently devouring his own box of Rainbow-Os. Saying that these things are not bad is like saying that getting all the way to the Clean World was not hard—a complete understatement

"These are the best things I have ever tasted," I say, giving him a 'thumbs up'.

"That's just the beginning. You haven't even tried bacon yet," says Luke. "It's made from pigs."

"Cow juice and pig parts—yummy, yummy," I joke.

There is no one in the room to stop us, so for the next hour or so, all we do is stuff our faces with all the new foods. I would never have imagined I was missing so many tastes and flavors—all kinds of different meats that surprisingly taste so different from volve.

No one mentions Marty's or the Commander's death, but I know it's on everyone's mind. For me, the shock has faded into the back of my head, and the whole incident seems very surreal—like something that happened to someone else—but the truth is, I really don't know how to feel. When someone you thought hated you, sacrifices herself for you, it's hard to hate her anymore. But also, since you thought she never liked you, you never had the chance to get to know her and develop any kind of love for her that would make you sad about her death. And as for Marty. Had I really known him? He went through so many transformations in the short time we traveled together. Am I remembering the wrong him?

It's true. I was devastated right after they died, but now, just like the shock, it has faded to the back of my mind and left me wondering if I am really sad for the commander or

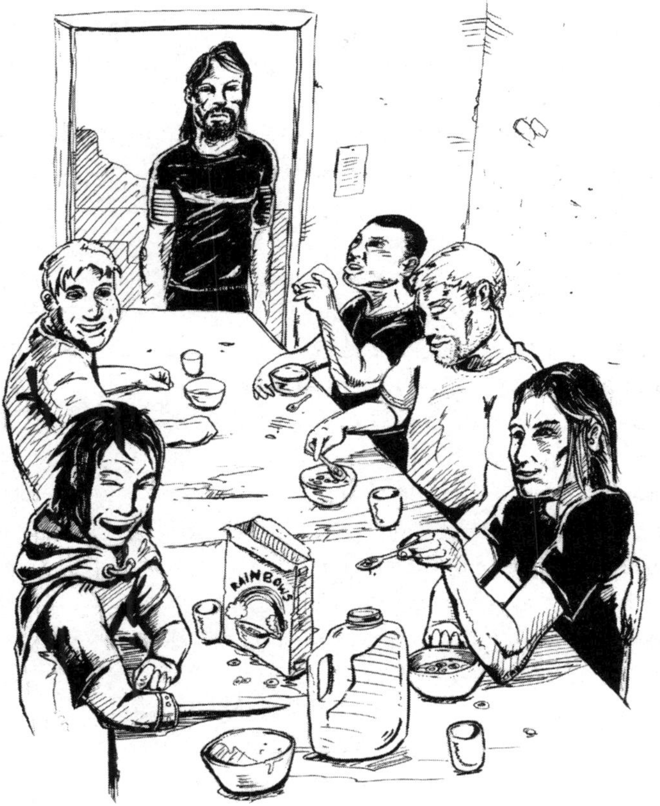
RAINBOWS

if Marty's death really tore me apart. The Commander died with satisfaction—the smile on her face as she died proved that. Maybe she is already in a better place, somewhere that the government she so hated can never get to her.

Even the commander's death doesn't take as much space in my mind as does the conversation with my father. It went well up to the point where I asked about my mother. What could possibly be so awful that it could end the first conversation a father has with his son in fifteen years? I guess I must drown my sorrows in food, since I eat everything the others put in front of me.

Just when my stomach feels as though it's expanded to the size of a small whale (one of the few meats I haven't tried this morning), and the stash of food has successfully diminished, footsteps can be heard in the hallway. After several seconds of the sound, my dad steps into the room. He gives me a hesitant smile. I wonder if he thinks I am mad at him for walking out on me. That really couldn't be further from the truth, as I am definitely not mad—if anything, I am simply curious.

"Hey," I say, somewhat awkwardly. Getting used to having a dad is going to take some time. I don't even know how I should greet him. I don't know his beliefs, his habits, or what he finds acceptable, so I take the safe route.

"How are you doing?" I say. My dad had used that greeting yesterday, so it must mean it's the one he is most comfortable with, and the one I should use with him.

"Good, but we need to talk." My friends just stare at us—the tension in the room is unbelievable. I just need to relax and stop acting as though my dad is a bomb that could explode at any second.

"Okay, talk. Let's talk," I say, agreeing with him because I don't know what else to say. I wait for him to say something. After several silent seconds he speaks, pointing with his eyes at the door.

"Alone." He isn't smiling—instead, he looks very tense, and I realize that my dad is like a bomb. He needs to tell me something, or he will explode if he doesn't.

"I see how it is," says Zeleng, faking indignation and strolling towards the door. The others follow, laughing, but I don't get what's funny until just before the door shuts behind them when I hear Zeleng say, "Zane has to have a daddy talk."

My dad walks over to the table and sits down across from me. I am suddenly aware of the huge pile of trash and crumbs that litter the table.

"I am sorry about walking out on you yesterday. I was kind of mixed up emotionally, but I have thought about it and I am ready to tell you." He brushes the hair out of his face and rubs his eyes. I can tell by the bags under his eyes that he didn't sleep very well. Something is bothering him enough that after having had a happy reunion with his long lost son, he still couldn't sleep.

"No problem," I say, again taking the safe route. I pick my fingernails. I don't know why it's so hard to look into his eyes. I think it must be because it's like looking right into myself.

"It is a problem, though. You're my son and you have a right to know." He takes a deep breath, but doesn't say anything.

"What problem?" I ask, trying to sound curious without prying too much. I can tell this is hard for him, but the truth is, I want to grab him and shake him until he spills whatever he is going to tell me.

"When I hacked NAWC, they took you and I fled to the rebels and ...," he pauses, squeezing his eyes shut, either from the pain of the memory, or because he doesn't want me to see him crying. "Your mom didn't come with me when I fled. She stayed with NAWC."

I stare at him trying to understand what he is saying. I don't yet know the implications, but I see no positive outcome from this conversation.

"You see, her parents were important among NAWC and they drilled it into her head that NAWC is supreme, and is always right, and not to be questioned. So naturally—when I hacked NAWC—she was furious with me, but even when they took you, she didn't doubt NAWC. She blamed me, refusing to come with me to the rebels."

The food that had tasted so good has formed a painful lump in my stomach.

"What you need to understand is, your mom is a good person—she just was raised by people who were unaware of the dark side of NAWC. She has a good heart, trust me, I know. All I want is for you not to hate her." He looks at me with an expression of desperation.

"Why, where is she now?" How can I not hate someone who sides with the people who sent me to a life of hardship in the Wasteland, and how can I not despise a person who sides with the group who killed the commander?

My dad gives me a pained look, as if he knows what I am thinking, and he takes a long time to answer. He runs his fingers through his hair.

"You'd think after fifteen years a man would get over

this, but really that couldn't be further from the truth. No man deserves to lose his wife and son within days of each other." He puts his head in his hands. I somewhat understand what he is saying, but why is he so distressed? This happened so long ago.

"But where is she now?" I ask for the second time. My dad looks up at me from the table and stares me straight in the eyes. This time I see the true agony that gives his eyes that look of sadness, and I wonder what could possibly make him look so hurt, so beaten down.

"Zane, what surname have they given you down there?"

"Stellafilius."

"Starson. Of course...," he trails off. He trips on his next words at first as though his mouth is rebelling at what he must say.

"That is not your real last name. Your real last name is Frazer. Zoe Frazer is your mother."

In the moments it takes me to comprehend his words I get to watch my father fully deteriorate, his last bits of strength flowing out of him, his resolve not faltering, but collapsing, his upper body following suit as he slumps miserably against the table. But then my father's words are clicking in my mind as well and it is like the clicking of a loaded gun heard inches from his ear. The sound brings forward intense feelings of fear and hopelessness. The noise that smothers one in a veil of constricting inner turmoil. My body acts as if it knows the full world-shattering implications of the circumstances before I have fully worked out anything but the bare and simple idea. President Fraser of NAWC is my mother.

"Do you understand now why they sent so many

soldiers after you? You are the most dangerous person to them on this entire planet, because you have a chance to break your mother's strict resolve and bring NAWC crashing down once and for all. The fate of this planet rests on your shoulders, Zane, and it is a burden I didn't want you to bear no matter how necessary it is."

I don't know why, but my eyes sting and anger wells up in my throat. Why did my life have to be so unfair? Not knowing what to do, I walk around the table and sit down next to my dad. He looks up at me, his eyes full of misery. I don't know how it happens, but the next thing I know, I am slumped against his shoulder and he has his arms around me. I want to forget everything. I want to wake up back in my room back at the wagon, but I know that won't happen. Sometime later, I don't know when, Zeleng, Auburn, Luke and Paul come back into the room, and before I know it, Zeleng is hugging me—for what reason I don't know—but I do know it makes me feel better. Even if my life sucks, I have Zeleng with me—Zeleng to always stick by my side—Zeleng who has lived through all odds and is hugging me. I don't even care about being cut to pieces by his arm—all I care about is being okay. I don't feel Auburn or Luke or Paul hugging me, but I know they are. In normal circumstances this would be awkward as hell, but these aren't normal circumstances. We have survived years in the harsh Wasteland—we have survived volve attacks, rains of trash and herds of treefs. Zeleng got his arm torn off. We have marched across the Wasteland, traveled in a barge, and finally, traveled millions of miles just to be in this spot right now. Possibly the most normal thing of my life right now is this giant group hug that signifies that no matter what, we are sticking together, and together we can make it.

My name is Zane, and I have escaped the Wasteland. I have made it to the Clean World, but I have found that it's bad all over, no matter if the place you are living in is clean or full of trash. You can't count on anything in life—your dreams become nightmares and your family is torn apart as fast as a volve tears off a hand. But I do know with all my heart that no matter what happens, you can fix it. No matter what, no matter if your hand is torn off or your parent is the leader of an evil organization, there is always hope, and rather than having a Clean World you hope to someday reach, you should make your own circumstances into the Clean World others dream of reaching. That is my challenge now.

Afterword

Despite the rather pessimistic message depicted in this book, I do not believe we are screwed. It is very unlikely that man-made environmental issues (minus nuclear war perhaps) will cause humans to go extinct. We will live on. We will not completely wipe ourselves out, but the kind of world we live on into is not so certain. The Wagons, Barges and Cities, the cobbled together civilization that struggles to live on in a world no longer beautiful is one possible fate, but is not the only fate. We children currently are growing up in a world familiar with the beauty of nature, but it is, alas, a choice whether or not we preserve it for our children. And honestly, what gives us the right to take greedily now and condemn those who come after us to a life in a world greatly affected by climate change and pollution, a world no better than the Wasteland? We might not have a planet to escape to, but we do have a Clean World. Why not keep Earth beautiful?

That being said, the world, if we want to maintain this beauty, is going to have to start being more like the Wasteland, and I don't mean that Earth should look more like the trash-covered landscape of the Wasteland, but rather in the way that our lifestyle needs to mirror those of the Nomads—communal living, sharing of resources and saving of supplies. The Wagons were a well-oiled group of people efficiently working together. Only in being more like Nomads can we preserve our Clean World for posterity.

About the Author

Lucas Bleyle, when not writing books is nowhere to be found. He is somewhere in the woods with a group of friends from dawn to dusk, cobbling together a fort. He also enjoys such things as the satisfaction of popping open an umbrella, seeing people nodding along while he speaks, and listening to uncontrolled saxophone duets. Lucas, now 14, lives in Ames, Iowa, with his parents, four siblings, two dogs, a cat, a fair amount of mice, and the occasional fellow crashed on the couch. He completed *The Scavengers* as an eighth grader and it is his first novel.

About the Illustrator

Blaine Garrett is a Minneapolis based fine artist and illustrator. As one-fourth of the Dim Media artist collaborative group, he has created a number of painting series and murals around the Twin Cities. As an illustrator, he has worked on 'zines, comics, and illustrated novellas such as Dim's "Blue Flame" series. His favorite medium is Black Cat India ink.

More of Blaine's artwork can be found at his website: http://dimmedia.com

Made in the USA
Middletown, DE
30 July 2015